P9-BYK-680

Duets™

**Two brand-new stories in every volume...
twice a month!**

Duets Vol. #105

Talented author Carol Finch returns to Hoot's Roost,
Oklahoma, where there are quite a few single
cowboys who don't give a hoot about marryin'.
But that all changes when the Ryder men meet
the women of their fantasies. Enjoy Carol's funny,
romantic Double Duets stories about the
BACHELORS OF HOOT'S ROOST—
where love comes sweeping down the plain!

Duets Vol. #106

Popular Jennifer Drew kicks off the month
with a fun story about an adventure writer who
hates to travel and desperately needs a stand-in
for a book tour. Jennifer always "gives readers a
top-notch reading experience with vibrant characters,
strong story development and spicy tension," says
Romantic Times. Dianne Drake delivers a quirky tale
about a hero determined to write a romance novel.
Problem is, he doesn't have a romantic bone in his
body! Luckily the heroine is there to help out!

Be sure to pick up both Duets volumes today!

"You're doing it again," Miranda said.

"Doing what?" Vance asked innocently.

"Staring at me as if you can see..." Her gaze flicked away. "I don't like it when men look past the uniform."

"Then try pinning the badge someplace besides on your chest," Vance teased. "Look, Officer Jackson, I'm trying my darnedest to stay out of your way, but I find you attractive. Now, if you want to arrest me for that, then fine. I'll plead no contest."

Miranda stared into his ruggedly handsome face and felt the unwanted jolt of attraction. "Okay, since you're being honest I'll return the favor. I like the looks of you, too, even if you don't take things seriously and you drive the most pathetic excuse for a vehicle that ever cruised the highway."

"Thank you for the comment, ma'am," Vance said, his lips twitching. "Even if you think I'm stupid, it's nice to know you don't find me hideously ugly while you're handing me warnings and tickets."

Miranda broke down and smiled. She just couldn't help it. The man was a charmer when he wanted to be!

For more, turn to page 9

"So you'll be playing cowboy." Mackenzie frowned. "What am I supposed to do? Sit here and twiddle my thumbs?"

"That's the general idea, yes," Gage confirmed.

She smirked. "Typical male response."

"Well, I'm a typical male. What kind of response did you expect?"

"Not interested in this setup. Let me hear plan B," she demanded.

"There's no Plan B. You'll be in charge of the house." He knew that would get a rise out of her, but he could deal better with her temper than those forbidden sensations that hammered at him.

Her eyes narrowed. "I'm the domestic help?"

"You got it, Mac. I bring home the bacon, you cook it." Before she could offer a smart retort, he cleared his throat and added, "Um, there's more. I have to explain your presence to the community."

"I'm supposed to be your temp housekeeper?" she guessed.

"No, you'll be playing the role of my wife. We're madly in love, by the way."

"Wife?" she crowed. A moment later she threw back her curly dark head and laughed out loud.

That was not *quite* the response he'd expected...

For more, turn to page 197

HARLEQUIN DUETS

ISBN 0-373-44171-1

Copyright in the collection:
Copyright © 2003 by Harlequin Books S.A.

The publisher acknowledges the copyright holder
of the individual works as follows:

FIT TO BE FRISKED
Copyright © 2003 by Connie Feddersen

MR. COOL UNDER FIRE
Copyright © 2003 by Connie Feddersen

This edition published by arrangement with Harlequin Books S.A.

® and TM are trademarks of the publisher. Trademarks indicated with ® are registered in the United States Patent and Trademark Office, the Canadian Trade Marks Office and in other countries.

Visit us at www.eHarlequin.com

Printed in U.S.A.

Carol Finch

Fit To Be Frisked

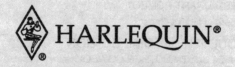

HARLEQUIN®

TORONTO • NEW YORK • LONDON
AMSTERDAM • PARIS • SYDNEY • HAMBURG
STOCKHOLM • ATHENS • TOKYO • MILAN • MADRID
PRAGUE • WARSAW • BUDAPEST • AUCKLAND

Dear Reader,

Welcome back to Hoot's Roost, Oklahoma! Although Cousin Wade and Quint Ryder have found the women of their dreams in my first Double Duets, #81, Vance, the practical joker of the family, is still footloose—until he plays a prank on a lady cop. When she fines him for stupidity the fireworks explode.

Miranda Jackson is a by-the-book rookie cop and she doesn't find the handsome cowboy's playful attitude the least bit amusing. Furthermore, she has her life all planned out and she has no intention of becoming sidetracked by this unexplainable attraction to a man who is her exact opposite. *A practical joker and a cop?* It'll never work. Yet she's thinking very seriously about arresting Vance for theft—because the fun-loving cowboy has stolen her heart.

Happy reading,

Carol Finch

Books by Carol Finch

HARLEQUIN DUETS

SILHOUETTE SPECIAL EDITION

HARLEQUIN HISTORICALS

This book is dedicated to my husband, Ed,
and our children—Jill, Kurt, Christie, Jeff and Jon—
with much love. And to our grandchildren—
Livia, Kennedy, Blake and Brooklynn.
Hugs and kisses!

1

VANCE RYDER HEARD SIRENS wailing behind him, but he couldn't see the flashing lights because his old clunker farm truck was caked solid with mud. All Vance had was a peephole on the windshield to see where he was going. It looked as if he'd have to talk his way out of a traffic ticket before he got this bucket of rust into Hoot's Roost to replace the bald tires and exhaust system that had more holes in it than a slice of Swiss cheese.

Shouldn't be too hard to get off with a warning, he mused confidently as he pulled the old truck onto the shoulder of the road. Hoot's Roost's police department was accustomed to dealing with farmer/stockmen and their beat-up equipment. For certain, the law officers in the area tended to overlook minor infractions because they'd seen their share of rattletrap trucks, tractors and machinery moving from one field to another.

In fact, Vance predicted that his old school chum, Turk Barnett, was the officer who'd pulled him over just to chitchat. Turk could talk your leg off if you let him and he got lonely while he cruised the streets during his long shifts.

Vance killed the engine and bounded from the

truck. He stopped dead still when a sharp, female voice said, "Freeze! Stay where you are!"

Startled, Vance pivoted on his boot heels to see a female officer pull her gun and crouch in shooting position. Was she nuts? Obviously so. He wasn't a gangster and Hoot's Roost was not the crime capital of Oklahoma. This was cattle country.

"Put your hands on top of the truck, sir," the cop commanded authoritatively.

Vance did as he was told then squinted into the bright sunlight to survey the shapely silhouette of the woman in blue who approached him as if she expected him to grab a pistol from out of nowhere and shoot her full of lead. Her weapon was trained on his head, but Vance's gaze was fixed on her well-endowed chest.

Wow! This lady cop was some kind of built and he had trouble raising his fascinated eyes from her bosom. When he did he found himself staring at a pair of mirrored sunglasses and a pouty mouth that looked all too kissable—but not the least bit friendly. She snatched off her glasses and tucked them in her breast pocket, and he found himself gazing into a pair of cedar-tree-green eyes that were fanned by long curly lashes.

Whoa, mama, this didn't look like any cop Vance had ever encountered. He began to wonder if there might be an advantage to being arrested by her on a regular basis.

"Don't ever climb from your vehicle until you've been asked to do so," she lectured as she stared at him over the barrel of her police-issued pistol. "Do you understand, sir?"

Vance nodded stupidly. He studied Officer Gorgeous for a long befuddling moment. Ah, now it was beginning to soak in. This had to be a prank, he decided. Since he'd been dubbed the practical joker of the Ryder family, his ornery cousins had probably decided to have him placed under mock arrest. His birthday was just a week away so he figured Cousin Quint and Cousin Wade probably decided to give him a *prank* for a gift. After all, Vance always enjoyed a good joke, even if it was played on him.

As the supposed lady cop with the killer body approached, Vance turned sideways to flash his patented Ryder grin. "Cute, darlin', you really had me going for a minute. Did Cousin Q and Cousin W send you out here?"

"Excuse me?"

The dark-haired bombshell was playing her role to the hilt. "C'mon, I know my cousins sent you. You're my birthday gag gift, right?"

She stared at him as if he was off his rocker. "I need to see your license and insurance verification."

Still grinning good-naturedly, Vance reached into his hip pocket to extract his license from his wallet. He glanced over the top of her head to stare at the patrol car. "Turk's in there, isn't he? Should've known he'd be in on this. Yo, Turk! You can sit up now. You're busted."

But Turk Barnett didn't raise his head and show himself. Vance's gaze swung back to the cop who was checking his ID. "This isn't a practical joke?"

"No, sir," she said as she stuffed her weapon into its holster. "This is a 705, 734, 736, 743 and an 804 traffic violation."

Vance frowned. "What the heck does all that mean?"

She looked him squarely in the eye. "Basically it means that this vehicle is an unfit pile of junk that doesn't meet safety regulations and the mud on your windshield and rear window obstructs your vision. You're dangerous to other motorists," she admonished. "I want you to remove this truck from the state highway immediately, sir."

Vance surveyed the pile of metal and bolts that he and his cousins used to plow through creeks to repair downed fences and to haul mineral and cattle cubes to their livestock. "Okay, so one headlight is missing and it's a little muddy—"

"A *little?*" The cop smirked distastefully as she appraised the jalopy that had more dents than a bumper car. "If this state still required vehicle safety inspections this junk heap would be in a salvage yard. Now, Mr. Ryder," she said as she returned his license, "I want you to turn this thing around and head back down the graveled road."

Vance flashed another charming smile—it was as well received as the first one. "I'm on my way to the service station to mount new tires and replace the muffler," he explained as nicely as he knew how.

"Not today you aren't," she informed him. She flipped open her ticket pad and grabbed a pen.

"Aw, c'mon, Officer," he cajoled. "Don't give

me a ticket. I've driven this truck into town plenty of times. This is rural America and traffic jams aren't a problem out here in the boondocks.'' To prove his point he hitched his thumb toward the highway. ''No one has even driven past since you pulled me over. There's no one here for me to endanger.''

Her green eyes narrowed on him. ''Are you questioning my authority, Mr. Ryder?''

''Vance,'' he corrected then grinned charmingly. ''No, I'm just saying that I've never had a problem with the other officers in Owl County. You must be new here.''

''I am, but regulations are still regulations,'' she maintained aloofly. She directed his attention to the graveled road to the west. ''Now then, turn this thing around and take it back the same way you came or I will write you a ticket instead of letting you off. And don't use the highway until this vehicle has been washed and those dangling headlights have been plugged back in their sockets.''

She slapped the warning in his hand then spun on her heels. Distracted, Vance watched the hypnotic sway of shapely hips encased in trim fitting blue slacks. His attention momentarily shifted to the long braid of glossy brown hair that glided between her shoulder blades, but ultimately, his gaze dropped to the exceptionally fine shape of her fanny.

Mmm, Officer Good Body looked as terrific when she was walking away as she did when she was coming toward him. Too bad she was rigid and unfriendly. Probably didn't have a personality worth mentioning, either, he predicted. Definitely not Ms. Congeniality of the Police Pageant.

Vance slid onto the seat and switched the key. The engine sputtered, coughed a couple of times then growled to life. Exhaust fumes fogged around the old truck. Vance shoved the gearshift into Reverse then backed into the bar ditch to turn around.

He was more than a little surprised that Ms. By The Book didn't stop him for an improper U-turn. But she just sat there in her black-and-white, staring him down through her sunglasses as he veered around her to hang a right onto the gravel road.

A devilish grin pursed Vance's lips when he saw Cousin Wade barreling toward him. The original plan was for Wade to pick up Vance in town so they could gather farm supplies while the rattletrap truck was being repaired. Then they'd grab a quick lunch at Stephanie's Palace—the restaurant owned and operated by Cousin Quint's new wife, Steph. Vance recalled that Wade had been champing at the bit all morning, anxious to complete their chores so he could meet his new wife, Laura, for lunch.

Every time Vance saw Cousin Wade—the former woman-hater of the family—drooling all over himself because he was so crazy over his new wife Vance chuckled in amusement. It was downright pathetic the way Wade and Quint mooned over their wives. In fact, there were times when his formerly macho cousins acted so sappy that it creeped him out.

When Wade thrust his arm out the window to flag him down, Vance pressed hard on the brake, reminded that adding a quart of brake fluid might not be a bad idea, too.

Wade glared at Vance. "What are you doing? Forget how to get to town?" He glanced anxiously at his watch. "I told Laura I'd meet her at noon. If you make me late you're gonna hear about it."

Vance swallowed a grin when inspiration struck. He hopped from the old truck. "Switch vehicles with me, cuz. I forgot something back at the ranch. You take the clunker truck to town and I'll be right behind you."

"You better be right behind me," Wade threatened as he hopped from his black extended cab truck and brushed past Vance. "Today is our sixth month anniversary, ya know."

"Gee, it's not like you haven't mentioned it about a dozen times this morning," Vance said flippantly.

Impatient, Wade slammed the clunker truck in gear, whipped around and headed for the highway. Vance chuckled in amusement as his cousin roared off in a cloud of smoke. He was anxious to see how Wade fared when he met up with the latest addition to HRPD.

Ah, nothing like a good prank to start the day off right, he mused.

OFFICER MIRANDA JACKSON glanced in her rearview mirror then muttered under her breath when she saw the same clunker truck barreling down the highway, defying her order. Apparently that handsome cowboy she'd encountered didn't think he had to take her seriously.

Well, so much for giving that rascal a warning, she mused as she hit the switch. Lights flashed and sirens wailed. This time she'd give him a ticket and impound his truck and just let him try to talk her out of it!

When the truck eased onto the shoulder behind her, Miranda stormed back to confront Vance Ryder. She blinked in disbelief when the driver rolled down the mud-splattered side window to stare curiously at her. Another raven-haired hunk of cowboy, who bore a strong family resemblance to Vance, flashed her a winsome smile.

"Is there a problem, Officer?"

Miranda jerked herself to attention to address the driver. "The problem is that I just sent Mr. Vance Ryder back in the direction he came, in this truck, because the vehicle is in violation of several traffic codes…" Her voice trailed off when a shiny black 4X4 truck pulled up beside her. The tinted window slid downward and she silently fumed when Vance grinned playfully at her.

"Everything okay here?" he asked with mock innocence.

Miranda was tempted to grab her nightstick and whack the mischievous cowboy over his handsome head. His devilish dark eyes twinkled with amusement and she knew he was silently taunting her. He thought he'd pulled a fast one on her, did he? Well, they'd just see about that.

When he waggled his thick brows and flashed her another one of those lady-killer grins her temper snapped. "Get out of that truck, Mr. Ryder." Both men opened their doors. "Not you, *him!*" she ordered as she made a stabbing gesture at Vance.

"Wha'd I do?" Vance asked, lips twitching.

"Don't play games with me," she said warningly. Miranda grabbed her pad and quickly wrote out a ticket.

"Hey! There's nothing wrong with the truck I'm driving," Vance objected hotly.

"What is going on here?" Wade demanded, glancing at his watch again. "I'm on a tight time schedule. May I go now?"

"How about we forget the ticket and I escort my cousin and the clunker truck into town," Vance suggested. "I'll lead Cousin Wade all the way to the service station with my emergency lights flashing. That suit you, Officer?" He had the audacity to toss her a wink and another sexy smile.

Miranda didn't appreciate being the object of manipulation and flirtation. But just as before, those ebony-colored eyes slid up and down her body, lingering momentarily on her chest. Well, this bozo was going to find out real quick that she expected to be taken seriously. She was a law officer and he'd better show her some respect!

"Fine, Mr. Ryder, you lead your cousin to town," she muttered as she thrust the ticket at him. "And wash that pile of junk while you're there so you and your cousin can see where you're going. If this happens again, I will impound the truck."

Wheeling around, Miranda stalked back to the squad car.

"A hundred-dollar fine!" Vance yowled, his eyes bulging in disbelief. "For what?"

Miranda pivoted to toss him a goading smile. "You've been fined for stupidity, Mr. Ryder. Don't ever pull a stunt like that on me again."

With extreme satisfaction, Miranda drove off, leaving Vance staring after her with his jaw scraping his broad chest. Thought this was funny, did he? Well, he could have himself a hundred-dollar laugh. Next time maybe he'd think twice before he tried to make her look like a fool.

BY THE TIME VANCE ESCORTED Wade to Pinkman's Service Station he was fuming mad. "A hundred freakin' bucks," he scowled as he slid across the seat so Wade could drive his black pickup. "That lady cop has no sense of humor whatsoever. None of the officers have ever pulled us over in the jalopy. Man, she's a stuffed shirt, if ever there was one."

"I'll say she is," Wade agreed with a grin.

Vance shot him a glare. "That's not what I meant."

"Sure it is. I saw you checking her out. Hell, your tongue was practically hanging out of your mouth while you watched her walk away."

"Oh, stuff a sock in it," Vance growled. "I was only gaping at her in shock. Where does that idiotic female cop think she's patrolling? Downtown Chicago?"

Wade arched a dark brow and grinned unsympathetically as he cruised toward the restaurant to meet his wife for their anniversary lunch. "That's a good lesson for you, joker. You gotta watch who you're fooling with. Just pay your fine and get over it.''

"I most certainly will not!" Vance huffed indignantly. "Just because she's a knockout in a cop uniform doesn't mean she can go around handing out citations that no other law officer in these parts would consider ticketing."

Wade chuckled as he pulled into a vacant parking space. "A knockout, huh? So you do admit it."

"As if you didn't notice she was built like a supermodel," Vance said, and smirked. "You may be loco over Laura, but no man could overlook a woman with a body like that lady cop has."

"I agree she's stacked. So are you gonna ask her out after you pay your fine?" Wade asked as he piled from the truck.

"Not on your life," Vance said adamantly. "The day I get interested in a gung ho cop is the day you have my permission to shoot me."

"Right," Wade said as he made a beeline for the restaurant. "A cop and a practical joker. It'd never work."

"Damn right it wouldn't." Vance followed his cousin through the door to pan the interior. "I like fun-loving females whose natural reaction is to smile, not look down their noses at you and scowl. Besides, that lady cop is so staunch and defensive that she'd never be a bit of fun, even out of uniform."

Vance was certain his cousin hadn't heard a word he said. The instant Wade saw his blond, blue-eyed wife waving at him from the corner booth he strode toward her like a dog going to heel. It was nauseating to watch those two lovebirds together. Of course, watching Cousin Quint and his new wife, Steph, wasn't any better. They couldn't keep their hands and eyes off each other, either.

Speak of the devil, Vance mused as Cousin Q sauntered from the kitchen, holding hands with the redheaded queen of cuisine. Dining with these four was sure to ruin Vance's appetite.

"What's wrong with you?" Quint stared curiously at Vance as he cozied up in the booth beside Steph.

"Oh, don't mind him," Wade said, grinning. "He's bent out of shape because he had a run-in with the new police officer. She's a real pistol, by the way."

"Pistol, hell," Vance muttered. "She's an assault weapon and she'll mow you down if you get in her line of fire."

Laura and Steph stared worriedly at Vance. "What happened?" Laura asked.

Wade waved off their concern. "You know the joker. He tried to play one of his dumb pranks and the new lady cop didn't think it was the least bit funny. She fined him a hundred bucks for stupidity."

Quint burst out laughing. "That'll teach you to be more selective, cuz. Serves you right."

For sure, Vance was getting no sympathy from this quarter. Even Laura and Steph commenced giggling.

Vance sulked his way through lunch while the

lovebirds cooed at each other. Well, maybe his family thought he should pay the hefty fine and chalk it up to a prank gone sour, but Vance wasn't letting it go. Ms. Gung Ho hadn't heard the last from him on the subject. He'd go over her head and talk to the chief of police. Tate Jackson needed to know that a member of his force was harassing one of the lifelong residents of the community. Tate was a reasonable man who'd lived in Hoot's Roost for fifteen years. He would make certain that his new officer wasn't overstepping her bounds.

"Where are you off to in such a rush?" Wade asked when Vance dropped a ten spot on the table and vaulted to his feet.

"I'm going to swing by the police department before I pick up the old truck."

"Let it go," Quint advised.

"Like he said," Wade chimed in. "All you're gonna do is make that lady cop madder than she is now. She'll be gunning for you every time you show your face in town."

Vance ignored the advice and strode across town square. He cast a distracted glance toward the circular fountain where a concrete owl hovered in perpetual flight.

Although Vance was usually a happy-go-lucky, carefree kind of guy he wasn't going to let that rookie cop get away with this. He just had to make sure he got to tell his side of the story first.

When Vance breezed in the door of the police station he flashed the dispatcher a friendly smile. "Hi, Maggie, how's it going?"

Maggie Davidson grinned back at him. "Fine, handsome. What are you up to? No good, as usual?"

Vance braced his elbows on the counter and flashed her a high-voltage smile. At least she reacted favorably, he thought. Unlike that green-eyed monster of a cop.

He and Maggie had dated casually for a few months before she got stuck on a man who eventually became her ex-husband. Vance decided to pour on the charm and ensure that he had one ally in enemy camp.

"You know me, darlin', I'm a harmless, law-abiding citizen who wouldn't hurt a fly." He graced her with a trademark grin. "Is Tate in his office? I'd like to chat with him for a few minutes."

"Sure is. Go on back. I'll let him know you're on your way."

"Thanks, good lookin'. Seeing anyone at the moment?"

Maggie shrugged and propped her chin on her hand. "Not seriously. You?"

"Nope. Maybe we can do a little two-stepping at Hoot's Tavern Friday night."

She beamed with delight. "Love to."

Vance ambled down the hall, remembering that he'd always had fun with Maggie in the old days. In addition, it never hurt to have a friend in the right place. Plus, he could quiz Maggie about the new officer and find out what caused that chip on her shoulder.

"Come in," Tate Jackson called out when Vance rapped lightly on the door.

Vance strode inside to pump Tate's hand then he plopped into the creaky wooden chair across from the chief's desk that was piled high with files and red-tape forms.

"What can I do for you, Vance?" Tate asked.

"I came to file a complaint," Vance replied. "I had a run-in with the lady cop on your force this morning."

Tate rocked back in his chair and his graying brows flattened over his eyes. "Did you? What kind of run-in?"

Vance tried to keep his voice neutral, but it wasn't easy when the image of that high-and-mighty bombshell cop popped to mind. "She slapped me with a ticket when I tried to bring my old farm truck into town for repairs. I told her I was on my way to the service station, but it didn't faze her. I don't know where she hails from, but she seems to think that we should follow the same regulations here in the outback that apply to the traffic-congested metropolis."

Tate steepled his fingers under his chin and nodded pensively. "I see. Didn't cut you any slack, did she?"

"None whatsoever," Vance confirmed. "That old truck might look like a bucket of rust, but it's necessary equipment on the ranch. My cousins borrow it all the time. We haul barbwire, tools, cattle feed, you name it. There's times when I have to take it to town for repairs, but that rookie ordered me to turn it around and drive home."

"Hmm," was all Tate had to say in response.

"She wasn't the least bit understanding," Vance went on. "She fined me a hundred bucks to let me bring the truck to Pinky's station for tires and a muffler. You'd think there was a toll road between my ranch and town and she's in charge of collecting payment."

"A hundred dollars, you say?" Tate murmured. "That does sound a little steep. Let me see the ticket."

Yesss! Good ole Tate was on Vance's side. That was all the encouragement Vance needed. "And I'm sorry to report that your lady cop has a holier-than-thou attitude that's going to alienate townsfolk," he tattled.

Tate studied the ticket for a moment. "I suppose you gave her the good-ole-boy routine, but she didn't bite."

"She sure didn't. I climbed down from the truck and she yelled 'Freeze!' Heck, you'd have thought I was about to take potshots at her or something. Then she pulled her gun on me and flashed it around to intimidate me. We're talking loose cannon here, Chief. I'd hate to think what would happen if someone committed a serious offense," he added. "Then she started spouting code numbers at me. I have no idea what she was ranting about."

Another rap rattled the door and Tate glanced sideways. "Come in."

Vance inwardly cringed when the object of his frustration materialized in the doorway. The cop with those dazzling green eyes and a body to die for stopped in her tracks. Her narrowed gaze bounced from Tate to Vance. He tossed her a smug grin. *Bring it on, Ms. Smarty-Pants. We'll see who walks out of here with the reprimand.*

2

"I WONDER IF I MIGHT HAVE a word with you, sir. After you finish your conference, of course," the lady cop said politely.

Vance sincerely hoped Tate called this cop on the carpet. The prospect provoked him to smile in devilish delight.

Tate arched a questioning brow. "Does this have anything to do with the incident Vance is discussing with me?"

The lady cop nodded and that shiny braid of dark hair curled over her shoulder to brush the swell of her breast. Vance tried not to notice, he really did. But damn she was built like nobody's business. Too bad that she had the disposition of a snapping turtle.

"Yes, sir, it does," she told her superior.

"Then take a seat, Miranda, and let's get this situation squared away."

Miranda. Didn't that just figure, Vance mused. The knockout female had decided to enter a profession in which she could *Miranda* everyone. Well, he'd like to read her a few rights and tell her what she could do with herself and her hoity-toity, by-the-book attitude.

"Vance was just telling me about your confrontation on the highway this morning. He objected to the hefty fine.''

Didn't that just figure, Miranda mused, keeping her expression carefully controlled. No doubt this practical joker had decided to take the incident a step farther by tattling to her boss. The rat.

"I'm sure he objected," she commented, "but I maintain that he got exactly what he deserved for turning that unsafe vehicle over to his cousin to drive to town after I sent Mr. Ryder back the way he'd come."

When Tate leveled a pointed stare on Vance, Miranda noted that he sank a little deeper in his rickety chair. Obviously the stool pigeon purposely omitted several important details.

"You didn't mention that, Vance," Tate said stonily.

"I was just getting to that part when we were interrupted," Vance mumbled, shooting Miranda a fulminating glance.

"Of course you were," she said, then sniffed.

Vance braced his hands on the armrest and jerked upright. "Hey, *I* was here first to give my report. *You* were out of line."

He glowered at her from beneath bunched brows. Refusing to be intimidated, she glared right back at him.

"So I suppose you didn't mention that you took devilish delight in trying to make me look like a fool in front of your cousin," she countered. "Well, the joke's on you, Mr. Ryder. The next time I pull you over you better show some respect!"

"I will not be bullied by a gun-toting female who's itching to blow my head off over a stupid vehicle violation!" he snapped.

"I was not itching to blow your head off...*then,*" she retaliated, green eyes flashing. "*Now,* I'm thinking about it."

"I don't have to take this abuse from you, lady," Vance flared.

"Of course you do. You invite abuse and it would be rude of you not to accept it," she sniped at him.

When Vance bounded from his chair and Miranda stamped forward to confront him—nose to nose and toe to toe—Tate pounded his fist on the desk, demanding attention.

"Park it, both of you," he boomed. "Let's not allow a minor infraction to escalate into World War Three, shall we?"

"She fined me for stupidity!" Vance roared as he plunked into his chair. "How professional is that?"

Miranda swallowed uneasily when the chief's gaze zeroed in on her. Okay, so that wasn't very professional of her, she'd admit it. But this handsome hunk of cowboy had ticked her off royally. She couldn't say exactly what there was about him that got her hackles up. It was just a knee-jerk reaction. She was intensely aware of him and this ridiculous attraction made her megadefensive.

"You fined him for *stupidity?*" Tate repeated incredulously.

"He deliberately provoked me. Plus, I should have arrested him for sexual harassment," she blurted out. "He tried to flirt with me to get out of the warning and ticket."

"That's a mistake I'll never make again, believe you me, lady. I've met rattlers with better dispositions." Vance crossed his arms over his broad chest and glared laser beams at her. "You can't take a joke worth a flip, either."

She let him have it with both barrels blazing— figuratively speaking of course. "And you don't have enough brains under that dirty cowboy hat to know when to be serious and not come on to a female officer."

Vance scowled at her. "I resent that dumb cowboy comment."

"Enough already!" Tate blared as he vaulted to his feet. His thick chest swelled like a bullfrog as he glowered first at Vance then at Miranda. He sucked in a steadying breath then appraised the two antagonists who were glaring each other down like gunfighters at twenty paces.

It was a long moment before he said, "First off, Miranda, fining a man for stupidity, even if he deserves it, won't hold up in traffic court and you know it."

Vance smiled so smugly at her that she gnashed her teeth, crossed her arms and glanced the other way.

"Secondly," Tate continued, "flirting with a law official is inappropriate and you know it, Vance."

So there, thought Miranda, wishing she could childishly stick out her tongue at that cocky cowboy. He would never have gotten to first base with her anyway. No matter how attractive he was—in a rugged, back country sort of way—he wasn't her type. If he'd come on to her while she was dressed in civilian clothes she would have made use of her years of tae kwon do instruction and left him flat on his butt, gasping for breath.

"Now then," Tate said as he dropped back to his chair to drum his beefy fingers on the desk. "I'm not going to react rashly, which is apparently what you both did during the altercation this morning. I'm going to give this situation some thought before I decide how to handle it."

"Sounds fair to me, Uncle Tate," she took grand satisfaction in saying.

"*Uncle* Tate?" Vance hooted, owl-eyed.

When Tate Jackson nodded, Vance wilted back in his chair and inwardly groaned. He was sunk for sure. Tate was usually a fair man. But coming from a close-knit family himself, Vance always stood behind his cousins when trouble arose. True, Vance and his cousins, even the absentee Gage Ryder, delighted in razzing each other until hell wouldn't have it. But when the chips were down they became the Four Musketeers. All for one and all that jazz.

No doubt, Tate felt the same connection to his niece, even if Ms. Serious Britches was aloof, defensive and snippy. She also seemed to crave a position of authority so she could lord over the males of the species.

No question about it, Tate would side with Miranda and Vance would be doing time in the slammer, just because of his clunker truck and a harmless prank. Wouldn't that be a fun way to spend his up-coming birthday?

"You will both report back to my office at ten o'clock sharp on Saturday," Tate decreed. "That will give you three days to cool down. In addition, you will abide by whatever decision I make con-cerning the incident. Agreed?"

"Yes, Chief," Miranda said so sweetly that Vance feared he'd hurl his lunch.

"Fine, Chief," Vance muttered, knowing he was doomed.

Tate couldn't possibly be impartial where his gor-geous but prickly niece was concerned. Vance would have to turn all his ranch duties over to Cous-ins Q and W while he rotted away in the calaboose. If he was lucky, maybe Stephanie would deliver meals from her restaurant and Laura could drop off some reading material from the high school where she taught. Yup, Tate would pretend to think it over for three days, but he'd still lower the boom on Vance.

Tate's niece, for crying out loud! No wonder the trigger-happy lady cop hadn't been booted off the force already.

"Now, both of you scram, I have a pile of reports to fill out," Tate grumbled as he stared at his clut-tered desk. "And try to stay out of each other's way and out of trouble. *Please.*"

Vance nodded grimly as he surged from his chair. However, he was too consumed by frustration to no-tice the chief's wry smile or detect the snicker he camouflaged with a cough. Obviously Chief Jackson found the situation highly entertaining.

It took considerable restraint on Vance's part not to breeze through the door and let it slam in Miranda's face. Instead he bowed like the gentleman his mother instructed him to be and swept his arm forward. "After you, Officer Jackson."

"Thank you, Mr. Ryder," she replied in the same overly polite tone.

Vance decided that he'd made a tactical error by permitting the knockout female in uniform to precede him down the hall. He had to stare at her shapely backside and the mesmerizing glide of her hips. The unruly man in him wanted to let loose with a wolf whistle, but the sensible side of his brain kept chanting that this was the very last female on the planet that he wanted to be physically attracted to. The only thing the woman had going for her, as far as he was concerned, was her alluring looks. Unfortunately her attitude and personality worked as effectively as the pesticide he needed to spray on his pastures this afternoon.

Vance made a mental note to warn his cousins to take a wide berth around Officer Miranda Jackson, lest they ended up in his position. Since she was the chief's niece, the townsfolk were obviously stuck with her. The thought was almost enough to make Vance consider selling his ranch and taking up residence beyond this bombshell of a barracuda's legal jurisdiction.

DRIVING THE JALOPY TRUCK that now boasted new tires and a muffler that didn't leave a vapor trail of fumes, Vance headed to his ranch. This time he could plainly see the patrol car trailing him because he'd taken time to wash the truck—as ordered by the High Priestess of the police department—the previous day. Vance was certain the reign of terror had only begun in Owl County. That vindictive lady cop was out to get him, no doubt about it.

"Damn," he muttered when lights flashed behind him.

What was it this time? he wondered sourly. Expired license tag? Naw, that was too easy. Leave it to Miranda Jackson to dig up some obscure vehicle code and stick it to him, despite what her dear uncle had said about mutual avoidance at yesterday's meeting.

Swearing under his breath, Vance waited for Miranda to climb from her car and approach him. He couldn't muster the good-natured smile he usually wore as he studied her in the side mirror. This female brought out the worst in him.

When she strode up to the truck he flung up his hands in supplication. "Guilty as charged. Just write me up."

"I'm not going to give you a ticket," she said, surprising the hell out of him.

"So, what's the problem now? Surely you aren't pulling me over to chitchat. I got the distinct impression that you don't have much use for me, judging by our yelling match in the chief's office yesterday." He smiled goadingly. "Oh, excuse me, make that *Uncle* Tate's office."

Her chin came up as she whipped off her mirrored

sunglasses to give him the full benefit of her death-ray glare. "Look, Mr. Ryder, I only stopped you to apologize for losing my temper at headquarters. I overreacted. It was unprofessional and it's never happened before. For some reason you rub me the wrong way."

"Well, not to worry, *Randi*," he said, knowing it would probably irritate her to be addressed by an abbreviated form of her name. "I'm not planning to rub you the right way, either. Far as I'm concerned, the less we see of each other the better."

"My sentiments exactly," she gritted out. "You obey the laws around here and there will be no reason whatsoever for us to engage in conversation…"

Her voice trailed off when Wade Ryder drove by and honked his horn. A few moments later Quint whizzed by, waving and grinning. Vance pulled his Resistol hat down on his forehead, slumped on the seat and cursed colorfully. No doubt, his demon cousins would taunt him unmercifully when he met them at the ranch to begin their afternoon chores.

"If you're through with me, officer, I have work to do."

"I'm definitely through with you," she announced, stepping away from the window. "I will abide by whatever decision the chief makes about our…um…incident."

"Ditto," Vance said, "but I expect to get the short end of the stick since you've got family and professional connections."

He watched her thrust back her shoulders and jerk up her chin. His gaze immediately dipped to her well-endowed chest. It was beyond comprehension that he found this female so damn attractive when she bugged the hell out of him. She was so distant and reserved that he had the ridiculous urge to draw a reaction from her—like tormenting a guard at Buckingham Palace until he snapped.

Vance had never had a problem relating to people or dealing with women. Normally he got along with everyone—male and female alike—because it was his objective in life to draw out a smile. He joked around, enjoyed making folks laugh and he tried not to take himself, or the world, too seriously.

He'd learned that technique after getting his heart crammed into a meat grinder by Shawna Karmody a few years back. Since that humiliating affair Vance enjoyed the company of women, enjoyed casual sexual gratification and used corny jokes and playful pranks to remain at an emotional arm's length.

Too bad he found nothing amusing about dealing with Miranda Jackson. And yet, he couldn't keep his eyes off her. She drew his attention and held if fast. What kind of self-defeating complex did he have going here?

"You're doing it again," Miranda said, jostling him back to the present.

Vance jerked his gaze off her full breasts. "Doing what?"

"Staring at me as if you can see…" Her gaze flicked away, unable to maintain visual contact. "I don't like it when men look past the uniform. It's insulting and degrading."

"Then try pinning that badge someplace besides on your chest," Vance teased, and then grinned scampishly when her face flushed beet red. "Look, Officer Jackson, I'm trying my damn...er... darnedest to stay out of your way and to see you impersonally, but you might as well know that I find you attractive.

"I don't particularly like you and you definitely don't like me, but there you have it. Right smack-dab out in the open. Now, if you want to arrest me for that, then fine. I'll plead no contest. But just because I can't seem to help liking what I see, doesn't mean I plan to throw myself at you. I do have some restraint. Are we clear on that, ma'am?"

Miranda stared into his ruggedly handsome face, into those entrancing midnight-colored eyes, and felt the unwanted jolt of attraction jarring her entire body. "Okay, since you're being honest I'll return the favor. I like the looks of you, too, even if you don't take things seriously and you drive the most pathetic excuse for a vehicle that ever cruised the highway. You're good-looking and I'm sure you know it. Same goes for your two cousins."

"Three, actually," he corrected, lips twitching. "But Gage is out of the country, breaking foreign hearts as we speak, I suspect. And thank you for the compliment, ma'am. Even if you think I'm stupid, it's nice to know you don't find me hideously ugly while you're handing me warnings and tickets."

Miranda broke down and smiled when he grinned playfully. She just couldn't help it. The man was a charmer when he wanted to be. His smile was contagious and those devilish eyes lured her into their dark, shiny depths.

"Well, I guess that's that. Now we can attend the chief's upcoming meeting without going for each other's throats," she said, taking another step away from more the unwanted lure of Vance Ryder.

"Fine with me." He poked his head out the window and extended his hand. "Shall we shake on it and call a truce?"

Miranda placed her hand in his—and felt the sizzle of electricity humming through her body. She quickly extracted her hand from his grasp and noted her palm was sweating. For heaven's sake, what was the matter with her? Since graduating from the academy she'd learned to handle a variety of tense and dangerous situations. So why was dealing with this particular cowboy different? Why did he affect her to such unprecedented extremes? She'd never felt such an intense reaction to the presence or the casual touch of a man before.

It was *so* unlike her. She lived for the job. Yet, since the moment she encountered Vance Ryder her hormones had gone completely haywire. This was absurd. She didn't even like him very much and he admitted he didn't care much for her, either.

She and Vance were like protons and neutrons bouncing around inside the same atom, repelling each other, colliding with each other. They were absolutely nothing alike. They had nothing in common. They approached life from opposing directions. She took life, and her job, seriously and he didn't seem capable of taking anything seriously—

except their previous shouting match in Tate's office.

Vance flexed and clenched his fist then clamped his hands around the steering wheel. He took his gaze off her and stared through the recently washed windshield. "I need to get going."

"If the blinkers don't work on this bucket of bolts, please use hand signals when you veer onto the graveled road," she instructed, falling back into police mode. "Have a good day, sir."

Vance glanced sideways at her and her heart gave an unexpected lurch when his obsidian eyes twinkled and he flashed one of those smiles that no woman could resist.

"You, too, Officer," he said in a low, raspy voice that drifted down her spine like a seductive caress.

When the truck rumbled off, its engine sputtering, Miranda pivoted on her heels to return to her squad car. She sincerely hoped that after the Saturday meeting at headquarters she wouldn't see Vance Ryder—except at a safe distance. She had no intention of getting interested in that cowboy. After all, she was only going to be employed by HRPD until Uncle Tate gave her the nod to take a position in Oklahoma City.

Miranda had her life planned out. Had a promising career ahead of her. She intended to follow in her dad's and her two brothers' footsteps. A family of cops serving in the same jurisdiction. It was all she'd ever wanted, all she'd dreamed about.

For sure, she wasn't going to get sidetracked by

a down-on-his luck rancher who drove a beat-up truck and probably had the ambition of a slug.

On that determined thought Miranda slid beneath the steering wheel then cruised off to ensure the speed demons around Hoot's Roost observed traffic codes.

VANCE INWARDLY GRIMACED when he put on the brakes and saw his cousins leaning leisurely against the fender of Quint's red pickup. Those two rascals were lying in wait, ready to tease the hell out of him for getting stopped two days in a row by the same lady cop. He didn't want them niggling him for information because, as much as he didn't approve of Randi Jackson and her gung ho attitude, shaking hands with her and staring too long at that gorgeous bod of hers set off disturbing explosions of sexual attraction. It was insane. Plus, he'd gotten aroused just watching her walk toward him.

Jeez, if ever there was a more unlikely pair, he and Randi were it. He smiled easily and often. She didn't. He looked for amusement in everything he did. She took everything megaseriously and stood behind her badge like a protective shield. But, man was she hot. The way she filled out her blue uniform should've been a full-fledged crime.

"So, cuz," Wade said playfully, "how's your on-going battle with law working out?"

When Quint snickered, Vance glared at the demonic duo. "Don't wanna talk about it. We've got work to do."

"So, are you busted or not?" Quint asked, ignoring Vance's thunderous scowl. "Or is the officer in question the only one busted?"

"Knock it off," Vance growled. "She's an officer of the law and her bustline is not open for discussion."

Again, his wicked cousins snickered. Vance seriously considered punching the grins off their faces.

"Surely you realize we aren't going to lift a finger to help you hook up the spray rigs to the tractors until you tell us what happened yesterday when you marched yourself down to the police station and explain why you got stopped today."

"Do you have to pay the hefty fine or not?" Wade quizzed.

"I don't know yet," Vance mumbled, resigned to giving his report before any work got done. "But since I discovered the lady cop is Tate Jackson's darling niece, I expect to pay through the nose. Tate is reserving judgment in the matter until the end of the week."

"His niece?" Wade and Quint parroted in unison. "You are kidding."

"No, for once, I'm not." Vance grabbed the five-gallon jugs of pesticide from the back of the clunker truck.

Wade retrieved the garden hose, crammed one end into the top of the spray tank, and then switched on the water. "Tate's a bachelor, right? Never had kids?"

"Not that I know of," Quint said as he checked for clogs in the spigots on the spray rig. "I guess that means his niece is pretty special to him."

"That'd be my guess." Vance climbed onto the supporting beam of the rig to pour the concentrated chemicals into the tank. "Most likely, I'll have to pay the fine and apologize for yelling at Randi during our three-way conference."

Wade's gaze leaped to Vance. "You yelled at her in front of the chief of police? Are you nuts?"

"Must be," Quint diagnosed. "You might as well have pinned a note on your chest that said—Fine Me—Big-Time. I'm An Idiot."

"Well, she yelled at me first," he said defensively then frowned. "I think. We were both yelling at each other. I don't remember who started it, but Tate put a stop to it."

Wade glanced at Quint. Both men snickered again. Damn them. It was going to be a long afternoon, Vance decided.

3

MIRANDA SWITCHED ON the sirens and lights when she saw the dark blue extended cab pickup whizzing toward town. The driver was doing eight miles over the speed limit and she intended to call him on it.

When the truck pulled over, Miranda swerved off the road and climbed from the squad car. She opened her mouth to ask what the big rush was all about then snapped her jaw shut when she glanced through the open window to see the spic-and-span version of the dusty cowboy she'd encountered for the fifth time in three days.

"Great," she muttered sourly. He was like a curse that wouldn't go away.

Vance rolled his eyes, sighed audibly and lifted his hand, palm upward. "Just gimme the blasted ticket. I was speeding. I'm late for a date. I'm guilty," he said, staring straight through the windshield—anywhere but at her.

Miranda frowned pensively. Vance definitely deserved a fine for speeding, but if she gave it to him she predicted her uncle would think she *was* out to get this cowboy. Damn, she prided herself in going by the book—until the morning she clashed with

Vance and allowed her fierce reaction to interfere with her job.

Although it went against the grain she decided *not* to ticket Vance, for fear he'd twist this incident against her during the conference with the chief. "Just slow this thing down, speed demon," she ordered brusquely.

He nodded then cast her a quick sidelong glance. "Yes, ma'am. Sorry, ma'am."

Well, at least he was showing some respect. No corny jokes, no teasing grins. No flirtation or appraising stares. So why did she feel a little disappointed that he wouldn't even look at her? He was going out on a date. Why did she care? She didn't. It didn't bother her in the least. Right?

When Vance put the truck in gear and cruised off Miranda stood by the roadside, watching the taillights disappear over the hill.

Wasn't there some law of nature stating that five chance meetings in the course of three days defied probability? She'd been in Hoot's Roost for almost two months, encountering a variety of citizens while on patrol. And then wham! She couldn't turn around without bumping into Vance Ryder.

"Well, surely that's the last I'll see of him before Saturday's meeting," she muttered as she hiked back to her car.

She had only two hours left on her split shift. Then she could return to the garage apartment she'd rented, treat herself to a warm, relaxing bath, watch a movie on TV then bed down for the night. Tomorrow she'd psyche herself up for her final confrontation with Vance Ryder. Life would return to normal and she'd focus on moving forward with her career.

That wasn't asking too much, was it? Of course not…so why did the prospect of Vance turning all his country charm on his date cause this unfamiliar twinge in the pit of her belly? There was nothing—absolutely nothing—between them, she told herself as she flicked on her headlights and cruised off.

VANCE TWIRLED MAGGIE Davidson around the dance floor at Hoot's Tavern, telling himself that he was having a good time. Maggie was personable and attractive. She was good company. They'd grown up together and they shared similar backgrounds and interests. So why were visions of Randi Jackson—naked—buzzing around his head? Sheesh, what was the matter with him? And why hadn't she given him the ticket he deserved?

He thought about that for a minute and decided it wasn't because she'd decided to go easy on him. But rather, because she didn't want *him* to have the slightest leverage to use against her when they met with Tate.

"You okay?" Maggie asked as she led the way back to their table, after the fast-tempoed song ended.

"Great." Vance flashed a wide smile. "Couldn't be better."

"You seem kinda distracted," Maggie observed.

"Well, maybe a little." Half-truth. He was distracted—a lot. "I have to meet with the chief and the lady cop in the morning to find out how much lighter I'll be in the wallet.''

Maggie chuckled. ''I heard about that. Or rather, I heard the yelling coming from the chief's office. Miranda is a do-gooder. She's nice and all that.''

Nice wasn't the word Vance would've used to describe her, but he kept his mouth shut.

''I think she's trying to overachieve, to prove herself to the rest of the men on the force. Her dad and older brothers work for OCPD,'' she informed him. ''Tate is giving her the chance to gain her footing before she's promoted to the big city. You know, learn the ropes out here in the boonies where the crime rate isn't horrific.''

''I suppose Miranda is Tate's pride and joy,'' Vance said glumly.

''Of course. He adores his niece and nephews. He's bragged on them for years. Plus, Miranda graduated with flying colors from the academy. Good at self-defense and a real sharpshooter, so Tate says.''

Wonderful. The woman was a bombshell *and* a walking lethal weapon. ''What about her mom?'' Vance asked curiously.

''She bailed out early on,'' Maggie imparted before she sipped her drink. ''Couldn't handle the stress, according to Tate. The chief thinks Miranda is out to prove that she can not only handle the pressure but excel at it.''

Vance swallowed a sip of beer. ''Not me. The only problem I care to resolve is which gate to open to which pasture so my cattle will have plenty to eat.''

"Yeah, right. Like I don't know how hard you work and how well you did on the rodeo circuit." Maggie smirked at him. "Of course, leave it to you to shrug off the pressure of making a go of your ranch when the agricultural economy is tight."

"Still, you don't see me haring off to battle the criminal elements of society."

The words barely passed his lips when shouts broke out at the bar. Vance swiveled in his chair to see two hired hands from a neighboring ranch throwing punches at each other. Customers were scattering like quail to avoid flying fists. Vance, who'd participated in his share of bar room brouhahas during his rodeo heydays, reflexively bounded to his feet to separate the brawlers before they destroyed the place.

"Hey, cool your jets," he ordered the two men who held each other in hammerlocks. They ignored him and wrestled each other to the floor to deliver one power-packed blow after another. As they rolled sideways a table crashed to the floor, along with four glasses of beer.

Vance cursed when beer catapulted onto his chest. "Jake, knock it off!" He grabbed one of the men and gave him a hard upward yank. "Now you and Fred kiss and make up. The way you're going at it you'll have everyone in here thinking you don't love each other."

Well, so much for teasing both drunkards back into good humor. They weren't paying attention. When another table teetered off balance Vance reached over to snatch up the full pitcher of beer before it hit the floor.

"Damn it!" he yelped when the brawlers banged into the back of his knees. He staggered to catch his balance, but more beer slopped down his shirt and dribbled on the crotch of his jeans. Before he could set aside the pitcher a flying elbow gouged him in the kidney. His legs buckled and he hit his knees. Scowling, he twisted around—and accidentally caught a fist in the eye.

"That does it!" Vance roared as he set aside the pitcher. No more Mister Nice Guy. He'd tried to cajole these yahoos into ceasing and desisting, but they wouldn't cooperate. He was left with no choice but to knock some sense into them.

Vance reared back and punched out Fred's lights. The drunkard wilted on the floor in a tangled heap. Vance cocked his arm to throw a punch at Jake, but when he heard that tormentingly familiar female voice yell *Freeze!* he froze.

But Jake didn't. He busted Vance right in the chops.

His head was still spinning while he watched Miranda—lady cop to the rescue—storm toward him. When Jake threw another punch she tried to whack him over the head with her nightstick. Unfortunately Jake teetered sideways and the blow caught Vance upside the head.

Groaning, he collapsed on the floor and watched stars explode behind his eyelids. Next time somebody started a brawl Vance definitely was not going to step in to intervene. He was getting too old for this stuff.

Miranda grabbed Jake by the back of his shirt and gave him a good shaking. "Get on your feet," she barked at him.

Miranda felt as if she was on display as she dragged Jake to his knees then squatted down to check on the third brawler who lay unconscious on the floor. Her credibility was at stake here, she realized. She was a woman and the newest addition to the police force. She had to take command of this situation so the townsfolk would gain confidence in her abilities to quell disturbances.

As for Vance Ryder, Miranda had no choice but to presume the man was a habitual troublemaker—in addition to being a speed demon, a defiant practical joker and incorrigible flirt. The man didn't seem capable of making wise choices in life.

But oh, how she wished she hadn't been the officer closest to the tavern when the bartender called for police assistance.

Grimly Miranda slapped the cuffs on all three men. Vance braced himself on his elbows, glared at her and said, "Wait just a damn minute!"

"You have the right to remain silent," she muttered at him. "And I prefer that you do. Just clam up, Vance."

The glower he directed at her as he rolled to his feet indicated he'd like to give her a punch in the nose—just like he'd obviously done to the other cowboys. Damnation, this man just kept making her life difficult, kept tormenting her emotions, challenging her authority.

The crowd parted like drapes as Miranda marched her prisoners out the door. "I'll send another officer to take statements so don't anyone leave," she called over her shoulder.

Once outside, Miranda shoved the men into the caged back seat. Vance ended up in the middle. He hurled visual daggers at her via the rearview mirror.

"I didn't do a blasted thing wrong back there," he growled.

"What? Assault and battery don't count in your book? Sorry, but they count in mine," she replied.

"I was trying to break up the fight," he insisted.

"Really? When I walked in you clocked the man on your right."

"Would you please tell the cop that I wasn't involved?" Vance demanded of the men who bookended him.

Miranda glanced at the other two brawlers who simply glared at Vance.

"Well, damn," Vance muttered. "Framed. This is a fine how-do-you-do."

Vance said not another word—thank goodness—when she pulled up to headquarters. He didn't resist when she herded him and the other men into the holding tank.

Breathing a sigh of relief, Miranda propped herself against the counter and glanced at the dispatcher working the night shift. "Better call the chief," she said grimly.

While the dispatcher made the call Miranda piv-

oted toward the front door. She still had a half hour
left on patrol and she didn't want to be within shouting distance when Uncle Tate showed up to handle
the alleged brawlers. Why did she have to be the
one who locked Vance in the slammer? She could
almost hear Vance tattling to Tate that this latest
fiasco proved she was out to get him.

VANCE PACED THE HALL, waiting for Wade to show
up. His cousin had been less than pleased when the
call came to bail him out. Apparently Wade had
more *pleasurable* pursuits planned for the evening
and didn't take kindly to being roused out of bed by
his irate cousin. Maggie Davidson had arrived fifteen minutes earlier to inform the chief that Vance
had only tried to stop the fracas before property was
destroyed and that all he got for his efforts was a
drenching in beer, a black eye, bruised jaw and a
knot on his head.

"I'm really sorry about this," Maggie had said
when Vance exited the grungy cell.

Vance had carefully inspected his swollen eye and
muttered a few curses to that lady cop's name.
"Why don't you drive my truck to your place and
I'll pick it up when Wade gets here. No need for
you to hang around."

Patting him sympathetically, Maggie pushed up
on tiptoe to give him a peck on the cheek that hadn't
suffered a jarring blow. Offering him a consoling
smile, she'd left headquarters.

Ten minutes later Wade arrived. "You don't look
so good, cuz," he said candidly.

"Thanks." Teeth gritted, Vance stalked toward the door. "Let's go."

"Where to next? Are we stopping by to shoot the policewoman on our way home?"

Vance flashed his grinning cousin a black scowl. "Don't tempt me. We're stopping by Maggie's place to get my truck. Then you can head home. Thanks for coming. If I'd known I'd be in and out so quickly I wouldn't have disturbed you at all."

"Is the meeting still on for tomorrow?" Wade asked as he cranked the engine of his pickup.

"Oh, yeah, and you can bet I'll have something to say about Randi the Robo Cop's complete mishandling of the situation at Hoot's Tavern. I was cuffed, stuffed and subjected to police brutality."

"Mind filling me on the details of what happened?"

"Don't wanna talk about it," Vance snapped.

He didn't break the silence when Wade pulled into Maggie's driveway, just slammed the door and got in his truck. Vance felt like putting his foot through the floorboard during the drive home. But the way his luck had been running he figured he'd get pulled over again and this time he'd go for that woman's throat!

One thing was for double damn sure, he mused as he begrudgingly observed the traffic laws—to the letter—on his way home. This insane fascination for Randi Jackson was over. Done. Kaput. As soon as he walked out of that morning meeting with the chief he never wanted to see her again—ever. She was the curse of his life. No woman, no matter how attractive and challenging she was, was worth this kind of torment. After tomorrow, Vance vowed he'd run—screaming—the other way when he saw her coming.

MIRANDA ENTERED THE CHIEF'S office with a deep sense of foreboding. Tate was ensconced behind his desk, looking as sober as a judge who was prepared to hand down a sentence of execution. Vance, she noted, didn't spare her the slightest glance, just sat there steaming and brooding.

He looked awful, she noticed. His eye and jaw had turned black and blue and there was a sizable knot on his forehead—compliments of her nightstick.

She'd read the statements taken at the tavern and discovered that Vance had tried to break up the fight. Needless to say she felt like an idiot for thinking the worst about him. She'd been intent on clearing the area and, from what she'd been able to determine during the altercation, Vance had been part of the problem, not the solution.

Another difficult lesson learned, she mused as she sank into her chair. Maybe she wasn't good cop material if she kept jumping to ill-founded conclusions. Maybe she didn't have her dad, uncle and brothers' instincts for keeping law and order. She was a failure at her first major assignment and she'd never wanted to be anything but a top-rate cop.

Miranda knew she was as good as gone from the force, even if her uncle was in charge here. Furthermore, she didn't want to be an embarrassment to a man with his upstanding reputation in town.

"Well," Tate said for starters, "we certainly had an eventful evening, didn't we?"

Vance shot Miranda a murderous look. With his bumps and bruises he looked menacing and unapproachable, but she tried not to flinch. "Yes, sir, I'm afraid so. I—"

Tate's meaty hand shot up to silence her. "I've given the previous situation serious consideration, asked for Wade's take on the incident and I've taken into account the fiasco from last night as well."

Miranda slouched in her chair when her uncle pinned her with a stony stare. She'd goofed up. She knew it. He knew it. Vance knew it. She'd be lucky indeed to get a security job position at a bank in some podunk town in the middle of nowhere.

"You two seem to have gotten off to a bad start," Tate remarked. "In my experience on the force I've discovered there's always at least two sides to every story." He stared at Vance, then at Miranda as he drummed his sausage-link fingers on the desk. "Rehashing last night's altercation at the tavern will only make both of you defensive and I'm in no mood to listen to another shouting match. In my opinion, and mine is the only one that counts here," he added emphatically, "you both did the right thing."

Miranda's jaw dropped open. Never in her wildest dreams had she expected Uncle Tate to defend her conduct. But it didn't seem to sit well with Vance because he sent her another disdainful glare.

"Witnesses verified that Vance tried to stop the fight before the tavern was trashed," Tate continued. "Miranda tried to follow standard procedure by clearing the area and letting backup take the statements. Any ill feelings between you two are outside the letter of the law. This will have to be worked out on a personal basis because this appears to be a personality conflict between you."

Tate leaned on his forearms on the desk and stared Miranda and Vance down. Miranda hadn't the slightest idea where her uncle was going with this.

"I plan to view this conflict between you as an internal affair because Vance is an old friend and Miranda is my niece and a member of my staff. I'm going to resolve it and this is how it's going to go down." Tate focused his attention on the battered cowboy. "Now then, Vance, you need to understand that it isn't easy being a rookie, as well as the first and only policewoman on this force. My niece is trying to gain the respect of her co-workers and the citizens of the community she's sworn to serve."

"Right," Vance said, and snorted. "She's trying to ruin my life. I have to wonder how many other lives she plans to destroy to meet her monthly quota."

The look Vance hurled at Miranda indicated she'd never have *his* respect. Not that she blamed him. From his standpoint he'd been the abused victim and he wanted to see her pay for her role in last night's foofaraw.

Tate heaved himself from his chair and strode around the desk to loom over Miranda and Vance.

He crossed his thick arms over his bulky chest—a gesture that implied that he wasn't going to be swayed by forthcoming comments and objections. Miranda wisely kept her trap shut. Vance did likewise.

"Since Miranda needs to gain a feel and understanding for life in this rural community, a community unlike the city where she grew up, I propose *you* familiarize her with life on the ranch and introduce her to the folks in town."

Vance nearly came unglued. "No way in Hades!" he crowed.

"In other words," Tate went on, ignoring the loud objection, "your sentence will be public service for one week and you will not pay the fine." While Vance sputtered, Tate's gaze riveted on Miranda. "To ensure that Vance understands what it's like for a woman on the force, he will accompany you on the evening shifts while you're on patrol. You'll be taking shorter shifts, which will mean a smaller salary for the week."

Miranda gaped at her uncle. "You want us to spend our days and evenings together for a week?" she choked out. "The man hates my guts. This won't work."

"*I* hate *you?*" Vance spouted. "I suffered unprovoked police brutality, in addition to being stopped three times on the highway. You think so little of me that you're out to get me. You even ruined my date—on purpose."

"That's ridiculous!" she erupted. "I couldn't care less how many women you go out with!"

"Quiet—" Tate cut in, but he wasted his breath.

"I can't work with Ms. Gung Ho, Chief," Vance muttered in frustration. "It'll be a race to see who murders whom first. I'll pay the fine. Gladly. Someone else can play nursemaid to Randi the Robo Cop. She might be your precious niece, but she's my worst nightmare."

"As if you haven't made my life miserable in the course of four days," Miranda said heatedly. "My job is on the line and all you can think about is how horrible it would be to spend a week in my company. It would be horrible for me, too, you know!"

"Children, simmer down," Tate broke in loudly. "I'm not finished yet. Just sit back in your chairs and take a deep breath. Your sentences are not negotiable. There will be no appeals. I'm judge and jury here, so pipe down."

A week with Randi underfoot? The thought was inconceivable. Vance wanted his normal life and his easygoing disposition back. He wouldn't get it with this witchy woman breathing down his neck. No telling what she'd screw up at his ranch. Plus, she'd likely get him killed while he was riding shotgun in the squad car. After all, she had a knack of pissing people off. He knew that from firsthand experience.

"I'd rather serve jail time," Vance declared.

"And I don't want to join Peter Pan in Neverland," she said huffily. "He's never grown up to take life seriously—"

"*Peter Pan?*" he crowed indignantly. "I'll have you know that I'm taking *this* seriously."

Tate surged upward, his muscled arms slashing through the air like machetes. "That's it! Silence!"

Vance frowned curiously. If he didn't know better he'd swear the chief was biting back a snicker.

"In addition," Tate went on eventually, "you two have graciously volunteered to co-chair the HRPD's annual town-wide garage sale that benefits our new youth center. If the event is a flop then you'll both receive equal blame. Any questions?"

"Yes," Vance said. "I'm feeling suicidal. Can I borrow your gun?"

"Here," Miranda offered generously. "Use mine."

Vance sneered at her and she sneered back.

"I'm giving you another few days to cool off before I throw you together for this assignment," Tate announced. "Come Tuesday morning, Miranda will report for ranch duties at seven sharp."

"Oh, goody gumdrops," Vance muttered sourly. "I can't think of anyone I'd rather spend my birthday with."

Tate didn't look the least bit sympathetic. "You can grab a bite of supper and begin patrolling at seven in the evening. Now skedaddle from my office. I have work to do."

Disgruntled, Vance exited posthaste. He didn't do Miranda the courtesy of holding open the door, either. He only had a few days of freedom before he faced a solid week with that dark-haired albatross clamped around his neck.

Vance wondered how long it would take for the chief to run him to ground if he decided to skip town. He definitely needed more than a few days to gird himself up for a week of having that lunatic woman following him around like his own shadow.

Tate certainly knew how to dole out the worst conceivable brand of punishment, Vance thought sourly. A scalding dip in the bubbling fires of hell wouldn't hurt as bad as a week in the company of Randi Jackson.

INSIDE THE OFFICE, Chief Tate Jackson was having himself a good laugh. He'd never seen two individuals so determined not to like each other and yet so obviously attracted to each other. It had taken tremendous effort to keep his serious "cop face" from slipping off during Vance and Miranda's animated protests. If his instincts were on the mark, the week of togetherness was exactly what Vance and Miranda needed to come to grips with their explosive reactions to one another.

Tate chuckled as he picked up a stack of folders and got to work. He knew he was handy with police-issued pistols, but he thought perhaps he also had a knack with Cupid's weapon of choice—a bow and arrow. If things worked out the way he predicted they would, he just might try moonlighting as a matchmaker.

4

DRESSED IN BLUE JEANS, a T-shirt and her OCPD windbreaker jacket—a gift from her dad and brothers—Miranda reluctantly climbed from her car at seven o'clock sharp. She fully expected Vance to test her mettle, but she hadn't expected to have his two cousins on hand to witness her inadequacy at handling ranch chores.

"Why are they here?" she asked as Vance approached, wearing leather chaps and a bulky denim jacket that emphasized his rugged good looks and muscular physique. She tried to ignore the tantalizing effect the man had on her—but it wasn't easy.

"They're here to ensure we don't kill each other," Vance replied as he appraised her choice of clothing. "No boots?"

"I don't own cowboy boots. Tennis shoes will have to do."

He grinned wickedly. "Well, good luck getting the fresh manure out of those treads."

He started to take her arm to escort her downhill to the pipe-and-cable corral then obviously decided against making physical contact. He'd made it perfectly clear that he thought she was a jinx and the curse of his life. Well, those feelings were mutual.

That day she met Vance would go down in the annals of history as the worst day in her personal and professional life.

"C'mon, I'll introduce you to Cousin Quint, formerly the ladies' man of the family. He has a nearby ranch and he married Steph after Thanksgiving last year. She owns the Palace restaurant and the food's terrific in case you haven't tried it yet."

"Steph, restaurant, Quint," she repeated. "Copy that."

Vance, she noted, almost smiled at her determination to remember names and familiarize herself with the citizens of Hoot's Roost.

"You've already met Wade. He claimed to be a woman-hater until he met and married Laura last summer. She teaches math and computer science at the high school," he informed her.

Miranda systematically filed the background information. "Got it."

He halted her in front of his cousins. "Miranda Jackson, HRPD, this is Quint Ryder," Vance introduced. "And I'm sure you remember Wade."

Wade tipped his hat politely. "Nice to see you again, Officer Jackson."

"Pleasure to meet you, ma'am," Quint added, flashing her a smile.

She studied the three similarly dressed cowboy cousins who towered over six feet and made her five feet six inches seem small in comparison. Obviously well muscled physiques, striking good looks and devastating smiles ran in the Ryder family. "Please call me Miranda,'' she insisted as she offered them a cordial smile.

''And this is Frank,'' Vance said, gesturing to the blue heeler that was wagging his stub of a tail. ''Wade's cow dog is the only one around here who has the good manners to shake hands.''

On cue, Frank lifted a paw and waited for Miranda to hunker down for the formal introduction.

''Best cow dog this side of the Red River,'' Wade boasted proudly. ''Or at least he was until my wife tried to turn him into a house dog. Frank's been suffering an identity crisis since Laura showed up to pamper him.''

Miranda noticed how the big cowboy's voice softened when he mentioned his wife. Clearly the man was deeply in love. She couldn't imagine how it would feel to be in love. She'd never been remotely close to experiencing those emotions.

Her gaze drifted to Quint. ''What about your wife, the restaurateur? Steph, right? Married three months?''

Quint's whiskey-colored eyes widened in surprise. ''You know Steph?''

''Not yet, but Vance mentioned her fabulous restaurant so I'll want to try it out.''

''Enough chitchat. We have cattle to separate and haul to Cousin Gage's ranch.'' Vance glanced down at Miranda. ''You *do* ride, don't you?''

Miranda shifted uneasily. ''Um…no.''

Vance's grin turned mischievous. ''Perfect.''

''He means that you won't have to unlearn any

bad habits," Quint put in as he sent Vance a sur-
reptitious glance. "Isn't that right, Cousin V?"

"Sure, what else?" Vance said with a nonchalant
shrug.

When Vance ambled toward the string of horses
tethered beside the gate Miranda glanced anxiously
at Wade. "I've heard Vance is the practical joker of
your family. He isn't going to put me on the wildest
bronc he's got is he?"

"Probably not. Most of his jokes are playful and
harmless," Wade assured her. "Like the time he left
red construction paper hearts on my pickup seat
while Laura was working as my temp housekeeper.
Then he disguised his voice and called to say I'd
won a honeymoon vacation to the Bahamas, long
before we'd even had our first date."

"Or the time Vance stocked our honeymoon
apartment with aphrodisiacs and left a bed as the
only stick of furniture in the place," Quint added
wryly. "Then there were the Christmas lights he
strung outside the apartment and glowing neon sign
that read. Do Not Disturb."

"In high school there were the usual pranks of
adding extra gas to our tanks to make us think we
were getting great mileage and nailing our shoes to
the floor," Wade recalled.

"Don't forget that trick he pulled on the baseball
coach with breath mints and water," Quint reminded
him. "The poor man's mouth turned green while he
was engaged in a heated dispute with the home-plate
umpire."

"And there was the time on the rodeo circuit

when Vance—'' Wade clamped his mouth shut
when Vance flashed him a silencing frown. "I guess
the joker doesn't want you to hear the list of his
offenses."

Vance drew the paint pony to a halt in front of
Miranda then glanced at his cousins. "Why don't
you round up the cattle in the west pasture while
Randi and I bring in the herd from the south. We'll
take Frank with us."

When Wade and Quint mounted up, Miranda
noted the ease with which they settled in their saddles. She doubted she'd look as relaxed on a horse.

"Ready, Calamity Jane?" Vance asked, directing
her attention to the stirrup. "Nothing to this. This
horse is well trained to move cattle. All you have to
do is stay aboard. Heaven forbid that you fall off
and end up with a black eye, swollen jaw and knot
on your noggin."

"About that knot," she said as she approached
the pinto mare. "It was an accident."

"Or an opportunity too good to pass up," he said,
and smirked.

Miranda wheeled on him. "Look, pal, I'm going
to do my level best to handle everything you throw
at me this week and try to get along with you. So
can we *please* get past that night at the tavern and
serve this sentence as amicably as possible?"

"Sure, just as soon as I get over that wisecrack
about Peter Pan," he said darkly. "I may be fun-
loving, but I take proper care of my cattle, horses
and ranch. Just because I try to inject enjoyment into

my work doesn't mean I shirk my duties and behave irresponsibly.''

''I can see that you don't,'' Miranda assured him. ''You have a well-manicured place that's indicative of pride, hard work and commitment.''

Her compliment took the defensiveness out of his stance and expression. He even smiled at her. Miranda wished he hadn't because the woman in her responded instantaneously. Even with that black eye and discolored jaw she still found him absolutely irresistible.

Enough of those inappropriate thoughts, she chastised herself. She turned to stuff her foot in the stirrup. Her body went on red alert when Vance clamped his hands around her waist to steady her and guide her onto her perch.

When she glanced down he tipped back his head to stare at her with that endearing one-eyed squint. ''Sorry, Officer, I wanted to make sure you got settled in the saddle without mishap.''

''Well, uh, thanks.'' Miranda yanked her attention away from those full, sensuous lips and toyed with the reins. ''How many gears does this mare have?''

''Just two.'' He grinned wryly. ''A plodding walk and a hell-for-leather gallop. Hold her to first gear and you've got nothing to worry about.''

Miranda watched Vance mount up with grace and experienced ease. The man was definitely in his element. She, however, was not. He probably wanted to see her fail—big-time. Wanted to see her swallow her pride and nurse a few bruises after she cartwheeled off the pinto and bit dust. He'd probably laugh his head off when she went flying. Well, she'd stick to this saddle like glue, she vowed resolutely. She'd already made a fool of herself in his presence more times that she cared to remember. She was *not* going to do it today.

VANCE HAD TO ADMIT RANDI was a real trooper. Even when the cattle herd cut and ran and her pinto mare shot off to stop the stampede Randi held on tightly. Of course, her face turned baby-powder white and she clamped her teeth together in grim determination. But damn if he didn't admire her for tackling the unfamiliar chores and attempting to do her very best.

Things progressed without mishap until the Black Angus bull abruptly turned tail and headed for the creek. The bull, it seemed, decided he wasn't in favor of being confined to the corral. He thundered toward Randi and her mare who stood directly in his escape route.

"Oh, my God," Randi squawked as the cantankerous bull charged toward her.

The pinto reared up when the bull sideswiped it. Vance's heart missed several vital beats while he watched Randi somersault backward over the horse's rump. He nudged his sorrel gelding and raced toward her. Damn it, if he killed the chief's niece on the first day he'd be penitentiary bound.

Vance dismounted before his horse skidded to a stop and raced to Randi. She lay sprawled facedown in the grass, her breath coming in shallow hitches.

"You okay?"

"Don't...know," she wheezed. "Can't breathe yet."

Vance liked the way she didn't go into instant panic mode after she got the wind knocked out of her. She just lay there, waiting to get her breath back.

He slid his arm around her shoulders, turned her over and eased her upright. "Put your head between your legs, cowgirl," he murmured. "You'll be fine."

"I'm lousy at this," she choked out then did as he instructed. "Lousy cop, too."

"Aw, don't be so hard on yourself. That's what I'm here for."

She raised her head and managed a wobbly smile.

"I'll probably make a lousy assistant cop while I'm riding with you. You'll have your chance to poke fun."

He hadn't meant to brush his forefinger over her bloodless cheek or sink his hand into that mass of dark, silky hair that lay like a braided rope on her shoulder. It just sort of happened naturally. It felt good to touch her. Too good.

Vance jerked his hand away. Her deep green eyes locked on his and he swallowed hard when desire pelted him. He wanted to taste those cupid's bow lips, but he denied himself. Knowing this bristly cop, who was out to prove herself to the world—and to the men in it—she'd probably take offense and he'd get his face slapped. As if he didn't have enough bumps and bruises already.

"I'm okay now," she squeaked, offering him an anemic imitation of a smile.

She didn't look or sound very okay, but Vance hoisted her to her feet, nonetheless. When her legs folded up he hooked his arm around her waist to offer support. He had to admit that he admired the way she sucked it up and didn't whimper and whine. He could easily visualize her taking those self-defense lessons at the academy. She'd give her all and she'd never let a man know she was hurting or let a hard fall slow her down. She'd likely swallow a howl of pain and get back on her feet—even if it about killed her.

"Why don't you go up to the house and lie down for a few minutes," he suggested. "No shame in that. I had my bell wrung plenty of times when I bucked off a rodeo bronc. Stuff happens, ya know, and sometimes you just need a breather."

"No, I agreed to do this job and I'm going to do it."

She inhaled a fortifying breath and Vance cursed himself soundly when his gaze helplessly dropped to her breasts. The woman could barely stand up and he itched to cop a feel of the lady cop. Man, he was such an insensitive jerk.

Scowling at himself, Vance helped her into the saddle. He glanced sideways to note that Frank had chased down the bull and nipped the big brute's heels until he rejoined the herd.

When the cattle converged from both pastures, Vance motioned for Miranda to dismount. "The next order of business is to cut the weaning calves from the cows for transport to a distant pasture. Then we'll make another cut of marketable calves from the combined herds, work them and haul them to the stockyards.''

"Marketable?" Miranda questioned. "What's that mean?"

"We'll package the seven- and eight-hundred-pound steers in groups to sell to feedlot buyers. Heifers, too, but they don't command the same prices as feeder steers,'' he explained as he strode over to the clunker truck to grab two leather whips. "My cousins and I will evaluate and sort out the calves, then pen up the newborns for branding and inoculations. Your job is to open and shut the pasture gate to filter out the cows.''

"And the bull?" she asked, casting the ton of beef on the hoof a wary glance.

"Nope, we're taking him to service the cows at Cousin Q's ranch. We rotate our bulls to protect against inbreeding.''

When Vance walked over to speak to his cousins Miranda heaved a pained sigh and rolled her strained shoulder. Of course, she hadn't told Vance that she'd hurt herself. Pride wouldn't allow that. She just gritted her teeth and toughed it out.

Positioning herself by the metal gate, Miranda watched, impressed, as the Ryder cousins directed calves into the loading chute for transport and cut out other calves for branding and injections. She was able to stand aside and watch the interaction between the Ryder cousins, noting the playful camaraderie they employed while working. Occasionally she caught the teasing comments Vance made that kept his cousins grinning, while they went about their tasks. She couldn't help but wonder why Vance was unable to direct that playful attitude toward her.

Probably because he hated her and she'd criticized his easygoing manner one too many times.

Miranda jerked to attention when one of the cows trotted toward her. She managed to open and shut the pasture gate several times without incident. But to her dismay, she wasn't agile enough to shut the gate before one of the small calves darted around a cow and shot through the opening like a cannonball.

Her gaze instantly flew to Vance who muttered and scowled. She fully expected him to chew her out royally. Instead he said, "Don't worry about it. I'll bring back the calf."

Miranda watched him hop the fence to gather a lariat from the clunker truck then bound onto his horse. Fascinated, she watched him gallop after the runaway calf—with the loop of the lariat circling his head. He roped the calf on the first attempt, stepped down to secure the small calf's legs then draped the bawling animal over his saddle. When he returned, Miranda opened the gate to let him deposit the calf in the designated pen.

"Nice work, cowboy. Sorry about that. I won't let it happen again. Now that I know how sneaky those little buggers can be, I'll be ready and waiting."

"Good, because time-consuming delays will make it hard for us to finish up before dark. I'm on

patrol duty tonight, ya know,'' he said with a teasing wink.

Miranda inwardly winced at the reminder. She decided, right there and then, that she wasn't going to
be the cause of another delay. She'd throw herself
in front of an escaping calf before she'd interrupt
this precisioned process again.

Ten minutes later she was forced to put up or shut
up. Another calf zipped around a cow and scrambled
toward the open gate. Miranda launched herself at
the calf. The animal bawled its head off and kicked
her in the thigh, but she brought it down and
rammed her elbow in its wet nose. While the calf
recovered from the stunned blow, Miranda surged
to her feet to slam the gate shut.

Vance froze in disbelief, his goggle-eyed gaze
fixed on the woman who'd just tackled a two-
hundred-fifty-pound calf before it escaped and had
to be chased down.

''Did I see what I thought I saw?'' Quint chirped,
incredulous.

''Think so.'' Wade glanced at Vance. ''Wha'd
you do? Threaten to clean her plow if she let another
calf get past her?''

''No,'' Vance mumbled. ''Jeez, I knew she was
about half crazy, but I didn't realize she was a daredevil, too.''

Quint chuckled as he turned his attention back to
the task at hand. ''Damn, those self-defense classes
at the academy must be something else. Didn't know
some of the techniques used for steer-wrestling also
applied to taking down escaping criminals.''

"She could've hurt herself—badly," Vance muttered. "That was above and beyond the call of duty."

Wade chuckled in amusement. "Nice to know how devoted she is to the job. I'll sleep better tonight knowing how well I'm being protected by HRPD's finest."

Well, maybe his cousins were properly impressed, but Vance was just frustrated that Randi had risked injury to stop the calf from hightailing it north. She'd scared him. She'd triggered protective instincts he hadn't realized he had—didn't *want* to have—for *her.*

She was a pain in the patoot. The proverbial thorn in his paw. He didn't want to admire, respect or worry about her. That signified that she meant something to him. She didn't. They were polar opposites. Their approach to life was diametrically different. She took everything seriously. And to the extreme.

Damn, he'd almost stopped breathing when he'd seen Randi dive at that calf that outweighed her by at least a hundred and twenty pounds. He'd had a horrible vision of dragging her trampled body back to Tate and hearing himself say: Here you go, Chief. Sorry I got your niece killed in the corral because she was trying too hard to live up to my expectations.

An hour later, when the feeder calves had been loaded in trailers and the weaning calves were penned up, Vance breathed a tired sigh. He'd watched Randi throw herself in front of another oncoming calf and he had suffered another near coronary. At that point he'd called time out and given her quick instruction on where and how to use the whip so she didn't have to tackle a runaway calf.

The woman might not know jack about ranching and farming, but she'd certainly taken very seriously the sentence Tate handed down to her. That get-the-job-done, do-or-die attitude of hers was admirable, but it was making him nervous. He didn't want to consider how he'd react if he had to sit by and watch her handle some crazed criminal that was avoiding arrest. The thought gave him the heebie-jeebies.

Criminey. This was *not* going to work, just like he'd told Tate. After one morning with Randi, Vance was ready to call it quits and pay the fine. The woman was affecting him on too damn many levels and he was so aware of her that it was driving him nuts.

"What's next, boss?" she asked as she walked toward him.

Vance noted the grimace that bracketed her mouth and the limp she was trying very hard not to favor. It upset him all over again. He wasn't accustomed to being upset. He was the kind who shrugged, smiled and got on with life.

"You're hurt," he blurted out accusingly.

She forced a cheery smile. "I'm fine."

"Are not, damn it," he growled down at her.

Randi tipped her head back to study his black scowl then glanced at Wade and Quint. "I thought you said Vance was the happy-go-lucky joker of the family. Doesn't look happy now."

Vance's arm shot toward his pickup. "Just load up, Calamity Jane," he demanded.

She opened her mouth to protest his sharp tone, clamped her lips together then did as she was told.

"Sheesh, you're in a mood," Wade teased. "She's really getting to you, isn't she, hotshot?"

"She is *not* getting to me," Vance denied huffily.

"Oh, gimme a break," Quint said, and smirked. "I've seen the way you've been looking at her for the past two hours. She's definitely getting to you."

"I saw you grimace when she defended the pasture gate," Wade put in gleefully. "You're showing all the signs of a man with a woman on his mind."

"Can you blame me?" Vance erupted uncharacteristically. Funny, this tormenting teasing between cousins had been more amusing when he was dishing it out rather than taking it. "The Robo Cop defied injury and death, right in my corral. I'll be a basket case after riding patrol with her. No telling what brave deeds she plans to attempt in the name of truth, justice and the American way."

"If you ask me, she's trying to prove herself competent and worthy to you. Hmm, wonder why that's so all-fired important to her?" Quint remarked.

"Good question," Wade said, smiling wryly. "Could it be that you're getting to her, too?"

"Are you two yahoos going to stand here harassing me or are you going to help?" Vance demanded crankily.

"Harassing is more fun," Wade replied devilishly.

"I have to agree with Wade," Quint seconded.

Swearing ripely, Vance shouldered past his cousins to climb into his truck. Dealing with this gutsy, fearless female was problem enough. Being hounded by his evil relatives was turning his stomach. Vance was beginning to wonder if he'd be able to get through the first day of his tortuous sentence without murdering one—or both—of his cousins. And don't forget the very real possibility of getting Ms. Eager Beaver killed in a ranching accident, he mused uneasily.

EXHAUSTED, BRUISED AND unwillingly impressed by Vance's commitment to his ranch, Miranda made use of his shower then changed into her uniform. There hadn't been time to rush back to her apartment before she reported for patrol duty. There had been time at lunch, however, for her to make some hurried requests by phone. The secretive arrangements were her way of apologizing to Vance for the comedy of errors that had befallen him.

After contemplating the incidents of the past week Miranda decided the blame rested entirely on her shoulders. If she hadn't taken her job—and herself—so seriously, hadn't been so defensive about her physical attraction to Vance, they wouldn't have ended up handcuffed together for seven long days and a considerable portion of the nights.

Fact was, Vance wasn't what she'd expected. He was diligent, skilled and got on well with his family. He and his cousins combined forces to manage their ranches and help each other with various tasks. Part of the reason the Ryders could pull it off, she realized, was that Vance had a knack of neutralizing difficult situations with laughter and smiles. As much as Miranda loved her dad and brothers she wondered if they could work together with such ease.

Well, one day she'd have the chance to find out, she mused as she applied a thin coat of makeup. She was determined to fulfill her dream of joining her family at OCPD.

After a quick self-inspection in the bathroom mirror, Miranda veered into the hall. Earlier she'd taken time to admire Vance's spacious home and countrified décor. Pictures of Vance and his cousins during their rodeo career hung on the walls of the paneled den. Trophies and silver belt buckles lined the shelves. She wondered if that scar she'd noticed on the underside of his chin was a battle scar from his wild rides on broncs while he traveled the suicide circuit.

Oh, yes, she'd been paying close attention while Wade and Quint filled her in on Vance's past, during their short breaks. She'd discovered that the older generation of Ryder men had deeded their ranches over to their sons and headed south with their wives to a retirement village in Texas. They were living on the royalties of the oil wells that dotted these sprawling ranches.

She'd also learned that Vance had never wanted to do anything but excel on the rodeo circuit before he returned to run his ranch. According to Wade and Quint, ranching was in the Ryder blood. It wasn't a job, they insisted, it was a way of life.

Miranda could relate to that because she'd never wanted to do anything except follow in her dad and brothers' footsteps. You might even say she was *driven* to it.

"Should I strap on my six-shooters?" Vance asked as he followed her down the hall. "How much gunplay can I expect while patrolling with you?"

"You can leave your guns at home," she told him as she led the way out the front door. "I'll be the only one packing hardware on the night shift—" Her voice dried up when Vance snagged her arm and turned her to face him on the front porch.

"One request," he murmured, staring somberly at her.

The feel of his lean fingers on her forearm was as gentle as a caress. She tried very hard not to respond to his touch. It was like trying not to breathe.

Damn, he was so easy on the eye, so big and brawny and totally male. The scent of his cologne threatened to lure her closer, but she stuck to her guns and kept her distance.

"What's your one request?" To her dismay, her voice wobbled in helpless reaction to his devastating presence.

"Don't scare me to death the way you did while we were separating cattle."

His husky voice caused gooseflesh to pebble her skin, but Miranda willfully ignored the reaction and flashed a smile. "Not to worry, cowboy. I can guarantee that won't happen."

His shoulders sagged slightly. "Good. I didn't like knowing you were hurt this morning but were too proud to admit it. I'm pretty sure I'll like you a whole lot better without any bullet holes in you, so no daring heroics for my benefit, okay? I've already recognized the fact that you're no lightweight, despite what I said in a snit of temper.''

His roundabout compliment and the teasing hint of concern flattered Miranda.

''You aren't afraid to take risks and you don't mind getting your hands dirty with hard work,'' he added as his dark gaze skimmed over her face. ''You don't hover on the perimeters of life—you dive in headfirst. I respect those qualities and I can relate to them. But I still don't like seeing you hurt.''

She was so flattered and pleased that she very nearly caved in and pressed an impulsive kiss to that sexy mouth that had driven her crazy each time she ventured close enough to appraise the shape and texture of it.

''For the record,'' she murmured unsteadily, ''I don't hate you and I'm not out to get you.''

When he smiled rakishly her heart slammed against her ribs—and stuck there momentarily. ''Maybe I'd like it better if you *were* out to get me,'' he said in an ultrasexy voice as he inched closer.

He was practically standing on top of her, crowding her space, surrounding her with that magnetic male aura and staring at her mouth as if he wanted to devour her. She wondered how it would feel to have those sinewy arms wrapped around her and give into this fierce, illogical attraction that was growing by leaps and bounds.

Just one taste and touch. What could it hurt? *You*

could like it too much, came the voice of caution. *And that would be dangerous.* This, she reminded herself, isn't the kind of danger you're equipped to handle so back off.

Swallowing hard, Miranda retreated from temptation. She pivoted to scuttle down the steps on legs that suddenly felt like cooked noodles. "We better get going," she chirped. "I'm a stickler for punctuality."

"Figured as much," Vance said as he followed her to the squad car.

Miranda didn't try to engage in conversation during the drive, just let silence reign supreme. She just kept sneaking peeks to study Vance's profile in the dash lights. Of course, she'd been guilty of sneaking peeks at him every chance she got during the day. She was too aware of him, too aware of her attraction to him.

Now that she'd come to like him he was even more difficult to resist. But she had to resist that playful charm. She predicted he could be a heartbreaker if a woman began to care too much. Quint Ryder might have been a former ladies' man of the family, but now that he was out of circulation she suspected Vance held the title and she didn't doubt for a minute that he could live up to the family reputation.

When Miranda pulled up in front of Stephanie's Palace, Vance stared questioningly at her. "Why are we stopping here? Checking for a liquor license or something?"

"Nope. This is where you get out, cowboy," she said.

He frowned suspiciously. "Now look, Calamity Jane, you upheld your end of the deal today and I sure as hell intend to uphold mine. I'm not about to lounge around at dinner while you're wolfing down a stale sandwich from Hoot 'N' Holler and patrolling the streets."

"Get out, Vance. I'm giving an order, just like the ones you gave me at your ranch. I obeyed them to the best of my abilities. I expect the same consideration from you. Now go!"

He opened his mouth to protest then clamped his jaw shut. "Okay, fine. But if you don't come back in an hour so I can take my tour of duty I'm gonna be spitting mad. Got it?"

Miranda nodded. "Got it. Now beat it. I'm going to check the alleys to ensure the other downtown businesses are secured for the night."

The instant he stepped from the car she whizzed off, before his guilty conscience could nip at him again and he tried to climb back inside. As for Miranda, she desperately needed some breathing space—some downtime away from the kind of temptation she'd never faced...until she ran headlong into Vance Ryder.

5

WHEN MIRANDA DROVE OFF, Vance stood by the
curb until she disappeared from sight. Well, hell,
he'd pretty much put her, and himself, through the
paces during the day and now she was letting him
off easy by allowing him to enjoy a leisurely meal.
He'd have Steph dish up one of her fancy gourmet
dinners-to-go and take it to Randi when she picked
him up.

With that plan in mind, Vance entered the ritzy
restaurant then stumbled backward in disbelief when
dozens of people—his cousins included—bounded
from their chairs to yell, "Surprise! Happy birthday!"

Vance stood there like a thunderstruck idiot while
his friends, neighbors and family converged to shake
his hand and pat him on the back.

Several minutes later, Vance cornered his cousins.
"I thought you said you were throwing me a small
family party this weekend," he reminded them.

"We still are," Wade replied. "This was Randi's
idea. She set it up."

Vance's jaw dropped open and his eyes popped
like boiled eggs. "She did? When?"

"She called Steph at noon to make the arrangements," Quint reported.

"Then she called Laura at school and asked her to make the phone invitations during her planning hour," Wade added. "She also paid for the cake the chef prepared in your honor and bought the dinner you're about to eat."

Vance was floored—and that was putting it mildly. Randi had gone to all this expense and effort for him? He was stunned that she even remembered that he mentioned his birthday during their heated debate in Tate's office.

Why had she done this? Hell, she couldn't even be here to reap the benefits of a superb meal and fancy cake. And furthermore, he suspected she had no intention of swinging by to pick him up this evening. She intended for him to party until the restaurant closed at ten.

Feeling like a jerk for working her like a field hand all day, while she secretly set up this wingding, Vance put on his happy face and enjoyed the celebration in his honor. But it didn't set well, knowing she'd outdone him. Plus, he knew she'd taken a pay cut for the shorter shifts she'd be working this week. She'd spent hard-earned money on him.

Well, he wouldn't be so hard on her tomorrow, he promised himself as he settled in for a mouth-watering feast. Man, this was something. No one besides family had ever gone to so much effort to recognize his birthday. He wouldn't forget her thoughtful gesture, either.

MIRANDA TRUDGED TO HER cracker-box apartment after her five-hour shift on patrol. Sitting for long hours in the squad car—after straining muscles during ranch chores—made her body stiffen like cured plaster. Every tendon and joint screamed in complaint until she half-collapsed in her recliner.

Ah, well, it was worth it to know she'd surprised Vance and compensated in some small way for getting them into this mess with the chief. No doubt, Vance had hooked up with one of the women attending the party and was celebrating his birth by practicing procreation.

The thought stung more than it should have. She and Vance had nothing going—except her itsy-bitsy, teeny-weeny one-sided infatuation that was so inappropriate that it didn't bear thinking about.

The abrupt rap at the door brought Miranda upright in her chair. "Who's there?" she called cautiously.

"The birthday boy. Open up."

Miranda wasn't sure she wanted to open up—physically or emotionally—at the moment. She was too tired. But neither did she have the heart to ignore Vance on his birthday.

Wincing, she hobbled to the door to find Vance holding two foam boxes.

"A late dinner and a slice of birthday cake." He invited himself inside then surveyed her apartment approvingly. "This is where Steph lived until she hooked up with Cousin Q. You've fixed it up nice."

Miranda blinked. "This is where you strung all the colored lights and removed all the furniture, save the bed?"

"Yup," he said as he walked over to set the containers on the small drop-leaf table. "Deep down, Quint appreciated the prank. He and Steph didn't show their faces in public for three days. Good thing I stocked the kitchen with enough food to tide them over during their lovefest."

"Considerate of you, joker," she said, lips twitching.

"That'd be me. Considerate, helpful and cheerful." He motioned her to the table. "Come take a load off. Bet you didn't bother with supper, did you, Ms. Super-Duper Cop?"

When Miranda shook her head he sighed then said, "That figures. Now sit down and eat. I'll fix you a drink."

Miranda sank tiredly into the chair and lifted the lid of the box. The appetizing aroma made her mouth water and her empty stomach growl in anticipation.

Vance thrust a fork and glass of ice water at her. "No booze in the fridge," he observed. "You a teetotaler?"

Miranda nodded, her attention fixed on the fabulous food.

"Great, Patti Perfect, you have no flaws or vices whatsoever, I suppose?" he asked as he straddled the vacant chair backward and draped his arms across the back.

"Overachiever," she mumbled between delicious bites.

"Already pegged you as that," he replied with a smile and a wink. "You've got the face of an angel and the heart of a lion. Anything else I should know about you since we'll be partners on my ranch and on your police beat?"

"Single-minded dedication," she admitted before she wet her whistle. "Strong sense of fair play and strict attention to rules and regulations." She peeked up at him from beneath her lashes. "*Usually*. You're the exception. I suffered momentary lapses of sanity during our first few confrontations and now we're both paying for it. Sorry about that."

"You're forgiven," he said with a chuckle. "What else? What about scandalous affairs with married men that put you on this straight and narrow path to pursue this honorable quest for perfection?"

"None of your beeswax, buster," she said darkly.

"What about a boyfriend waiting in the big city to slide a ring on your finger after you've landed a job alongside your dad and brothers?" he quizzed her.

She arched a brow at that. "I didn't realize you were an expert at investigation and interrogation."

When he grinned she inwardly groaned at the radioactive impact this man had on her. He was pure hell on her defenses.

"Turnabout is fair play, I always say. My cousins told me that you grilled them for information about me today."

Miranda took offense. "I most certainly did not! They spilled their guts with no encouragement from me. They talked and I listened."

He narrowed his eyes at her. "Answer the question."

"No, there's no man waiting in the wings or anywhere else for that matter. I've focused entirely on my career."

He nodded thoughtfully. "I figure that a girl raised by a family of cops will turn out one of two ways. Either she'll run wild in rebellious defiance or she'll try to live up to her family's noble calling and become the personification of excellence." He stared her straight in the eye. "You'd be the do-it-right rule-follower, correct?"

"What is this? Your countrified version of the Spanish Inquisition?" she asked huffily. "Look, I'm tired and I can't deal with you when I'm not at my best. You require too much energy and mental attention. Can we call it a night?"

He smiled at her defensive tone. "Okay, I'll stop teasing you. But there's just one more thing, Calamity Jane."

Her breath clogged in her throat when he made her mouth the focus of his profound concentration. Oh, God, she couldn't deal with the sensuality that radiated off him in tidal waves, especially when she was weary and vulnerable. She might slip off this righteous pedestal her family designed for her. It would be so easy to fall—for him.

Miranda fidgeted nervously when his eyes, like hypnotic obsidian flames, bore down on her from beneath that thick fringe of long lashes. "You aren't going to do something stupid, like kiss me, are you?'' she asked, her voice wavering with the internal conflict of wanting and not wanting.

"Darlin'," he said with a killer smile, "stupidity became my middle name when I met you. I haven't been the same since."

And then he was hoisting her from her chair and wrapping those sinewy arms around her like a warm cocoon. The instant her body came into full contact with his muscular length her hormones leaped into full-scale riot—and he hadn't even kissed her yet. He just kept staring at her with those eyes that were as dark and shiny as the devil's own temptation. Apparently he was waiting for her to pitch a fit if she didn't want to be kissed. The choice, it seemed, was hers to make.

She really should object, should push him back into his own space. Or better yet, give him the benefit of her self-defense techniques by breaking his hold. But like an idiot she just focused her curious attention on that tempting mouth and wondered if he'd give her a hit-and-run kiss or suck her into the vortex of sensuality that went by the name of Vance Ryder.

Hit-and-run would've been much easier on her senses, she decided after his mouth slanted over hers in gentle possession. But in less than a heartbeat the tenderness melted beneath an eruption of desire that Miranda had tried to pretend didn't exist between them. But there it was, right in her face, burning in the pit of her stomach, channeling in all directions at once, making her crave the forbidden.

Suddenly she was arching into him and he was

pressing her hips against his as his tongue delved deeper to taste her completely. The world wobbled on its axis and her brain short-circuited. Sensation after fiery sensation blazed through her weary body, regenerating energy and heat that fed on themselves until the intensity of it set her aflame. Wow! Kissing Vance was like being caught in a thermonuclear blast!

She was kissing him back with frantic desperation, clawing at the pearl snaps on his Western shirt, needing to explore the hard muscled wall of his chest. In response, he tugged the hem of her shirt from her slacks and skimmed his hands over her waist—without breaking the fervent kiss.

Someone moaned in helpless surrender. She prayed that it wasn't her. She'd never caved in like this before, never wanted to gobble a man alive the way she wanted to feast her hands and lips on Vance.

Before she realized it she was *sitting* in the empty foam box of food and *wearing* his birthday cake on her butt. But it didn't matter because his skillful hands were gliding up her rib cage and skimming across her bra to arouse her nipples to hard, aching peaks. And then he dragged his mouth from hers and dipped his head to suckle her through the flimsy fabric of her bra. The nearly intolerable burning sensations got even worse.

He raised his head and said, ''Damn, woman, I knew you set me off, but not quite like this.''

He delivered another lip-blistering kiss as he wedged his hips between her legs and pressed closer. He was hard as stone and she was hot and aching and craving the intimate contact like a hopeless addict. Sweet mercy! Who was this woman who was climbing all over this gorgeous hunk of cowboy and begging for more? This turbocharged male was gunning down her usual inhibitions like crumbling clay pigeons at a trap shoot. She'd been the farthest thing from a pushover—until Vance Ryder invaded her world and introduced her to combustible desire.

Miranda couldn't breathe without inhaling the scent of him, couldn't think past the web of pleasure he weaved around her like a sorcerer's spell. Her head fell back as his hot, moist lips glided down the column of her neck and his roaming hands slid upward to cup her breasts. She gasped when she felt his mouth against one bare nipple then the other. He flicked at her with his tongue and she whimpered in aroused torment.

The room spun in dizzying circles as his lips scorched a fiery path up her throat and over her flushed cheeks to reclaim her mouth. His kiss was so demanding and possessive that she felt as if she'd had the wind knocked out of her—just like this morning, only a zillion times worse. When he pressed his hips precisely into the cradle of her thighs she arched helplessly against him. Then she kissed him as if there was no tomorrow—and he was her *last* request.

Miranda was shocked by the intense feelings of wild desperation and desire that hammered at her. Shocked but powerless to defend against sensations of overwhelming need that rocked her. Then, when she felt so completely out of control that she was on the verge of screaming: *Take me—now—because I can't stand not knowing what it would be like to be swept away by you,* he lifted his head and stepped away.

Vance gasped for air and willed his shaky legs not to fold up beneath him. He stared at the enticing sight of her partially bared body and felt another blast of unholy desire rip through him. She'd braced her elbows on the table where he'd deposited her. Her long shapely legs were still spread to accommodate him when he'd eased himself against her because *not* being as close as he could get—even while fully clothed—had not been an acceptable option.

Holy kamoley! he thought as he stared into her wide green eyes and watched her breasts heave in attempt to draw breath. Nothing had ever hit Vance this hard so fast and just kept coming at him like bullets spitting from a howitzer. Damn, there was nothing leisurely or casual about his desire for Randi and the intensity of these feelings shocked him.

As birthday kisses went, this one took the cake. Literally. Thanks to him, she was sitting in it.

Dazed by his wild, instantaneous reaction to her, burning from this obsessive need to have her, right here, right now, Vance stumbled back a step. He told himself to breathe, to clear his head and not to look at her for another second or he'd lose control all over again.

He wheeled around and stared at the door while his body throbbed with unappeased desire. "Thanks for throwing me the party,'' he croaked. ''That was…uh…mighty…uh…nice of you.'' He cleared his throat. ''See ya tomorrow.''

And then he was outta there. Running for his life, to be more accurate. He was afraid to stand still too long for fear the unleashed emotions she incited would overtake him and send him racing back inside her apartment to finish what he never should have started.

Damnation, he'd known she was intensely passionate about her job, but he hadn't expected to be dragged into that turbulent undercurrent of emotion he'd tapped into. She'd set him on fire and he was very much afraid that he couldn't run fast enough, or far enough, to douse the flames of wanting her that were burning in his wake.

Vance inhaled a bracing breath of cool evening air. He desperately needed to find a place to cool off—pronto.

FILLED WITH PURPOSE the next day, Vance climbed from his truck to approach his cousins who were waiting for him at Quint's ranch. ''You gotta help me out,'' he said without preamble.

''With what?'' Wade asked as he draped his arms over the corral fence behind him.

''I want one of you to haul Randi around in your pickup while we're repairing fences this morning.''

Quint's lips pursed in amusement. ''Why's that? Does it have something to do with the fact that you borrowed my truck to swing by her apartment last night after the party?''

"Did something happen we should know about?" Wade razzed him.

Something had definitely happened and it had kept Vance tossing, turning and breaking out in a cold sweat all night.

"Did she give you a birthday kiss that was too hot for you to handle? Could it be that the joker's wild about the gorgeous cop and he's running scared?" Quint quizzed him unmercifully.

"Oh, shut up," Vance said with a scowl.

His cousins erupted in gales of laughter, made smacking noises with their lips, and then cackled again. Muttering under his breath, Vance wheeled toward the barn to gather barbwire and fence posts. By the time Randi showed up for work Vance intended to be ready to leave. He couldn't take much more of his cousins' teasing.

And they called *him* the joker of the family? Well, there was nothing amusing about the intimate images of Randi that he'd been seeing the whole livelong night. She'd had the starring role in his hottest fantasies.

He'd gone to his cousins in desperate need of help and they'd tormented him unmercifully.

What he needed was a day away from temptation and it looked as if he wouldn't get it. He'd have to sit on his hands to keep them off her, he decided grimly. Today was going to be the ultimate test of restraint and he'd better pass it. How? He had no idea. After last night wanting her had become a constant thing, a gnawing craving that wouldn't go away.

"It's gonna be one hell of a day," Vance growled as he tossed the fencing tools and supplies in the clunker truck.

BRIGHT AND EARLY IN THE MORNING, Miranda approached her uncle's home. "Uncle Tate, I need a favor," she announced when Tate opened the door and motioned her inside.

"What's up, kiddo?" he asked curiously. "I have to be at headquarters in a few minutes, so make it snappy."

Miranda glanced around the tidy, compact home and hesitated in making brief eye contact. "I request some other form of reprimand for my involvement...I mean my unprofessional behavior for ticketing Vance and tossing him in jail."

Tate smiled as he appraised her rigid, military stance. She tried to relax but just couldn't get it done.

"Some assignments aren't to our liking, you know. Difficult as this might be, it's good exercise in self-restraint."

"Yes, sir, I understand, but I can't have Vance in the squad car with me or ride with him in his pickup while commuting from one set of ranch duties to the next."

"Too close for comfort?" he asked perceptively.

He didn't know the half of it! Miranda could feel the heat streaming into her cheeks when flashbacks of her reckless behavior last night leaped out at her.

Tate rocked back on his heels and clasped his hands behind his back. "As luck would have it,

Vance will only be riding shotgun with you for one more night.''

She nearly collapsed at his booted feet in relief. *Thank you, God!* ''Thank you, chief, I—''

''—because I'm making arrangements for a code 5 to investigate the possibility of drug trafficking,'' he explained.

''A *stakeout?*'' she tweeted. ''With *Vance?*''

Tate nodded. ''You'll be keeping surveillance in a house that sits across the street from the suspected drop-off and pickup site. We believe we have an upstart drug ring trying to take root and we want to nip it in the bud. So far we've only noted activity at night, which will work out perfectly since you're helping Vance during the day and you'll both be available to keep surveillance at night.''

''But, sir...Uncle Tate—'' she tried in vain to protest.

''I've given Mr. and Mrs. Preston, the elderly owners of the home, a rental car and an expense-paid vacation at the hotel of their choice until we can collect evidence,'' Tate continued as he walked over to grab a suitcase that set on his couch. ''Glad you dropped by. It'll save me a trip.''

He handed the luggage to her. ''You'll find several sets of clothes similar to the Prestons' usual attire, plus some wigs, stage makeup and photographs so you can duplicate their appearance as best you can. It will help that you and Vance won't be showing up at the house until almost dark so the neighbors and suspects will have difficulty distinguishing between you and the Prestons. I'll drop off their car at your place so you can use it tomorrow night.''

''A stakeout? Using a civilian?'' she chirped. ''Isn't that irregular?''

Tate shrugged nonchalantly as he scooped up his hat. ''I've done it a few times before. We're understaffed at the moment, since one of the officers is on vacation. This will work perfectly. You and Vance are already paired up and I need a couple to go undercover.''

Like a doomed prisoner on her way to the gallows, Miranda walked from the house with a suitcase of disguises in hand. This could not be happening. She'd go crazy if she had to share the same house with Vance. She was already going crazy after that lip-sizzling, heart-stopping kiss that had left her half-naked and wanting him beyond bearing last night.

VANCE MANAGED TO MAKE IT through the day with Randi helping him string wire and clip it to the new posts. He'd made the decision to suffer through evening patrol duty by pulling his hat over his eyes and pretending to catch a few z's while Randi cruised around town.

But curiosity got the best of him and he found himself monitoring Randi while she settled a domestic dispute between a middle-aged couple that resulted in the wife hurling her husband's clothing onto the lawn. Vance also watched her deal compassionately with a four-year-old boy who'd gotten lost and needed a police chauffeur to take him safely home.

An hour before they went off duty, Randi pulled over a rattletrap car with four male occupants. When she approached the vehicle Vance rolled down the window to monitor the conversation.

To his frustration he heard wolf whistles as she halted by the driver's window. He couldn't hear what she said in response, but he did hear the male guffaws wafting in the breeze. That did it. She didn't have to tolerate that kind of disrespect and he didn't have to sit here and listen to it.

Vance was out of the squad car in nothing flat. He bore down on the four juveniles who had their baseball caps turned backward on their heads and were leering at Randi whose shapely physique was spotlighted by the headlights of the squad car.

He could tell right off that she resented his interference. Her head snapped up and she flashed him a get-your-butt-back-in-the-car stare. He disregarded the silent command because his protective instincts were in overdrive.

"I believe I heard the officer ask for your license," Vance growled. "Hand it over."

The boys lapsed into silence while Randi checked the license and wrote out a ticket for speeding and reckless driving. When the foursome cruised off Randi rounded on Vance like an attack Doberman. "I told you to stay in the car!" she all but yelled at him. "That was the deal. You ride along, not participate. I can do my job."

"Well, I can't do mine," Vance flared. "I'll be

damned if I'm going to sit by and watch those little creeps treat you with disrespect.''

''It didn't bother you when *you* were the one coming on to me,'' she retorted as she stamped back to the car.

She definitely had him there. ''Yeah, well, I'm a grown man and I'm attracted to you. I couldn't help but act like an idiot. Those young punks stepped over the line with those catcalls and rude gestures.''

She stopped and stared at him over the top of the car. Even in the semidarkness he could see her eyes flash like a traffic light. ''You don't get it, do you? I deal with this kind of behavior and reactions from males all the time. I also dealt with it from fellow male students at the academy. I have learned to handle it.''

''Well, I don't like it,'' he grumbled.

''Neither do I but I have to live with it and do my job in spite it. I can't help what I look like on the outside and I'm not changing professions because of it. This is what I do, why I have to act tough. I also have to be a rottweiler in this dog-eat-dog world where I work and you're going to have to sit tight next time.''

''Well, *excuuuse* me for feeling protective,'' Vance growled. ''It's natural instinct and reflex. You might as well tell me not to breathe while you're at it.''

She whipped open the door and plunked on the seat. ''You only have to restrain yourself for—'' she glanced down at her watch ''—forty-five minutes and this will be the end of our patrol duties.''

Vance looked at her in surprise as he sank onto the seat. "It is? Tate is letting me off the hook?"

"No," Miranda muttered as she put the car in gear. "We've been assigned a stakeout, beginning tomorrow night."

"Good, that has to be better."

It had to be easier than watching Randi deal with males who saw her as a woman rather than a law officer... Hell, he'd been guilty of that not so long ago. Well, he'd had an epiphany tonight and it made him ashamed to be a man when he watched other males behave like jackasses in Randi's presence.

"No, it will not be better," she said as she cruised the highway. "We have to disguise ourselves like an eighty-year-old married couple and we'll be stuck in a house every night until we have enough information to make a drug raid." She shot him a pointed glance. "That, of course, is privileged information that you'll have to keep under your hat until this case is closed."

"And you can't stand being in the same house with me, *why?*" he quizzed her.

"For the same reason, I suspect, that you weren't all that thrilled about having me with you in your truck all day," she tossed back.

Vance shifted awkwardly. "Okay, so last night was a little unnerving for me and facing you this morning wasn't easy. Obviously it wasn't easy for you, either." He glanced out the side window, counting the electric poles as they whizzed past. "And I'll admit I got a little carried away with that...um...birthday kiss."

"A little?" She kept her gaze trained on the road.

"All right. A lot. I stepped over the line. But correct me if I'm wrong, but you seemed as involved as I was."

"I was," she finally whispered.

"You was *what?*" he probed.

"Involved." She didn't look at him.

He sighed heavily, removed his hat and raked his hand through his hair in a gesture of frustration. "You know as well as I do that this isn't going to work."

"What isn't?" She pulled onto the side of the road and half-turned to look at him.

Desire slammed through him when he stared into her enchanting face and lost himself in those mystifying green eyes. *"Us,"* he said, his voice rough with feelings he was fighting like the very devil.

"Right. Whatever it is, it's just physical. We're too different."

"Precisely." He leaned in close, drawn against his will. "What you do for a living bugs the hell out of me and makes me afraid for you."

"News flash, cowboy. The farming and ranching profession falls into the high-risk category, too. You face daily danger with animals, machinery and equipment. I don't want to have to worry about you getting hurt, either." She leaned toward him. "I don't want to get involved with you because this is just a temporary position for me. Besides, I'm not the casual kind of woman who suits your easygoing lifestyle."

He could feel her minty breath against his cheek,

see her eyes flaring slightly, hear the sudden hitch in her voice. Common sense bade him to battle what he was feeling, thinking, wanting.

But he couldn't resist her. This maddening woman had gotten under his skin, occupied his thoughts and made him ache until hell wouldn't have it. There was no help for it. He was just going to have to kiss her again.

And so he did. Sane or crazy, there were just some things a man had to do to survive. And he wasn't going to survive another second if he didn't kiss her.

In the time it took to blink he was tantalizing her with his mouth and his tingling caresses and she was tugging at his shirt, desperate to get her hands on his chest. They were like drowning swimmers locked in each other's arms. His mouth twisted over hers, devoured hers. His arms were like steel bands mashing her against him. And then his hand was under her shirt and he wanted her out of that uniform and beneath his pulsating body—right this very minute.

Locked in a desperate embrace, they toppled sideways on the seat. Vance twisted to pull her beneath him—and accidentally slammed his elbow on the horn and his knee against the siren switch. The electrified silence shattered.

Swearing colorfully, he levered himself up and over to his side of the car—where he should have stayed in the first place. Had he lost his friggin' mind? He'd been sitting there listing the reasons he and Randi shouldn't take this ill-fated attraction to another level, and she'd been in complete agreement. Then poof! All sensible thought went up in the smoke of smoldering passion.

"I'm sorry," Vance growled huskily then grabbed his hat that had toppled to the floorboard.

"Ditto. Really stupid. Inexcusable," she panted as she rearranged her clothing. "I'm on patrol, for Pete's sake."

Vance gestured grimly toward the lights of town. "Better drop me by to pick up my truck. Just don't tell the chief that I cut patrol duty short."

Miranda made fast tracks to town—and cursed herself with every mile she logged in. This latest lust attack, while on duty, was the last straw. "I won't tell Uncle Tate that you won't be on the stakeout, either," she assured him.

"Breaking the rules?" he teased. "Sure you can do that?"

"In the name of self-preservation, yes," she said determinedly. "I didn't learn a thing in self-defense that makes it possible to handle you so I'm going to cut my losses. This cannot happen again."

"Amen to that," he agreed. "But I'm still doing the stakeout."

"No," she said emphatically.

"Yes, damn it," he insisted. "We'll just keep our distance and see this through."

She heaved a frustrated sigh, grabbed the sack that contained Vance's disguise from under the seat and tossed it to him. "Fine, but make sure you come dressed in this stuff when you arrive at my apartment for duty tomorrow night."

Vance grabbed the sack then climbed from the car to retrieve his truck at her apartment. When she was alone, she breathed a gigantic sigh of relief. Things were getting out of hand between them. She had to put a stop to it. The self-control that she'd taken for granted for years wasn't holding up well against that devastating cowboy.

Miranda decided that she'd do what she usually did when she encountered a difficult situation. She'd just try harder. That had worked for her before. She could only hope and pray that it would work for her now.

She glanced skyward when she noted the flicker of lightning in the bank of clouds building up in the west. Maybe she should get out of the car, stand in the middle of the road and wait for a lightning bolt to strike her. Surely that kind of electrical shock therapy would jolt her back to her senses so she could overcome this obsessive compulsion for Vance.

6

_____

Dressed only in her undies, a toothbrush clamped between her teeth, Miranda dashed from the bathroom to answer the phone. *"Hewwo,"* she said, frothing at the mouth.

"It rained last night," came Vance's abrupt announcement.

Miranda pivoted toward the bathroom to rinse her mouth then said, "Thanks for the weather report. Does the time and temperature accompany this courtesy call?"

She was striving for flippant and breezy, which was the exact opposite of how she felt when she heard Vance's voice.

"I can't work at the ranch in this mud and slop so we'll meet downtown and I'll introduce you to my friends and acquaintances, just as Tate requested," Vance said hurriedly. "We'll grab coffee at Hoot 'N' Holler at nine bells then we'll make the rounds."

She stared at the phone when Vance hung up suddenly. With a sigh she replaced the receiver.

Since she was in for a round of howdy-dos Miranda decided to make a good impression by dressing in a colorful blouse and skirt and curling her long hair rather than containing the thick mass in a braid. She applied a liberal coat of makeup to conceal the circles under her eyes—compliments of steady work and very little rest. Not to mention the constant torment of fighting her maddening attraction to Vance.

Half an hour later Miranda strode into the convenience store for a welcomed cup of coffee that she doctored with plenty of cream and sugar. She stopped short when she saw Vance enter the store. He skidded to a halt and gaped at her. "Something wrong?" she asked self-consciously.

"Uh, no. You look...nice." This he said while he stared at the air over her left shoulder.

My, Vance was acting weird, even for Vance.

Miranda barely had time to sip her coffee before Vance clutched her hand and dragged her to the counter to introduce her to Chet Walker, the manager, and then to the customers. Miranda pasted on a friendly smile, but she gave up trying to remember all the names that Vance rattled off. She couldn't possibly familiarize herself with everyone in town overnight.

She only managed four sips of her coffee before Vance shepherded her from the store and practically frog-marched her across town square to Martin's Farm and Feed Store. To her surprise, the place was jam-packed with farmers and ranchers. With expansive gestures of his arms, Vance assembled everyone into a single receiving line and tugged her from one person to the next, rapping out names and family connections so quickly that he gave her an instant headache.

The customers—most of them of the male persuasion—were friendly and welcoming, even after they discovered she was the new cop on the force. Miranda was particularly glad to meet the owner's wife. Leta Martin—age fifty, or thereabout—was bubbly and petite and she invited Miranda to stop by anytime to chitchat or to join her for lunch.

Then off they went to Jenkins Pharmacy, the clothing store, tag agency—and every shop that faced town square. Miranda felt as if she was being towed along behind a whirlwind and her throat had dried out after so many pleased-to-meet-yous. In addition, her feet were killing her. The dress shoes weren't built for a swift hike and she could feel blisters forming on her heels.

"What is this? A race against the clock?" she asked when Vance whisked her out of the furniture store then practically shoveled her into the beauty shop.

"I want to hit all the stores before I drop you off at the high school so Laura can introduce you to the other teachers," he explained before he guided her toward the two beauticians for another quick round of how-do-you-dos.

Miranda managed to schedule an appointment for a haircut before Vance dragged her back to the sidewalk.

"That about covers downtown." He stared toward the fountain in the middle of the square. "You can mix and mingle with the teachers while I pick up supplies at the farm store then we'll have lunch at Steph's place before driving back to my place to make flyers announcing the annual town-wide garage sale we got roped into spearheading. We'll call it an early day before we start the stakeout tonight.''

Miranda set her feet when Vance tried to tow her off, but he uprooted her like a weed. ''Hold your horses, cowboy. I really don't think the stakeout should include you. I'm having more second thoughts about it.''

''I take my orders from the chief and he said I should be there, so I'm there, like it or not.''

She decided this was the safest place—in public—to say, ''I've proved that I can't trust myself to be alone with you so let's not invite more trouble by being stuck together in a house during a stakeout, shall we? We both agree that this is a dead-end relationship, despite these lust attacks. I don't want to tarnish my professional résumé because I can't keep my hands off you.''

He glanced down at her for the first time in an hour and his eyes burned over her like a blowtorch. Heat pooled in her belly and fanned out in all directions. Damnation, one searing look from Vance and she was a captive of the red-hot memories they'd made together in a blaze of passion.

''I don't trust myself with you, either, darlin', but a deal's a deal. We decided this is just physical so it'll wear off eventually. We'll just have to make the best of it.''

''Right.'' Miranda nodded and sighed audibly.

"You're right. We're mature adults. We can lick this thing."

Vance grabbed her hand, ignored the buzz of pleasure and veered toward his pickup. "By the way, you look better than nice. You look sensational." He sounded casual and nonchalant, didn't he? Sounded like his old suave self?

"Thanks, Vance, you look pretty terrific yourself. Nice butt," she added with a cheeky grin. "I noticed several women at the stores we blazed through at record speed were checking you out. Denim becomes you."

"There, ya see?" he said, shooting her a quick sidelong glance. "We're moving ahead. You know, getting stuff out in the open so it doesn't drag us down. Give us a couple more days of straightforward honesty and we'll be just friends who can speak our minds without causing hard feelings."

"Sure, we'll be buddies, pals," she agreed confidently. "This has to be better than the way we started out. All tense and frustrated and unsure of our footing."

It sounded great in theory and Vance vowed to get past these *hard* feelings that assailed him each time he looked at Randi's luscious body and allowed his thoughts to detour down the wrong avenues.

He chatted her up during the drive to the high school, giving her a brief history of the community that had once been a notorious hideout for an outlaw gang during Indian Territorial days. He explained why the town had been named for owls—an Indian legend dating from way back when. Then he dropped Randi off at school where Laura waited to escort her through the hallowed halls of his alma mater.

Feeling as if he had himself under control again, Vance strode into the feed store—and was set upon by every bachelor in attendance. He cringed at the wolfish grins and suggestive waggle of eyebrows that accompanied the mention of Randi's name.

"Man, that is one hot cop," Judd Allen, a neighboring rancher, purred. "She can arrest me any ole time she pleases."

"She can pat me down with no objection from me," Brandon Spears remarked. "Hell, I might break a few laws, just to get her all to myself."

"Zip it, you bozos," Vance muttered. "Show some respect."

The comment earned him several surprised stares.

"What's up with you, Vance?" Clay Kirby teased, gouging him in the rib with an elbow. "You sweet on her or something?"

"Of course not. I was asked to introduce her around town, is all." The words rang false as they tumbled off his tongue, but he was determined to believe exactly what he said.

"Well, then, when in pursuit of that sexy lady cop may the best man win," Judd declared. "Give us her address and phone number."

Although he felt uptight and territorial Vance rattled off her address and number. But when the men began rhapsodizing over the startling color of her green eyes and began speculating on her vital statistics Vance just couldn't take it anymore. He stalked to the counter to pay for his farming supplies then hightailed it back to his truck. He sat there, telling himself that he didn't care how many of his friends and acquaintances asked Randi out. He was still trying to convince himself of that when Randi reappeared on the front steps of school.

"I REALLY LIKE YOUR COUSINS' wives," Miranda commented as she set up the surveillance equipment near the upstairs window of the house her uncle had secured for the stakeout.

"Yeah, they're real sweethearts," Vance mumbled behind her.

She cut him a curious glance, then broke out in a chuckle when she became distracted by the old-fashioned clothes and the rest of the disguise that made him look like someone's grandfather. "You've been in a sour mood since this morning. You didn't have much to say the whole time we were making up the flyers for the garage sale, either. What's wrong?"

"Nothing. Everything's swell. Couldn't be better. Except for this dumb disguise that makes me look like a bald-headed old geezer with dorky glasses that are about the size of a windshield," he grumbled. He gestured back and forth between her outdated attire and his. "I'm beginning to think your uncle has a wicked sense of humor. We're tramping around here like a couple of old fogies and he's probably at headquarters, laughing his head off."

"Maybe so, but we still have a job to do—at his

command,'' she replied. "I'll take the first shift up here.''

"Fine. I'll go downstairs and watch the college basketball playoffs on the tube until it's my turn to man the binoculars.''

Having said that, Vance wheeled around and groped along the wall of the dark room to return downstairs.

Miranda sank down on the chair to focus the telescope and binoculars. She wished for more activity, something to distract her from this constant battle of emotions that bombarded her. She was trying very hard to get a handle on the crazy attraction Vance held for her, but when he was constantly underfoot she was constantly aware of him.

Just buddies? Pals? Right, as if saying the words would change her feelings for him. Well, she just had to gut it out until this week was over. Then maybe he'd be out of sight and out of mind—if she didn't go out of her mind first.

Miranda sighed in frustration and forced herself to pay attention to business. She had procedures to follow. She couldn't sit here woolgathering about a man who was all wrong for her.

Only two hours into her surveillance shift a car drove past, cut its light, and then moved slowly down the alley. Miranda perked up immediately. She adjusted the telescope to ID the car. She blinked in surprise when she recognized the vehicle as the one she'd pulled over the previous night on patrol. Miranda could barely make out the silhouettes of four suspects in the car. When the door opened the interior lights didn't flick on to give her a better view of the occupants. However, she saw a shadow scurry out the passenger door and skulk toward the back of the house under surveillance.

She very nearly came out of her skin when Vance whispered, "What's going on? I thought I heard something." Heavens! She hadn't realized he'd returned to the room. Some observant cop she was turning out to be.

Willfully she ignored the feel of his warm breath against her neck, ignored the tantalizing scent of his cologne. "Remember the rattletrap car I pulled over last night? Four juvies?"

"Yeah, vividly," he murmured.

"Well, the same car is in the alley and one of the passengers just crept toward the back door."

"Bringing stuff in or carrying it out?" Vance questioned.

"Can't tell. I need to move to a better position."

"Don't even think about it," Vance growled quietly. "If anyone is going to belly-crawl to a better position it'll be me."

"This is my job," she told him without taking her eyes off the vehicle. "You're only along for the ride, remember?" Hurriedly she popped to her feet like a jack-in-the-box, grabbed the collar of his outdated shirt and stuffed him in the chair she vacated. "Jot down the time and activity on the open file on the laptop. Keep your eyes glued to the scope," she instructed.

"Damn it, Rand," he muttered.

"Just do it." She picked her way along the wall,

using the night-light in the hall as her guide. "I'll be back as soon as I can."

Randi discarded the frizzy gray wig and oversize glasses on the way downstairs. By the time she breezed through the back door she'd shed the billowing housedress and had drawn her pistol. Wearing black shorts and a clingy knit shirt that didn't hamper movement she skulked around the corner of the house.

She swore under her breath when the neighbor's dog commenced barking its head off. By the time she ducked behind the car parked in the neighbor's driveway a dark silhouette emerged from the front door of the house under surveillance.

Posted lookout, she guessed. Thanks to that yapping dog the occupants were on guard.

Refusing to make a rookie mistake or blow her cover Miranda backtracked past the yapping dog then raced down the alley to approach the familiar vehicle from the opposite direction—on the posted lookout's blind side. At a dead run Miranda zipped across the street.

When light suddenly streamed from a nearby window she dived headlong into shrubs to prevent being spotted. She winced uncomfortably when a stabbing branch gouged her leg.

Inhaling a quick breath, she slithered toward the clump of overgrown grass and weeds that lined the alley. She'd only made it to the second fenced yard when the car lumbered toward her—sans headlights. She sprawled on her belly in the grass as the vehicle rolled past her. Miranda cautiously raised her head to check the license plate, but she couldn't get a positive ID in the darkness. Still, she was certain it was the same vehicle she'd stopped for speeding the previous night.

When the car pulled from the alley Miranda scrambled to her feet and jogged to the back of the house under surveillance. Well, damn, no wonder it was difficult to reconnoiter the back of this house from the upstairs window across the street. The porch was overgrown with vines, providing effective cover for anyone approaching from the rear.

At least she had a pretty good idea who was muling drugs or making purchases, she mused as she retraced her steps around the block to reach the two-story house. The tip would give her the opportunity to monitor the activities of the juvies while she and her co-workers were on patrol.

"What the hell took you so long?" Vance demanded when she came through the back door.

"You're supposed to be manning the telescope," she said as she brushed past him. "I had to circle the block because of the posted lookout. Did you log in the activity?"

"My God!" Vance crowed, his gaze transfixed on the scrapes on her legs. "You're bleeding."

"I had to do a half gainer into a shrub to avoid detection." She shrugged nonchalantly. "No big deal."

"No big deal?" Vance echoed as he grabbed a paper towel to blot the blood dripping down her leg.

The instant he put his hands on her bare thigh all sorts of sensations leapfrogged through her body. "Gimme that. I can do it myself," she insisted.

Vance sat back on his haunches and glared at her while she cleaned the minor injuries. "What's with you, crime dog?" he asked sarcastically. "Didn't you get enough attention growing up? Do you have to perform daring heroics in hopes of getting your photo splashed on the front page, either as the cop of the hour or a fatal statistic?"

"I'm just doing my job," she declared.

He stared at her so long that she fidgeted uneasily. Those ebony eyes burned into her until she couldn't take it anymore. "I better get back upstairs," she said, dodging his probing gaze.

He rose quickly to block her path. "I can't do this anymore," he told her gruffly.

"Then call one of your cousins to pick you up and take you home," she suggested.

"I don't mean this." His arm swept up in an all-encompassing gesture. "I mean *this*. This thou shalt *not* thing. Those skintight spandex clothes are driving me crazy."

His head swooped down and he kissed her. Plundered her mouth, robbed her of breath and stole the thoughts right out of her head was more accurate. Her arms fastened reflexively around his neck and she hung on to him, as if her very life depended on it. Her senses exploded. The taste of him demanded another taste. And another.

The feel of his muscled contours that blended into the curves and planes of her body set off burning sensations each place they touched. When her wandering hand encountered the tight, flesh-colored wig that made him appear bald she yanked it from his head and raked her fingers through his raven hair.

Then she clenched her fist in those thick strands and held him, just so, so she could feast on his mouth and mate her tongue with his.

She didn't object when his roaming caresses mapped the curve of her fanny and he fitted her to his hard arousal. More than likely she would have objected, if he *hadn't* pressed her tightly to him. She was *that* needy and desperate to be as close to him as she could get.

She liked knowing that he was as aroused as she was. Needed to know that he wanted the forbidden as much as she did. That still didn't make it right or sensible, of course. But there was consolation in this mutual desperation that picked the darnedest times to erupt like Mount Vesuvius.

"I have to get back to the surveillance room," she panted when she finally came up for air.

"I'll go with you," he said on a seesaw breath.

He grabbed her hand, snatched up his discarded wig and pulled her up the steps to the darkened room. And then he was kissing her again and her body went into nuclear meltdown. She should have her eyes glued to the telescope. Should have, but didn't. All she could think about was getting her hands under his outdated shirt and feeling those rippling muscles flex and contract beneath her hand.

As if he considered turnabout fair play, he pulled off her tight knit shirt and brushed his palms over her taut nipples. Fire blazed through her body as he bent his head to suckle her. Her breath escaped her lips in a ragged moan of helpless surrender and she gave into the hungry sensations he aroused in her.

"I must be going nuts," she mumbled aloud.

"Nice of you to join me," he said shakily. "I'm already there."

Vance glided his hand beneath the waistband of her shorts and found her hot and wet against his prowling fingertips—and he nearly lost it. He wanted to be inside her, surrounded by her heat. Now. He wanted those long, well-toned legs wrapped tightly around his hips. He needed to satisfy this insane craving that intensified with each passing hour of every day that he was with her.

His lips locked on hers, he walked her backward toward the bed and took her down with him. Hell, it wasn't his bed. It wasn't even his house—and he didn't care. He just needed to feel her beneath him, needed another taste of that sensuous mouth and another touch of that incredible body that had tormented him to no end the moment he saw her coming through the back door, wearing clothes that clung to her like a coat of paint.

"What's wrong with us?" Randi gasped as she writhed against his roaming hands.

"I wish I knew," he managed to get out—barely—before he kissed her again and settled himself on top of her.

"I've got to stop." She turned her head sideways, dragged in a panting breath and said, "Damn it, Vance, I'm on duty."

The bark of the neighbor's dog forced Vance to roll away from temptation to check the window. He was breathing hard, as if he'd just run a marathon. His body throbbed and pulsed in rhythm with his thundering heartbeat. Sexual torment nearly blinded him and he had to give his head a shake to get his eyes uncrossed so he could stare through the binoculars.

There, on the street below, he saw a long-haired teenager dash from the house under surveillance and plunge headfirst into the sleek sports car that slowed down only long enough for the door to open and shut before it sped off without headlights. Only when the car was two blocks away did the lights flick on.

"What is it?" Randi wheezed as she came to stand behind him. He could feel her bare breasts pressing against his back and he wondered when and where he'd lost *his* shirt. It was probably in the same place where he'd lost his head over this gung ho policewoman who was the last person on the continent, maybe even the western hemisphere, that he needed to be involved with.

"See the dark sports car?" He gestured south. "Some kid dashed from the bushes and jumped in before it raced off."

"I'll log it in."

He glanced sideways to watch Randi, still nude from the waist up, tapping the keys of the laptop. She was so absorbed in what she was doing that she forgot she wasn't fully dressed. But Vance hadn't forgotten. Another doubled fist of desire suckerpunched him.

Damn it to blazing hell! He had to cram his hands into the pockets of his outdated slacks to keep from making a grab for her. His timing was lousy and this maddening obsession for Randi was totally inappropriate. He felt like a pressure cooker that was all steamed up and about to blow.

"I'm going back downstairs." He lurched around and headed for the door as fast as he could get there, without tripping himself up in the darkness.

"Vance?" Her quiet voice stopped him in mid-step.

"Yeah?" He didn't look back, couldn't deal with another moment of visual torment. Her alluring image was already scorched into his eyeballs.

"I shouldn't have let things go so far. I just wanted us to be friends," she murmured.

"Yeah, me, too," he grumbled. "So much for mission impossible."

VANCE DECIDED HE WAS turning into a nutcase. He'd kept a slippery grip on his willpower for three tortuous days and nights—while running his ranch operation during daylight hours and playing detective with Randi after dark. He'd kept his distance from her as best he could. And vice versa. They'd made an unspoken pact, it seemed. She didn't look directly at him while they were living in each other's pocket and he didn't look at her.

They didn't spend more than a few minutes in the same room while changing guard on the surveillance equipment, either. The tension between them was so thick Vance swore he could slice it with a wire cutter and he kept counting the hours until he completed the sentence Tate handed down.

In one of those rare moments when Randi was out of sight—but still driving him out of his mind—Vance strode into his house to perform the menial tasks of starting the dishwasher and tossing in a load of laundry. He braced himself against the churning washing machine and inhaled several cathartic breaths. One more night, he encouraged himself. He could get through this.

His moment of silence was broken by the sound of boot heels clicking against the tiled floor.

"Yo, cuz?"

"Where are you?"

Wade and Quint. Great. The torture team. "I'm in here!" he called out reluctantly.

His cousins appeared in the doorway and Wade said, "Randi wanted us to tell you that she's taking off early today. She finished the list of chores you gave her to do in the barn."

"She said she had a hair appointment before supper," Quint reported. His lips quirked as he studied Vance astutely. "You okay? You look stressed out."

"To the max," Wade insisted.

"I'm fine. Perfect." Vance mustered a smile. His gaze dropped to the gold bands on his cousins' ring fingers and he cursed sourly. He was not going for the gold, he promised himself. If his cousins wanted to carry the Olympic torch for their wives, then dandy-fine. But he wasn't going to get reeled in by this jumble of emotions Randi kept sucking him into. He was going to finish this frustrating assignment and get his freedom and his life back.

He didn't want to wear one of those goofy smiles that plagued his married cousins when their wives crossed their line of vision. He didn't want Randi underfoot anymore because trying to restrain himself was exhausting.

"So, this is the last day of your sentence," Quint

commented. "No more public service after dark. Right?"

"Yup."

"I hear tell that Randi caused quite a stir among those of the male persuasion when Laura introduced her around the high school," Wade reported. "Laura has several bachelor teachers pawing the dirt, ready to race over to Randi's apartment and ask her for a date the moment she has some spare time on her hands."

"Good." Vance surged forward then wedged past his cousins. "Glad to hear it."

"Sure you are," Quint taunted as he dogged Vance's boot heels. "That's why you've been so hard to live with lately."

He'd been *hard*—period—but he didn't dare mention that to his satanic cousins. "Why don't you two take a hike? I've got book work to catch up on. Bills to pay. A life to lead."

"Your life won't be a bit of fun, starting tomorrow," Wade predicted.

"Think not?" Vance threw over his shoulder. "Ha! A lot you know, Einstein. I'll have more fun than you can imagine, just you wait and see."

Now, all he had to do was convince himself that he wasn't going to miss having Randi around and everything would be hunky-dory.

7

AFTER MIRANDA KEPT HER BEAUTY appointment she decided to hike across town square to treat herself to one of Stephanie Ryder's scrumptious meals before reporting for duty at the stakeout. The moment she entered the restaurant Stephanie flashed a smile and motioned her to a table.

Miranda had taken an instant liking to the vivacious redhead who appeared to be juggling her career with married life. Plus, she was craving the company of a female rather than being surrounded by men—one man in particular.

"Hey, Miranda, good to see you again. What can I get for you?" Steph asked.

"I'd like your special of the day," she replied as she slid into the booth.

"Coming right up." Steph glanced across the restaurant. "Since the supper crowd hasn't arrived to keep me busy, may I join you?"

Miranda smiled warmly. "I'd like that. There aren't enough women in my line of work and gabbing with you would be a welcome change."

"Then let me give Laura a buzz to see if she can join us." Steph retrieved her cell phone and punched in the number. "She's tutoring a few students after school and she might be about finished."

After a quick call to invite Laura to a gab session Steph strode off to grab drinks and place Miranda's order. She returned a few minutes later with two cups of coffee and a basket of warm rolls.

"Quint tells me that you've been giving Vance fits." She beamed in impish delight. "Good going, Miranda. About time that man got all shook up."

Miranda couldn't recall the last female confidante she'd had—if even at all. She usually kept her own counsel, but this...thing...with Vance needed airing and she felt as if she was going to burst if she didn't discuss it with someone.

"The man is turning me into a lunatic. How can I be attracted to him when we have totally different approaches to life, different aspirations?" she blurted out, exasperated.

"I know what you mean," Steph commiserated. "I felt the same way when I became reacquainted with Quint after a dozen years." She flicked her wrist toward the elegant interior of the restaurant. "My career was my life. I had visions of moving back to hotel and restaurant management in Dallas. But I couldn't get past Quint, no matter how I tried. I know I made the right decision because he means more to me than my job." A dreamy smile touched her lips. "It seems love makes up its own rules and sets its own time schedules."

"Well, I'm not in love with Vance," Miranda said emphatically. "I..." Her voice trailed off when Laura breezed through the door, zigzagged around

the tables and parked herself in the booth beside
Miranda.

"Wha'd I miss so far?" Laura said, all eyes and
ears.

Steph snickered in amusement. "Miranda was
just telling me that Vance drives her nuts, but she
doesn't love him."

"Well, of course not," Laura said with an elfish
grin and a dismissive flick of her wrist. "Who'd be
interested in a gorgeous hunk of cowboy who has a
terrific sense of humor and a knock-'em-dead smile?
Who'd want to wake up in the morning and see that
ruggedly handsome face staring back at you? He's
too fun-loving and playful and he'd tease you out
of your blue mood when you're having a bad day.
Couldn't have that."

"Exactly," Steph agreed, straight-faced. "And
who'd want to end up living on his sprawling ranch
where you could get completely away from your
demanding job in town? And who'd want a man that
half the women in town moon over because he's
such a prize catch?"

Miranda frowned darkly at Steph and Laura. "I
know what you're trying to do, but your reverse psychology isn't working. All I've ever wanted from
life is to serve on the same police force with my
dad and brothers."

"I hear you, girlfriend," Laura said, blue eyes
twinkling. "That's truly admirable. As for me, I
wanted to be out from under my four brothers' dom-
ination. They were always trying to run my life and
make my decisions for me. They had that protective

brother complex going. They screened my dates, plotted out my life and practically smothered me. I had to move to Hoot's Roost to get control of my own future.''

Miranda frowned pensively. ''Now that you mention it, I dealt with the same sort of thing. For as long as I can remember it was a given that I'd attend the academy and join the force. I thought it was all my idea, but...'' She shrugged uneasily when she realized that family expectations had been predetermined for her at an early age and she'd fallen into line without understanding how it had happened.

''I'll bet it was tough to have a date when your dad and brothers were cops. Pretty intimidating for a would-be boyfriend, I suspect,'' Steph remarked.

Miranda squirmed on the seat. ''Yes, well, there weren't all that many date invitations. I just thought guys didn't find me interesting.''

''Not interesting?'' Steph hooted. ''Hello? Have you looked at yourself in the mirror lately? From the gossip flying around town, every eligible bachelor is standing in line to go out with you.''

Laura thrust her hand into her purse then waved a piece of notebook paper in Miranda's face. ''See this? This is the list of fellow teachers who want me to put in a good word about them. Not interested, my eye!''

''I said *interesting*,'' Miranda corrected. ''As in enjoyable to be with. As in endearing personality and character traits. The looks are just packaging, after all.''

''I totally agree,'' Laura and Steph said in unison.

Then Steph said, "I felt the same way about myself until a few months ago. I didn't think a man could see past the wrapping to what was inside. But the Ryder men aren't that shallow. They have their own devastating good looks to contend with. They realized early on that they held magnetic appeal for women who were looking for a low maintenance husband. Unfortunately I think all the Ryder cousins learned their lessons the hard way and they're cautious of feminine traps and snares."

"Take Vance for instance," Laura remarked. "He went gaga over Shawna Karmody, the spoiled rich girl who was only using him to get back at her daddy who was planning out her life without her consent. She liked Vance's looks just fine, but she had plans of her own and they didn't include hanging out in this podunk town for long. She was baiting Daddy so he'd *pay* her to drop Vance like a hot potato. She took the money and flew off to the Big Apple to make her start in modeling and run in the fast lane with the fashionable crowd."

"Quint told me that Vance didn't know Shawna was leaving town until she was already gone. After that, he decided not to take women seriously again," Steph reported.

Miranda hadn't known, and could only imagine, how it would feel to be used to such extremes. To care and to be discarded so heartlessly would be extremely painful.

"Oh, before I forget," Laura said, jostling Miranda from her pensive musings, "Wade and I are hosting a family party for Vance tomorrow night at our place. We'll be getting him gifts, but you don't have to bring anything except yourself.''

Miranda tried to decline the invitation. ''I don't think—''

''You definitely should come,'' Steph broke in. ''You planned the surprise party for Vance and you didn't even get to join in the celebration. Please come by tomorrow night.''

Miranda didn't think it was a good idea. She doubted Vance wanted to see her after he put in his last evening in her company tonight. She wasn't sure she wanted to see him again, either. It was wearing her out trying to maintain a safe physical and emotional distance from him.

''Then it's settled,'' Laura decreed in her I'm-the-teacher-and-what-I-say-goes voice. ''Be there about eight.'' She glanced at her watch. ''I better get back to school.''

Laura bustled off before Miranda could object to being railroaded into attending the family party. When a waitress arrived to set a plate in front of her Miranda devoured the delicious food and decided to worry about the party later.

When Steph strode off to tend her duties Miranda stared pensively at her silverware. She wasn't a complete idiot. She knew what Laura and Steph were trying to do. They were hopelessly in love and thought the whole world should be head over heels, too. But this was different. She and Vance had clashed and then they had been thrown together for a solid week. Despite their maddening physical attraction, she was *not* in love with him and he wasn't in love with her. Unrequited lust maybe, but definitely not love.

Just because she was besieged by erotic tingles when Vance came within five feet of her didn't mean she wanted to spend her life with him, to alter her grand plans. Besides, moving on to join her family would be safe, familiar, expected. This thing that she and Vance had for each other was probably just a passing fancy.

Or so she tried to reassure herself.

Miranda fidgeted uneasily when Laura's comments about being dominated by her brothers came back to haunt her and she realized the similarity in their background. Miranda tossed money on the table to pay for her meal then exited the restaurant.

She couldn't help reviewing her past and wondering if perhaps she had been brainwashed by a household of cops. Had she been living to meet her family's expectations and desires for years? She'd made social and personal sacrifices left and right, trying to live up to the noble image, trying to follow the Jackson footsteps. Good grief, who was she *really* and what did *she* want from life?

Well, Miranda decided as she strode to her car. She better find herself quickly or she would become exactly as Vance tauntingly described her—Randi the Robo Cop.

What if he was right? What if she'd been programmed for the line of duty? Take away the years of psychological preparation and physical training, take away the badge...and who was she?

Miranda gulped hard as she headed home to

change into her disguise. She'd never busted loose her entire life, never strayed from the straight and narrow. She *had* taken herself too seriously, just as Vance insisted.

Maybe she should take lessons from Mr. Happy-Go-Lucky. Maybe she should let her hair down and have herself a wild, reckless fling. Heck, maybe she should make time to have a personal life while she was at it.

Well, that's what she'd do, she decided as she entered her apartment. She'd give into this uncontrollable attraction for Vance and cut loose for once.

Miranda smiled in wry amusement, wondering if Vance would freak out if she actually came on to him. Probably. Well, too bad. She needed to know if she was actually a repressed rebel, a self-restrained diva or a tunnel-vision cop. She was going to find out for sure...real soon.

VANCE TUGGED ON THE SKINTIGHT cap that made him appear bald, save the thin ring of gray hair above his ears then mashed the gray mustache against his upper lip. With the black-rimmed glasses in place, he glanced in the mirror to ensure the pasty makeup he'd applied had concealed the bronzed tan on his face and didn't appear streaky and blotchy.

He was damn glad this was the last night he'd have to wear this outdated getup and smear on this face paint. And thank goodness his cousins hadn't seen him disguised as an old man. He'd never hear the end of it.

He wondered how this stakeout would proceed

when he was officially off the hook tonight. Who'd be playing his role? Turk Barnett? Probably. Turk would be spending his evenings with Randi. Vance winced, annoyed by this insane spurt of jealousy. He should be jumping for joy, anxious to have his life back. He *was* pleased…wasn't he? Of course, he was. It was what he wanted—freedom from the woman who was constantly close enough to touch and yet impossibly wrong for him.

Vance checked his watch then whizzed outside to bound into his pickup. He drove into town—ever mindful of the speed limit, thanks to his run-ins with Randi. He parked by her apartment and hurriedly climbed beneath the steering wheel of the old Buick. An amused smile quirked his lips when she hobbled outside, wearing a floral housedress that concealed her shapely figure, the frizzy gray wig that reminded him of an oversize Brillo pad, the pale-colored support hose and orthopedic shoes. Her chalky makeup and painted-on wrinkles made her look every bit the senior citizen she portrayed.

"Hello, dear," he greeted Randi when she plopped into the Buick. "You look fetching, as usual."

"Good evening, honeycakes," she said saucily. "Did you remember to take your dose of Viagra and Rogaine today?" She squinted at him through her unstylish glasses then patted his skinned head. "No apparent improvement up here. What about elsewhere?" Her pointed gaze dropped to his lap.

Vance did a double-take. This was a new twist. She was cracking jokes. And wasn't she more casual and nonchalant than usual? What happened to the uptight, do-it-right cop he encountered on most occasions?

"What's up with you?" he asked as he navigated the armored-tank-size Buick through town.

"Just settling into my role as an old married lady... Stop frowning," she instructed. "It's causing your makeup to cake on your forehead."

"Sorry, granny. I'm just puzzled by your behavior. Just when I think I've got you figured out you turn weird on me."

"Maybe this role-playing is causing an identity crisis and I'm just trying to figure out who I am."

Vance cast her a quick sidelong glance, noting the pensive look in her eyes. But then it was gone in a flash and she reverted to cop mode.

She patted the oversize pocket of her flouncy housedress. "Uncle Tate told me to bring along the department's camera tonight. It's been three days since the last suspicious activity. The chief has a twitchy feeling that tonight we might see some action. That's the MO for this upstart drug ring that's trying to infiltrate Hoot's Roost."

Vance pulled into the driveway of the two-story house and felt himself getting tense and frustrated. He didn't want to be on hand again to watch Randi thrust herself into harm's way in the line of duty. Once had been enough, thank you very much.

"I'll take the first shift at the upstairs window," Miranda volunteered as she stepped from the car. "You can watch tonight's round of basketball playoffs. No need for you to miss part of the game if anything does go down tonight.''

Vance followed her through the door, walking with his usual slump-shouldered shuffle. ''Just don't get yourself hurt,'' he cautioned.

''You're such a sweetheart, fussing over me like that,'' she cooed. ''Watch it or you'll have me thinking you actually care.''

''Well, maybe I do, damn it,'' he muttered.

''You're such a kidder, Vance.'' She closed the door and tossed him a flippant smile. ''I know what you really think of me. You think I'm a royal pain in the butt and you can't wait to be rid of me.''

''Just because we're pretending to have been married for a half century, don't get to thinking you know what I think and how I feel. I'm serious,'' he insisted. ''I want you to be careful tonight.''

''*Serious?*'' she asked in mock amazement. ''I better log that into the laptop so I'll have it on record.''

''Quit clowning around, Randi.'' He couldn't believe he had to say that to *her*, of all people. ''If anything big happens, just call for backup, okay?''

''Why?'' She nailed him with an unblinking stare. ''Because you don't think I'm good enough at my job and you don't have confidence in me to do it right?''

''No, because I—'' He slammed his mouth shut.

''Because you what?'' she quizzed him.

''Because I *do* care, damn it all,'' he blurted out. ''There, I've said it. I don't just have the hots for you because you've got a great bod. I like it that you are self-reliant and independent. Plus, you've got goals and aspirations and I admire that.''

Her fake eyebrows elevated in surprise. ''Thank you. What brought this on?''

''It's our last night together.'' He couldn't meet her gaze a second longer so he stared at her fuzzy wig. ''I just want to go on record by saying that you've got grit and style and, despite our differences, I respect you.''

''I've gotten attached to you, too, cowboy,'' she murmured before she pivoted toward the stairs. ''But let's don't get mushy and sappy because you're too much of a distraction already and I can't deal with that right now. I've got work to do.''

Vance grinned in pleasure when she admitted she felt a little something for him. He knew this attraction was going nowhere, but he was glad they could at least part company tonight on an honest note. He hoped they could handle future encounters with mutual respect and civility.

Everything was going to be okay, he convinced himself as he plunked into Mr. Preston's favorite chair to watch the game. He'd almost gotten in over his head with Randi. It was just having her in such close quarters that bothered him most. But in a few hours he'd have his own space again and he could breathe without drowning in her alluring scent.

Oh sure, there was a part of him that would always wonder if the chemistry between them would've been as spectacular as he imagined. And yeah, the playful side of her nature that he'd glimpsed briefly this evening intrigued him. But this was for the best, he told himself. By the time they connected to make further arrangements for the town-wide garage sale next month he'd have moved on. Same for her. They'd have gotten past this flare-up attraction.

Although Vance lounged in his chair and watched the basketball game, his gaze kept straying to the window to monitor the traffic that cruised down the residential street. He became fully alert when he saw the same rattletrap car he'd seen on two previous occasions drive slowly down the street.

Another pickup or delivery, he predicted as he discreetly stationed himself beside the window to keep surveillance. Sure enough, the car veered around the corner and switched off its headlights.

He was exasperated but hardly surprised when Randi flew down the steps and headed for the back door. All his protective instincts hit a flashpoint when she said, "Call the chief and ask for backup. I intend to get a positive ID tonight so we can make a move if the situation presents itself."

"Rand—" he tried to protest—in vain.

"Just do it," she requested as she hurriedly jerked off her wig and housedress and slipped out the back door.

Swearing profusely, Vance snatched up the phone. "Get over here, pronto," Vance told Tate. "That daredevil niece of yours thinks she's a one-woman SWAT team."

"I'll be there as soon as I can, but it may be a few minutes," Tate said.

That wasn't good enough for Vance. The police

station was four miles from the older residential section of town. Randi could get her damn-fool head blown off before Tate arrived on the scene.

Grabbing the car keys and Randi's discarded disguise, Vance dashed outside to climb in the Buick. He didn't switch on the lights, just followed the same route the rattletrap car had used to enter the alley behind the house suspected as a drug site.

If something went wrong, Vance vowed to provide backup because he had to do his best to keep her safe, civilian or not.

RANDI HAD COME PREPARED to silence the yapping dog that had forced her to take a longer, more time-consuming route a few days earlier. She tossed bite-size pieces of raw meat and biscuits over the fence before she blazed across the lawn and raced across the street. She needed to be in position to make the ID tonight and to eyewitness any exchange of money for dope that might take place on the back porch.

Crouched beside a tree, Randi waited for the old car to creep past her hiding place in the alley. Thankfully there was enough light streaming from the neighboring house to confirm a match on the license plate. Like a darting shadow, she shot to the opposite side of the alley to take a better position for monitoring activity.

With extreme satisfaction she watched the youth riding shotgun exit the car and skulk toward the back door of the house. There was just enough interior lighting from the house that was under police surveillance for her to get a snapshot and description of the burly, long-haired man who appeared on the porch. He dangled a plastic bag containing a white substance in front of the youth like a carrot before a mule.

She frowned curiously when the man snatched the bag away when the youth reached out for it. With the bag tucked behind his back, he mumbled something to the boy before closing the door. Grumbling inarticulately, the youth returned, empty-handed, to the waiting vehicle.

As the car cruised to the far end of the alley another vehicle arrived. Randi suspected drug mules were lining up like jets on a runway to pick up and deliver the goods. Her mouth fell open when she recognized the old model Buick that belonged to the Prestons.

She muttered under her breath when Vance leaned across the seat to open the passenger door for her. "Get in," he said in a clipped voice.

Scowling, she crawled into the car, tossed the camera in the glove compartment and tucked her pistol under the seat—so she wouldn't be tempted to use it on Vance for disobeying orders. "This isn't standard operating procedure."

"Tough. Tate can't get here fast enough to back you up in case you have trouble." He thrust the wig and housedress at her. "Now, which way did they go?"

Miranda figured she'd get suspended over this breech in policy, but the grim countenance on

Vance's face indicated he was sticking to her like bandage adhesive.

"The other vehicle turned left from the alley," she reported as Vance took off in slow pursuit. "Don't get too close."

"I know how to do this," he grumbled. "I've seen it done in the movies and on TV for years."

"Right. Everybody's a police expert, thanks to TV shows and movies." She poked him on the arm and gestured to the right. "Pull into a driveway so you can flick on your lights. Otherwise, you'll tip off the driver that he's being followed."

"Good idea." He whipped into the nearby driveway then hit the lights before he backed out.

When the car they were tailing pulled into the alley behind the convenience store, Randi motioned for Vance to circle the block. "Don't pull in behind them. They might have spotted us and are trying to set a trap. Swing around and park at the service station next to Hoot 'N' Holler. I'll take it from there."

"Why would those punks be pulling into Hoot 'N' Holler? I've known Chet Walker, the manager, most of my life," Vance mused aloud. "Surely he isn't distributing dope on the side."

"You'd be surprised how many clean-cut criminals appear to lead law-abiding lives and then end up doing time. It just goes to show you that you never know for sure."

Vance pulled to a stop beside the gas pump at the station then stared at Miranda. "You know this bugs the hell out of me. I want to be there with you, just in case something goes wrong."

"This is what I do," she reminded him, though she was truly and sincerely touched by his concern. "Not to worry. I'll be fine."

"You damn well better be fine. If you're not, I'll be ready to shoot you myself." He clutched her arm, giving it a gentle squeeze. "I'll be sitting here on needles and pins until you get back. I really need for you to be okay."

It was totally unprofessional, but she leaned over to kiss him hard and fast then said, "I will be now. You're magic kisses always get my adrenaline pumping and put all five senses on bravo alert."

Miranda, with her disguise back in place, headed for the convenience store to investigate. Thankfully no one but the manager was inside. She wandered into a nearby aisle, pretending to read the labels on the items on the shelves.

Well, this is a big help, she thought dryly. If she needed to get her hands on hemorrhoid ointment, indigestion medication, bandages and antibiotic salve—in a hurry—she'd know exactly where to look.

Suddenly the back door crashed against the wall and two juveniles burst inside—carrying guns and wearing ski masks and muddy trench coats. What in the world was going on? This wasn't what she'd anticipated. These two yahoos appeared to be robbing the place.

Miranda muttered a curse when she realized she'd left her weapon under the seat of the car after she crawled in beside Vance. Fat lot of good that would do her now. Fine cop she was. Couldn't even keep track of her weapon unless it was strapped on her hip.

"Hands up, pal," one of the would-be thieves shouted at Chet Walker.

"Get over here, old lady," the second thief blared at her.

Miranda did a double-take when she realized the weapons were, in actuality, toy pistols. The untrained eye might not notice, but she certainly did. Her dad and brothers had given her toy pistols as gifts when she was a kid. Then they gave her the real thing when they deemed her old enough to take target practice. Well, at least she and the perps were on a level playing field, she mused. They weren't playing with real bullets and lethal weapons, either.

She also noticed how nervous the juvies were. First-timers, she guessed. They were bouncing around like jumping beans.

Miranda gave herself a mental slap and ordered herself to portray the role of a frantic senior citizen so she could divert attention away from the manager. "Oh my God! Oh my God!" she howled clutching her chest. "Is this a holdup?"

When the perps wheeled toward her, the manager used the distraction to hit the alarm switch beneath the counter. It was the antiquated variety that beeped like a foghorn, startling the young perps.

"Open the cash register," the first thief demanded shakily as he swung his pistol back to the manager. "Make it fast."

Miranda knew she had to act quickly to ensure the civilian wouldn't become a hostage or lose his

cash. "The cops are here already." She didn't
bother to mention that she was the only cop in sight.
"Oh, thank God!" she howled in a grating nasally
voice. To draw even more attention to herself she
waved her arms in frantic gestures.

She heard the sound of squealing tires. The smell
of burning rubber wafted through the back door that
was still standing wide-open. Obviously the driver
of the getaway car had decided to save himself from
arrest and let the two juvies inside the store take all
the heat.

When the manager wisely ducked behind the
counter and crawled into a hidey-hole the boys pan-
icked. Left behind, they darted this way and that,
unsure what to do next.

"You might as well throw down those guns,"
Miranda suggested. "The cops will go easier on you
that way."

Apparently the young perps didn't think much of
that idea. One of them rushed over to hook his arm
around her neck and wave the toy pistol in her face.

"Don't shoot!" Miranda squealed and tried to
look properly horrified.

"You're gonna get us outta here, old lady, so
don't croak on me. Got it?" the kid panted nervously.

"Got it, but if that's gonna work, you better get
your friend over here, too."

The kid glanced down at her in confusion. "Why
should I do that?"

"So I can provide cover, just in case the cops
outside start shooting at you."

The boy swallowed audibly. "Right. Good thinking, Granny." The kid motioned his partner over beside him and Miranda breathed an inward sigh of relief. She was in control of the situation. Now, if she could just resolve it without anyone getting hurt.

"Now what?" the kid asked.

"You need to bookend me so the cops can't get a clear shot at either of you without wounding me," she instructed. "We'll go out the door together."

"Then what?" the first thief said apprehensively. "If I'd known this was going to turn out like—"

"Just calm down, sonny," Miranda instructed in her nasally voice. "You didn't actually steal anything, so there's no need for anyone to get hurt. Just do what I tell you and you can skedaddle without a scratch on you."

The boys huddled close to her as she started toward the door. She had to make certain the boys weren't injured, given that they were packing plastic pistols and were obviously grossly inexperienced at robbery. For sure, she didn't want one of her fellow officers to take a shot when these nervous kids hit the panic button and tried to outrun the law.

Damn, she thought, when one of the boys leaned away to open the door. She couldn't take them down simultaneously before they stepped outside—as she'd hoped. She'd have to wait for the prime opportunity to present itself.

As Miranda and her captors exited the front door she wondered if Vance would appreciate the irony of this situation. For once she wasn't following by-the-book procedure. She was going to have to wing it and make certain these jittery juveniles came out of this alive—but still got struck by the fear of God so they'd keep their noses clean after this misadventure was over.

8

VANCE WENT BALLISTIC when he heard the alarm clanging. The damn thing was so loud that people poured from the filling station and restaurant to determine what was going on. Instinctively Vance took off running, determined to rescue Randi.

"What the hell? Vance, is that you?"

Vance skidded to a halt when he recognized Cousin Wade's voice behind him. He wheeled around to see Wade, Quint and their wives staring incredulously at him.

"What are you doing in that getup?" Quint questioned. "If this is one of your practical jokes, it isn't funny, cuz."

Just then, three squad cars wheeled into the parking lot—lights flashing and sirens wailing.

Chief Jackson bounded from the seat and glared at Vance. "I thought I was supposed to meet you at the house. Then I got the call from HQ to report the robbery. What the blazes is going—?"

The sound of squealing tires and the sight of the rattletrap car peeling out from behind the convenience store distracted the chief.

Vance's arm shot toward the getaway car. "Put someone on that car's tail," he said hurriedly.

"Robbery suspects, the same bunch we ID'd at the stakeout."

The chief gestured for one of his men to follow the getaway car.

"Stakeout?" Quint parroted.

"Robbery suspects?" Wade hooted.

No sooner were the words out of Wade's mouth than the door burst open and two juveniles wearing ski masks and long coats shepherded Miranda—in her elderly woman disguise—outside. Vance nearly had a seizure when he realized the punks held one pistol to her neck and one to her ribs.

Suddenly he was confronted by his worst nightmare. He had the unnerving feeling that Randi was about to blown to be kingdom come after he'd told her specifically that he wanted her to remain in one piece. Damn it to hell!

MIRANDA FELT THE JUVIES—who were clamped up against her—flinch when they stepped outside to see the squad cars and onlookers who'd gathered around the convenience store.

"Don't panic," she said confidentially. "Tell the chief of police that you want a getaway car or you'll whack me."

"Are you sure that's how this is supposed to be done?" the first would-be thief asked as his wild-eyed gaze leaped from one police car to the other.

"Of course I am," Miranda insisted. "I watch all the cop shows. Now make your demand."

"We want a getaway car or the old lady gets it!" the second thief yelled so close to the side of Miranda's head that he nearly pierced her eardrum. She winced.

"What if he won't give us one?" the kid said worriedly.

"He'll do it," she assured him quietly.

"Just take it easy, boys," Chief Jackson called out as he positioned himself a few feet away from the squad car. "You can have a car, but let the woman go."

"Forget that," the first kid called back. "She's our insurance that you won't take potshots at us."

"Good comeback," Miranda whispered. "Now tell the chief you want my husband's car that's sitting in the parking lot at the service station."

The second kid glanced at the old Buick and frowned. "What do we want with that old thing? It probably won't do seventy on a straightaway."

"Nondescript," Miranda informed him. "When you're on the lam you can't be driving a flashy sports car or squad car. You'll be spotted and pulled over before you have time to form your plans."

"Okay, okay, we'll take the granny-mobile," the first kid muttered. "Damn, this was all mistake. I never should've let myself get talked into this initiation test."

Miranda remembered watching the burly man dangle the sack of white substance in front of one of the juvies then snatch it away. So sending the kids to rob the store was an initiation test, was it? Well, that oversize goon was going to pay dearly for talking these kids into committing a crime to ensure their allegiance to his drug ring.

"We want the old lady's car!" the first kid called out.

"Fine, take it," the chief called back, then motioned everyone away from the old Buick.

Vance supposed he went a little crazy in that tense moment when the punks marched Miranda across the parking lot. He lurched forward, only to have Cousin Q and Cousin W grab his elbows to hold him in place.

"Down, boy," Wade growled in his ear.

"You might look harmless in your old geezer getup, but those punks might panic if you go barreling at them like Lone Ranger to the rescue."

"That old lady is Randi in disguise," Vance said between gritted teeth.

Quint squinted at the hostage. "Well, hell, you're right. But Randi's a cop. She's trained to handle these situations."

Vance didn't care if she held the world title for defusing hostage situations. He wanted her safe—and in his arms—and watching this scene unfold was driving him bonkers.

Vance strained against his cousins' fierce grasp on his arms when both punks—with Randi clutched tightly between them—veered toward the passenger side of the car. When the boys ducked down to slide into the car all hell broke loose.

To Vance's openmouthed amazement, Randi simultaneously elbowed both boys in the solar plexus. When they reflexively doubled over her arms shot upward, catching them in the chin. Before they knew what hit them they were flat on their backs—

and disarmed. Their weapons were tucked in the pockets of Randi's housedress.

"Jeez, Granny," one of the boys howled as he held his hand to his injured nose. "That hurt! Where'd you learn to do that?"

"Toldja I picked up a few pointers by watching those cop shows on TV," she said before Chief Jackson raced forward to slap on the cuffs. "And let this be a lesson to you, boys. Crime doesn't pay and you should be thankful you didn't rob that store because then you'd be in more trouble than you are now. If you cooperate with the chief you might see the light of day before you're as old as I am."

Vance nearly collapsed in relief when the chief and Randi escorted the punks to the squad car. Still, his pulse was pounding so rapidly that he swore he was about to have a stroke.

"Wow, I'm impressed," Wade commented as he eased his grip on Vance's arm. "That was really something, wasn't it?"

"Damn, she's good, isn't she?" Quint chimed in. "She laid out those young thugs and they never saw it coming."

When Randi and the chief took off in the squad car, Wade and Quint turned on Vance. "Okay, cuz, so what's really going on around here?" Wade wanted to know that very second.

"We want all the details," Laura insisted as she and Steph converged on him.

"Your getup gives me an inspiration for the restaurant," Steph said, lips twitching. "A Halloween costume-party night might be fun. By the way,

Vance, I love that bald head cap and mustache on you. Really gives you a snazzy new look.''

Quint chuckled. ''Flashy clothes, too. Even if they haven't been in style in twenty years.''

Vance was in no mood for the playful teasing. He felt wrung out. Watching Randi being held hostage had scared the living daylights out of him.

''First off, I'm not at liberty to discuss any details,'' he told his curious family. ''Secondly, I just want to go home. Quint, how about dropping me off at Randi's place so I can get my pickup.''

''Sure, be glad to,'' Quint said then leaned over to give his wife a quick kiss. ''I'll see you at home, Red.'' He waggled his dark brows suggestively. ''Maybe we can play cops and robbers after you close up the restaurant.''

''Hardy-har-har,'' Vance said, and scoffed.

''Oh, lighten up.'' Wade chuckled at Vance's sour expression. ''If Randi wasn't in the heat of this showdown you'd be cracking corny jokes to beat the band.'' Wade grabbed Laura's hand and pivoted toward town square. ''C'mon, darlin', let's go home and get out the pistols and whips.''

''Boy, you four are a barrel of laughs,'' Vance grumbled.

''We have to be,'' Quint said as he directed Vance to the pickup. ''You aren't living up to your reputation as the joker these days.''

Vance decided his joker status had been shot all to hell after his dealings with Randi. She had him so tied up in knots that he couldn't tell which way was up and he couldn't crack wise to save his life.

During the drive back to his ranch to wash off the face paint and change clothes Vance kept reliving the hair-raising incident Randi had endured. He wanted to take her in his arms and assure himself that she was all right, but she was wrapping up the case and, most likely, being praised to high heaven by her uncle. Then Tate would give her a glowing recommendation and send her off to OCPD so she could join her dad and brothers.

And where'd that leave him? he asked himself as he cruised down the graveled road. He'd have his life back and Randi would move on to her dream job.

He should be pleased to have dodged the bullet that plugged his lovesick cousins through the heart. Vance still had the freedom to do as he pleased, with whomever he pleased. In fact, Maggie Davidson had invited him over for a home-cooked meal tomorrow night and he could accept. Or he could meet up with some fun-loving female at the honky-tonk. He could play the field the way he usually did.

Too bad that returning to normal didn't hold the same appeal that it once did.

"Hell's bells," Vance burst out as he veered into his driveway. It suddenly dawned on him that *normal* for him these days was *aching* to have Randi in his arms. That woman had turned his life upside down and left him wanting what he knew he shouldn't have. Damn, how'd he get in this mess?

Even better question: How did he get *out* of this mess?

RANDI SWITCHED OFF THE SHOWER and twisted water from her hair. After the adrenaline high she'd ridden during the thwarted robbery attempt she was exhausted and ready for a good night's sleep.

After the boys had sung like a couple of canaries to get off with lighter punishment, she'd buzzed around headquarters, filling out paperwork and debriefing Tate on the information she'd picked up. She'd been on hand when Turk Barnett brought in the two juveniles who'd zoomed off in the getaway car. Plus, another cop on patrol had arrested the driver of the black sports car—the one she and Vance had spotted during the stakeout. The driver had been waiting to rendezvous with the kids after the robbery.

The unplanned sting on the drug ring had produced scads of evidence that resulted in several arrests. Randi had received praise galore from Uncle Tate and her co-workers, but the satisfaction of a job well done hadn't filled the empty space in her chest.

Bottom line, she had no excuse to see Vance Ryder again. If she knew in her heart that it was for the best, how come these feelings of loneliness and loss assailed her?

Randi stepped into her pink cotton panties and pulled on an oversize T-shirt that served as sleepwear. She padded barefoot to the small living area to switch off the lamp. A quiet rap at the door had her switching on the lamp again. When she looked through the peephole she saw Vance, decked out in his country and western regalia, standing on the porch.

When she opened the door he didn't wait for an invitation, just strode inside. "Just wanted to make sure you're okay," he murmured, as he looked her over from head to toe.

"I'm fine." She shifted self-consciously from one bare foot to the other. He looked good enough to gobble up in one bite. She looked like a wet mop wrapped in a wrinkled T-shirt.

"Well, I'm not okay," he said abruptly. "You scared me spitless tonight."

And then he swooped down, picked her up off the floor and crashed his mouth down on hers in a kiss that stole the breath from her lungs. And that's all it took to detonate the explosion of her senses and leave her kissing him back with wild desperation. Her arms clamped around his neck as he wrapped her bare legs around his hips. He kissed her again with an urgency that left her light-headed and she savored the taste and feel of him.

"We're all wrong for each other," he rasped when he finally broke the scorching kiss.

"I know," she wheezed as she met those midnight eyes that bore straight into her.

"You make me so crazy that I can't see straight, can't think straight," he growled as he pulled her tightly against the hard evidence of his arousal.

"Ditto."

His hands glided up from her hips to frame her face. "And if I can't have you right now I think I'll go crazier than I already am. If you're totally op-posed to going to bed with me then you better say so.''

She liked that he was asking permission. Of course, he had no idea what he was letting himself in for and she probably should tell him. She'd never been so tempted. Never felt anything remotely close to this kind of chemistry for a man. She'd never felt so reckless, hungry and ready to appease the needs churning through her.

Miranda was tired of fighting this impossible attraction, even if she knew they weren't meant for each other and that he was way out of her league.

His forehead dropped to hers as he exhaled a ragged breath. ''Sure is taking you a long time to answer. Is that a no? Do you want me to leave?''

''No.''

''*No,* you're not interested or *no,* you don't want me to leave? You need to be very clear about what you want, Calamity Jane,'' he rasped.

''I want you to stay,'' she whispered achingly. ''Because I want you.''

He walked backward so he could sit down on the sofa, but he didn't release her. His hand curled beneath her chin, forcing her to meet his gaze head-on. ''Maybe you should know that I'm the one taking the giant risk here.'' He smiled crookedly at her. ''I saw what you did to those punks tonight, ya know. If I make a wrong move I fully expect you'll clobber me where it hurts the worst.''

The teasing remark prompted her to smile, easing the tension so she could say what needed to be said. ''I've seen and heard things on duty that shocked and embarrassed me the first few times, but I haven't actually done this before,'' she admitted.

"I sorta figured that out after I discovered you had three cops as bodyguards while you were growing up. As for the stuff you've probably seen, keep in mind that I'm not into perversion so don't expect really kinky stuff from me.''

"So, you don't mind messing around with a rookie?''

His reply was a tender kiss that would've knocked her socks off if she'd been wearing them. Damn, the man could kiss like nobody's business when he took it seriously.

"I want you. Hell, I can't seem to remember when I didn't want you,'' he murmured against her lips. "I want you any way you want me. However much or little you want, Randi. You call the shots.'' He chuckled and winced. "Bad choice of wording, after watching you in action.'' His smiled faded. "I just need to be with you tonight.''

The way he was staring at her, as if she were the sun in his universe, made her go hot all over. Her inadequacies as a woman melted away, giving her an unprecedented sense of feminine confidence. "Okay then, I want the super-duper-deluxe passion package.'' She shifted against the hard ridge of his arousal that pressed against the fly of his jeans then flashed him the kind of smile she'd seen other women use as a come-on. "Give it, cowboy. I want the best you've got.''

He chuckled scampishly as his hands sneaked beneath her T-shirt to trace the elastic leg band of her panties. "Better be careful what you wish for, rookie." He eased her off his lap and stood up. "C'mon, you can't get the super-duper-deluxe package of passion except on a bed. This sofa would definitely cramp my style."

To her surprise he hooked one arm around her waist and one under her knees and carried her toward the small bedroom. Without releasing her he laid her gently on the sheets and towered over her like a shadowed fantasy come true.

Miranda waited with trembling anticipation. She heard the pearl snaps popping open on his shirt, heard the quiet hiss of his zipper and her heart started pounding like a jackhammer. The striptease in the dark was enough to drive her insane. But she really would like to view the unveiling in full light sometime in the near future. Until then, she'd settle for *touching* all that rippling muscle. Not a bad consolation, she figured. Hands-on experiments had always been her style.

Her gaze dipped to his white briefs that contrasted his shadowy form. She gulped when he shed the last article of clothing and she held her breath when he stretched out beside her. When his hand glided up her thigh Miranda jerked away, startled by the intensity of her reaction to him.

"Relax, sweetheart," he whispered against the pulsing vein in her neck. Slowly he peeled the shirt over her head and tossed it aside. "I won't hurt you. That's a promise."

Miranda felt herself melting beneath his gentle caresses and whispering kisses. Given their previous reactions to each other she'd sort of expected him to pounce. But instead, he aroused her by tantalizing degrees, making her burn from inside out, making her arch helplessly toward his skillful touch.

The man was definitely a connoisseur of passion, she decided. He knew exactly where and how to touch to launch her inhibitions into outer space. When he plucked at her nipple then suckled her she nearly came off the bed. Mercy! She could barely draw breath and when she did manage it, the musky fragrance of his cologne bombarded her. She was so intensely aware of him, aware of what he was doing to her that unfamiliar sounds kept tumbling off her lips.

It didn't take long to reach the point that she didn't care what he did to her, so long as he *kept* doing it. The sensations streaming through her hypersensitive body were incredible, compelling, and she was blown away by each and every one of them.

Vance couldn't get enough of the alluring feel and taste of her. Those muffled noises she made encouraged him to pleasure her until he became the focal point of her rioting need. He couldn't remember wanting to arouse and satisfy a woman as much as he wanted to arouse and satisfy Randi. It mattered to him the way nothing ever had. Now that he'd discovered the textures and contours of this woman behind the badge he was mesmerized by her.

When he trailed leisurely caresses from the peaks of her breasts to her navel he could feel her lush body quavering in response—and that turned him on to the extreme. He pulled off her panties and cast them over his shoulder. His hand glided lower, finding her hot and damp against his fingertips. Desire slammed into him with the impact of a head-on collision when he felt her burning his hand like liquid flames.

He dipped his head, letting his lips follow the erotic path of his hands. He traced her heated flesh with his tongue and fingertips and felt her clutching his shoulder so tightly that her nails bit into his skin like spikes.

"Vance, do something!" she demanded on a shattered gasp.

He smiled and did something else to shock and pleasure her. He felt her shimmering around his lips and fingertips and knew she was as ready as she'd ever be to accept him. He hurriedly grabbed for the protection he'd placed on the nightstand, and then settled himself between her silky thighs.

He was doing an admirable job of taking it slow and easy—until she grabbed hold of his hips in impatient urgency and pressed him against her. Sensual wildfire blazed through his body, frying the circuits in his brain. Instinctively he drove into her then felt her flinch, heard the sharp intake of her breath. But then she pulled him down on top of her until he was buried to the hilt.

Ah, finally, he was exactly where he wanted to be—so deep inside her that they were practically sharing the same body, the same breath.

"About damn time," she said as she nipped at his shoulder. "I thought you'd never get where I wanted you most."

When she arched toward him his body moved on its own accord in ageless rhythm. The wild desperation he thought he'd learned to control when he was with her returned full force. He wanted—no, he *needed*—it harder, faster, and deeper because that seemed to be what *she* wanted. Sensation after incredible sensation lambasted him as he clutched her as tightly as she held on to him.

Sex maniacs, he thought fleetingly. That's what they were. Fire and dynamite. Highly explosive. Dangerously volatile. It was a wonder they hadn't set the sheets aflame the way they were burning up in this wildfire of passion.

And suddenly the world disintegrated around him and he was scattering in about a million directions at once. Pulsating release left him shuddering and gasping for breath.

Holy kamoley! Who was the rookie here? Vance swore he'd discovered things about passion he hadn't known. Sure, he'd had his world rocked a time—or three—in his younger days. But making love with Randi…

No, no, no, the voice of self-preservation yelled at him. *Having* sex *with Randi.* Making love indicated…well, he couldn't think about that right now because he couldn't think rationally. Sex was casual. Sex was fun. This was loads of fun, but there was nothing casual about it. This was—

"Well," she said, breaking into his thoughts.

He waited, expecting her to add something more, but she didn't. She just draped her arms over his shoulders and stared up at him with a look he couldn't interpret.

"Disappointed?" he asked huskily. *Shut up, Vance. What are you looking for? A personal evaluation of your prowess? Jeez, you're so pathetic.*

"No," she whispered, a tender smile hovering on her lips. "Definitely worth waiting for. Sure glad I hooked up with someone who knows what's what."

He felt a stupid grin quirking his lips. Coming from Randi, that was quite a compliment. "Thanks, Officer, you were pretty good yourself. I like being *Miranda-ed*. You sure know how to read a guy his rights."

She giggled at his corny joke. "Yes, well, you handle a firearm like a pro."

Vance grinned as he traced the curve of her lips, fascinated by this playful side of her personality, wanting to see more of it. "Thank you, ma'am. I do *aim* to please."

She giggled then said teasingly, "However, being a law officer and all, I'm required to ask if you've registered with the proper authorities. We have certain rules about carrying concealed weapons, you know."

Vance dropped a kiss to her smiling lips. Ordinarily he was in a hurry to get up and get moving, but he didn't want to be anywhere except as close to this intriguing woman as he could get—for as long as she'd have him.

"Where do I go to get my permit?" he asked as he moved sensuously against her.

When she smiled impishly and said, "Cowboy,

you're already there," need hammered at him like hailstones. He moved above her with hungry intent and she responded eagerly, enthusiastically.

Of course, he should have expected that because Randi did nothing halfway. When she let loose she was a sensual wild woman and everything male inside him responded instantly. She gave her all to him and he reciprocated because anything less than being totally involved wasn't an option for him. At least not where she was concerned.

That was his last coherent thought before mind-blowing passion swamped him. Intense pleasure engulfed him as he and Randi skyrocketed through space without leaving the tight circle of each other's arms.

When he finally collapsed in exhaustion he wrapped her in his arms and held her close to his heart. With her luscious body tucked familiarly to his he felt as if he'd come home, as if he'd found the elusive place where he belonged.

Vance hadn't slept this well in weeks, but he konked out in nothing flat when he had Randi nestled possessively against him. He figured that living out a forbidden fantasy simply had this effect on a man.

A FEW MINUTES AFTER THREE in the morning Vance awoke and eased off the bed. He had to get home, he told himself. First off, he didn't want Randi to suffer embarrassment when his pickup was seen sitting in her driveway at dawn. Secondly, his demon cousins would be showing up bright and early to inoculate the calves they planned to wean and move to Wade's pasture. Vance wasn't sure he wanted to explain where he'd been all night because Wade and Quint were notorious for teasing.

Crawling around on all fours in the dark, Vance rounded up his clothes and hastily put them on. He decided he must have put his underwear on backward because they felt uncomfortable. But he didn't take time to make the adjustment since he didn't want to take a chance on waking Randi. Considering the evening she'd had, she could use the rest.

Still on all fours, Vance crawled from the miniscule bedroom then tiptoed to the door with his boots in hand. He slipped outside and walked to his truck in his stocking feet. When he drove off, he was struck by the sensation that he'd left something important behind—like his heart or something.

Egad, where'd that thought come from? He couldn't let himself go gaga over Randi. She'd only be here for a short time, padding her résumé before she moved on. Just like—

The painful memory and suppressed humiliation of dealing with his old flame stiffened Vance's resolve. If he had the good sense God gave a gnat he'd back away and play it cool. His relationship with Shawna Karmody had taught him a hard lesson and he wasn't going through that heartache ever again. He might have been known for his ability to make folks laugh and smile, but there was obviously something about him that made it easy for a woman to walk away. Apparently he possessed some flaw that didn't invite strong, lasting commitment.

It didn't matter that Randi was the best time he'd ever had and that being with her seemed necessary—natural even. And never mind that he'd gotten an odd twinge in his heart when she'd shared the playful, teasing side of her nature with him during their intimate encounter. She'd captivated him, devastated him—and left him wondering if maybe they weren't as mismatched as he tried to convince himself that they were.

The chemistry between them was phenomenal. She'd touched places inside him that he'd kept private and protected for years. But nothing changed the fact that she had her sights set on bigger and better things in the city.

They might have had one glorious night together but she'd still be just as gone in a few weeks and he'd be here nursing a wounded heart if he wasn't careful.

Resolved not to get all mushy and sentimental over the one—and probably the only—night in Miranda's bed, Vance drove home. He didn't bother turning on lights when he walked into his room, just crashed into bed. The emotional roller coaster he'd been riding all evening took its toll. He fell asleep about five seconds after his head hit the pillow.

9
___

Vance groaned wearily when he was awakened by the incessant pounding on his front door and heard his cousins shouting at him to rise and shine. He scrubbed his hands over his face, glanced at the digital clock that indicated he'd overslept, then yelled, "All right already. I'm coming!"

"Yo, cuz, there's been a change of plans!" Wade called as he came through the front door.

Vance threw back the covers and stood up, wishing he hadn't forgotten to lock the door when he came dragging in so late last night. To his dismay, his cousins barged into his room—and stopped cold in their tracks. Quint's eyebrows nearly rocketed off his forehead and he jerked back so suddenly that the paper cup in his hand tilted, spilling coffee down the front of his shirt.

Wade's mouth opened and shut like a trap door then he threw back his head and laughed hilariously. A second later Quint cackled like a nesting hen.

"What the hell's so damn funny?" Vance muttered at his loony cousins. "If you two don't get a grip you're gonna split a gut."

It was a long moment before Wade and Quint toned down their loud guffaws to muffled snickers.

"Nice panties, cuz," Wade said. "I expected a lace bikini thong, though, not the no-nonsense pink cotton variety."

Vance glanced down his torso then gasped in horror at the garment he'd mistakenly pulled on at Randi's apartment at three in the morning. He couldn't remember the last time he'd felt the heat of embarrassment pooling in his neck then climbing upward to burn his cheeks. Another wave of humiliation blasted him when Quint and Wade glanced curiously toward the master bathroom.

"Gee, we didn't catch you in the middle of someone, did we?" Wade asked, his eyes glinting with pure deviltry. "Where is she and what's *she* wearing?"

Vance snatched up his discarded jeans and stepped into them, lickety-split. "Get outta my room. A man oughtta be entitled to a little privacy. Instead, you two bozos just trotted in here like you own the damn place."

"So if she's not here," Quint said, blithely ignoring the demand to leave, "where did you spend part of the night?"

Wade smiled wickedly. "The *best* part of the night, no doubt."

Vance's arm shot toward the door. "Get out!"

His evil cousins didn't budge from the spot. "So, is exchanging undies something new with you or is it standard practice for your sleepovers?" Wade asked.

"Damn it," Vance shouted. "If you breathe one word of this to your wives, I'll—"

"You'll what?" Quint challenged. "Do us in?"

"'Course he will," Wade said, broad shoulders shaking with barely contained amusement. "He's already *done* the lady cop."

Vance did something he hadn't done since he was thirteen years old. He took after his cousins with murder in his eyes. Back then, their taunts and roughhousing had gone from playful nudges to painful punches and he'd pounded on them. But this was ten times worse. They were making the night he shared with Randi sound like a careless tumble. He couldn't stand for it. They'd apologize or he'd deck them, so help him he would!

"Hey!" Wade yelped when Vance's forearm shiver slammed him up against the wall and vibrated his teeth.

"Ouch!" Quint hissed when Vance shoved the paper cup against his chest and soaked him to the skin.

"Damn, Cousin V," Wade said. "What happened to the old days when you used corny jokes to ease a tense situation?"

"Dunno," Vance growled. "Must've lost my sense of humor."

"Bet I know whose apartment you left it at, along with your jockey shorts," Quint dared to remark.

"Now you listen to me, you brainless bozos," Vance snarled. "You don't like the color or style of underwear, that's one thing. I can take the razzing. But you leave Randi outta this, hear me? I don't want her embarrassed. Do we understand each other?"

Biting back ornery grins, Wade and Quint nodded. "Right. Mum's the word," Quint promised. "No poking fun at the lady cop. She's off-limits to our off color jokes."

"Exactly," Vance growled, tempted to punch the teasing smiles off their faces because they still weren't taking him seriously. "Breathe one word and it will be your last breath." He stepped back, but not before he flashed his cousins his I'm-not-kidding-around glare. "So what's with this change of plans?"

"Gage called last night," Wade reported. "Said he'd be home in a couple of weeks after doing some jet hopping to clear his trail—"

"Yeah, whatever that means," Quint cut in. "You know Gage, he's always so secretive that you never know what he's doing or where he's been."

"Thanks for the commentary, cuz," Wade said caustically. "Anyway the gist of the request was that Gage wants us to spiffy up his house and make sure the heating, plumbing and appliances are operational. He says he's toting a valuable package and he'll be keeping it under wraps for a while, but we're not to spread that around town."

"A package?" Vance grabbed some clothes from the closet and quickly got dressed.

"That's what he said. My guess is that he's in charge of protecting some classified documents or something," Wade presumed. "At any rate, we'll get the cattle moved to my pastures, double-check the fences then give Gage's house a thorough going-over."

Vance headed toward the door. His cousins arched curious brows and stayed where they were. "What now?" Vance demanded impatiently.

"You gonna wear those girly panties all day?" Quint asked.

"Yeah, as a matter of fact I am. Might even buy some more just like 'em. Got a problem with that?"

Quint shrugged and grinned. "Hey, whatever lights your fire, cuz. Just curious, is all."

Vance wheeled around to wag his forefinger in his cousins' grinning faces. "If I hear even one smart-ass remark about getting in a woman's pants, I'll knock your teeth down your throats, guaran-damn-teed."

"Whew, he sure is touchy all of a sudden, isn't he?" Quint said as he followed Vance down the hall.

"Must've gotten in touch with his feminine side last night," Wade said and snickered.

"Yeah, talk about sensitive and emotional."

"Shut the hell up!" Vance ranted in frustration.

But it didn't do any good, of course. His cousins gave him hell all the livelong day. He really hadn't expected anything less.

One good thing, though, Vance mused several hours later, the razzing kept his mind occupied. He only thought about Randi a few dozens times. It could have been worse. He could have spent the day by himself, with nothing to distract him from vivid, Technicolor memories and emotions too complex to sort out.

I can't be with her again, he told himself resolutely. He'd been left behind before. He'd been left holding his bruised heart in his hands while townsfolk whispered behind his back and sent him sympathetic glances. He wasn't going through that again. He was already standing on an emotional cliff where Randi was concerned. Seeing her again might send him over the edge. He simply had to steer clear until she left town.

MIRANDA CAME SLOWLY AWAKE to see sunlight streaming through the slats of the mini blinds. Memories flashed in her mind and she smiled, remembering the inexpressible sensations, the taste and feel and scent of Vance.

She glanced sideways to notice the empty space beside her and her smile fizzled out. She supposed she should be grateful that he'd ducked out like a thief in the night, sparing her the speculations of her neighbors or passing motorists who might recognize his pickup sitting in her driveway. But part of her— the foolish, romantic part of her that had gotten stuck on Vance—was disappointed she couldn't wake up beside him. That might have made it seem as though the unprecedented night meant more to him than a sexual conquest.

She was honest enough with herself to realize that her feelings for Vance went deep. Otherwise she would have sent him on his way last night. She hadn't had the nerve to say: I think I might be falling in love with you and for the first time in my life it feels right. If he truly felt the same connection he'd be back, she told herself. He'd call and they might even have an official date. They'd be seen around town as a couple, starting with the family birthday party Laura had planned for the evening.

But Vance didn't call that afternoon—or the next. The jerk. Miranda didn't see handsome hide or raven hair of him while on patrol duty or while she was off duty. Miranda lost count of the times she'd picked up the phone to call him and then reconsidered at the last moment.

When a full week passed and she hadn't heard from him, Miranda had to accept the demoralizing realization that she'd only managed to make herself a challenge to Vance Ryder. Now that he'd gotten what he wanted—all that he wanted, obviously—she held no interest for him.

That thought pulverized her pride as nothing else could. Miranda vowed that when they eventually crossed paths she would show no reaction whatsoever. She'd become as indifferent as he was. She'd think of their night together as an experiment in passion. They'd had sex, for the sake of mutual gratification, and that was that.

Miranda fastened the belt that held her pistol, cuffs and nightstick around her waist and prepared herself for another evening of patrol duty. On the outside she might appear calm and rational and unaffected by Vance Ryder. But that didn't mean that way down deep she didn't want to pound him over the head, cuff him to the nearest fence post and shoot him for not loving her back.

As for the briefs Vance had left behind—when he made off with her panties, as if they were his prize—she hung them on a hook in the bathroom. They served as a reminder that the only kind of *briefs* that interested or concerned her these days were the legal kind that passed across the chief's desk.

VANCE CONDUCTED HIS getting-over-Randi phase with regular visits to Hoot's Tavern. He cracked his corny jokes, made his acquaintances laugh and two-stepped around the dance floor with various sundry of available women.

And he went home every night alone. In spite of that adage that claimed the best way to get over one woman was to lose yourself in the arms of another, the words didn't ring true to Vance. It seemed he was just hanging in limbo until Randi packed up and moved to the city.

Distance was the only solution, he'd decided, and time was the cure. In addition, he'd made all sorts of bargains with himself if he could stay away from her until she left town. Yup, wait it out. That was the plan he was sticking with.

Vance exited the restaurant after sharing a delicious meal of oriental cuisine with his cousins and their wives and breathed in the fresh evening air. It was the perfect night—no wind, a dome of twinkling stars. Too bad he didn't have a certain someone to share it with.

Distracted, Vance pivoted and accidentally stumbled into the customer entering the restaurant.

"Oh, sorry—" His breath evaporated in his chest when he realized the person he'd reflexively reached out to steady on her feet was Miranda Jackson. He snatched his hand off her forearm as if he'd been bitten. All those nightly pep talks about getting over her and not needing to see her, not needing to hold her, not touch her went up in a puff of smoke. Seeing her again was the instantaneous and intense reminder that she'd become a vital part of his life and he'd been missing her like crazy.

"Randi..." he murmured. Helplessly he feasted on the sight of her, committing every swell and curve, every enchanting feature of her face to memory.

"Vance?" She tilted her head in that infuriatingly aloof way that he remembered from their first encounters. The cool-as-a-cucumber Robo Cop had overtaken the wildly sensuous woman who still haunted his dreams. Now she was just a walking badge, dressed in her blue uniform, doing her job and determined to remain emotionally detached— especially from him.

For several moments they simply stared at each other and Vance couldn't think of a single, solitary thing to say—except all those things that would give his feelings away. That he couldn't do because he knew the dreams of promotion meant more to her than hanging out in this one-horse town with a cowboy.

The restaurant door swung open and Quint and Wade breezed outside. Vance inwardly grimaced. Just what he needed to make an awkward situation worse.

"Hey, Randi, good to see you again," Quint said

amicably. His gaze bounced to Vance then resettled on Randi. "So, how have you been?"

"Can't complain," she said with a shrug.

She wouldn't complain. She never did, thought Vance.

Wade studied her crisp uniform. "Are you off duty or just on a dinner break?"

"I'm on break," she replied. "If you'll excuse me, I'm short on time. But it really was a pleasure to see you again."

When she disappeared into the restaurant Vance discovered that he could finally breathe again.

"What was that all about?" Wade asked. "You and Randi looked so stiff in the spine I'd swear someone stuck mortar in your vertebrae."

"No joke," Quint commented as he critically appraised Vance. "You two have a falling out or something?"

"Gotta go." Vance made a beeline toward his pickup.

Wade and Quint were on his trail like bloodhounds. Figured. When a man needed time alone to regroup no one would ever cut a guy some slack. Before he could dive into his truck and lock the doors, Wade and Quint grabbed his arms and pulled him to a stop.

"Did she dump you?" Wade asked flat-out.

"Dunno. I guess I dumped her first," Vance mumbled.

"What?" Quint crowed. "You spent one night with her and then bailed out? Tell me that even you wouldn't do something that stupid."

"Well, she's not a permanent fixture in Hoot's Roost," Vance told his nosy cousins. "As soon as the chief gives her the nod she'll have a position at OCPD and rejoin her family. If you think for one minute that I'm going to let myself get so attached that watching her walk is gonna bring me to my knees then think again. Been down that road. I'm not taking that trip again."

"How do you know she wants to leave?" Wade quizzed him. "Could be that she's waiting for a good reason to stay."

"What kind of good reason?" Vance said, and snorted. "Like a marriage proposal? Nuh-uh. She'd turn me down flat. That job at OCPD has been her dream for years. I know exactly where I stand. In second place behind her career."

Wade arched a dark brow. "Marriage? I didn't mention marriage. Did you mention marriage, Quint?"

"Nope, sure didn't. Vance must've given the matter prior consideration or he wouldn't have brought it up. But it sounds like a plan to me. I can fit the ceremony into my social schedule. Just name the day, cuz."

Wade rolled his eyes. "It's beyond me why you don't put a ring on the finger you've been wrapped around. You seem to be the only one around here who doesn't realize that you're hooked. The first thing you need to do is go see her and apologize for being a jerk."

"It's about time you got over yourself," Quint added. "You need to admit that you're intrigued by a strong-minded, highly motivated woman and stop being intimidated by that. She's nothing like the other women who fawn over you and cater to you. She's stuck in your head and that's when you *know,* cuz o' mine.''

"You shouldn't let the best thing that's come along in your life get away from you, just because you're too much the coward to find out how she feels about you," Wade said.

"Coward? Gee, thanks so much for the insult."

"You're welcome," Quint said.

"You might want to think about what we've told you while you're spending all your evenings alone." Wade suggested before he turned on his heels and ambled to his truck. Quint was a step behind him.

Vance was left alone with his thoughts. Unfortunately he didn't much care for them so he hopped in his truck and tried to outrun them.

It was, he soon discovered, a complete waste of his time.

ONCE INSIDE THE RESTAURANT, Miranda inhaled a steadying breath and tried to compose herself. She hadn't counted on being knocked for a loop when she'd seen Vance standing under the street lamp, staring up at the night sky. The impact he'd had on her senses and her emotions had very nearly prompted her to lurch around and run in the opposite direction. But she'd gathered her nerve and confronted him with a cool, remote façade that belied the feelings bubbling inside her.

Yes, she definitely had it bad for Vance Ryder

and it was going to take more than a week to get over him. Maybe even a month—and that was an optimistic prediction.

"Hi, Randi." Steph strode toward her, wearing a welcoming smile that went a long way in calming Miranda's jittery nerves. "Did you see Vance? He just left."

"Yes, unfortunately," she mumbled.

Steph came to a halt and narrowed her gaze. "Okay, what's going on?"

Miranda smiled ruefully. "Precisely nothing."

"Hey, Randi, good to see you…uh-oh." Laura slowed her step as she approached. "I know that look. I wore it myself a few times when Wade was giving me fits."

Miranda's shoulders slumped. She might've been able to put up a good front for Vance and his cousins, but other women, apparently, could see right through you and pinpoint where you hurt the most.

"Come over here and sit down." Steph motioned Miranda to a corner booth. She signaled the waitress to bring Miranda the special—on the house. "Sit," she commanded.

Miranda found herself bookended by the two women. There was definitely something to be said for the comfort provided by female support groups.

"Okay, spill it," Laura said in her authoritative teacher voice. "What did my meathead cousin-in-law do?"

"He didn't do anything," Miranda blurted out miserably. "That's the problem. I thought the night we—" She swallowed hard and forced herself to continue. "I thought we had something special going. Then he never called, never came by, just disappeared from my life."

"Ah-ha," Steph said thoughtfully.

"That would explain his uncharacteristic silence at supper tonight and at his party," Laura said. "No corny jokes, no teasing, no nothing. Just your everyday average bump on a log."

"You're in love with him, aren't you?" Steph quizzed.

Miranda smiled faintly. "You two missed your calling in police interrogation. You cut to the chase like real pros."

"Thanks," they said in unison. Then Laura said, "Men are more complicated than they like to think they are. But we can tell you from personal experience that the straightforward approach is best with Ryder men. If you want Vance then go get him."

Steph sank back in the booth and stared her squarely in the eye after the waitress placed her plate on the table. "Okay, bottom line. Do you love him or not? And don't dodge the question this time."

Reluctantly Miranda nodded.

"Then *tell* him," Laura advised. "He may feel the same way and is afraid to let you know."

"It's the not knowing that's the worst," Steph insisted. "Don't stand around twisting in the wind."

"Just because he hasn't called you doesn't mean you can't call him," Laura said. "We are millenium women, after all. Sometimes you have to give a guy a full dose of in-your-face honesty, especially the old-fashioned Ryder men. This is an equal opportunity world we're living in, ya know.''

"Food for thought," Miranda said before taking a bite of the entrée.

"Now then, I'm going home to be with Wade because he's the one I want to spend my life with." Laura stood up and draped her purse strap over her shoulder. "I highly recommend commitment," she encouraged before she walked away.

"And I'm going to leave the restaurant in the capable hands of my chef so I can go home to hug the stuffing out of the only man I want to spend my life with," Steph announced as she slid from the booth.

"Vance is a good, hardworking, honest guy. And he was a laugh a minute until he encountered you and couldn't figure out what to do with himself. I think you've got him right where you want him, so put him away," Steph added before she walked off.

Miranda finished her meal and wondered if she possessed the courage to walk right up to Vance and tell him how she felt. Confound it, there were all sorts of manuals and handbooks to guide cops through procedures. Why wasn't there a how-to book on being in love?

Her tormented thoughts scattered when the police radio on her belt sounded off. "Officer Jackson, Code 1 at HQ with the chief," the dispatcher said.

Miranda left a generous tip and exited the restaurant. She wasn't sure what her uncle needed to discuss—Code 1, *at her convenience*—but she had a few minutes left before she resumed patrol duty.

There was only one way to find out, she supposed. Go ask him.

According to Laura and Steph that same policy applied to her relationship—if you could call it that—with Vance. *Go ask him.*

10

"WELL, YOUNG LADY," Tate said as Miranda strode into his office. "Your dad called a while ago, bursting at the seams with pride and praise for your accomplishments." He motioned her into a chair. "He's got a job waiting in the city."

Knowing she had her family's praise and respect and a dream job waiting didn't trigger the reaction she would have expected. For the first time in her life it didn't matter that she had her family's approval and that she'd lived up to family tradition.

Praise and promotion were Pyrrhic victories if she couldn't share them with Vance.

True, she hadn't known him very long, but he'd become so important that *not* having him around made her restless and edgy. She couldn't pinpoint the precise moment that her career became a distant second, but there it was. Without Vance there was an emptiness inside her that nothing satisfied or filled.

"Something wrong, hon?" Tate asked, watching her astutely.

Miranda jerked to attention and forced a smile. "No, of course not. I'm glad the family is proud of me and the promotion came through."

Tate nodded. "You did a fine job on that drug case. And be sure to convey the department's gratitude to Vance for his assistance. Good man. I've always liked him."

"Yes, sir," she murmured neutrally.

Tate sank down in his chair and propped up his booted feet. Hands clamped behind his neck, he winked at Miranda. "You know, a good cop relies on instincts. Sometimes you just have to go with what feels right."

"So I've been told, sir," she said.

"You never want to let the bad guys get away. That also applies to the good guys, too, you know."

She lifted her head to note his amused smile. "Sir?"

"Leave off with the *sir,*" Tate insisted. "We aren't talking cop to cop now. We're talking uncle to favorite niece."

"I'm your only niece," she said, chuckling.

"Favorite, all the same." He stared meaningfully at her. "I'd have to be blind in both eyes not to see that you and Vance throw off sparks when you're together. Why do you think I paired you up for a week of constant togetherness?"

"For punishment?"

"Naw, that was the excuse. The reason was because you and Vance were too stubborn to figure out what was going on."

"Uncle Tate—"

"Can it, hon," he interrupted. "I'm doing the talking here and you're doing the listening. I've known for a long time that your dad has pushed you to follow his footsteps, same for your brothers. He lives for his job, especially after your mama bailed out on him. You missed out on a lot while growing up. I tried to tell your dad to back off and let you breathe, but he thought he had to prove a point to your mom." His gaze zeroed in on Miranda. "Now, *I'm* telling you that some of the empty places in your life can't be fulfilled with a career. There's more out there, Miranda. You can have it both ways if you give yourself a chance."

"What are you suggesting?" she asked curiously.

He smiled wryly. "Don't play dumb. Smart girl like you knows what I'm talking about. Don't be afraid to be the woman behind that badge and don't you dare hide behind it, either. If you're wondering if Vance might be what you want and need then you better figure it out for sure before your dad packs you up and moves you to the city. You with me so far?"

Miranda smiled at her uncle's roundabout lecture that was beginning to sound amazingly like the one Laura and Steph delivered over dinner. "So if I want…oh, say, an incredibly handsome rancher then I'm supposed to just go get him and browbeat him into thinking he wants me too, even if we don't have diddily squat in common?"

"Nothing in common?" Tate scoffed. "You patrol Hoot's Roost. He lives in Hoot's Roost. Same geographical location. He's a man and you're a woman. That's always a plus. I noticed he all but came unglued the night you allowed yourself to be taken hostage. That means he's emotionally involved. So are you, so don't deny it.''

"I can't deny it, but—''

"No buts,'' he broke in. Tate stood up then braced his hands on the desk to stare directly at her. "You need to hightail it to Vance's ranch and figure out what direction you really want your life to take. Not what direction your *dad* and *brothers* have decided it should go. What is it going to take to make *you* happy?'' His arm shot toward the office door. "Now, scram, kiddo. And don't come back until you decide what you want to do with your life.''

"Yes, sir.'' She gave him a saucy salute.

He reached over to grab a pair of cuffs, tossed them to her and grinned. "Here. You might need an extra set to pin him down so he'll listen with both ears.''

Lips twitching, she tucked the cuffs in her pocket. "If you think it's such a great idea to throw myself at Could-Be-Mr. Right, how come there's no Mrs. Tate Jackson?'' she dared to ask.

The smile that encompassed his face nearly threw Miranda off balance. Her uncle practically glowed like a firefly. "There will be a *Mrs.* in a couple of months,'' he informed her. "She's the pharmacist at Jenkins Drug Store. She's been dissolving Love Potion Number Nine in my iced tea since last September. Now, skedaddle. I told Cynthia I'd stop by her place after I finished up here.''

Miranda followed Tate from the office, knowing she planned to take his advice. She was going to walk out on a limb, going to stop fighting the attraction for Vance. She'd prove to him that she could be all woman, even if she was a cop.

So what if seducing a man wasn't her forte? She'd come up with a creative approach. She'd have to because she suspected that women with a lot more know-how than she had going for her had worked their wiles on Vance.

First things first, Miranda told herself during the ride home. She had to make herself look the part of the seductress and this uniform had to go.

VANCE HAD TRIED EVERYTHING he could think of to fall asleep. He'd taken a long, relaxing shower and watched a movie that was a major yawn. He'd even read the small print in the classified ads of the newspaper. Still, here he lay, hands cushioning his head, staring into the darkness of his bedroom.

Every time he closed his eyes Randi's image flashed across his mind in a succession of vivid memories. Randi diving for an escaping calf in his corral. Randi pulling over speeders on the highway. Randi crouched on the sidewalk, giving a lost and frightened boy a comforting hug before taking him home. Randi flouncing around in that frumpy disguise that made her appear decades beyond her age…Randi being held at gunpoint…

Vance thrashed in the sheets then flopped onto his stomach and crammed his face in the pillow. He had to admit that Randi was pretty amazing in action, even if she'd scared a few years off his life during that hostage situation. But he could deal with her job, if he had to. He just couldn't deal with not being with her.

When the doorbell rang, Vance levered up to glance at the illuminated clock on the dresser. One o'clock in the morning? His first thought was that Gage had arrived prematurely in the dark of night, toting the mysterious "package" he'd mentioned to Cousin W and needing assistance in stashing it someplace for safekeeping.

Vance snatched up his jeans and stuffed his legs into them then hurried down the hall. Bare-chested and barefoot he zipped across the living room to open the door.

His eyes bugged out and his breath logjammed in his throat when Randi strolled inside, wearing a shrink-wrap red dress that glittered and shimmered with every step she took. The eye-catching scrap of fabric emphasized every feminine curve and swell of her voluptuous body. Her dark hair tumbled over the spaghetti straps on her bare shoulders and curled enticingly against the diving neckline that show-cased her breasts to their best advantage.

The tight dress hit *her* at midthigh and hit *him* with an attack of pure lust. His body clenched and hardened in one second flat. His mystified gaze made another slow, attentive sweep from the top of her head to the soles of her spiked heels.

Whoa, talk about visual impact! Vance thought as he wobbled on his legs. She definitely had his attention and his masculine appreciation.

It took a long moment before he could drag his devouring gaze off her gorgeous body and register the fact that a leather holster, complete with pistol, cuffs and nightstick hung low on those shapely hips. Now here was the sum composite of a woman cop and *this* package was enough to make a man want to throw himself at her feet and beg to be arrested and frisked.

When he finally got around to meeting her gaze she arched a brow and smiled seductively at him. His pulse immediately went off the charts and his body throbbed like a bongo drum as she sashayed past him with the kind of walk that would've done Mae West proud. He caught a whiff of her perfume and sighed audibly. She looked incredible. She smelled heavenly.

And he was a goner. Cousin Q and Cousin W were right. If he let this woman get away from him he was crazy. He'd *go* crazy if he lost her.

He watched the hypnotic sway of her hips until she pivoted on those skyscraper high heels to face him again. "You modeling the new police-issued uniform?" he asked when he finally recovered his powers of speech.

She flashed him an impish smile. "Yes and I'm conducting a survey to see if John Q. Public approves."

Vance raked her up and down again. "Put me down for a definite yes. But I don't think that outfit is going to look that sensational on your uncle. He doesn't have the legs for it..." His voice trailed off when she moved a step closer. His gaze, and his thoughts, transfixed on her incredible body—accentuated by that sparkly-glittery, painted-on dress.

He was caught totally off guard when she slapped a cuff on his wrist and said, "Vance Ryder, you're under arrest. Come with me."

As she led the way down the hall he said, "Nice of you to let me grab my boots and socks before you haul me away. Would you mind clueing me in on what I've done wrong this time?"

She flicked on the light then panned the spacious room. "Nice room, by the way. A little too masculine-looking for my tastes, but very nice," she complimented.

She towed him over to the bed and then hooked the free handcuff to the wooden bedpost. He gaped at her incredulously when she grabbed his free hand, slapped on another set of cuffs and secured it to the other bedpost. Leaving him tethered like a horse, she scooped up the pile of dirty laundry that he'd left strewn around the room.

"I want to make sure no one grabs the wrong articles of clothing by mistake—or on purpose." She slam-dunked the garments into the laundry hamper then sent him an accusing glance.

"It was a mistake," Vance assured her. "It was dark and I pulled on the wrong underwear. I may have a reputation as a practical joker, but if you think I took your undies as a prize you're wrong."

"I'm relieved to hear that." She gestured toward the bed that he was tied to. "Make yourself comfortable, cowboy. You aren't going anywhere for a while yet."

Arms outstretched and hooked to the bedposts, he sprawled out and watched her with fascinated curiosity. Slowly, deliberately, she unbuckled the police-issued belt that held the tools of her trade and let it drop to her feet.

While Vance stared at her with openmouthed astonishment, Randi stepped out of her high heels and instantly felt better. Those impractical shoes pinched her feet and she was glad to be rid of them. She dug her toes into the plush carpet and cocked her hip in what she hoped was an attention-grabbing pose. Apparently it was, because Vance's obsidian eyes ran the full length of her. Then a rakish grin quirked his lips.

"I may be a little slow on the uptake, but you aren't, by chance, trying to seduce me, are you?"

"Maybe. What are my chances of success?"

"Pretty damn good," he assured her. His smile turned devilish. "You gonna lose that red-hot red dress? That'd be another step in the right direction. There isn't a man alive who can resist a striptease."

Miranda tugged down the spaghetti straps and let the slinky garment ride dangerously low on her breasts. She was rewarded with a tormented growl and a stare that visually ate her alive.

"First police brutality and now the torture rack. How'd I get into so much trouble with the law?" he rasped.

When she noticed the bulge pressing against the fly of his jeans she smiled in feminine satisfaction. She was getting to him the same way he got to her. That was certainly good to know. This relationship wasn't based entirely on sex, at least not from her standpoint, but it was more than obvious that the chemistry between them still threw off hot sparks.

On hands and knees Miranda crawled onto the bed. She perched between his sprawled legs and flashed him an impish grin. His eyes widened and his nostrils flared as he made another visual feast of her.

"You're driving me crazy, just like you always do," he growled. "I want both my hands free so I can taste you, touch you. Turn me loose."

"I think I should turn off the light first," she said, glancing pensively toward the wall switch.

"Whatever makes you more comfortable. Just gimme the key to these damn cuffs," he ordered impatiently.

She shook her head as she scooted away to switch off the light. "Sorry, no key. I intend to have my way with you tonight. When you touch me I can't think straight so that means you have to be restrained."

"Yeah? I get to you, do I?" he asked, grinning in masculine satisfaction.

"Boy, do you ever, cowboy, and you're going to pay the penalty for theft," she insisted as she resettled herself between his thighs.

"Theft?" His voice hitched when she reached up to unzip his jeans and pulled them out of her way.

"Stole my heart," she confessed as she divested him of his briefs.

"I did—?" He groaned when her hand folded around him, stroking him from base to tip. "Oh, man…"

"All man," she corrected before her moist lips whispered over his aching flesh.

"Randi," he whispered shakily, "you're playing with fire here."

"I live for danger. Plus, a good cop should familiarize herself with the weapon she plans to handle, I always say."

Vance would have chuckled, but the feel of her hands and lips on his ultrasensitive flesh robbed him of breath. She was driving him right to the edge of self-restraint with her seduction and he ached to touch her as intimately as she was touching him.

"You stole my heart, too," he admitted on a ragged breath. "Just what is the police code for robbery?"

"Two-eleven," she murmured as her left hand glided over his muscled thigh.

"You're killing me." He clenched his teeth when she flicked at him with her tongue. "What's the code for murder?"

"One eighty-seven," she whispered back.

He groaned when the ungovernable sensations she aroused left him arching helplessly toward her hands and lips. "I can't take much more of this. What's the code for I love you?"

Her caressing hands stilled and she looked up at him. "Are you saying that because you want to have sex with me?"

He shook his head. "We aren't going to have sex," he told her.

She frowned, puzzled. "Why not?"

"Because I can't have sex with you. Turn me loose."

She sank back on her heels. "You have me totally confused here."

"Turn me loose," he commanded.

Randi reached into the bodice of her dress to grab the key then unfastened the cuffs. And suddenly she found herself flat on her back while Vance loomed over her. He pinned both of her wrists with one hand and peeled off her dress with the other.

"Let that be a lesson to you, Officer," he told her. "Never believe a cornered criminal because he'll say anything to get free."

When his hand glided over her body she moaned, totally defenseless against his skillful caresses. "So does this mean we are going to have sex after all?"

"Nope," he whispered as his lips skimmed over her nipple. "Now, go ahead and ask me why I can't have sex with you."

"Damn it, Vance," she moaned when he teased her with the flick of his tongue then took her nipple into his mouth and suckled her until she arched off the bed in tormented pleasure.

"Ask me," he ordered before he gave the same erotic attention to her other breast.

"Okay," she wheezed. "Why can't you have sex with me?"

"Because having sex with you isn't enough," he murmured against her ultrasensitive skin. "I can't settle for anything less than making love with you... Now, say it, damn it."

"Say what?" The feel of his hands and lips roaming over her body was making it impossible to form coherent thought. Suddenly she couldn't remember where they were in the conversation—and could care less.

"Say you love me. Say you'll stick around town and give our love a chance." He braced his hands on either side of her shoulders and stared down at her with eyes that burned all the way to her soul. "Tell me that I mean as much to you as your life-long dream."

She looked into his shadowed face, into those glittering ebony eyes, and saw the truth of her emotions staring back at her. She looped her arms around his shoulders and drew his head toward hers. "You mean *more*," she assured him before she kissed him. And when she broke the kiss, she said, "I've gotten mighty attached to this one-horse town, and incredibly attached to you. I'm also recommending a life sentence for you, cowboy. No chance for parole. And none of this stick-around-a-while-and-see-how-it-works-out business. If you really want me, then marry me. The ceremony, the ring on the finger, the whole shebang."

Vance chuckled as he bent to brush his lips over hers. "Gotta be by the book, does it, Officer Good Body?"

"I mean business," she assured him. "I take this love I feel for you more seriously than my job. And you know that I can't do anything halfway. If you can't handle the whole package then you better run for your life, right this very minute."

A killer smile spread across his lips as he eased

between her thighs and brought his mouth within a hairbreadth of hers. "I'm not going anywhere, sweetpea. I don't ever want to miss you the way I missed you last week, either. I felt like I was walking around with a hole clean through my chest and I was surprised no one else noticed. Even my worst days, *with* you in my life, are better than my best days, *without* you in it. You push all my buttons when no one else has ever been able to. I'm not ever letting you go, because I'm crazy in love with you."

And when he came to her, giving all of himself to her, and she offered all that she was back to him, Vance knew this was one life sentence he wouldn't appeal. She *loved* him, totally, completely.

She'd dressed up in that sexy little number and come after him. She wasn't going to leave him behind to take the promotion. She was serious about him and he felt exactly the same way about her.

No more single life for him. No, sirree. He was sailing off on the Good Ship Lollipop and joining the ranks of his married cousins. He'd probably be wearing the same sappy smile when *Randi* crossed *his* line of vision. But he didn't care because the week he'd spent without her had been pure hell and he didn't want to go through that again—ever.

That was his last sane thought before a multitude of extraordinary sensations demanded his complete and undivided attention. He lost himself in Randi, in the ineffable feelings she triggered inside him.

And the most potent emotion among them was love.

RANDI RAISED HER HEAD from the solid wall of Vance's chest and squinted at the digital clock. It was 7:00 a.m. She reached across Vance to grab the phone. As she dialed the number, Vance pried open one eye and gave her the kind of smile that tempted her to forget the call and let him fulfill the sensual promise in those dark eyes. But the call had to be made, she reminded herself.

The phone rang twice before Miranda heard the familiar voice on the line. "Jackson here."

"Dad, it's me."

"Ah, my little trooper. I guess Tate told you that I have the paperwork in order. Your brothers and I will be out to move you to the city next weekend."

Miranda dropped a kiss to Vance's sensuous lips then refocused her attention on the phone call. "Dad, what would you say if I told you that I didn't want to be a cop anymore. What if I decided I wanted to be a ballerina?"

"A ballerina?" he howled in disbelief. "What the hell are you talking about?"

"Or what if I wanted to be an archaeologist or a beautician? Would you be supportive?" she asked while Vance's skillful hands swept over her body, threatening to sidetrack her.

"No," he said adamantly. "You're a cop's daughter, a cop's niece and a cop's sister. I didn't raise a damn archaeological ballerina/beautician."

Miranda smiled ruefully. Yup, sure enough, her life had been predestined. "Okay, then what would you say if I told you that I want to be a cop in Uncle Tate's jurisdiction and marry a real live cowboy?"

"I'd say you need to see the police department's shrink," he grumbled.

"I'm not crazy," she assured him then smiled adoringly at Vance. "I'm just crazy in love."

"You can't be in love right now. I've got everything planned!" her dad yelled in her ear.

"Plans change, Dad. I'll let you know when we've decided on the wedding date. Bye."

"Miranda, wait! I want to have this guy checked out!"

She smiled impishly as her gaze ran the full length of Vance's magnificent body. "Don't bother. I've already checked him out thoroughly. He's perfect for me. Talk to you later, Dad."

Her dad's voice was still blaring from the phone when she replaced the receiver.

"Didn't take it well, did he?" Vance murmured as he cuddled her close.

"Not particularly." She angled her head to peer up at him. "But what's the worst he can do?"

"Shoot me," Vance supplied.

Miranda moved provocatively against him. "Can't happen. I'll be guarding this great bod of yours with my life."

"That's mighty reassuring, darlin', but I don't think Daddy is interested in giving you away to me. I think we should make a run for it before Daddy comes after you. What say we fly off to Vegas for a few days? No ranch chores and no patrol duty to distract us. Just you and me on a fantasy getaway in the fantasy capitol of the world. How soon can you be packed?"

"In fifteen minutes. I only have one more thing to do before we leave."

"What's the one thing?"

When Vance tried to roll off the bed, Miranda latched onto his arm and towed him back to her. *"You."*

"Sweetheart," he purred huskily. "If you *do* me the way you *did* me all night, I won't *be* worth shooting."

"Then problem solved with my dad and brothers." She looped her arms around his neck and brought him down on top of her. "I love you."

"You better. If I'm gonna find myself in a showdown against three blood-thirsty cops, I want that 'I love you' on paper."

"It'll be signed, sealed and delivered," she promised him. "And if Daddy keeps pitching a fit I'll just remind him that a good cop always gets her man."

"You've got him, Officer Good Body," he said playfully. "Now what are you gonna do with him for the rest of your life?"

Miranda showed him—in slow, deliberate detail—and the joker went wild.

Carol Finch

Mr. Cool Under Fire

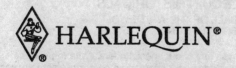

TORONTO • NEW YORK • LONDON
AMSTERDAM • PARIS • SYDNEY • HAMBURG
STOCKHOLM • ATHENS • TOKYO • MILAN • MADRID
PRAGUE • WARSAW • BUDAPEST • AUCKLAND

Dear Reader,

Welcome back to Hoot's Roost, Oklahoma, where love comes sweeping down the plain!

I've saved the best for last in this special Double Duets volume. Cousin Gage, the mystery man of the Ryder family, is assigned as a bodyguard for a woman who delights in giving him fits. But Mr. Cool Under Fire gets a little rattled—never mind hot under the collar—when his involvement with Mackenzie Shafer becomes personal rather than professional. She's getting to him big time.

Enjoy!

Carol Finch

Books by Carol Finch

HARLEQUIN DUETS

36—FIT TO BE TIED
45—A REGULAR JOE
62—MR. PREDICTABLE
72—THE FAMILY FEUD
81—LONESOME RYDER?*
    RESTAURANT ROMEO*

*Bachelors of Hoot's Roost

SILHOUETTE SPECIAL EDITION

1242—NOT JUST ANOTHER COWBOY
1320—SOUL MATES

HARLEQUIN HISTORICALS

592—CALL OF THE WHITE WOLF
635—BOUNTY HUNTER'S BRIDE

Don't miss any of our special offers. Write to us at the following address for information on our newest releases.

Harlequin Reader Service
U.S.: 3010 Walden Ave., P.O. Box 1325, Buffalo, NY 14269
Canadian: P.O. Box 609, Fort Erie, Ont. L2A 5X3

1

GAGE RYDER GLANCED DOWN into the face of the woman who had fallen asleep on his shoulder. He'd worn her out completely.

He hadn't worn her out the way men liked to boast about wearing out a beautiful woman, he thought wryly. No, this particular woman disliked him intensely and it was only exhaustion that prompted her to use his body as her mattress and his shoulder as her pillow.

If Mackenzie Shafer were awake—which she'd be in another few minutes—she'd be assailing him with verbal zingers. But she was his assignment so he had to tolerate that sassy mouth.

Gage signaled the pilot, requesting a reduction in air speed and altitude to insure a safe exit from the unmarked plane. He eased away from Mackenzie to make last-minute preparations for the drop. A crooked smile pursed his lips as he watched Mac snuggle into her chair and sigh tiredly in her sleep. He'd give her another couple of minutes of rest— and give himself a few moments of peace and quiet before she raised hell with him again.

With experienced ease Gage strapped the harness and parachute pouch on his black flight suit then eased open the hatch. Below him was nothing but thousands of feet of darkness. But in the distance he could see the makeshift drop zone his three cousins had provided at his request. Gage grabbed two over-size duffel bags and attached them to small parachutes and emergency lights then heaved them from the plane.

He pivoted around and inhaled a bracing breath. It was time to wake the sleeping dragon.

"Hey, Gidget," he said as he pulled her sluggish body into an upright position. She was still in a semiconscious state as he fastened her harness over her dark jumpsuit. "Wake up. This is where we get out."

"Where're we going this time?" she mumbled as he shepherded her toward the open hatch.

"To meet my family, so be nice, for once."

Gage grinned as he raked the curly tangle of hair from her face and crammed a Kevlar helmet on her head. Any moment now her sleep-logged brain would register the fact that there were no steps to descend from the aircraft and she'd come to instant alertness—and outrage. Sure enough, a moment later her eyes shot open wide and she latched on to him like a cat sinking its claws into a tree trunk.

"Oh, my gawd!" she howled when she realized they were about eighteen hundred feet above the ground—and Gage had a parachute strapped on his back. "I thought you said the pilot was dropping us off! You tricked me, you sneaky jerk!"

He ignored the insult and gestured southwest. "See those lights below us?"

She nodded nervously, her eyes still as wide as saucers. "You can go on ahead and I'll stay here to make sure the pilot lands the aircraft safely."

"Sorry, Gidget, but we're going down together."

"Absolutely not!" she screeched at him. "I am not jumping out of this plane!"

"It'll be fun," he enthused. He hooked his arm around her waist when she tried to back away. When she hit another level of panic he dug into his pocket. "Here, put this little pill under your tongue and you'll be good to go."

She glanced frantically from him to the open hatch. "I don't care if that pill can make me fly," she sounded off. "Or at the very *least,* make me light as a feather. I am *not* getting off this aircraft! *Capisce?*"

Gage quickly tucked the pill under her tongue— and jerked his fingers out of the way before she bit him. Despite her resistance he shifted her closer so that he could attach her harness to his. "The pill will make you high as a kite, which is about the best we can hope for."

Without giving her time for further protest—and it looked as if one was forming on her lips—Gage made a flying leap from the plane. The rush of air whizzed past them as they plunged headlong into the abyss of darkness like an anchor dropping straight to the ocean floor.

"Ohmigod! Ohmigod!" Mackenzie shrieked in horror.

Gage clamped one arm around her and assumed skydiving position—knees and free arm bent. "Just relax. I've got you," he tried to reassure her as he tucked her head against the side of his neck.

"If I survive this, I swear I'm going to kill you!" she railed at him as she wrapped her arms and legs around him and hung on for dear life. "I...*ooofff!*"

Her voice dried up when Gage pulled the ripcord

and the canopy of the parachute caught in the air, abruptly jerking them upward. He knew the instant the little white pill kicked into Mackenzie's system because she sagged heavily against him. Good, if she wasn't resisting his maneuvers, it would make landing easier.

Thanks to the pilot, a fellow operative, Gage had managed to secure a vortex ring parachute designed with four cloth sections that rotated during descent, making speed and direction easier to control, especially while he had Mac wrapped around him. That was a good thing because there was just enough wind speed to blow him off course if he didn't pay attention to business.

He was doing a fine job of paying attention to business until Mac stirred provocatively against him and pressed a kiss to the side of his neck. Her seductive gyrations and the feel of her velvety lips against his skin derailed his train of thought. He'd planned to pull gently on both guide ropes as he approached the lights below and touch down at a fast-walking speed without so much as a bump. Being airborne qualified, he'd made plenty of jumps and smooth landings—until he'd leaped from an aircraft with Mac plastered against him and she started rubbing against the male parts of his anatomy.

He'd witnessed a variety of side effects that little white pill had on folks the past few years, but he was totally baffled and unprepared for Mac's reaction to the medication. Plus, he was shocked by his elemental response to this woman that he'd viewed as the kid-sister type for almost a decade. Suddenly he had an alarming new perspective of her. That was *not* good. Keeping Mac alive and protecting her from harm was his assignment. His *only* assignment—and there could be no fringe benefits.

"Oh, hell!" Gage jerked to attention and tried to maneuver the parachute eastward when he realized he was heading directly toward the cattle pond that was a hundred yards from the lights of the drop zone. But it was too late to make the necessary adjustment. His near perfect landing was about to become a splashdown. He released the balance ropes and covered Mackenzie's face with his hand so she wouldn't take on too much water.

Although Gage managed to land in shallow water the drifting parachute tugged him forward, causing him to stumble and stagger. Gooey mud and pond scum sucked at his feet.

In the near distance he could hear his cousins shouting at him. Thrown off balance by Mac's limp weight, Gage reared back, hoping to keep her face above water—and he ended up plunking backward into the sticky goo.

"Well, wasn't that fun? Can we do it again?" Mackenzie asked in a slurred voice. "Gee, you sure know how to show a girl a good time."

Gage was eternally thankful when Cousin Wade and Cousin Quint grabbed his elbows and dragged him ashore. Between Mackenzie's dead weight and the sucking mud Gage was having trouble finding his footing.

"Next time I ask you bozos to set up a landing zone for me don't put the target so damn close to a pond," Gage muttered the moment his feet landed on solid ground.

"Hey, cuz," Quint Ryder said, "we kept you out

of the trees, didn't we? You're getting awfully picky in your old age. And you're welcome, by the way.''

"Thanks so much,'' Gage said ungratefully. He unhooked Mac's harness from his, pried her loose from his body then glanced around. "Where's Cousin Vance?''

"He drove off to pick up the bags you dropped out earlier,'' Wade reported then turned his attention to Mac. "Who's your friend?''

Gage didn't reply, just deposited Mackenzie in Wade's capable arms so he could unhook his own harness and step free of the parachute.

"It's a woman?'' Wade hooted as he steadied Mackenzie's swaying body against his hip. "I thought you said you were bringing home a *package* to stash away for safekeeping.''

"I did. She's it.'' Gage hastily rolled up the parachute. "She's my latest assignment.''

Quint Ryder chuckled in amusement as he watched Wade prop up the unsteady female. "Tough work if you can get it, Cousin G. How long will you be guarding the goods?''

"Until the threat against her has been neutralized.''

"The threat?'' Cousin W parroted. "As in…?''

"Kidnapping, ransom. Or worse,'' Gage replied. "Hey, watch it, she's…'' His voice trailed off when Mackenzie's wobbling legs folded up like a lawn chair and dumped her unceremoniously at Wade's booted feet.

Gage muttered sourly at his cousins. "Don't just stand there staring at her, as if she's some unidentified specimen of bug. Show some respect.''

"Oh, sure,'' Wade smirked. "Like you didn't

throw her off a plane and dump her in a pond. That's taking good care of her all right.''

Gage dropped the rolled parachute and dashed over to check on Mackenzie since his cousins made no effort to haul her back to her feet. ''Hey, Gidget, you still with us?''

No response.

He pulled off her headgear, allowing the wild mass of raven hair to tumble over her shoulders.

Quint flicked on his flashlight as Gage unzipped her wet jumpsuit and peeled it away. ''Whoa, cuz, this is *sooo* not a *Gidget*. This is a *goddess*. I should know. I married a goddess, and this is another one. Who the hell is she anyway?''

''Mackenzie Shafer,'' he said as he shed his flight suit and tossed it aside. ''She's my associate's daughter. He doesn't want her to become bargaining power for a nasty group of individuals who are putting excessive pressure on him.''

Gage scooped Mac's limp body into his arm and pivoted toward one of the pickups that had been used to provide lighting for the drop site. ''But this information goes no further. As far as anyone else around Hoot's Roost is concerned, Mackenzie Shafer is my wife. We've come home to meet the family.''

''Wife, huh?'' Wade said, lips twitching. ''Interesting cover. Not a long-lost cousin? Business associate, temp housekeeper or live-in lover?''

Gage scowled at the teasing question. Although he'd come to his family for assistance with this particular assignment, he should've known better than to expect cooperation without the playful haranguing indigenous to the Ryder cousins.

Gage and his cousins were as close as brothers and they backed each other up when the going got tough. However, they'd razzed each other to no end since childhood and the habit seemed impossible to break. Now it looked as if it was Gage's turn to become the brunt of jokes and torment. But he could endure the harassment so long as he kept Mac safe.

She could be a real pain in the keister with that smart mouth and feisty temperament. But after living in such close quarters for over two weeks he'd sort of adjusted to having her underfoot. Things had been going as well as could be expected—until they made that parachute jump. The feel of her lush body rubbing suggestively against him had reminded him that he'd been without a woman for a while now. Worse, the incident was a blatant reminder that Mac had become a desirable woman, but he sincerely hoped he could revert to viewing her as the girl-next-door type of female. No question, after those unnerving few minutes while they were aloft, she'd distracted the hell out of him. Obviously. Otherwise, they wouldn't have touched down in the stock pond and received a muddy dousing.

Gage was jostled from his troubled thoughts when the bright headlights of a speeding pickup nearly blinded him. He halted in his tracks—with Mac's lifeless body draped in his arms—and watched Cousin Vance Ryder bring the pickup to a skidding halt.

"Hey, Gage, good to see you again." Vance hitched his thumb toward the truck bed. "I found your gear. So where's the mysterious package...and who's this babe?"

"They're one and the same," Quint spoke up. He

grinned wryly as he surged forward to open the pickup door for Gage. "This is his pretend wife, *Gidget*."

"Gidget?" Vance crowed as he stared into Mac's flawless face. "I thought Gidgets were supposed to look like pixies with freckles on their noses and cropped haircuts."

Gage vividly remembered his first introduction to the scrawny, flat-chested teenager with the super-short hairdo and expressive violet eyes that dominated her face. "She was a Gidget when I first met her years ago," Gage explained. "The nickname just stuck. So did the nickname *Mac*."

Vance studied Mackenzie's shapely physique that was emphasized by the form-fitting knit shirt and jeans. "I'd qualify her as drop-dead gorgeous. She isn't actually *dead*, is she? That'd mean you aren't too good at your job, cuz."

"I sedated her before we jumped from the plane," he retorted. "She wasn't the least bit thrilled about coming with me." And that was putting it mildly.

Wade chuckled as he strode around to slide beneath the steering wheel of his pickup. "Gee, I can't imagine why she'd object. You didn't even give her a parachute."

"That's because I didn't want to have to chase her all over the night sky. No telling where she might've drifted off to." Gage eased a hip onto the bucket seat and shifted Mackenzie's lax body onto his lap. Her head dropped against his shoulder and he tried to ignore the whisper of her breath against his neck. *Kid sister*, he chanted silently when his unruly body reacted to the feel of her supple feminine form pressed familiarly to him.

"We'll take you back to your ranch and help you get settled before we gather your parachute and collect the other trucks," Quint said as he and Vance piled into the back seat of Wade's extended cab pickup.

"We checked out everything at your house, as you requested," Vance commented. "The place is shipshape. Food in the pantry and the fridge. All appliances are operational. Now what's this about a wife?" he asked in the same breath.

"I—" Gage's voice fizzled out when Mac moaned aloud and shifted in his lap. To his embarrassed dismay, she looped one arm around his neck and spread a string of warm kisses along the column of his throat.

"Mmm, Justin, I've waited a long time for this," she mumbled groggily. "You taste as good as you look."

Gage inwardly cringed when his cousins snickered.

"Why is she calling you Justin?" Quint questioned.

"Justin Sayer is an alias," he explained as he battled his response to the featherlight kisses fluttering against his neck. "That's who I am to her."

"Gee, looks like you're a lot more than an alias to her," Vance taunted. "She's got a severe case of the hots for you."

The comment drew several more snickers.

"Actually she doesn't like me at all," Gage insisted as he grabbed her roaming hand that skimmed across the breadth of his chest. "She's trashed because of the medication I gave her before the jump. You'll meet the real Mackenzie Shafer when this stuff wears off. She's a spoiled little rich girl and she can filet you with her tongue when the mood strikes.''

''Better debrief us, cuz,'' Wade requested as he circled around the herd of cattle that had bedded down near the pasture gate. ''You're usually secretive about your assignments, but if you want us to provide backup for this one we need to know what to expect.''

Gage tried to subdue his rioting hormones when Mac's free hand slid off his shoulder and she clumsily unbuttoned his shirt to rake her nails over the hair on his chest. Damnation, it was hard to concentrate on conversation when her wandering caresses were driving him crazy. He was truly baffled by her reaction to the medication. She'd gone from belligerent and hostile to amorous in less than an hour.

''Her father is a client and close associate at the U.S. Consulate in Russia,'' Gage explained. ''Daniel Shafer was appointed by the government to represent the U.S. commercial interests in St. Petersburg. During our attempt to gather intelligence we came across highly sensitive information that indicated ties to the Russian Mafia. The money-laundering network is linked to fraudulent imports to the U.S.''

Vance gave a low whistle. ''Damn, Gage, don't tell me that you and Daniel Shafer stepped on the toes of foreign crime bosses and they're coming after you.''

Vance didn't know the half of it, but Gage couldn't go into detail without divulging classified information. ''Something like that. We know too

much, but we can't blow this case wide open until
the info passes through the proper channels at specific governmental agencies.

"We learned from another undercover operative
that Mackenzie was targeted as a hostage to keep
her father silent. I had to extract her immediately.
She was on her way to take her bar examination.
Needless to say she was irate when I whisked her
away without telling her where we were going."

Gage became distracted once again when Mackenzie's head lowered to trail kisses across his chest.
Jeez! She was getting him all fired up and he was
begging to have the old Mackenzie back. This alter
ego of hers was as dangerous as the assignment that
had landed in his lap—literally.

"She's almost a lawyer?" Quint questioned from
the back seat. "Brains *and* beauty, huh? I like that
in a woman."

"Well, this particular woman has more degrees
than a thermometer," Gage reported as he fidgeted
on the bucket seat. "Since her father has served as
attaché, ambassador and consul at various locations
around the world she's been home-schooled by the
best money can buy. She enrolled in college at age
sixteen and she speaks five languages fluently." He
ought to know. She'd cursed him in all five of them.
"Since she had to meet the requirements of six different universities, worldwide, she accumulated
credit hours galore before she graduated summa cum
laude from Harvard."

"Damn, what is she?" Vance asked incredulously. "The female version of Einstein?" He piled
from the truck to open and shut the pasture gate.

"Close," Gage said. "She's already had a dozen

job offers from elite corporations and private practices back east. With her background, family connection and extensive résumé she can name her own salary. Naturally she's been giving me hell about interrupting her life since we began hopscotching across the U.S. of A. by plane, train, bus and automobile to lose the tail that's following us."

Vance hopped back into the truck. "What'd I miss?"

"Cousin G was telling us that hit men are after his exceptionally bright, gifted and pretty package," Wade said as he cruised toward Gage's ranch house.

"That's why you decided to hole up in the outback of Oklahoma, where everyone knows everyone else," Quint surmised. "Unfamiliar faces draw quick attention and suspicion. We'll know the instant trouble arrives."

"Precisely," Gage confirmed as he stared anxiously toward his home. He needed Mac off his lap—and fast. "Since Justin Sayer only has a post office box for an address in New York he'd be hard to locate."

"As I see it, you have only one potential problem to resolve," Wade said pensively.

"Just one problem?" Gage said, and smirked.

The most pressing problem was the curly haired woman who had his hormones so revved up that he could barely sit still. She was so smashed that she was touching him just about everywhere. Damn, he couldn't wait to tuck her into bed for the night. He couldn't think straight when those soft lips and wandering hands were igniting the fires of lust—the very last thing he should feel toward this particular woman.

"One problem in *this* neck of the woods," Wade clarified.

"What's the one problem?" Gage asked, his voice a little on the unsteady side, thanks to Mac's arousing caresses.

"Dexter Nolan," his three cousins said in unison.

Gage groaned aloud. "Hell, I almost forgot about Dex."

"In that case, let's refresh your memory," Quint insisted. "You were generous enough to let Dex live in that old cabin on the north end of your ranch, rent free, under the pretense of keeping watch for rustlers, stray cattle and horses since you're away on business so much."

"Nice gesture on your part, by the way," Vance said wryly. "But the problem is that Dex is a little paranoid."

"A little?" Wade scoffed. "That's an understatement if I ever heard one."

"If you recall," Quint continued, "Dex served in Desert Storm just a little too long and never readjusted to civilian life. He's convinced that a surprise attack could occur at any moment and he remains on constant alert."

"Dex always has a pair of binoculars draped around his neck so he can watch for incoming hostiles. He also keeps a camera handy for visual evidence," Vance added.

"Last month Dex nearly freaked out when the DEA choppers were running surveillance along the river to search for ditch weed." Wade snickered in amusement as he veered onto the graveled driveway that led to the house. "Dex thought we were under attack and he came tearing down from the hill in his beat-up truck to warn us.''

"Yeah, and it took a pint of Jack Daniel's to calm him down and reassure him," Quint recalled. "He was sure we were on the verge of nuclear war."

"Five'll getcha ten that Dex spotted your plane and parachute while he was keeping surveillance with his night vision goggles," Vance said. "Personally I think he spends way too much time wearing those NVGs. They make him spookier than he already is."

"Having Dex on our side might work to our advantage," Gage said optimistically. "If suspicious characters show up to case our ranches he'll let us know."

"Right, now all you have to do is figure out how to explain why you parachuted into your pasture at night with your 'package' in tow," Quint remarked. "Thanks to your line of work, you're accomplished at tap dancing around the truth."

Yes, he was, Gage mused. Mostly he operated on a need-to-know basis. In the early years, lying used to go against his grain, but he'd learned through experience that honesty and espionage didn't make good bed partners. The truth could get you deepsixed and Gage had gotten exceptionally good at concealing information as well as emotion.

He'd been dubbed Mr. Cool Under Fire, but he was here to say that he was anything but cool while Mac was under the influence of medication that transformed her into a seductive siren. No matter how many times he reminded himself that Mac was his close associate's daughter and that he was to treat her like a kid sister his male body wasn't buying it.

Gage swallowed a sigh of relief when Wade stopped the truck. "Vance, carry Gidget into the house and I'll grab our luggage. Since Quint and Wade are married I won't ask them to handle Gidget while she's in this weird mental state. I don't want to get them in trouble with their new wives."

Gage frowned curiously when his cousins chuckled. Vance said, "Actually I'm married, too."

"Get outta town. Since when?" Gage demanded. "Why wasn't I informed of this?"

"Because the practical joker pulled a fast one on all of us," Wade reported, grinning as he watched Mackenzie caress Gage's partially bared chest. "He and the well-stacked lady cop flew off to Vegas for a long weekend and decided to tie the knot while they were there."

"Lady cop?" Gage chirped. "Vance and a cop? No fooling?"

"No fooling," Quint assured him. "They had the shortest, most intense courtship on record and set the whole town, not to mention the Ryder family, on their ears."

"We had a two-day engagement," Vance announced with a goofy smile that stunned the hell out of Gage. "I'm serving a life sentence and loving every minute of it. Nowadays, Randi is the only woman I want to get my hands on, so *you* can carry your gorgeous package and *I'll* grab the luggage."

"I'm the only Ryder cousin who isn't hitched and wearing a lovesick smile? Good thing one of us still has some sense left." Gage shouldered open the door and resituated Mackenzie in his arms. To his frustration she looped her arms around his neck and slathered kisses to the underside of his jaw.

"I want you, stud muffin," she purred sluggishly.

Wade burst out laughing as he veered around Gage to unlock the front door. "Gee, *stud muffin,* are you sure this woman hates you? We're getting an entirely different impression." Green eyes gleaming with deviltry, he stepped aside to let Gage pass. "Damn good thing you've had martial arts training or else I'd be worried about leaving you alone with Gidget. *You* might be the one who needs a bodyguard."

Quint tossed Gage a wink and a grin. "I'd sure hate to see her take advantage of you and ruin your reputation."

"Just call my new wife if you need assistance," Vance teased. "She'll have Gidget arrested. She's good at arresting people, ya know. She even arrested me once."

Gage frowned darkly when his evil cousins continued to hover around him, watching Mac shower him with kisses. "Thanks for the assistance. I can take it from here. You can remove the evidence of the drop zone in my pasture."

Quint patted Gage's shoulder affectionately. "All kidding aside, cuz, we're glad to have you home for a while. We'll give you time to get settled in with your *assignment* before you repay us for overseeing your ranch all these years."

"You're way behind on fence repair, branding and inoculating all these prize cattle we've stocked in your pasture," Wade reminded him playfully.

"Plus, you'll need to be on hand for the reception scheduled for the newlyweds." Quint flashed Vance a grin. "Vance has yet to be introduced to his new father-in-law and brothers-in-law. They're all cops and they aren't too thrilled about this sudden wedding."

"For sure, I can use backup and moral support." Vance grimaced. "I've been told, via the phone, that I better make double-damn certain that Randi's happy...or else."

When the door closed behind his cowboy cousins Gage made a beeline for the spare bedroom. He set Mackenzie to her feet and steadied her while he turned down the bed. He grabbed her with both arms when she swayed unsteadily beside him.

"Damn, remind me never to give you another one of those pills," he muttered as her head lolled against his shoulder and her glossy black hair tangled in his eyelashes.

He removed her boots and, leaving her fully dressed in her blouse and jeans, he tucked her in bed. Fascinated, he watched her stretch leisurely before she graced him with such a sultry smile that his knees nearly buckled beneath him. Although there was a dazed look in those amethyst eyes Gage felt himself tumbling into their mesmerizing depths. He tried not to study her so astutely, but it was impossible not to. She'd transformed into an extraordinarily beautiful woman.

When she raised up to clutch both of her fists in the collar of his shirt and practically pulled him down on top of her he didn't put up resistance, as he should have. Like an idiot, he just stared at her full, lush mouth and wondered how it would feel to have those velvety lips directly beneath his.

"Come to bed with me, Justin," she invited as she pulled him ever closer. "I want you."

"I'm gonna pretend I didn't hear you say that," he wheezed, feeling himself growing hard and needy as he braced himself above her. "Now gimme a break and go to sleep."

She pulled herself up again, her fists anchored on his shirt collar—and kissed the breath clean out of him. She might have smelled a bit like his stock pond, but she tasted like heaven on his lips. Gage responded instantaneously.

Forget about that kid sister and girl next door mantra he'd been chanting, he mused as he returned her kiss with reckless abandon. This would be the first and last time he kissed Mackenzie Shafer. She was so zonked from the medication that she was behaving as if she actually liked him, and she was coming on to him as if she were wildly attracted to him.

Gage found himself deeply involved in the demanding wallop of a kiss—which was part adrenaline rush, part frustration and an excessive amount of forbidden desire. A guy was entitled to an occasional fantasy, wasn't he? Besides, the seductive siren who'd overtaken Mac's luscious body—which was pressed intimately against his—intrigued and dazzled him.

As fantasies went, this was a real humdinger. Mac was kissing him for all she was worth and her restless hands were roaming over him, spearing into his shirt to rake over his chest and belly, causing hungry need to churn inside him.

"Get naked with me, Justin," she whispered when she finally came up for a breath of air.

"You've tempted me enough already," he muttered as he unclamped her hands from his neck and defied the urging of his unruly desires. "Go to sleep, *please.*"

Her reply was another smoldering kiss that sent erotic sensations sizzling through him and left him questioning the self-restraint he'd spent thirty-four years perfecting. Damn, if he didn't pry himself loose and put some distance between them—PDQ—he didn't want to be held accountable for what might happen next.

While Gage was fighting for self-control and telling himself that it was time to break this scorching kiss, Mac's head flopped backward and her hands dropped away from his shirt. She'd finally konked out. Thank God.

Breathing hard, Gage rolled off the bed and stared down at Mac for a long, confused moment. She'd been sixteen years old when he'd first met her. A woman-child whom he'd easily written off as Daniel Shafer's kid. The kid who came and went from colleges to visit various U.S. Consulates around the world. She'd had a chip on her shoulder and an obvious dislike for him—though Gage never had figured out what he'd said or done to tick her off. And then wham! Mackenzie was all over him. And he'd enjoyed it way too much.

He grinned in amusement at the Dr.-Jekyll-Ms.-Hyde female who'd taken up temporary residence in his life. The next time Mac decided to lambaste him with her rapier tongue he'd remember this kiss. It would take the sting out of her hostility toward him.

Impulsively he leaned down to brush his lips over her lush mouth—just one last time. "I guess we'll see the real Mac Shaver in the morning, won't we, kid?''

Gage did the brotherly thing by pulling the sheet up to her chin, patting her curly head then turning off the light. After the sexual torment she'd put him through he could use a cold shower.

2

MACKENZIE BATTLED HER WAY through the haze of grogginess then swallowed with considerable effort. Her mouth felt as dry as Death Valley and the dull throb in her skull made her reluctant to wake up.

She eventually pried open one heavily lidded eye and stared up at the ceiling. She had no idea where she was. The past two weeks had been a road trip from hell. Justin Sayer, resident demon and personal tormentor, had dragged her from one locale to the next, as if they were fugitives trying to outrun the law.

With fiendish, paranoid dedication he'd constantly kept watch over his shoulder and checked them into fleabag hotels under assumed names. There was always an adjoining room with an adjoining door so he could get to her in a flash in case of trouble. Of course, there hadn't been a bit of trouble, just two weeks of putting her through exhausting paces to appease her father's obvious neurosis. Daniel Shafer wanted her buried in obscurity until this supposed threat to her life died down.

What was her father thinking when he sent the very last man on the planet that she wanted as her personal protector? A stranger she could have dealt with easily. But *not* this man, she mused as she drifted back to sleep.

Several hours later Mackenzie finally dragged herself from bed then blinked in surprise when she noticed a pair of faded jeans and chambray work shirt draped over the chair that sat in the corner of the bedroom. Lord, what now? she wondered as she headed across the hall to the bathroom. For two weeks Justin had made her wear one disguise after another. Blond wigs. Red wigs. Unisex clothing and sunglasses. Now he'd obviously decided to dress her like a farmer's daughter. If he kept this up much longer she wouldn't remember who she was.

Finding the bathroom well stocked with necessities, Mackenzie peeled off the clothes she'd slept in and stepped into the shower. Ah, she lived for morning showers and evening baths. The soothing water and solitude eased the tension—and frustration, couldn't forget that—of dealing with Justin 24/7. As paranoid as he'd been she was surprised he wasn't standing guard at the bathroom door.

Ten minutes later Mackenzie grabbed a towel and wrapped herself in it. Revived and refreshed, she returned to the bedroom to dress. She jerked upright when a hazy flashback zipped through her mind. She remembered standing at the open hatch of the plane, disoriented from sleep, hearing Justin announce they were taking a flying leap. She'd come unglued while he stood there, cool as a cucumber, as if he took death-defying leaps into space on a regular basis. Obviously he did because he hadn't batted an eyelash at grabbing hold of her and skydiving from the aircraft.

Mackenzie donned her clothes and frowned at the fuzzy image of soaring through space with Justin's powerful body meshed tightly to hers. After that, the memories became jumbled and completely out of sequence.

When she plopped down on the edge of the bed to stuff her feet into the work boots Justin had provided for her the strangest image leapt to mind. Lost in troubled thoughts, Mackenzie squirmed uneasily. She could almost swear that she remembered being curled up on Justin's lap, living a secret fantasy that she'd repressed for years.

"'Bout time you got up, Gidget."

She started at the sound of Justin's rich baritone voice. She glanced over her shoulder to see him propped leisurely against the doorjamb. He was dressed in chambray and denim and his muscled arms were crossed over his broad chest. His casual smile sent a stab of longing through her—the kind of unrequited longing she'd battled for years. Damn it, this handsome hunk of masculinity incited so many emotions inside her that she never knew what to do with all of them. Resentment headed the list of feelings he aroused in her, but it was followed closely by her exasperating and unrealistic infatuation that had hounded her since adolescence.

She ignored the tumble of emotions and made an all-encompassing gesture with her arm. "Just where are we now and what charade will we be playing today?"

"We're at my Oklahoma ranch," he said, surprising her.

"Your ranch? I didn't know you had one." Mackenzie surged off the bed and, in typical Mackenzie Shafer fashion, strode off to investigate. "How long have you had a ranch?"

"I grew up here," he said as he followed her

down the hall. "It's been in my family for several generations."

Mackenzie halted at the door of the spacious master bedroom. Curious, she panned the masculine decor and noticed the laptop computer sitting on the desk. All sorts of odd electronic gadgets were attached to it. Her gaze drifted to the photographs that lined the dresser. She ambled across the room to pluck up the picture of Justin standing beside three men who bore a strong family resemblance—strikingly handsome men with raven hair and supremely athletic physiques. They stood at least six foot four inches in their cowboy boots.

"Your brothers?" she questioned curiously.

"No brothers or sisters. Those are my first cousins on my dad's side of the family." He scooped up the pile of clothes he'd worn the previous day. "You'll meet them and their wives tomorrow night. This is our final destination, by the way."

"For how long?" she asked as she studied the photo of Justin standing beside a man and woman whom she presumed to be his parents.

"Until the threat no longer exists." He tossed the wrinkled garments in the laundry hamper in the master bathroom then strode over to clutch her elbow. "C'mon, kid, you can look to your heart's content later. I've been waiting lunch on you and I'm famished."

Mackenzie allowed herself to be ushered down the hall, only because she was anxious to see the rest of the house where Justin Sayer grew up. Otherwise, she'd have protested being led around like a puppy—the same way he'd led her around for the past two weeks.

"Someone around here has excellent taste," she commented as she panned the sprawling living space that was furnished with two sofas and love seats, two comfy recliners and a big screen TV. "Must've been your parents."

"Thanks, Gidget. Never toss me a compliment, if you can help it," he said, chuckling. "My cousins were kind enough to stock the kitchen with food so don't whine to me if you don't like the sandwich fixings they provided."

Mackenzie stopped short to survey the expansive kitchen and dining room area. Sunlight splashed through the floor-to-ceiling windows and spread across the terra cotta tiles. Fascinated, she strode over to stare at the lush rolling hills that were dotted with cattle and horses then she scanned the thick clumps of trees that lined the winding creeks.

"My," she breathed appreciatively, "what an incredibly picturesque view."

"You like?"

Mackenzie dragged her admiring gaze away from the panoramic view to note that Justin seemed genuinely interested in her opinion of his home. Well, that was a first, she thought. Ordinarily this man was professionally cool and revealed very little of his emotions. Even when she ranted at him for dragging her all over creation and making her change her appearance he rarely blinked an eyelash. And suddenly, it appeared that her opinion mattered. Well, what do you know? At long last she'd stumbled across something that stirred a passion inside him. It didn't take a genius to realize his home meant something special to him. If only *she* meant...

She discarded that whimsical impossibility instantly. Justin Sayer regarded her as an assignment—paid for by her father. Furthermore, this gorgeous hulk of attractive male treated her as his kid sister. Always had. Which grated on her feminine pride like he wouldn't believe.

"Well?" he prompted.

"I love it. Think I'll buy it," she replied with the aloof aplomb he'd come to expect from her. "How much do you want for it?"

"You want the whole kit and caboodle? Livestock, too?"

When he smiled down at her, silver-gray eyes twinkling, she lost her foolish heart all over again. Damn it, why did he have to have such a devastating effect on her? Bedeviled by the expression on his ruggedly handsome face, she could only nod because she didn't trust her voice not to get all choked up. In these surroundings, Justin seemed different somehow. More relaxed and at ease. Less professional, more approachable. This was his *querencia,* his safe refuge, she realized with sudden insight.

"The whole shebang," she finally replied, unable to control the answering smile that spread across her lips.

He leaned down—so close that she could see the rare sparkle in his eyes at close range and count the crow's-feet that fanned away from those long black eyelashes. Her breath stalled in her chest when his gaze dipped to her lips. She wondered if he was about to kiss her. Justin? Not a chance. And yet, she was struck by the strangest sensation that she knew how it felt to have that sensuous mouth against hers, knew how it felt to breathe him in and lose herself in his kiss. Sheesh! She was really losing it, she decided.

"Even you and your daddy's money can't afford this place," he murmured as his gaze roamed over her face. "There isn't enough money in the Federal Treasury to persuade me to part with this ranch, Gidget."

And then he stepped back into his own space to tower over her. That nonchalant mask was back in place so quickly that it made her head spin. For a moment there, she swore he'd regarded her as a woman, not an assignment, not the child she'd been to him since they'd first met.

"Sit down. I'll put lunch on the table," he said briskly.

Gage wheeled toward the fridge to grab lunchmeat and condiments. All the while he mentally kicked himself for coming within a hairbreadth of kissing Mac. Hell's bells, he couldn't look at her this morning without thinking about the sensual woman he'd encountered the previous night. He felt as if someone had cracked him over the head with a crowbar, blurring his vision, making him see double. He stared at Mac and he saw one image overlapping the other. The snippy little imp who delighted in testing his temper and the provocative seductress who'd crawled all over him last night. Now, he couldn't respond normally to her. Inappropriate feelings of desire kept getting in his way. Well, this had to stop, here and now, he told himself resolutely. He was being well paid to protect Mac from harm, not have a flaming affair with her.

"So what's the plan?" she asked as she nodded her thanks for the food and drink he'd placed in front of her. "Are we going to hang out here until you get the all clear signal from Dad?"

Gage plunked into a chair to slap together a Dagwood sandwich. "Yes," he said, determined to get them started off on the right track. "I'll be helping my cousins with ranch chores since I've been away from home too much the past few years. There are corrals to build, fences to repair and cattle to sort out, inoculate and haul to stockyards or distant pastures. Plus, we have fields to plant for hay grazer and pastures to overseed with grass."

"So, you'll be playing cowboy. And what am I supposed to do? Sit here and twiddle my thumbs instead of pursuing my promising career in law?"

"That's the general idea, yes," he confirmed.

She smirked then wet her whistle. "Typical male response."

"Well, I'm a typical male. What kind of response did you expect?" he teased.

"You plan to resume your previous life and I'm supposed to hang in limbo, waiting for *you* to *allow* me to leave? Not interested. Let me hear Plan B," she demanded.

"There's no Plan B. You'll be in charge of the house." He knew that would get a rise out of her, but he could deal better with her temper than these forbidden sensations that hammered at him when he spent too much time staring at her.

Her eyes narrowed in irritation. "I'm the domestic help?"

"You got it, Mac. I bring home the bacon. You cook it."

"I thought you raised cattle, not hogs," she said smartly. "Some rancher you are, Justin Sayer. You don't even know a bull from a hog.'' She eyed him suspiciously. ''Or maybe the truth is that this *isn't* your ranch where we're holed up.''

Gage braced his elbows on the table, forced himself to stare at her gorgeous face and decided it was time to come clean. ''My real name is Gage Ryder and this *is* my ranch,'' he told her honestly. ''I have several aliases, depending on my assignments. Everyone around Hoot's Roost knows me as Gage. Get used to calling me that so it doesn't arouse suspicion.''

Her violet eyes nearly popped from their sockets and she almost choked on her bite of sandwich. Gage bounded up and darted around the table to smack her between the shoulder blades. When her face returned to its normal color and she sucked in a breath he took his seat.

''You aren't my father's bodyguard, attaché and/or advisor?'' she croaked when she recovered her ability to speak.

''Not exactly.''

Her gaze focused intently on him. ''Just *who* do you work for, if not for the government?''

''I work for an elite, low-profile organization that supplies specialized services for clients in the private, corporate and governmental sectors,'' he explained while she gaped at him in astonishment. ''The government contacts us for certain assignments because we aren't under the same scrutiny and don't get bogged down in red tape.''

''In other words, the government likes to use your company because you can play by your own rules,'' she paraphrased.

He smiled. ''You could say that. Your dad is my

contact. He teasingly refers to me as the male version of *Charlie's Angels*. Only neither of my bosses is named Charlie and, because of their experience in counterintelligence, they've accumulated extensive data that the Pentagon envies. It's taken two years to compile the information on the underground Russian network and syndicates infiltrating America.''

"And things were going fine until the Russian Mafia realized you'd infiltrated their network," she surmised.

"More or less," he replied. "Your dad was forced into hiding, despite his diplomatic immunity. He felt it necessary to whisk you off so you couldn't be used as a pawn, making him choose between your life and his patriotic commitment. The foreign crime bosses can't dispose of your father without international repercussions, but they *can* twist his arm into remaining silent by getting their hands on *you.*"

Mackenzie slumped back in her chair to digest the startling information. "Even my own father doesn't know exactly where I am, does he?"

"No, and that's for his own protection, as well as yours," Gage replied. "Even my own family doesn't know exactly who I work for. They've accepted the fact that I'm not at liberty to disclose much info. Most of it is classified…and I'm not sure why I'm telling you this." He sighed as he raked his hand through his thick raven hair. "Well, maybe I do," he admitted.

"Because you're hoping I'll stop giving you grief while we're stuck here indefinitely," she guessed. "Tell the kid just enough so she'll stay off your back, correct, 007?"

Gage couldn't help but respond to her saucy smile. She'd rarely directed genuine smiles at him and he'd discovered that he wasn't as immune to her as he should be.

"Um, there's more," he said, then cleared his throat.

Gage took a bite of his sandwich. "I have to explain your presence to the community. My cousins know I'm on assignment, but their wives don't."

"I'm supposed to be your temp housekeeper?" she presumed.

Gage sipped his iced tea as he met her disgruntled gaze. "No, you'll be playing the role of my wife. We're madly in love, by the way."

Her mouth dropped open wide enough for a pigeon to roost. "Wife?" she crowed. A moment later she threw back her curly dark head and laughed out loud. That was not the response he expected from Mac. "Oh, goody, we can have sex, sex and more sex and I can crawl all over you in private and in public and no one will think a thing about it..."

Her voice fizzled out momentarily. Then she gaped at him and emitted an ear-cracking shriek. "Oh, my gawd!"

Gage knew the exact instant when she remembered what had happened between them last night. The mind-numbing effects of the pill he'd stuffed in her mouth had worn off and her memory had cleared up. He'd hoped the incident would elude her completely. No such luck.

"That pill you gave me!" she howled. "Damn it, Justin...er...Gage!"

Mackenzie slumped in her chair and covered her flaming face with her hands. Fits and starts of memory flashed across her mind. She suddenly remembered curling up in Gage's lap and playing out her repressed fantasy of kissing and touching him. She vaguely recalled the hum of conversation going on around her while she boldly caressed Gage's masculine chest and spread kisses over his cheeks and neck. And later...

Mackenzie groaned aloud when she realized that she had kissed Gage's lips off before she fell asleep. That was no erotic dream. It had been reality. She was so mortified that she couldn't sit there another moment. Couldn't face him after that horrible pill had obliterated her inhibitions and left her coming on to him like a sex-starved nympho.

She was out of her chair in a flash, dashing toward the one room in the house that she was sure had a lock on the door. The bathroom.

"Mac, come back here!" he called after her.

She heard his chair hit the floor with a crash when he leaped up to give chase, but she didn't slow her swift pace. She locked herself in the bathroom then stared at her flushed reflection in the mirror. She looked like a wild witch with her naturally curly ebony hair streaming around her flamingo-pink face and her eyes as wide as serving platters.

"Mac, open the door," Gage demanded sharply.

"No, I'll be living in here indefinitely. Deliver my food via the bathroom window. I never want to see you again. I made a complete fool of myself!" she wailed in exasperation. He knew she had the hots for him now. She couldn't possibly play his adoring wife in public. It was too close to the truth and, smart as he was, he might see through her charade.

"Hey, kid, don't take it so hard," he insisted. "I knew that wasn't the real you. No hard feelings. It's forgotten."

"Do not call me kid," she muttered at the closed door. "I'm not a child anymore."

There was a pregnant pause before he said, "Believe me, after last night, I'm aware of that."

Groaning, Mac slid down the door and plunked on the floor. She'd never been so humiliated in her entire life. "Your cousins witnessed my outrageous behavior, didn't they? They saw me behaving like a nympho."

"Not to worry. I told them that you hated me and it was only the effects of medication. Now, come out here and finish lunch. We have some high-tech devices that will alert us to the arrival of unfriendlies to install this afternoon."

Sighing, she laid her head against the door. "Gage?"

"Yeah?"

"I'm dreadfully sorry I embarrassed you, and myself, in front of your family."

"Forget it. Everyone should have at least one embarrassing moment in his life. It's not like you stripped naked in front of me, ya know."

Mackenzie swiveled around to stare at the door that separated him. "What if I had?" she wanted to know.

"Mac..." he said warningly.

"Seriously. What if I had?" she demanded. "Answer me."

"Not until you open the door."

"No, I can't face you yet. Answer me!" she demanded.

"You really don't want to know."

"Don't tell me what I want," she shot back. "I *do* want to know how you would've reacted. Would you have had sex with me if I'd gotten naked and had thrown myself at you?"

She waited with bated breath—but to no avail. He never replied. He simply walked away. Despite her humiliation, Mackenzie was on a quest for information and she was like a pit bull when she was in woman-on-a-mission mode. She had to know so she unlocked the door and dogged his footsteps. Why it was important, she wasn't sure. Heavens, she wasn't even certain which response she wanted to hear from him. *No,* he wouldn't have taken advantage of her because she didn't interest him and he wasn't attracted to her. Or *yes,* he wouldn't turn down a quick tumble when a woman threw herself, naked, into his arms.

When Mackenzie reentered the kitchen she found Gage hunkered over his paper plate, engorging himself on another Dagwood sandwich. He didn't look up when she walked in, just pretended she didn't exist. Well, no more of that. He'd overlooked her for years and she was done with that, thank you very much. She was a woman now, not a child and it was high time he dealt with her accordingly.

"Yes or no?" she persisted relentlessly.

He still didn't glance at her. "Doesn't matter," he muttered. "Nothing happened. Nothing is going to happen. In public we'll be affectionate because that's what's expected. In private you stay in your own space and I'll stay in mine, *kid.*"

"You call me kid one more time and I'm going for your throat!" she said vindictively.

He ignored her. Damn, but he was good at doing that.

"Your father is a long-time associate. He specifically requested that I protect you and that's exactly what I'm going to do. There will be no naked bodies and no sex. You're like my kid sister and your dad is like a father figure to me."

Because her emotions were already in a tailspin the comment triggered the resentment she'd battled for years and she burst out with, "Right. You're the son my dad never had. He's thrown you in my face for years. Mr. Wonderful and Can Do No Wrong."

Hands on hips, she thrust out her chin and glared at him. "Well, how do you think it made me feel to be measured up against Mr. Super Duper Dynamo Spy and to find myself constantly lacking? I worked my butt off to make excellent grades so I could receive a smidgen of the praise Dad directed at you. But what I accomplished was never enough. I was the kid sister standing in your shadow. I wanted to outshine you, but who can compete with 007? Mr. Cool Under Fire. Mr. *Everything!* I tried and I failed! You had your own father. Why couldn't you leave *mine* alone?"

Mackenzie felt a jolt sizzle through her when Gage finally glanced up and stared at her with those intense gray eyes. "I didn't know you felt that way, Mac."

"Yeah, well, some observant spy you are, James Bond. You looked right past the obvious. I lost my mother years ago and all I have is Dad. But I don't really have him because of you. I know he loves me—"

"Damn right he does. Otherwise, you wouldn't be in hiding," he interjected.

"But I'm not *you!*" she shouted at him.

He had the audacity to grin at her. "Now that you have that off your chest, how about planting your fanny in your chair and chowing down on this meal I slaved over? You can finish your tantrum later, if you feel it necessary, but we have things to do this afternoon. The high-tech devices should be arriving within the hour."

"I'll sit down and shut up *after* you answer the question," she negotiated.

Gage delivered a hot, sizzling stare that nearly buckled her knees. Never in all the years she'd known him had he ever stared at her with such blatant masculine interest. It took her breath away and caused her pulse to shoot off the charts.

"Do we really need to make this situation more complicated than it is, Gidget?" he asked in a voice that crackled with sensuality.

His steel-gray eyes burned into her, daring her to **make** him answer the question directly. Confused, defeated—she wasn't sure which—she plunked into her chair and ate.

There and then, Mackenzie made up her mind to give Gage—and it was going to take time to get used to calling him that—what he expected from her. In private she'd be the feisty, mouthy brat he preferred to deal with. In public, however, she was going to live out her secret fantasy. And since it was Fantasy Impossible she'd take the opportunity to explore her adult feelings for Gage. She'd let this unproductive fascination run its course. She'd purge this infatuation by fire and maybe move on to the promising career awaiting her once the danger passed.

She'd finally outgrow Gage Ryder, overcome her childhood resentment and embrace her new life. Now that would be an accomplishment she could anticipate.

"That smile of yours is making me nervous," Gage said, jostling her from her contemplative musings. "What are you thinking, Mac?"

He was worried? He had every right to be worried. To compensate for years of bottled frustration she intended to ambush him from every direction at once. Then they'd see how well Mr. Cool Under Fire held up. It was going to be a hoot playing devil and angel, alternately, and watching Gage try to respond to her split personality.

His dark brows bunched over his gray eyes. "Answer me," he demanded impatiently.

With supreme satisfaction she flashed a wicked smile, threw his own words in his face and watched him wince. "You don't really want to know, 007, so don't ask."

He stared at her for a long moment. "You're planning to make my life miserable, aren't you?" he deduced.

"Who? Harmless, dim-witted little ole me?" she drawled, smiling innocently and batting her eyelashes for effect. "How could I possibly make life difficult for an incredibly capable man like you?"

When the doorbell rang Mackenzie watched Gage bound from his chair. "That's probably the package I've been expecting from headquarters. We'll place the gadgets in position as soon as you finish eating."

Mackenzie gulped down the rest of her meal and

put away the leftovers. She wasn't sure where they were going or exactly what they'd be doing, but for the first time in two hectic weeks she felt that she had herself together. She had a plan, an objective—to drive the imperturbable Gage Ryder as crazy as he'd made her the past few years.

3

————

"WHAT ARE THOSE THINGS? New millennium spy gadgets?" Mac asked curiously as she swung onto horseback.

"Exactly," Gage confirmed as he stuffed the jewelry-box size sensors into the saddlebag. "They save manpower and they can be linked to my computer for constant surveillance."

Mac reined her horse toward the pasture gate. "Are we going to bury them or dangle them from tree limbs?"

"Bury them." Gage watched the ease with which Mac sat a horse. He suddenly recalled that Daniel had mentioned giving his daughter riding lessons during one of his extended stints as an attaché in England. Although Mac had been trained on English saddles she'd made the transition to Western saddles with graceful ease.

What Gage noticed most, however, was that Mac looked exceptionally fine in those tight-fitting faded jeans, with her long legs wrapped around a horse. He wondered how those world-class legs would look wrapped around his waist.

Gage jerked upright so quickly, when bombarded by that forbidden thought, that his horse shifted skittishly beneath him. Damnation, after last night's erotic encounter and their morning conversation

Gage was having serious difficulty keeping his mind on professional matters.

That was not good. In fact, it was terrible. He didn't want to see Mac as the lovely, desirable woman she'd matured into. He wanted to focus on that scrawny kid with wide lavender-colored eyes and no breasts worth mentioning. Unfortunately the Gidget of yesteryear had metamorphosed into a ravishing beauty whose long, curly ebony hair made him itch to run his fingers through those spring-loaded tendrils and kiss those velvety-soft lips.

"Whoa, boy." Gage wasn't sure if he was talking to himself or the high-spirited palomino gelding that was prancing beneath him, anxious to stretch his legs into a wild run across the pasture.

Gage reached over to latch the gate then chewed himself out royally for fantasizing about things that were not going to happen. He was a professional, damn it, and Mac was his assignment, double damn it. He'd accomplished several difficult missions in his career. He wasn't going to let this one defeat him or compromise his integrity.

"Race you to the pond," Mac challenged then plunged off before he could accept or decline.

Gage nudged his eager mount and charged after Mac. He'd let her win, of course. It was the least he could do after she'd confided that she'd been competing with him for Daniel's affection and resented Gage's intrusion into her relationship with her father. Gage hadn't a clue that Mac begrudged his friendship with Daniel. Like she'd said: Some spymaster he was if he couldn't see that she'd felt left out and that he'd stolen her thunder.

To make a good showing, Gage gave the palo-

mino his head and let the gelding run nose to nose
with Mac's strawberry roan mare. Both horses
leaped the obstacle of a narrow creek bed without
breaking stride and galloped toward the pond.

Suddenly, a flashback from his youth flared in his
mind. He saw himself racing his cousins, cross-
country, without a care in the world, except to win
bragging rights. He'd missed being home, sharing
an easy camaraderie with his cousins.

His thoughts trailed off as he watched Mac curl
herself over the horse to ease into the lead. With
that long black hair flying in the wind Gage couldn't
decide if she reminded him more of a witch on a
broom or a siren at full sail. Unfortunately both sce-
narios seemed to fit her. She intrigued him, even
when he didn't want to be intrigued or fascinated by
the woman she'd become.

Gage gasped in alarm when Mac jerked the mare
to a skidding halt and the horse reared up to paw
the air. But Mac didn't so much as flinch, just threw
back her head and laughed at the thrill of defeating
him in the race.

"Well, *big brother*," she taunted as he trotted up
beside her. "Do you concede or do you wanna make
this contest the best two out of three?"

"My horse is carrying additional weight," he explained.

She grinned mischievously. "Excuses, excuses.
Admit it, you can't keep up with me."

"You're right. You won fair and square," he con-
ceded. "Whaddaya want? A trophy to prove it?"

"Yes, just like the ones I noticed sitting in your
bedroom. I presume that you and your cousins used
to rodeo and were very proficient at it."

He shrugged casually as he led the way toward a grove of cedar and cottonwoods trees. "Rodeo scholarship in college. A couple of years on the suicide circuit," he informed her. "It's a hard and dangerous life. You should get a trophy, just for participating."

"That explains your occupation in the perilous world of espionage and intrigue. You must've inherited the restless gene that your cousins didn't get," she predicted.

"Suppose so," he admitted. "My cousins were ready to come home and assume control of their ranches after our tour on the suicide circuit. But I wasn't ready to settle down. I just sort of happened onto this job by helping an operative avoid getting shot full of holes. The organization made me an interesting offer and put me through six months of the most grueling and rigorous training imaginable. But I guess I always did love a challenge."

Gage wasn't sure why he was spilling his guts to her like this, but he rationalized that since she was playing the role of his wife she needed background information.

When she wheeled her horse around to trot away, he held up his hand like a traffic cop. "Hold up, Annie Oakley. I've got to bury the first sensor here."

Mac gracefully dismounted to untie the saddlebag. "Well, isn't this cute," she said as she pulled the small collapsible shovel from the leather pouch. "Haven't seen one of these babies since I took camping trips in the Alps while Dad was doing consultation in Switzerland years ago."

She unfolded the miniature shovel and set it on

her shoulder like a soldier holding a rifle. She gave him a saucy salute. "Where do I dig, sir?"

"I'll dig." He made a grab for the shovel.

"I can do it myself," she insisted, snatching the implement from his reach. "Where do you want the hole dug? And how do those high-tech sensors work?"

Gage gestured to a location near the copse of trees then inwardly groaned when Mac bent over to tend the chore. Denim stretched tightly across her shapely derriere. His gaze and attention focused on her like a laser beam. Flustered, he spun on his boot heels to retrieve a sensor and activate it.

"There's a miniscule camera attached to the computer chip that relays photos and coordinates to the ring of orbiting satellites. The info is bounced back to my laptop," Gage explained. "These electronic bugs are sound and light sensitive. We'll have a good view of the surrounding area, unless the live-stock decides to bed down on top of them."

"And all this state-of-the-art electronics will ensure the bad guys don't get the drop on us?" she asked as she stepped back to let Gage position the box in the hole.

"Exactly," he said as he buried the equipment.

"Mind if I ask how much this surveillance and personal protection duty is setting my father back?"

"Yes," he said. "It comes under the heading of NOYB."

"None of your business," she translated. While his back was turned she set her foot against his tush and gave him a playful shove off balance. When Gage scowled at her she chuckled gleefully. "My bodyguard has a blind spot. I'll have to remember that.''

When she sauntered off, Gage scraped himself off the ground. Mac had an impish streak a mile wide, he recalled. She took delight in tormenting him every chance she got. *That* he could deal with. *That* he was comfortable with. The sensual seductress who had kissed him breathless made him nervous.

''Speaking of guarding bodies.'' He quickened his step to capture her from *her* blind side and hooked his arm around her neck. ''You need to know a few self-defense...*ooofff!*''

Gage yelped in disbelief when Mac grabbed his arm with both hands, thrust her hip against his leg and then sent him cartwheeling over her shoulder. He landed in an undignified heap at her feet. He lay there, flat on his back, staring at the vault of blue sky and gasping for breath. Her smiling face, surrounded by a cloud of hair that burned like blue-black flames in the sunlight, appeared above him.

''Where...?'' was all he got out on a pained breath.

''Hong Kong,'' she replied. ''Martial arts classes, at Daddy's insistence. But that was before I knew you. So, now I'm thinking—hey, I don't need a bodyguard at all, because I know how to take care of myself.''

When she offered him a hand up Gage yanked her off balance. Quick as a cat, he turned the tables on Little Ms. Know It All and left her flat on *her* back—beneath him. His hand came around her throat, making her gasp for breath. ''Don't get too cocky, kid,'' he growled at her. ''When you put a man down you've only completed half the battle—''

Her uplifted knee caught him in the crotch and he howled in pain. She shoved the heel of her hand against the underside of his chin, snapping his head back with enough force to cause stars to explode behind his eyes like fireworks. While he was trying to recover from the counterassault, she heaved him away and rolled agilely to her feet.

"I know lots of stuff, 007," she said as she dusted herself off. She assumed a martial arts crouch of readiness. "Bring it on if you want to take the risk of never fathering children and singing soprano for the rest of your life."

Gage huffed and puffed and dragged himself onto all fours. Damn, he had taken Mac for granted— every which way—for years. She was no slouch in the self-defense department.

"Okay, kid," he wheezed as he staggered to his feet.

"I told you not to call me that," she huffed indignantly.

He ignored the objection—again. "You can take care of yourself one-on-one. How are you in a crowd of unfriendlies?"

Mac shrugged as she strode back to the horses they'd tethered by the trees. "Never been tested. Maybe you and your cousins should try me, if it'll make you rest easier."

Gingerly Gage walked back to his horse. He'd lost Round Two with Mac—first the horse race then the self-defense test. He told himself that it was good for her self-esteem, since she had that resentment factor working against him for years. She deserved to gloat—a little. But she was not prepared to go head-to-head with the kind of underworld Mafiosos who might have been sent to abduct her and use her as a pawn against Daniel. Hoodlums played dirty and their consciences were nonexistent. Gage sincerely hoped this situation would be resolved before Mac encountered the kind of trouble that he doubted she could handle with a few hand-to-hand combat tactics.

"Where to next?" Mac stared curiously at him from her perch atop her mare. She scanned the lush pastures that were filled with grazing cattle then inhaled a breath of country air. Gage's attention went directly to the full swells of her breasts that were outlined in the clingy knit blouse she'd opted to wear, instead of the loose-fitting chambray shirt he'd laid out for her. "I thought I'd dread this whole hiding-out-and-lying-low fiasco, but I love your wide-open spaces," she confided.

Gage pulled himself into the saddle. "I hope you like KP duty just as much. While I'm helping my cousins, you'll be in charge of domestics. I wasn't kidding about that."

"In your dreams, cowboy," she said, and smirked. "This is your assignment, remember? It's your duty to ensure I'm fed, clothed and protected. You wanna eat? Fix it yourself. I'll do *my* laundry and you can do your own."

Gage reined his horse south to place another sensor in position. "Why am I not surprised that you plan to be difficult and uncooperative?" he muttered.

"You've never made life easy for me and I'm returning the favor—in spades," she said breezily.

Although Gage had trained himself to be patient he wished Daniel and the other operatives working to compile more evidence to turn over to the FBI and CIA would hurry it up. But government bureaucracy was like a lumbering elephant. Arrest warrants for the international underworld didn't happen overnight. Therefore, he was stuck with Mac until the documents and warrants were signed, sealed and delivered.

Damn, and here he'd thought gathering intel was painstakingly difficult. Dealing with Mac was proving to be much harder on him.

MACKENZIE STARED AT HER reflection in the bathroom mirror then added a touch of rose blush to her cheeks. She'd fussed over her hairdo and selected the most form-fitting blouse and skirt from the limited supply of clothing Gage had packed for her before he spirited her away from her apartment. She rolled up the waistband of the knit skirt so that it hit her midthigh and tried to decide if she looked sexy or sluttish.

Tonight was her first official introduction to the Ryder cousins and their wives and she wanted to make a good impression. She didn't know what sort of women Gage usually had on his arm, but she presumed the women shouted class, style and sophistication. She could play that role with ease because she'd hosted and attended balls and banquets with her father, and other dignitaries, for years. Although she preferred casual and relaxed, she could definitely do suave and sophisticated if the situation demanded.

Mackenzie gave herself a final inspection then strode off. Playing the role of Gage's adoring wife was going to be a snap. She could let her guard down and react to him naturally for a change. If she made him uncomfortable by staring at him, as if she'd like to have him for dessert, then so be it. No matter what else happened he was not going to see her as the kid-sister type tonight. Oh, no, he was going to have to deal with the woman she'd become.

When she ambled into the living room she saw Gage, dressed in a colorful Western shirt, boots and jeans that emphasized his powerful physique. The suits she was accustomed to seeing him wear concealed the muscled details of his masculine body, but this shirt and butt-hugging jeans emphasized his broad shoulders, trim waist and nice derriere.

Hearing her approach, Gage pivoted around. Mackenzie decided to add a seductive swing of hips to her walk. It paid off, she noticed. Gage's gaze swept from the top of her head, across the diving neckline of her blouse and down the length of her legs. She saw his gray eyes flare in surprise and male approval. Good, all that extra primping had paid off. She had his attention—as a woman.

"Damn, kid, you look sensational," he murmured as his gaze flooded slowly over her a second time. And third.

Mackenzie tossed her head and struck what she hoped was an attention-grabbing pose. "Thanks, sweetie pie. You don't look half bad yourself. I suggest you come up with a better pet name for me than kid. Keep it simple but familiar. Isn't that what you spy guys prefer? Like maybe *Keni* instead of *kid?*" She smiled pensively. "Kendra Ryder. How's that grab you, sugar?"

"Kendra it is," he agreed as he reached into his pocket to retrieve a simple gold band.

When he slipped the ring on her finger an odd sensation coiled in the pit of her stomach. She glanced up to see his raven head bent over her left hand. When he raised his gaze, her attention zeroed in on his oh-so-kissable mouth. She had the wildest urge to kiss him and retest her reaction to him. Her memories of kissing him—while under the influence of medication—didn't come equipped with details of her reaction to him. She might not remember if there was a spark and sizzle, but during this charade she intended to find out if her secret fantasy was as good in reality as in her dreams.

"When it comes to responding to questions about our relationship, follow my lead," he requested. "We'll keep it as close to the truth as possible."

She flashed him a nonchalant smile then sauntered past him. "Not to worry, *dahling,* I've been studying to become an attorney, you know. I've learned to put advantageous spins on the law for a client's benefit. I can also twist facts to my advantage. So let your cousins fire away with questions and I'll conjure up believable answers."

"Good, because I've no doubt that they'll grill you." Gage took her arm to escort her outside and led her toward the shiny bronze-colored extended cab pickup that had spent more time sitting in the garage than logging in road miles because he wasn't home much.

Once she'd settled herself on the seat Mackenzie didn't bother pulling down the hem of her high-riding skirt. The tactic worked like a charm, she noticed with impish satisfaction. Gage's gaze immediately dropped to the exposed lengths of her bare legs. If this masquerade as husband and wife accomplished nothing else, she was going to continue to remind him that she'd grown up. He was going to get a reality check during this assignment.

Mackenzie crossed her legs, causing the skirt to shift a few inches higher then braced her elbow against the armrest. "So, brief me on your cousins and their wives, sweetheart," she requested.

Gage dragged his betraying eyes off those million-dollar legs and that daring neckline that showcased her full breasts. He told himself to concentrate on the upcoming get-together with his family. But damn! Keni looked good enough to eat. Her curly dark hair cascaded over her shoulders and lay enticingly against her breasts. It was impossible to cling to his previous perception of her and he didn't know why he bothered trying. Any man with eyes in his head would take one look at her and realize this was one hot package of femininity.

Unfortunately she was Daniel's precious daughter. Like an overly confident imbecile, Gage had thought he could play the role of husband during this assignment. Big mistake. Horrendous mistake. Seeing that shiny gold band that he'd asked Quint to pick up for him symbolized privileges he wasn't really entitled to. Especially not with Gidget. But one look at her and he wanted breathless kisses and all the hot, wild sex he could get.

"Yoo-hoo. Anybody there? This is no time for woolgathering, 007," she taunted him. "I need some facts."

Gage shook off the inappropriate thoughts that were leapfrogging around his mind and concentrated on offering information. "Cousin Wade is my age," he rapped out. "He married a school teacher whose family owns Glori software."

"Really? Cool. I've used some of their programs to write mock grants and other legal documents in my classes."

"Wade was the woman-hater of the Ryder clan after his first marriage went sour. But he's nuts about Laura. They've been married about seven or eight months," Gage expounded.

"Quint was dubbed the ladies' man until he tangled with the redheaded queen of cuisine who owns the restaurant where we'll be meeting my cousins for dinner. Quint had a hard time convincing Steph that he was sincere about her." Gage grinned wryly. "I was on hand to organize her abduction the night Quint wanted her brought to his ranch so he could propose."

"Dragged her, kicking and screaming?" she asked. When he nodded she laughed in amusement. "I guess not all of your assignments are a matter of international security."

"That one wasn't," he agreed. "As for Vance, the practical joker, he got arrested by a lady cop and lost his heart. They flew off to Vegas recently for their nuptials. I haven't met her yet."

"So, you're the only bachelor left in the clan?"

"Until today." Gage wiggled his ring finger that now boasted a matching gold band. "We met in—"

"Paris," she supplied smoothly. "I was doing my international internship last semester. I've done three of them to broaden my horizons, but I've decided to focus on counseling clients on estate planning, probate, trusts and such. But I'm also qualified in tort law to handle cases dealing with slander, libel, invasion of privacy, traffic accidents, personal injury and all that.''

Gage raised a brow. ''Anything else, counselor?''

Mac grinned elfishly. ''Well, I can also practice family law. You know, divorce, annulment, adoption. That sort of thing. I've been in college for what seems like forever, transferring from one place to another to be close to Dad.''

She eyed him curiously. ''So, how many assignments have you taken in which you've had to pretend marriage, 007? I'd like to know how many women you've had in bed before we tied the matrimonial knot.''

He smiled wryly. ''You're the first, dear.''

''Your first pretend wife?'' She stared him squarely in the eye. ''And just how many women have you seduced for information or to gain access to places you've wanted to infiltrate?''

He dodged the probing question by saying, ''You're good at cross-exam, sweetums. I've no doubt that you'll make a first-rate attorney after you pass the bar.''

''In other words,'' she countered, ''you've had women galore during your globe-trotting. Gee, that sure makes a girl feel special when she becomes your wife.''

''I'm sure you have a long list of beaus.'' An unfamiliar, inappropriate sense of possessive jealousy pricked him.

She tossed her head, causing her ebony hair to ripple over her shoulders and draw his attention to her bosom—again. Gage inwardly groaned. He could *not* keep getting distracted.

''So, are we talking about an extensive string of

broken hearts behind you, snookums?" he asked. "A husband needs to know how much comparison is going on inside your lovely head."

"Oh, dozens of comparisons," she said with a careless flick of her wrist. "But, if anyone asks, you're the hottest lover I've ever had, of course. So, tell me more about this policewoman?" Amazing how she could switch subjects without missing a beat. "What's her name?"

"Miranda, or Randi as Cousin Vance calls her. Brunette, She's about your age, I think," Gage informed her.

"A cop and a practical joker? Interesting combination."

"My thoughts exactly. I'm anxious to see Vance and Randi together. I'm told these family dinners are a weekly ritual. We'll be joining my family regularly. It won't take you long to get acquainted with everyone."

"If these family dinners get me off the ranch I'll be anticipating them." She stared somberly at Gaze. "I'm used to being on the move. I'll go nuts just hanging out."

"That's where perfecting your domestic skills comes in to play," he said as he veered past town square to find a parking space at Stephanie's Palace.

"We've covered that territory, *dahling*," she cooed caustically. "I've never done much cooking and I'd prefer to volunteer at a law office to while away the hours."

"Tough, kid. You're my responsibility and I need to know where you are and what you're doing constantly. I intend to eat, sleep and breathe you until this threat is neutralized."

"I'll wear a bug and tracking device. You can check on me with your fancy Global Positioning System on your high-powered computer."

"No." His tone brooked no argument. "Don't lull yourself into a false sense of security. Your dad's enemies are turning the continent upside down to find you. I've covered our tracks as best I can, but the underground syndicate is as high-tech as my organization. So don't get *too* comfortable. Got it?"

She glared at him before climbing down from the pickup.

"Damn it, Keni." He scowled as she stalked off without waiting for him. He caught up with her in five long strides and grabbed her arm. Reflexively, he scanned the street—a habit he'd picked up years earlier. "Control your temper," he muttered at her. "For the benefit of folks in Hoot's Roost and my family, you're supposed to be nuts about me. Play your role for a couple of hours. Then you can bite my head off if you still feel like it."

He felt the rigidity drain from her body as she turned to face him directly. Gage inwardly winced when her agitated frown transformed into a saucy smile. That elfish expression worried him to no end. Although she was stylish and sophisticated, when need be, she had a wicked, rebellious streak that spelled trouble for him. Always had.

Gage braced himself and tried not to respond when she looped her arms over his shoulders and brushed that U.S.D.A. prime choice body against him. He caught a whiff of her hair, of her alluring perfume. Desire hit him like a doubled fist and he had the unmistakable feeling that the self-control he'd taken for granted for years was about to desert him.

"You're definitely going to pay later, sugar plum," she drawled as she pulled his head down to hers. "But if the loving wife is what you want for two hours, then a loving wife you'll get."

When she kissed him for all she was worth and molded her curvaceous body tightly to his she fried the circuits in Gage's brain. Hungry need exploded inside him like a grenade. For a moment Gage forgot they were standing on the sidewalk in his hometown. She tasted so sweet, so welcoming that everything male in him responded and ached for more. Mindlessly he made a feast of her mouth.

"Well, if it isn't the newest newlyweds of Hoot's Roost."

Gage raised his head to see Cousin Wade and Laura strolling toward them, hand in hand.

"Maybe you two better head home and forget about dinner," Wade teased wickedly as he drew his wife possessively to his side. "Laura, this is Gage's new wife." He waited for Gage to make the introductions.

It took Gage a moment to recover his powers of speech and jump-start his brain. "This is Keni... uh...Kendra."

"Nice to see you again, *Kendra*," Wade said, grinning slyly. "You weren't feeling well the first time we met. I hope you're feeling better now."

Gage gave her high marks for responding to Wade's teasing. She smiled brightly and extended her hand to Laura then to Wade. "I'm feeling much better, thank you for asking." She cast Gage a quick glance. "I suffered a bad case of motion sickness," she explained to Laura. "Quick drops in altitude seem to have an adverse effect on me."

"Welcome to the family." Laura smiled warmly. "Wade tells me that you've graduated from law school. I know our business law instructor would love to have you as a guest speaker for his classes. Interested?"

"Absolutely," she enthused. "Name the time and day."

Gage did a slow burn. Damn the woman. Five minutes ago he'd specifically told her that she wasn't to go gadding about town without a chaperone. She was staying at the ranch where there were sensors circling the property that could alert him to the first sign of danger.

"I don't think—" Gage tried to object.

"I don't mind, darling," she interrupted. "It will give me something to do in between job hunting."

Gage's hands curled into fists when Mac sashayed toward the restaurant. He made a mental note to strangle his "wife" for defying him the instant he got her alone.

4

MACKENZIE WAS DELIGHTED to discover how warm, friendly and welcoming all the Ryders were toward her. They accepted her into their midst with open arms. Of course, she noted the sly glances the Ryder men discreetly cast in her direction. Obviously she'd provided plenty of amusement after she'd parachuted from the plane then crawled all over Gage during the jaunt to the house. But obviously Gage had ordered his cousins to keep their traps shut regarding that first humiliating encounter and they were abiding by his demand.

With keen interest Mackenzie studied the subtle nuances of intimacy passing back and forth between the couples. She took her cues from them to assume her role. She draped her arm over Gage's shoulder and stared at him intently each time he spoke. She cuddled up against him the same way Randi snuggled up to Vance in the padded booth. She even laid her hand on Gage's thigh, just as Steph did to Quint, and nuzzled his cheek, the way Laura did to Wade.

She felt Gage flinch each time she made an intimate gesture and decided he deserved to squirm. She enjoyed demonstrating her secret affection for him. All these years she'd concealed her infatuation by taunting and niggling him. If it made him nervous, then tough. He'd all but asked for it when he devised this phony-baloney marriage.

"Are you planning to set up a law practice in Hoot's Roost?" Randi questioned curiously.

Mackenzie shrugged. "Possibly. I don't want all these years of higher education to go to waste."

"We'd love to have you practice here. The only lawyer in town is well past retirement age," Steph remarked before sipping her mango tea. "I'll bet Lester LaFrantz would leap at the chance to hire you, even before you take your bar exam."

"I'll drop by to fill out an application," she replied, aware the comment aggravated Gage.

"I was hoping we could spend quality time together before you went job hunting, sweetheart," Gage put in, casting her a discreet warning glance.

Mackenzie traced her forefinger over his full lips then winked playfully. "As if I'd neglect you," she purred for the benefit of his family. "There are still several hours after dark to remind you how much you mean to me."

Her suggestive remark drew several snickers from Gage's cousins. As for Gage, he cut her a stony stare that warned her to watch her smart mouth. Fat chance of that, she mused impishly. She derived excessive pleasure from watching him fidget uneasily.

"I've got a great idea," Vance piped up. "Why don't you two join Randi and me for our wedding reception. The rest of the family will be arriving so we can make it a double celebration." Vance's onyx eyes danced with deviltry as he glanced at Gage. "Whaddaya say, cuz? We'll put your names on the invitations and presto! We'll celebrate both weddings at once." He looked to Randi for approval.

"Do you mind sharing the limelight with the other newlyweds?"

The attractive brunette nodded agreeably. "Sounds like a plan to me."

"I'm not sure that's a good—" Gage tried to protest.

"Then it's settled," Vance cut in quickly.

Mackenzie noted how Gage's ornery cousins bit back teasing grins when Vance put him on the spot. From the look of things Gage should be accustomed to being harassed, she decided. His cousins were as mischievous as she was.

"We can hold the reception at Gage's ranch, if you want," Mackenzie quickly volunteered, wrapping the noose a little tighter around Gage's thick neck.

"Now wait just a—" Gage erupted, only to be cut off by one of his enthusiastic cousins-in-law.

"I'll handle the refreshments," Steph insisted.

"I'll create the invitations on my computer," Laura offered.

"I'll handle the decorations," Randi volunteered.

Gage slumped in the booth. Damn it to hell! This charade was snowballing out of proportion. He sincerely wished he'd passed Mac off as his live-in housekeeper. But no, he'd tried to protect her reputation from gossip. The assignment was backfiring in his face.

"This will be a hoot," Mac said as she flung her arms around his neck and gave him a smacker on the lips. "I'll have the chance to meet all your friends and acquaintances, plus work with my new in-laws."

"Yeah, the hoot of Owl County," he muttered in

her ear. "I'll get you for this. When we get home you're toast."

Mac giggled as if he'd whispered a spicy suggestion to her. "Right here?" she said in feigned shock. "Really, wild thing, you keep that up and I'm going to think I married a sex fiend with stamina galore."

When his cousins burst out laughing, Gage clamped his hand over Mac's bare thigh and gave it a warning squeeze. "You're really asking for it, Mac," he hissed confidentially.

She smiled all too sweetly at him. "You're all bark and no bite, Mr. Guard Dog," she whispered in his ear. "Besides, if you leave marks on me, Daddy will have your head. After all, you're being highly paid for this assignment so don't damage the merchandise."

His hands curled to the exact size of a choke necklace. He'd really, *really* like to strangle her right about now. She was doing everything she could to piss him off.

"Gage? Is that you?"

He glanced up to see his old flame hovering beside the booth. Well, at least one thing was going right, he decided. Here stood the woman who'd taught him that romantic involvement was a waste of a man's time.

Sherry Palmer had three-timed him while he and his cousins were competing in rodeo competition during college. He'd returned to campus late one night to find Sherry intimately entertaining one of his good friends. Come to find out, another male acquaintance had also been playing footsies with Sherry while Gage had been out of town. Loyalty had not been Sherry's strongest suit. Gage had also questioned his ability to select so-called friends of the male persuasion. Friends who wouldn't betray him when his back was turned. And maybe, he thought with sudden insight, that was the reason he'd learned to trust no one but family.

"Hey, Sher, good to see you again." *Yeah, right.* He took grand satisfaction in directing the willowy blonde's attention to Mac. "Sher, this in my new wife, Kendra."

To his surprise Sherry didn't do Keni the courtesy of glancing in her direction. She kept her baby blues fixed on Gage. Her smile was pure seduction. "How nice for you. Come by and see me and we'll talk about old times, Gage. I'm working at the furniture store these days, so I'm never hard to find."

When she sauntered off, giving him the full treatment—one rolling hip at a time—Gage cast Mac an apprehensive glance. Sure enough, she was studying Sherry speculatively.

She turned her attention to Gage and elevated a perfectly sculpted brow. "Let me guess. Sherry specializes in bedroom furnishings, right?"

Wade chuckled. "I hear she personally tests every mattress she sells. So buyer beware."

"She's in between men at the moment," Vance reported.

"And Vance doesn't mean that *figuratively,*" Quint added, smiling wryly. "I've heard she has some kinky habits."

"Well, she's mistaken if she thinks she's going to get her hands on you," Mac said as she draped her arm possessively around Gage's shoulder then leaned in close. "You'll be much too busy for extracurricular activities, lover boy."

When Randi's pager went off she nudged Vance to his feet. "It's the chief," she said in explanation. "We're working on a string of B and Es. He must've gotten the results back on the fingerprints." She dropped a quick kiss to Vance's lips. "I'll run over to headquarters to check it out since we're in town."

"I'll come with you," Vance insisted as he grabbed Randi's hand. "Nice to have you with us, Keni."

"We better hit the road, too," Gage said.

"Same time next week," Quint reminded him. "We'll be working cattle at Wade's ranch in the morning. Be there at eight sharp."

Gage clutched Mac's hand and hoisted her to her feet. Before she could solidify any arrangements to speak at the high school, impulsively volunteer to wait tables for Steph or help with the town-wide garage sale that Vance and Randi mentioned, Gage half dragged her to the door.

"Sheesh, slow down, will you?" Mac fussed at him. "You'll have everyone in here thinking you can't wait to get me home and get naked. Now who's that blond vamp who was drooling all over you? Are all of your ex-girlfriends that obvious and aggressive?"

Gage waited until they were on the street to reply. "You don't have to play the jealous wife on Sherry's account," he assured her. "I want nothing to do with her."

"Hmm, I don't think the feeling is mutual," Mac replied as Gage shoveled her into the pickup and slammed the door. "Is she typical of your usual women?"

"I don't have usual women," Gage declared as he plunked on the seat then stabbed the key into the ignition.

"Just a string of meaningless affairs then." She clucked her tongue in disapproval.

He expelled a frustrated sigh. "Why is it that women think they need to hear the juicy details of a man's past relationships? You don't hear me demanding an account of your sexual habits, do you?"

"Go ahead and asked," she invited. "I've got nothing sordid to hide. My past is an open book."

"Well, maybe I don't want to know who you've been with. And maybe a three-day weekend is the longest relationship I've had in almost a decade. Now, can we get past the old history, Gidget?"

She turned narrowed violet eyes on him. "You really don't give a rat's patoot whom I might have been with in the past?"

"Nope, past is exactly that. Past." Okay, so he was a little bit curious about the men she'd dated, but asking would be an invitation for her to pry into his sex life. He didn't want to discuss it. Didn't want to know how many men had gotten their mitts on Gidget and if she responded as eagerly as she did to him.

"There's one good thing about being holed up at your ranch," Mac commented. "I can study the moods, habits and behavior of the male of the species. I might as well get something beneficial from this."

"Men don't have moods," Gage muttered sourly.

"Oh, right," she scoffed. "You've been in a rotten mood all evening because you didn't get your way every single minute."

"There is not going to be a speaking engagement at the high school, an interview with the local attorney or volunteer help at HRPD's annual garage sale," he growled as he headed out of town. "You'll have to renege on your offer to have that blasted reception at my ranch. I can't keep close surveillance with so many people running loose."

She stiffened rebelliously. "I most certainly will not. It's only for one night."

"What if a group of goons happens to show up the same night and snatches you away? Will it be worth it?"

Mac cast him a withering glance. "You are so paranoid."

"No," he contradicted. "I'm cautious. If you get kidnapped because you delight in spiting me at every turn, I promise I'll be royally ticked off. If I find you alive—and I can't guarantee that—then you can bet your sweet butt that I'm going to let you have it with both barrels blazing."

"Not gonna happen, 007," she said confidently. "You covered our zigzagging tracks across the country so well that I didn't even know where we were half the time. Besides, if a foreigner shows up in this one-horse town, asking questions about you or me, in Russian, it'd be a dead giveaway."

Gage pulled onto the graveled road then stamped on the brake. Parked in the middle of the road, he twisted sideways to give Mac his undivided attention. "You just don't get it. Just because the Russians want you doesn't mean they won't hire an English-speaking hit man to take you out. Maybe you should attend the International Hit Men's Conference so you'll realize goons come in all nationalities, colors, sizes and shapes," he suggested sarcastically. "They have one thing in common. They are demolition experts. They blow people away."

Mac crossed her arms over her chest and flashed him one of those stubborn stares that he'd come to recognize at first glance. "Fine. The Hit Men Association doesn't discriminate. But I still think you're getting carried away. I don't want to be stuck indoors indefinitely while you're out playing cowboy and yippie-ti-yi-yae-ing your way across the great outdoors. I need something to occupy my time."

He expelled an exasperated breath then shoved the pickup into gear. "Look, Ms. We Are The World, I don't want to see you hurt...or worse...just because you have to suffer cabin fever."

Mac gave him the silent treatment until they reached his ranch. When he shut off the engine she flounced from the truck and strode off. "Where the hell do you think you're going?"

"For a walk in the dark," she spouted off.

"Over my dead body!"

She stopped in her tracks, turned a quick one-eighty and glared at him. "Fine, whatever it takes. I need some space and some fresh air. I need to be *away* from you."

Gage knew that feeling so he watched her stalk toward the barn that was silhouetted in moonlight. When she was out of earshot his vocabulary dissolved into profanity. The woman was turning him into a headcase. He couldn't convince her to be careful and that irritated the hell out of him.

Okay, Gage relented as he climbed from the truck. He'd give Mac some breathing space—and himself as well. But he'd keep her on a short leash and refuse to let her out of his sight.

Gage dashed into the house to fish out his night vision goggles from his duffel bag. Pulling the NVGs into place, Gage hiked off to dog Mac's steps. Well, he mused, at least she was mad at him. He could deal better with her when she was in a snit than when she'd played that seductive routine at dinner. Now *that* was a megadistraction. Plus, his mind had detoured in the wrong direction each time she'd touched him.

There wasn't going to be any more of those kisses, either, he thought resolutely. It made his sap rise so damn fast he couldn't think logically. Trying not to respond to her was pure and simple torment.

Gage had been trained to handle a various sundry of situations. And Mac was right on the mark when she speculated there had been times when he'd had to play up to women who could open doors to places he needed to go. But that was just business. She was…well…he didn't know what she was besides a bona fide pain in the rear. If he had a lick of sense he'd contact his bosses and request another agent to tote her off to an isolated safe house.

And, by damned, maybe he'd make that call first thing in the morning—despite Daniel Shafer's specific request for Gage to guard Mac. Gage's time would be better spent accumulating intel since he'd been working this case for the past two years. Let some other chump follow around Ms. Persnickety and Defiant and see how he liked it.

MACKENZIE INHALED A DEEP breath of fresh air and exhaled slowly. The technique didn't relieve her bottled frustration so she grabbed another purifying breath. Dealing with Gage constantly wasn't easy because she was too sensitive to what he said and how he said it. He mattered to her as no other man ever had, and because he did, she reacted rather impulsively.

Halting, Mackenzie panned the rolling pasture and tree line that formed a natural boundary beside the hay meadow to the north. She allowed the peacefulness of the spring evening and the chirp of birds to settle over her.

Veering away from the herd of cattle, Mackenzie headed for the trees and the meadow beyond. Heaven forbid that she startled the cattle, caused a stampede and ran the livestock through the fences. That would give Gage one more excuse to chew on her hide.

While she was standing in the row of trees, watching the moon glow on the meadow a gloved hand clamped over her mouth. Although she elbowed her captor in the midsection she still found herself shoved facedown on the ground. Before she could sink her teeth into the man's hand he crammed a smelly rag in her mouth and rammed his knee into her spine, pinning her like a butterfly in an insect collection. None of her self-defense tactics were doing her a bit of good because she'd been taken by surprise. Gage would never let her hear the end of this!

Her captor held her in place with his bulky weight, grabbed her arms and secured them behind her back with duct tape. He ripped off another strip of tape and mashed it against the lower portion of her face. She erupted in a muffled squawk when he patted her down then rolled her onto her back to complete the frisk.

Mackenzie's eyes widened in alarm when she confronted the muscle-bound man dressed in camouflage overalls, a black turtleneck shirt, ski mask and combat boots. A nasty looking rifle was slung diagonally across his thick chest.

"Think I didn't see ya drop from that unmarked plane, sister?" He snickered as he duct-taped her ankles. "Been expecting you, missy...if that's what you really are."

Mackenzie shrieked indignantly when his hand drifted from her chest to lower abdomen.

"With all the cross-dressers running around these days ya never know for sure that whatcha see is whatcha get unless ya check. Yep, you're a woman, all right," he confirmed. "No male equipment." He tilted his masked face and studied her for a moment. "You a decoy? Well, we'll find out soon enough."

He scooped Mackenzie up in a fireman's carry and strode off. Her breath was forced from her chest in irregular spurts while her captor zigzagged through the trees.

She cursed herself soundly for being distracted by thoughts of Gage and being caught off guard. If Gage ever found her, he'd curse her up one side and down the other for not paying attention to her surroundings. And wouldn't that be a fun conversation? Provided she survived to have it.

WEARING NVGs, GAGE SCANNED the pasture and trees. He saw two coyotes trotting across the hill, but he found no sign of Mac and he was growing more anxious by the second. It was as if she'd disappeared into thin air in a matter of minutes. He broke out in a cold sweat when he had to face the realization that she might have been snatched right out from under his nose while he'd run into the house to grab his goggles.

Wheeling around, Gage raced back to the house again. He hit the front door at a dead run and barreled down the hall to check the laptop in his bedroom. To his relief or dismay—he hadn't yet decided—he saw the sensor on the northwest quadrant bleep. A vehicle was speeding across the pasture toward the section line. He probably couldn't intercept the vehicle before it reached the graveled road, but he could be on its tail if he laid rubber.

Gage grabbed his rucksack and raced to his pickup. By the time he reached the end of the driveway and headed west on the gravel road he had his dagger tucked in his boot and his Dirty Harry size handgun lying beside him on the seat.

How the hell could the bad guys have caught up with him so quickly? He'd taken every precaution in the codebook. Honestly, he thought he'd have at least a week or two before he had to maintain a high state of alert to spot incoming unfriendlies.

Gage snapped to attention when he veered north and spotted the lights of the vehicle a half mile ahead of him. Quickly, he shut off his lights and used his NVGs to see where he was going. The roller coaster adrenaline rush melted away when he saw the vehicle turn onto the dirt path that led to the dilapidated shack that was surrounded by trees.

Gage chuckled when he realized that Dexter Nolan had probably been out on one of his recon missions to check on terrorist infiltration and had captured Mac for questioning. Dex was definitely paranoid and about half off his rocker, having never fully recovered from the stress he'd suffered during heavy action in Desert Storm. He probably wouldn't torture Mac—too much—during his attempt to extract info.

Served her right, Gage thought as he followed Dex's old truck at a safe distance. He stopped on the path, grabbed his NVGs and watched Dex haul Mac from the clunker truck. With Mac jackknifed over his shoulder, Dex glanced this way and that, and then ducked into the cabin. Might as well allow Dex to give Mac a good scare before rescuing her, Gage decided. Maybe she'd be properly appreciative and humbled—for once.

Employing the stealth he'd acquired during his extensive training Gage circled to the back of the shack. If Dex was as nutty as his cousins claimed he'd become, the ex-vet might have booby-trapped or trip-wired the perimeters of his property. Keeping that in mind, Gage watched where he stepped.

Sure enough, he saw moonlight glinting across the silver wire that was stretched shin-high between the trees. Carefully, Gage stepped over the wire and kept his eyes peeled for an inner ring of protection. As anticipated, he spotted another trip-wire that was set ten yards from the cabin. Gage didn't disable it, just stepped over it to approach the back window. He inspected the window frame and noticed the alarm system Dex had installed. Damn, the wacky vet was thorough.

Gage angled his head to see through the blinds. Although the bedroom was dark light speared from the cramped living area. Gage swallowed a snicker when he saw Mac, bound up like a mummy, sitting in a straight-back chair. Dex was circling like a vulture, using a few scare tactics. Unfortunately Mac didn't look terrified; she looked mad as hell. Her eyes were narrowed and her shoulders were as stiff as a flagpole. Despite her gag, she was railing at Dex a mile a minute.

When Dex yanked the duct tape off her mouth she spit out the gag and lit into him with that sharp tongue of hers. Gage heard her demanding to be released or she'd slap a lawsuit on him so fast he wouldn't know what hit him.

Gage decided to circle around to knock on the front door before Mac mouthed off one too many times. Guarding every step, he crept around the small shack and rapped on the door.

"Dex! It's Gage Ryder. Better let me in!" he bugled.

A vicious snarl resounded from the other side of the door. He should've known Dex had found himself a man-eating dog to serve as an extra pair of eyes and ears.

"Gage?" Dex called out. "What are you doing here? Thought you were out of the country. How do I know it's really you?"

"Of course, it's me. I've been back for a couple of days. If you don't open the door I'll start making you pay rent."

The comment reassured Dex that it was his landlord. Only the Ryder cousins knew about the rent-free agreement.

The door creaked open and Gage smiled wryly at Mr. Camouflage. Through the slits in the ski mask Dex's dark eyes skimmed over Gage while the man-eating dog growled threateningly and sniffed at his boots.

"Who's your friend?" Gage gestured to the German shepherd as he stepped into the cabin.

"Hercules," Dex replied, then hitched his thumb toward Mac. "Caught a spy snooping around your place."

"I am not a spy," Mac snapped. "Gage, untie me before I lose all circulation in my hands and feet."

Dex yanked the ski mask off his red head. His flattop haircut was so neatly clipped that you could have landed an aircraft on top of it. He rubbed his hand over the week's growth of beard as he glanced back and forth between Gage and Mac. "You know each other?"

"Yeah, she's my wife," Gage announced.

Dex's bushy red brows shot up to his hairline. "Your wife? Hell, I didn't know you had a wife."

"Yup, she's new. I just got her," Gage reported. "I've been meaning to drive up and tell you that I'm back, but I've been kinda busy." He winked and waggled his eyebrows suggestively. "You know, being a newlywed and all, I've had other things on my mind."

Dex snickered as he spun on his heels. In less time than it took to hiccup he whipped out a knife that was damn near as big as a machete. "I can see why you might've been distracted," Dex commented as he whacked the tape from Mac's hands and ankles. "This one is a real looker, Gage." He tucked the dagger inside his overalls then turned directly on Gage. "I spotted an unmarked plane and parachute over your pasture a few nights back. By the time I got down there to check for tangos they were gone. I've been on high alert ever since. I think we've got unfriendlies infiltrating the place. You better keep your eyes peeled.''

Gage decided he'd have to give Dex the Cliff's Notes version of his assignment. The paranoid ex-soldier needed to be up to speed since he'd been trained to protect and secure.

''Dex, this is my wife, Keni,'' he said in quick introduction. ''She and I parachuted in the other night because foreign subversives are on her trail. I haven't informed the civvies in the area, of course. But being ex-spec ops, I know you'll report any suspicious activity. Keni needs protection. I'm hoping I can count on your help.''

Dex came to immediate attention and gave Gage a crisp salute. ''Damn right you can count on me.'' He glanced sideways at Mac who had come to her feet to survey his humble abode. ''You, too, sister. Sorry about absconding with you. Never can be too careful, ya know.''

''No harm done. I'm sorry I yelled at you,'' she said as she plucked leaves from her hair. ''You know, Dex, no offense, but this place could use a good cleaning. You probably spend a lot of time on recon patrol so I might be able to repay you for your surveillance assistance by spiffying up the place. Say tomorrow?''

She shot Gage a challenging glance, daring him to object. He noticed that she didn't offer to clean *his* house. But hey, if spring cleaning occupied her time then he had no complaint. ''Good idea,'' Gage agreed. ''Dex can do me a favor by keeping tabs on you while I'm working cattle tomorrow.''

''Don't mind playing bodyguard,'' Dex said then

glanced around the living area. "But you gotta watch what you touch, sister. Don't want anyone messing with my classified files and photos. I've got my own system."

"I wouldn't dream of pilfering your files," Mac assured him solemnly. "My father is a diplomat and I'm well versed in the necessity of protecting classified information."

"Well, okay." Dex scanned his cluttered living quarters. "I guess a little cleaning would be a good thing."

A *lot* of cleaning wouldn't hurt, Gage mused. "Then it's settled. I'll drop Keni off in the morning and pick her up before dark. You can protect her from every Tom, Dick and hit man who's trying to track her down and use her to twist her father's arm into cooperating."

Delighted to be a player in the intrigue, Dex lumbered over to give Mac a hug and a jostling shake that threatened to rattle her teeth. "I'll protect you, sister. Not to worry about that. You put up a damn good fight, for a female, when I grounded you. I'll show you a few tricks to protect yourself."

"Don't even start," Mac muttered a few minutes later as they hiked toward Gage's pickup.

"Hadn't planned to." He fell into step beside her. "That's a good lesson for you, though. Dex had you captured and extracted before you knew what hit you. He may have a few screws loose, but he's on our side and can help keep surveillance. Now, can we go home and hit the sack? I've got a long day of ranch duty ahead of me."

Eventually she said, "I'm sorry for storming off in a huff, but sometimes you bug me."

"That makes two of us. You bug me, too," he confided.

Mac leaned over to give him a peck on the cheek. "Thanks for coming to my rescue."

"You're welcome, kid. Next time you're PO'd at me, just yell at me and get it out of your system. It beats the hell out of sweating bullets, wondering if you've been abducted."

She arched a teasing brow. "Frightened you, did I? Nice to know I can get some kind of emotional response from you."

"More than you should," he mumbled. He had to accept the fact that he couldn't distance himself from the emotions Mac stirred in him. It was there, right smack-dab in his face.

"And another thing," he said impulsively. "You can cut out the kissing in public."

Her head snapped around and dark curls bobbled around her face. "You don't like the way I kiss? What's wrong with it?"

"Nothing's wrong with it." He cut a short corner and zoomed toward home. "It's too distracting. You've convinced my family and friends that we've got something going on, so you can ease off a little."

"Sure, whatever you say, 007. If you can't handle that part of the act, even when it doesn't bother me in the least—"

His hand shot out to grab her forearm. He took his eyes off the road to meet her mischievous grin. "Don't mess with me, Mac. You aren't in my league, despite what you think."

She pried his hand off her arm one finger at a time—all the while flashing him a smirk. "I think I can handle this burlesque-show of a marriage better than you can. You could kiss my lips off and it wouldn't affect me because I know it's an act. Although men have hair triggers on their lust, women have control over their hormones.''

"Is that right?'' he muttered into her confident smile.

"That's exactly right. All I have to do is remember I'm just one of a long line of women who've kissed you and it's a real turnoff. Most men think they're God's gift to womankind and that their moves are unique. Sorry to burst your bubble, but you kiss one guy and you've kissed 'em all. You couldn't knock my socks off unless you're wrapped in explosives.''

When the pickup came to a stop she bounded out and headed for the door.

"Hold it,'' he snapped at her. "I go in first. I *always* go in first. Understand?'' He sped past her to ensure the house was secure, since he'd raced off to the rescue without locking up. Pulling his weapon, he eased inside to look around.

Mac strode past him, rolled her eyes then made a beeline for the bedroom. "I don't know who's worse. You or Dex. Ask me, you both have a few screws loose.''

Gage took one step forward then jerked to a halt. She was tormenting him again. He wasn't going to succumb, just because she'd challenged his masculinity and ridiculed his professional caution.

"I wish I'd let Dex keep you overnight to torture info from you,'' he called spitefully.

"Wouldn't have worked,'' she said over her

shoulder. "I'd have charmed him until he told me everything he knows."

He smirked. "Think so, Mata Hari?"

"Guess we'll find out tomorrow if I'm as good at spy games as you are." She winked, grinned and shut the door.

Gage barreled down the hall and jerked open the door. His jaw sagged to his chest when he saw the tantalizing curve of Mac's bare back and shoulders peeking at him through the waterfall of raven hair. Holding her blouse against her breasts, she turned slightly to meet his stunned gaze.

"Yes?" she asked, lifting a taunting brow.

Gage felt himself go from annoyed to aroused in one-point-five seconds. He shut the door before he did something crazy—like peel away that blouse and look his fill. But that would prove what she'd said about a man's lack of willpower and hair-trigger lust.

Well, she was right, damn it. Much as he hated to admit it, she'd gotten under his skin. She inspired X-rated fantasies about stripping her naked and...

Gage lurched toward his bedroom, shut the door and shucked his clothes. He didn't want to want Mac the way he was beginning to want her. He didn't want to see her as a prospective lover.

Damn, this pretend marriage was the worst cover he'd ever dreamed up. Swearing, Gage flopped into bed, pulled the pillow over his head and prayed for sleep that was long in coming.

5

GAGE STEPPED DOWN FROM the pickup. Resistol hat pulled low on his forehead, work gloves dangling from his hip pockets, he headed toward Wade's corral. Funny how quickly he'd settled into the countrified world where he'd grown up. For years he'd lived in a world of suits by day and black clothing for surveillance by night. Talk about feeling as if he'd led a double life! Hell, there were times when he wasn't exactly sure who he was. But, for certain, the irregular visits home kept him grounded.

But dealing with Mac was still making him nuts.

Even though he knew Mac was in good hands—guarded by a paranoid ex-spec ops soldier, who remained on constant alert, it felt strange not having that violet-eyed terror beside him.

"Shake a leg, Cousin G," Wade called out as he set a bucket of medication and syringes beside the headgate that was attached to the squeeze chute. "I want to have these calves branded, inoculated and worked by lunch."

Vance hitched his thumb toward Wade. "Lover boy goes a little berserk when he can't meet Laura for lunch."

"So where'd you stash your better half?" Quint asked as he hooked up the branding iron to the neon orange extension cord that he'd strung from the barn to the corral.

Gage ambled downhill to join his cousins who worked side by side with impressive precision. "Gidget decided to clean up Dex's cabin today," he explained.

His cousins glanced up simultaneously and frowned. Wade said, "You left her with Dex? You sure that's a good idea?"

"Better than leaving her home alone." From habit, Gage scooped up the leather whip then climbed over the corral to move the first calf down the lane to the squeeze chute. "We had an incident last night. She went for a walk after dark and Dex captured her."

Quint chuckled in wry amusement as he dropped the metal gate behind the calf. "Did Dex scare her witless?"

"Nope. She was chewing him out royally when I reached the cabin. She doesn't get scared—she gets mad. I had to confide her situation to Dex and he's promised to act as her bodyguard while I'm away from home."

"Better be careful," Vance warned as he grabbed the lever on the headgate and secured the calf in place. "Dex hasn't been around a woman in years. All that bottled testosterone might come flooding out."

"Yup," Wade agreed as he grabbed an ear tag for the calf. "Dex could end up with a king-size crush on your wife. Sure would hate to see you and Dex square off in a showdown."

"The marriage is just an act," Gage reminded his cousins.

"Damned good one, too," Wade declared. "Gidget was laying it on thick last night. Ask me, it's more than an act."

"Nobody asked you, cuz," Gage muttered irritably.

Quint glanced at Vance, then at Wade. "Does our prodigal cousin seem a little testy to you?"

"Yup," Vance and Wade replied in unison.

"Testy. That's the word I'd use to describe him," Vance said. "I think this fake marriage is getting him all steamed up and he doesn't know what to do about it."

"Knock it off," Gage snapped. "When this assignment is completed Gidget will return to her world and I'll go back to mine. End of story."

"Right. You'll be back to your globe-trotting and she'll pass the bar exam with flying colors," Wade predicted. "You won't care if you ever see her again."

"Exactly," Gage said all too quickly.

"So, since you've decided on the no-touch approach to Gidget, are you going to take up Sherry on her not-so-subtle offer from last night?" Quint asked flat-out. "Ms. Bed and Mattress seemed pretty eager to let you try out the innersprings."

"Perfect solution," Vance teased as he unclamped the headgate to free the calf. "You get it on with Sherry and Dex gets the Big Crush going with Gidget."

Gage didn't appreciate the image of Mac and Dex that popped to mind. He didn't want to consider how quickly the sex-deprived ex-soldier would respond to the sweet taste of kisses more intoxicating than wine and the feel of Mac's curvaceous body pressed intimately to his. "Can we talk about something else?" he asked. Okay, *demanded*.

"Know what I think?" Vance said.

"Don't know. Don't care." Gage flashed his cousins a silencing glare. It was a wasted effort.

"I think you've got a thing for Gidget and you're either too stupid or too stubborn to admit it," said Quint.

"And I think you don't know what the hell you're talking about. Her father is a close associate. He entrusted her to my care and I'm giving this assignment my professional best."

"So you *do* care," Vance teased unmercifully. "Glad you admit it."

"I do *not* care!" Gage sounded off, alarming the calf and causing it to kick him in the shin. "Damn it!" He sucked in a pained breath then shoved his hip against the calf's rump to prevent being kicked again. "This is my job!"

"Fine," Quint said as he secured the calf then grabbed a syringe. "Then I'll relay the message Sherry gave me last night. She wants you to stop by and see her tomorrow night."

"Maybe I will," Gage muttered spitefully. "Then maybe you bozos will realize there's nothing between Mac and me."

"That'd convince me," Wade said. "How about the rest of you guys?"

"Sure thing," Vance agreed. "Go ahead and take a trial run on Sherry's mattress."

"That'll convince Gidget that it'd be a foolish mistake to get caught up in this temporary role as your wife," Quint remarked. "She's young, and all. She probably needs a wake-up call, just in case she starts thinking you're The One. Certainly can't have that.''

''Then Dex will be there to console her,'' Wade predicted.

There it was again. That tormenting image of Mac kissing Dex the way she'd kissed Gage. He didn't like the idea one damn bit, though he valiantly battled the unreasonable jealousy that knotted in the pit of his belly. And so he said, ''I'm going to call Sher.''

Work in the corral came to a grinding halt. His cousins stared at him from beneath the brims of their hats. Gage stuck out his chin. ''Just because you three clowns went soft in the head and got married doesn't mean I'm planning on it,'' he declared. ''I like my life the way it is. Every day is a new challenge and adventure. I don't want to spend my life sitting on a horse and staring at the butt end of cattle. And I don't need a woman driving me as crazy as Mac—'' He shut his mouth so fast that he nearly whacked off the tip of his tongue.

His cousins arched dark brows and grinned smugly at him.

''Oh, shut up,'' Gage snarled at them.

''Didn't say a word, cuz,'' Wade said, lips twitching. ''You're doing all the talking—''

When Wade's voice dried up, Gage followed his cousin's gaze to see Mac ambling downhill with Dex following at her heels like a devoted puppy. The sound of bawling cattle had overridden the racket of Dex's rattletrap truck. But suddenly there they were. Gage's narrowed gaze leapt from Mac's appealing physique, wrapped in knit and denim, to

Dex who'd scrubbed himself clean and shaved the stubble from his face.

Gage's attention shifted back to his smug-looking cousins who apparently thought their prediction of Dex fixating on Mac had come true. Well, hell.

Mac was all smiles as she halted a few feet from the corral. "Dex and I stopped to tell you we're doing lunch in town. We're also helping with the town-wide garage sale."

Gage blinked in surprise. Dex-the-Hermit was doing lunch in town and getting involved in civic projects? Man, talk about your overnight about-face.

"Not to worry, Gage," Dex declared. "I won't let her out of my sight. Nobody will get through me to get to her."

"That's swell," Gage mumbled. He noticed the way Dex's attention drifted to Mac's shapely physique. So did his cousins, obviously. Three toldja-so glances came Gage's way. "Uh, thanks, Dex. I knew I could count on you."

When Mac spun around to stride uphill, Dex stuck to her like her own shadow.

"Oh, yeah," Wade commented. "Dex has it bad. Gossip will be flying in town, for sure."

"I can hear it now," Quint put in. "Gage's wife is such a charmer that she lured Dex back into society. A real miracle worker, and all that."

"Good thing you don't give a flip," Vance teased. "But if some guy was panting after Randi like that I'd be tempted to use my stun gun on him."

"Are you yahoos gonna stand around flapping your jaws or work cattle?" Gage muttered. "We're burning daylight."

"Now he thinks he's John Wayne," Wade said, and smirked.

In order to shut up his demon cousins, Gage moved cattle down the lane, lickety-split, forming an assembly line of livestock that forced the other men to work fast and furiously. He was thankful for the reprieve from the razzing and glad to be busy enough not to think about Dex going gaga over Mac. But Gage was definitely going to have a talk with Mac about not encouraging Dex. The way that ex-soldier was watching Mac you'd think the sun rose and set in her luminous violet eyes. Sheesh!

MACKENZIE RINSED OFF THE dinner plates and put them in the dishwasher. She couldn't remember when she'd had a more productive day. Drawing Dex from his self-imposed shell and watching him become more at ease with each passing hour, while they gathered up donated goods for HRPD's charity garage sale and hauled them to the city park, was gratifying. Plus, Dex had been talkative at dinner this evening. It was Gage who'd sat at the table like a closemouthed clam, speaking in one-word responses and making little contribution to conversation.

"You better watch what you're doing with Dex."

Mackenzie started when Gage—and she hadn't even heard him enter the room—all but breathed down her neck. She pivoted to find him towering over her. His gray eyes reminded her of a thundercloud and his mouth was set in a grim line.

"And what, may I ask, is wrong with luring Dex back into society? The man's so lonely and isolated that he practically talked my leg off the whole live-long day,'' she informed him.

She reared back when Gage braced his hands on the edge of the counter, pinning her against the cabinet. He lowered his head until their faces were inches apart. ''It's not talking your leg off that worries me, kid,'' he muttered.

''I have told you repeatedly not to call me kid,'' she shot back, refusing to be intimidated by his looming presence.

''Fine, whatever.''

''Do *not* dismiss my request with a *whatever*,'' she smarted off. ''I'm making Dex my project, along with a few other civic activities to occupy my time.''

''Well, you did quite a job on Dex already,'' Gage growled at her. ''Even my cousins noticed that he's got the hots for you. And tonight, every time you graced him with a smile at dinner he practically melted on his plate.''

Her gaze narrowed on him. ''Just because Dex respects me and enjoys my company you think he has the hots for me? You are delusional.''

''No, I'm a man and I can sure as hell tell what other guys are thinking,'' he assured her sharply. ''Dex may be talking your leg off but he's fantasizing about getting your clothes off. So don't kid yourself, *kid*.''

Mackenzie knew the quickest way to make Gage back off was to come on to him. ''So, you're saying I shouldn't do something like this with Dex.'' She looped her arms around Gage's neck and pressed her hips against him—real seductive-like.

Ah, she lived for the day Gage made the first

move and pulled her into *his* arms. Would that day ever come?

She stretched upward and kissed him right on those sensuous lips. "And I probably shouldn't do this, either, right?" Her hands glided down to unbutton his chambray shirt then skied over the dark furring of hair on his chest.

She noted, with impish delight, that his nostrils flared and his eyes flashed. Good, because she could feel the sizzle and burn of desire that spread through her when she dared to touch him familiarly.

"Exactly right," Gage said roughly. "You try this stuff with Dex and he'd be all over you before you can blink."

"Unlike you who remains totally unaffected?" she murmured as she shifted closer. *Come on, Gage, give in, just a little.*

"Right, and I'm gonna tell your daddy that you're a tease if you don't cut that out." He frowned darkly at her, but he didn't push her hands away and she could feel his accelerated heartbeat beneath her splayed palm.

"Tattletale," she whispered before she pressed her lips to his. She felt him respond, though he was obviously trying not to. She savored the taste of him, the feel of his muscled body meshed against her. But before *she* lost control and had to admit that he was getting to her more than she was getting to him, she ducked under his arm and headed to the table to gather up the rest of the dishes.

"For your information, 007, you're way off base about Dex. We spent part of the morning cleaning up his cabin and then he gave me a crash course in unique ways to avoid and escape capture. He's a font of resourceful information and I learned a lot from him. Now I'm ready to rumble.''

"Learned things like what?" he asked shortly.

"Top secret stuff. Can't tell you," she said saucily.

"You can tell me. I have all sorts of security clearance." He picked up two bowls and carried them to the sink. "Dinner was good, by the way."

"Thanks, I got the recipe from Steph during lunch and I talked to Laura about speaking to the business law classes."

His dark brows snapped together over his steely eyes. "I told you that I don't want you running around unprotected while I'm helping my cousins."

"Not to worry. Dex volunteered to escort me wherever I want to go tomorrow."

"Tomorrow?" he echoed.

"Yes." Mackenzie scrubbed the bowls and crammed them in the dishwasher. "I also plan to stop at the lawyer's office to inquire about a job."

"Damn it, didn't you listen to one word I told you about laying low? You don't need to be high profile right now."

"I'll be careful and observant. Plus, I've got eagle-eye Dex. He wears so much hardware under his clothes that he's a one-man special ops squadron," she insisted.

He regarded her suspiciously. "How do you know what he's got under his clothes?"

"You mean besides the customary male equipment?" she teased outrageously. "He showed me his weapons, of course. Just to reassure me that if an attack comes he'll be well armed and well prepared."

Gage grabbed her elbow and spun her around so quickly that the dishrag in her hand slapped him on the chest. "Don't mess with Dex's mind. I'm not sure how stable it is."

"More stable than yours," she said as she wrested her arm from his grasp. "Since he thinks you and I are married he can let down and be himself around me. He feels safe and relaxed."

Gage's reply was a sarcastic snort.

"Plus, he doesn't treat me like a witless child and he provides interesting companionship."

"Yeah, well, if I start treating *you* like a woman then we'll both be in trouble," he grumbled.

Mackenzie smiled impishly. "*You'd* be in trouble," she corrected. "*I* can handle it. You're the one with intimacy issues. Not me. Heavens, you leapfrog all over the world just to avoid serious relationships."

"It's my job!" he erupted like Old Faithful.

"No, it's your *excuse*," she countered. "It's obvious that this Sherry person trampled on your heart and dented your male ego years ago. Now you're convinced that if you actually care about a woman you'll get your heart trounced on again."

Gage rolled his eyes ceiling-ward. "Great, now you think your Dr. Freud's sister. What did I do to deserve you?"

"I don't need a psyche degree to see that you're afraid of commitment," she declared. "Furthermore, I think you're afraid of me. You even kiss me as if you're half scared."

His massive chest swelled with indignation and his eyes narrowed dangerously. "Is that right?"

"Right on. If any kissing goes on around here I'm

the one who has to instigate it, even in public when we're supposed to be playing the lovey-dovey couple. At your insistence, might I remind you. Then you abruptly announced there shouldn't be any more kissing. But frankly, considering your world-renowned Casanova status, I expected to be blown away. But the truth is that I've kissed college nerds with better techniques... Oops, did I say that out loud? Didn't mean to.''

Mackenzie burst out laughing when he reared back as if she'd slapped him. God, she really had him going. She loved to torment him and push all his buttons. Perhaps it was immature and childish but somehow it compensated for her years of frustrated infatuation for this man who had looked right past her as if she were invisible to him.

''Well, let me tell you something,'' he scowled at her. ''If I ever decide to kiss the breath out of you, you won't be able to handle it. Guaran-damn-teed.''

''So you keep saying,'' she replied flippantly. ''As I said before, all talk and no action.''

He flashed her a naughty grin. ''I don't bite unless I'm asked to.''

Eyes dancing with mischievous challenge she tipped up her chin, gave him a daring grin and said, ''Okay, bite me.''

His eyebrows nearly launched off his forehead and he stared at her as if she'd sprouted a second head. ''Don't you ever quit?''

''Don't you ever deliver?'' she razzed him. ''Maybe I want to have a wild, reckless fling with you. Why not? Who'll know and who'll care?''

''*I'll* know, damn it. I don't become involved on assignment. It's the job, Mac. I *am* the job.''

"Well," she said before she sashayed across the kitchen, leaving him to finish cleaning up, "you've certainly given new meaning to being *married* to your job. Might as well make the most of it. We could get it on and have hot, rock-your-world sex every night if you weren't such a coward."

Mackenzie smiled in wicked satisfaction when she heard a plate shatter on the floor, followed by some pretty raunchy curses. She was sure Mr. Cool Under Fire was getting a little hot under the collar after their last encounter. Good. She'd rattled him. Nothing could have pleased her more.

Her plan was working like clockwork. She'd completed phase I of her mission. Gage had noticed she was a woman, not just an assignment. Phase II entailed getting him to initiate a kiss, instead of making her do all the work. Now that would be progress, she mused. Phase III, of course, was getting Gage Ryder to fall in love with her—when he had no inclination toward serious relationships. It would take some doing, but everyone was entitled to a dream, weren't they?

6
_____

FOR OVER TWO WEEKS GAGE watched Mac flit hither and yon with Dex, her devoted guard dog, at her heels. She'd thrown herself into organizing HRPD's community garage sale—which had raised scads of money for the youth center. She'd made a second visit to the school to speak to classes and she'd settled into a routine of working three afternoons a week at the local law office.

It was obvious to Gage that Mac was one of those people who always landed on both feet and hit the ground running. Of course, she'd grown up, learning to deal with one new set of circumstances after another because her father's assignments uprooted her then transplanted her in one country after another. She'd learned to adjust quickly and make her niche. She'd become acquainted with the locals in Hoot's Roost and you'd think she'd lived here forever. All Gage heard, when he ventured into town, was what a refreshing, delightful woman he'd married.

Delightful? Hell! The woman messed with his mind so frequently that most of the time he couldn't remember which way was up. She was disconcerting, that's what she was. It was starting to grind on Gage's nerves—ones he'd previously believed to be made of steel. Well, so much for that misconception.

"Hey! Stop dillydallying and roll out that barbed

wire,'' Wade called impatiently. ''This is your new stretch of fence and you're the one dawdling. Get your rear in gear.''

Gage grabbed the roll of wire, strung it out as he went and headed toward the corner post Wade and Quint had replaced.

Wade studied Gage curiously. ''What the hell's wrong with you? Getting itchy feet already?''

''Yeah, that's it.'' Gage grabbed the come-along to tightly stretch the new wire and secured it to the post.

''No, it isn't,'' Quint contradicted. ''You can't control Mac and it's irritating you to the extreme.''

''Didn't I tell you she was spoiled and head-strong?'' Gage shot back. ''You think you can keep her corralled at the ranch? Go ahead and try.''

''Did you inform her dad that she's defying your orders to remain low profile?'' Wade questioned.

''Yup, sure did.''

''And he said?'' Quint prodded.

Gage sighed audibly. ''He said to do the best I can because he knows Gidget is a handful. He also said it would be a while before this case is closed. Although he collected the necessary evidence and presented it to the G-men and Bureau boys, they're taking their sweet time about going after the crime syndicate. So we're stuck here for who knows how much longer.''

''You couldn't have left town anyway,'' Quint reminded him. ''Not with the wedding reception coming up.''

Gage groaned as he hiked off to roll out the next string of wire. ''Don't remind me. At least I managed to convince Mac to hold the reception at

Hoot's Tavern instead of my ranch. I can't risk someone using the festivities to case the place.''

"The whole family will be here for the wing-ding," Wade remarked, "so you'll have overnight guests."

Gage jerked upright. "Oh, damn!" That meant he and Mac would have to share the same bedroom. He'd had so much on his mind lately that he hadn't considered the complications of having his parents staying at the ranch.

Wade and Quint burst out laughing at the horri-fied look on his face. Quint said, "What's-a-matter, secret agent man, overlook that slight complication when you dreamed up your little masquerade?"

"Yeah, big-time. Hell!" Desperate, Gage ap-pealed to his cousins for help. "What am I going to do with Mac?"

"Gee, cuz, at your age I thought you already know what to do when you had a beautiful woman in bed," Wade teased wickedly. "But if you need pointers, I'll be glad to help."

"What's going on?" Vance asked as he climbed down from his clunker truck. "Sorry I'm late. Randi and I had a few arrangements to finalize for the re-ception." He frowned curiously at Gage. "What's wrong with you? You look like you've been gut-punched."

"It just dawned on him that he has to sleep in the same room with Gidget to keep up appearances when his folks arrive." Wade snickered wickedly. "He must be suffering from a bad case of perfor-mance anxiety."

While his cousins busted their guts laughing—at his expense—Gage stretched the second wire and secured it in place. "You knotheads just don't get it," he said, and scowled.

"Sure we do. On a regular basis." Vance grinned naughtily. "Deprivation. That's *your* problem, cuz. It's written all over you like a flashing neon sign. Obviously you didn't take Sherry, the Mattress Queen, up on her *standing* invitation—or however she prefers to do it."

No, he hadn't, Gage mused while his evil cousins treated themselves to a good laugh—again. Hard-pressed though he was to admit it, doing the horizontal Macarena with Sherry would feel like a betrayal to Mac. And, that was just plain insane. He owed her nothing except protection. He'd purposely stayed out of her way to avoid the temptation of wanting her that had him tossing and turning every cursed night. She had him tied up in so many knots that even the great Houdini couldn't get loose.

"You know," Wade said as he took a short break and propped himself against the corner post, "maybe, we should ease up on Cousin G."

"Why's that?" Quint sprawled on the ground to take a sip from the water jug. "I'm having fun teasing him."

"Yeah, making up for lost time and all that," Vance put in. "He hasn't been around for such a long stretch of time in years. He needs a steady dose of harassment. We have no choice but to catch up while he's in town."

"But think about it," Wade went on, waxing philosophic. "Here's a man who's trying to be professional and noble by keeping his hands to himself. Now me. I fought the good fight, but I couldn't resist Laura's innumerable charms." He gestured his dark head toward Quint. "Cousin Q couldn't back away from Steph, even after she claimed she never wanted to see him again in this lifetime. Hell, he practically had to *beg* her to marry him."

"Hey! I wasn't *that* pathetic," Quint huffed in offended dignity. "She was crazy about me. She just didn't want me to know it."

"And let's not forget the practical joker who couldn't keep his distance from the cop and couldn't crack wise again until she agreed to marry him. She took Vance right out of his game," Wade added teasingly. "Now, Gage is sticking to his guns and to his professional principles. Of course, all this admirable restraint is making him as cranky as a bear, but hey, he's got all those principles to cozy up with at night."

"Still, it's a damn shame that he doesn't know what he's missing by not having an official marriage with all the fringe benefits," Quint interjected.

Gage jerked off his work gloves, slapped them against his thigh then braced his fists on his hips. "Don't think I don't know you're trying to work your backward cowboy psychology on me. What I don't need is three wise guys making this situation worse. I plan to return Mac to her dad in the same condition I got her. Safe and sound. You three morons may need wives to lead you around by the nose to keep you happy, but I don't. I relish my freedom, damn it."

"*Uh*-huh," Wade said, lips twitching.

"I can come and go whenever I please," Gage maintained.

"Uh-*huh*." Quint's lips pursed in amusement.

"I answer to no one," Gage added defensively.

"*Uh*-huh," Vance said, biting back a grin. "Now that you've got that off your chest, let's get back to work. Randi is off duty tonight so we'll be chasing each other around the house. Do *not* call. We hate untimely interruptions."

Thankfully, the torture session ended and Gage's cousins granted him reprieve. They were hyping marriage and commitment to be a hallowed institution, but Gage wanted no part of it. His cousins could carry on family tradition and have themselves a houseful of kids. He'd dote over the little dumplings. But a wife and family weren't in the stars for him. He'd obviously been born with a streak of wanderlust.

No woman would convince him to settle down. All he needed was to circle back to home base occasionally, before flying off to various parts of the world. Besides, Mac had just completed college and her life and her career were ahead of her. All she claimed to want from him was a temporary fling. In addition, he suspected her outrageous flirtations and daring challenges were her way of getting even for the resentment she admitted that she'd harbored since adolescence.

He was not caving in to temptation, he vowed determinedly. His cousins could razz him and Mac could torment him, but it would change nothing. He'd been trained to withstand all sorts of pressure and temptation in the line of duty. Nobody was going to turn *him* into a lovesick marshmallow of a man. Having Mac underfoot was just one more test he had to pass. And, by damned, he'd do it with flying colors.

MACKENZIE SHIMMIED INTO THE slinky black dress she'd picked up for the reception and smoothed it over her hips. With her hair pinned atop her head she looked more sophisticated than she had in weeks. She'd taken to wearing a braid or ponytail while garbed in casual T-shirts and jeans. But tonight she would meet Gage's parents, aunts and uncles and she wanted to make a good impression.

Aware that Gage's parents would be spending two nights at the ranch, Mac had moved her meager belongings into Gage's room and lined up her toiletries in the master bathroom. Tonight should be interesting, she mused with an elfish grin. As of yet, Gage hadn't mentioned the new sleeping arrangement— probably putting it off to the last minute so she couldn't taunt him with it.

Well dressed and well shod, Mackenzie strode down the hall. She'd promised to meet Laura, Steph and Randi at Hoot's Tavern to oversee last minute preparations. When Gage had insisted the party be moved to the tavern, for security purposes, she'd given in. Besides, the local watering hole was guaranteed to hold a larger capacity of guests than they could squeeze into Gage's home.

Lost in thought, Mackenzie rounded the corner and collided head-on with Gage. She grabbed his arm to steady herself. When she glanced up she noticed his gaze had zeroed in on the plunging neckline of her dress and a spark of awareness shot through her. It was the first time in weeks that she'd been this close to him because he'd gone to tremendous effort to avoid her. She was heartened by the fact that he wouldn't be able to avoid her tonight, not with his family and friends at the reception, expecting them to appear the happily wedded couple.

"Damn, Mac, please tell me there's more to this ensemble than just that barely there dress," he criticized.

Well, so much for anticipating a compliment. Concealing her disappointment she stepped away then twirled in a circle. "You don't like the dress?"

His gaze slid over her—twice. "There isn't enough of it to like or dislike. It exposes too much skin," he muttered.

She smirked at his disapproving frown. "Don't be an old fuddy-duddy. This dress is the cutting edge of fashion."

"Ask me, someone *cut* too many *edges* off that dress."

"Well, I'm wearing it, whether you like it or not."

"Which I don't," he didn't fail to point out.

"Then you probably won't approve of the fact that I'm not wearing underwear, either," she said. "Too bad. Deal with it."

"That's more than I need to know." Way more.

Gage did his damnedest to meet her defiant stare, but his betraying eyes kept dropping to the exposed swells of her breasts and the extensive length of her well-shaped legs. She looked so incredibly sexy that she nearly blinded him. Desire razored through him, leaving him wondering how much more self-denial he could tolerate. Lord, it was going to be a long, tormenting night of portraying the adoring hubby without allowing himself to get sidetracked by forbidden temptation.

"Before I forget, we...uh...need to...uh...move your stuff to my room," he hem-hawed awkwardly.

She tossed him a saucy smile. "I already took care of that. We'll be bunking together. Think you can handle it?"

"Of course." *Not.* If Mac was in his bed then he'd have to make a pallet on the floor. No way could he trust himself not to touch her. He was already on the crumbling edge.

"Good. I was afraid you'd freak when it occurred to you that your parents expect us to be bed partners."

"I don't freak," he said indignantly. "I never freak."

"Oh, right, you secret agent types are prepared for everything," she said playfully. "Let's test that theory."

Gage didn't have time to gather his self-control before Mac flung her arms around his neck and bestowed a steamy kiss on his lips. And poof! His brain broke down and his body heated up. His hands glided over her butt, pulling her flush against him. He could feel the taut peaks of her breasts boring into his chest and his hands instinctively slid upward to brush his thumbs over her nipples. When she arched toward him he filled his hands with her breasts and groaned at the tormenting pleasure that pulsated through him. As he plunged his tongue into her mouth he wedged one leg between her thighs, feeling her sultry heat, causing her miniskirt to ride even higher, exposing her bare hip.

He had the wildest urge to rip off that sexy shrink-wrap dress and press his hungry lips to every satiny inch of flesh he unveiled. He wanted to feast on her, until he knew every part of her incredible body by taste and touch. And then he'd take her where she stood, right up against the wall. Hard and fast, until this tortuous desire for her had been appeased.

The blaring horn jerked Gage from his erotic fantasy. He blinked twice to erase the blinding red haze of passion that swam before his eyes and staggered away from the worst temptation he'd ever encountered. Kissing and caressing Mac was like handling a time bomb. One false move...and kaboom!

"That's Dex," Mac wheezed as she rearranged the dress he'd come dangerously close to peeling off of her in a moment of utter madness. "He's taking me in early so we can double-check the refreshments and decorations."

When she sauntered off in those skyscraper high heels and that come-and-get-me-if-you-think-you're-man-enough-to-handle-me dress and sans underwear—she hadn't been kidding about that—Gage half-collapsed against the wall. Swearing, he shed his work shirt and headed to the shower. Although he was looking forward to being reunited with his parents he wasn't anticipating the next round of torture Mac would probably put him through when they bedded down for the night.

Gage had been in worse situations, he assured himself as he stripped naked and climbed beneath the pulsating spray of water. But, for the life of him, he couldn't remember what those situations were. Visions of Mac in that eye-catching black dress that displayed her feminine assets—assets that he'd had his hands all over—kept bouncing around his head.

MACKENZIE STILL HADN'T COOLED down when she and Dex arrived at Hoot's Tavern. That arousing encounter with Gage assured her that when he let his guard down he became a sensual wild man. And he'd lit her fire, leaving her hot and bothered.

Inhaling a fortifying breath, Mackenzie turned her attention to the reception and dragged Dex over to chitchat with Laura, Steph and Randi. Although Dex ducked his head and nodded self-consciously the women drew him out of his shell and had him talking in no time at all. When Dex strode off to grab a ladder and string up the last of the wedding decorations the Ryder wives closed ranks around Mackenzie.

"You've done wonders with Dex," Laura remarked. "First he helped out at the charity garage sale. Now this. Impressive."

"Quint told me that Dex hasn't attended a social gathering in years," Steph commented.

"You have a local war hero here in your midst and no one has publicly recognized him," Mackenzie commented. "You should honor him at the Fourth of July celebration."

"That's a wonderful idea," Randi enthused. "Dex really is a nice guy and he deserves better than his self-imposed isolation."

"If I accomplish nothing else," Mackenzie went on determinedly, "I'm going to see that Dex becomes an active participant in this community."

"And we'll help," Steph volunteered.

Mackenzie smiled slyly. "I plan to do a little matchmaking this evening, but I think it would boost Dex's self-confidence if we took turns dancing with him first."

The Ryder wives nodded agreeably then Steph

said, "Hopefully that will squelch the gossip that's buzzing around town about you and Dex."

Mackenzie jerked upright. "Oh, for heaven sake." When the threesome nodded grimly, she sighed. "Gee, let me guess who's resorted to subterfuge. Sherry, the Mattress Queen?"

"None other," Laura confirmed. "I asked my fellow teachers about Sherry and the reports aren't good. I don't know what complex that diva has going, but she seems to have a compulsion for stealing other women's men."

"I was tempted to shoot her a couple of times last month when she cornered Vance outside the restaurant," Randi put in. "But now that Gage is back in town she seems determined to stir up trouble for him."

"Sherry gave Quint the message to have Gage give her a call," Steph grumbled.

Mackenzie silently wondered if Gage had taken his old flame up on her offer. He'd been away from the house a couple of evenings a week and had asked Dex to keep her company during his absences. The thought of Gage taking satisfaction in Sherry's all-too-willing arms hurt deeply. Yet, she honestly couldn't say she'd be surprised if Gage turned to Sherry. Until tonight, he'd been bound and determined to keep his distance from *her*.

She wanted to take up where she and Gage had left off an hour earlier. She wanted him to want her to such mindless extremes that Sherry was the very last thing on his mind. Darn it, why couldn't she attract the one man she desperately wanted to be interested in her?

By the time the colored lights and decorations had

been strung around the tavern and the refreshments were lined up for the countrified reception the Ryder men arrived with their parents. Although all the Ryder men looked devastatingly handsome, dressed in full western regalia, Mackenzie's gaze kept returning to Gage and her foolish heart squeezed in her chest. She nearly melted in a puddle when Gage swaggered toward her, wearing a smile guaranteed to break feminine hearts from eight to eighty. For appearance sake, he leaned down to buss his lips across her cheek.

"Don't pull another stunt like you did earlier," he growled softly. "You'll find out how dangerous I can be."

Despite her disappointment she manufactured a smile to greet Gage's parents. They embraced her enthusiastically and welcomed her into the family. But her heart ached, wishing this wasn't a charade, wishing Gage wanted her to be more than his assignment. Ah, if wishes were fishes, yadda, yadda.

When three men, dressed in police uniforms, arrived on the scene, Mackenzie's gaze reflexively shifted to Vance and Randi. Amused, she watched the cops descend on Vance who stood at rigid attention, as if prepared to do battle. Vance's new in-laws were obviously reserving judgment on his worthiness as Randi's husband until he'd been interrogated.

"C'mon, better make a show of force," Gage murmured.

Mackenzie was amused to see the other Ryder cousins converging on Vance as well. It was impressive the way this family rallied around one another. She'd never been a part of an extended family. It had just been her and Daniel. Again, she found herself wishing this wasn't a masquerade and that she was a part of this close-knit family.

"A little impulsive, don't you think?" Randi's father was saying when Mackenzie and Gage came within earshot.

"No, sir." Vance hooked his arm around his wife's waist and drew her possessively against him. "She's the most important person in my life and it didn't take me long to figure that out." He flashed a good-natured smile. "Surely I don't have to tell you how special she is. And by the way, I'm not giving her back, so don't ask."

The teasing comment was met with three stony stares. Obviously the three cops didn't possess Vance's lighthearted sense of humor—or approve of it. When uncomfortable silence stretched between the new in-laws Mackenzie stepped forward to introduce herself. She'd attended enough social functions on much grander scales and she knew how to hobnob. In the time it took to blink she had effectively guided one of Randi's brothers to the dance area. Laura followed her lead and latched on to Randi's other brother. Before the cops knew what hit them they were two-stepping in rhythm with the music, while the Ryder men gathered around Randi's father.

"Clever tactic," Steve Jackson said with a wry smile. "What are you? The family mediator?"

"More or less." Mackenzie grinned at the dark-haired cop who looked to be about Gage's age. "I've recently graduated from law school. Although I haven't been a part of the Ryder family very long I can tell you that your sister thinks Vance hung the moon and stars. And vice versa. We should all be so lucky to have what they've found together.

"So...what was Randi like as a girl? And please don't tell me that you refused to provide her with a normal childhood and groomed her to be a cop since her first birthday."

Steve chuckled. "You're good, counselor. We haven't completed one circle on the dance floor and you've already put me on defense. You gonna take on my younger brother, too?"

Mackenzie smiled playfully. "Sure, why not? I live for challenges."

"Obviously. You married into that cowboy family. Now which one of those Ryder cousins do you belong with?"

"She's with me." Gage loomed behind him. "I'm reclaiming my wife, if you don't mind, Officer. And by the way, lay off Cousin Vance. He's a good guy. Your sister is damn lucky to have him," he added pointedly.

"So your wife was just telling me," Steve replied. "And you're lucky to have this little lady. She's got spunk, style, a quick mind and exceptional beauty." He winked at Mac. "You don't happen to have a twin sister, do you?"

Gage arched a brow as the cop ambled off to rejoin his father. "Charming the pants off the cop, were you?"

Mackenzie shrugged nonchalantly. "Hard as it is for you to believe, some men actually find me stimulating and interesting company."

"I find you stimulating and interesting. I think we established that earlier tonight," Gage muttered as he held Mac at a respectable distance—no vital parts of his body touching hers. "But go ahead and bewitch all the Jackson men, if you need the validation."

"I don't need validation," she said defensively. "I thought it would be more diplomatic for me to reassure Randi's brother that Vance was her perfect match. I didn't think he'd punch me in the nose for saying so. *You,* I wasn't sure about."

"I can hold my own, kid," Gage assured her.

"Or you could let Sherry do it for you."

Gage missed a step and accidentally trounced on Mac's toe. "What's that supposed to mean?"

"It means that Laura, Steph and Randi warned me that Sherry has you in her sights. Since you've been mysteriously absent a couple of evenings a week—"

"So naturally, you presume that I was with her?" Gage cut in. "And if I were? It's not like I haven't heard the rumors that you've got something going with Dex."

"And if I did?" Her chin elevated a notch higher. "Why would you care? You constantly remind me that this is just an act. So, are you, or aren't you, 007?"

"Gage, there you are."

Speak of the devil. Gage watched Mackenzie's eyes narrow on him when Sherry showed up. The timing was perfect, he decided. After that unsettling encounter earlier it would be best if Mac presumed the worst. He could deal better with her if she was ticked off at him. Considering the close quarters he and Mac would be sharing, while his parents were at the ranch, it would be easier if Mac refused to speak to him in private.

"You don't mind, do you?" Sherry asked Mac,

but she didn't await a reply, just cuddled up to Gage and practically led *him* in the slow-tempoed two-step.

"That was really subtle," Gage said, smirking. He glanced over Sherry's dyed-blond head to note the hurt expression on Mac's face. Although this was for the best, guilt hammered at him for tramping on Mac's feelings. He knew what that was like.

Though Sher rubbed against him like a cat in heat, Gage was poignantly aware that whatever feelings he thought he'd had for this three-timing vamp had died years ago. These days, only one woman tormented his self-control and never failed to get a sexual rise out of him. That woman was currently dancing with Wade, he noted, determined to keep her in his sight.

"Your wife isn't what I expected," Sher murmured against his ear. "Never thought you'd rob cradles, handsome."

Gage didn't need to be reminded that he had nine years and scads of experience on Mac. It was just one of many reasons why he'd tried to keep his hands off her—and failed tonight. But he'd be damned if he'd allow this blond home wrecker to think he'd stoop to playing her games.

"Sorry, Sher, but I'm not messing up the good deal I've got with my wife. Go peddle your wares with someone who cares. I'm in love for keeps," he told her bluntly.

Sherry reared back, as if he'd slapped her. "Then you're a fool, Gage, because your wife is carrying on with Dex behind your back. I've seen them together all over town for weeks."

Although the jealous green monster threatened to take a bite out of him, Gage refused to react. He told himself it didn't matter that Dex spent so much time with Mac. He was the substitute bodyguard, after all. And this was—let's not forget—just a charade. Furthermore, he had a hell of a lot more faith in Mac's integrity than he did in Sher's.

When the song ended, Gage walked off to dance with Randi. Out of habit he glanced around the tavern to locate Mac. She was dancing with Randi's father. No doubt, she was making another pitch for Vance. Loyalty, Gage mused. Mac was quick to support and defend her friends and supposed relatives. Unlike Sherry who was too self-absorbed to concern herself with anyone. She looked out after Numero Uno.

Right there and then, Gage knew that, despite the rumors, there was nothing going on between Dex and Mac except friendship. No doubt, the ex-vet was infatuated with her, but Mac wouldn't betray a trust. It simply wasn't her nature.

Five minutes later Gage watched Laura and Mac tow Dex across the tavern to introduce him to an attractive strawberry-blonde. Gage smiled to himself. All you could accuse Mac of doing was ensuring there was someone for just about everyone.

THE MOMENT GAGE CLOSED the bedroom door behind them, Mackenzie headed to the bathroom to change into the oversize T-shirt that served as her nightshirt.

"Mac, that was a nice thing you did tonight," Gage commented as he shucked his Western-cut sport jacket.

"I did several nice things," she replied as she stepped out of her shoes. "Are your referring to the fact that I didn't grab one of the cop's sidearms and shoot you for allowing Sherry to cut in on us? She's a real piece of work, by the way.''

"I was referring to singing Vance's praises to his in-laws and introducing Dex to the librarian from Laura's school." He ambled over to check the print out from the sensors. "No unusual activity here tonight. That's a relief."

Mac stepped from her clothes and dressed for bed. She glanced at the spacious hot tub and decided that's where she'd bed down. Funny, before she left for the reception she'd anticipated making Gage squirm over the sleeping arrangements. But after the Sherry Incident she'd lost her sense of humor. She also decided she was wasting her time trying to make Gage fall in love with her. He didn't even want to fall into *lust* with her.

Starting now, she was going to tolerate these months of waiting to receive the okay to return to her life. She was going to discard this fanciful dream. Sometimes a woman just had to admit defeat and get on with her life. Gage Ryder would always be beyond her reach. He always had been. That hadn't changed during the time together—except *she* loved him more.

"What are you doing?" Gage asked when she reached up on tiptoe to grab two extra quilts from the walk-in closet.

"Making my bed in the Jacuzzi. Good night."

"Hold it, Gidget."

She glanced up from building her nest to see Gage leaning leisurely against the doorjamb—muscled arms crossed over his broad chest. He was studying her speculatively.

"What? No more teasing seduction? I figured you planned to make tonight a nightmare for me."

"Well, you figured wrong, secret agent man." Mackenzie heaved herself back to her feet then brushed past him to retrieve a pillow. "I've decided to play by your rules. That should make your day, Dirty Harry."

"You don't have to sleep in the tub," Gage said. "I can make a pallet on the floor."

Mackenzie smirked. "You've avoided me for weeks on end and ordered me not to make another pass at you. Terrified as you are of me, I won't risk sending you into cardiac arrest by sleeping in the same room."

"Mac—"

She shut the bathroom door in his face. How many reality checks did a woman need? How many blows to her feminine ego did she have to suffer before she acknowledged that the only man she'd ever wanted didn't want her back?

"I haven't been with Sherry," Gage said through the closed door. "She doesn't possess your character traits."

Mac plopped on her pallet. "I'm sure that's a point in her favor."

"I wanted you to know that I've been doing physical conditioning two nights a week to stay in shape."

Well, she mused, at least Gage hadn't turned to that blond-haired vamp for recreational sex. She'd rest easier knowing that.

She glanced at her makeshift bed, wondering how much rest she'd get tonight, while tossing and turning and telling herself to stop wishing for things that would never be.

7

GAGE HAD TO ADMIT THAT Mac played the perfect hostess while his parents were visiting. She'd charmed them with the same ease that she'd charmed the residence of Hoot's Roost. Although she played the loving wife for her audience of two Gage noticed the difference when she glanced in his direction. She'd retreated from him. She'd stopped teasing and tormenting him. He should've been pleased—but he wasn't. He hadn't realized how much he'd come to need his Gidget-fix. When she placed an emotional barrier between them nothing was the same.

"Let's drive into Steph's place for dinner tonight," Gage invited. "We haven't been seen in public together, with the exception of the family gettogethers, in weeks."

"No, thanks. I bought a book by one of my favorite authors while Dex and I were in town today. I'll just grab a sandwich this evening and read in my room."

Gage tossed aside his hat and frowned at her. "What's wrong with you? First you insist that you aren't the type to hang out with very little to do. Suddenly I can't drag you away from the ranch. Dex can, but *I* can't."

She glanced absently at him as she dusted the

furniture. "I've adjusted to this routine after almost three months."

"Damn it," he burst out. "I want the old Mac back."

She paused momentarily from her chore. "Well, too bad. Remember that adage about being careful what you wish for because you might get it? Well, you got it. I'm treating you like a stick of furniture. If you stand in the same spot you can expect to be sprayed with polish and dusted off." She took a swipe across the top of the big screen TV with her cloth then strode over to clean the end tables.

When he walked up behind her she elbowed him in the solar plexus. "Back off. You're crowding my space."

"C'mon, Mac," he coaxed. "Dinner and a movie. I'll even let you harass me to your heart's content."

The sadness he noticed in her smile and the lackluster in those enormous amethyst eyes really got to him. He wasn't sure why, but it did. Gage was reluctant to put a label on the emotions Mac aroused in him. When she wasn't her energetic, vibrant self he felt as if he were being deprived of something vital and necessary. Damn, when had that happened?

"Don't do me any favors, 007," she said flatly. "I'm trying to move on so don't bother trying to cheer me up."

He frowned, bemused. "Whaddaya mean you're moving on?"

"Nothing. Never mind. Buzz off," she snapped.

When she lurched around to walk away he snagged her arm and towed her back to him. The impulse to devour those pouty lips was intense. He hadn't tasted her in what seemed like forever. He hadn't been close enough to touch her in what seemed like an eternity. He wanted her—badly—but he refused to let himself do anything about it.

"Exactly where *were* you before moving on?" he questioned.

She sighed heavily and shook her head, causing the curly, raven ponytail to slither over her shoulder. "Cut out the third degree, Gage. Doesn't matter. It's not your problem."

"*You* are my problem." In more ways than one, he thought in frustration. His vivid dreams were haunting him nightly.

"Look, if you want to do dinner tonight then we'll do dinner. Just don't ask any more personal questions. This relationship is strictly business, after all."

When the phone rang, Mac lunged for it, using the incoming call as an excuse to get away from him. "Ryder residence," she said politely.

"Keni? Steph here."

Ah, a friendly voice, one that didn't get her emotions all stirred up when she was trying so damn hard to remain unmoved and unaffected by *his truly,* who was feeling sorry for her because she'd lost her pizzazz.

"Hi, Steph, what's up?"

"Girls' night out is what's up," Steph announced. "Quint decided on a spur of the moment poker night at our place so Gage is invited over here while the girls go into town to partake of a few cool ones at Hoot's Tavern. You game?"

Oh boy, was she! "I'm there," she enthused. "I'll tell Gage he's expected." She hung up the phone then whirled to face Gage's curious frown. "Poker night at Quint's. Girls' night out at the local watering hole."

"I was hoping we could spend some time together tonight," Gage said. "Something's been bothering you for weeks and I want to know what it is."

Mackenzie headed for the shower. *He* was bothering her. That and the realization that there would never be a *them*. They'd never truly be a couple. "Don't wanna talk about it, but thanks for offering a sympathetic shoulder and ear," she said on her way down the hall.

"We are definitely going to talk about this," he insisted as he followed closely in her wake.

"Not if I can help it." She closed and locked the door.

"Damn it, Mac—" She switched on the faucets—full blast—and drowned him out.

PROMISING GAGE THAT SHE'D STICK close to Randi, Laura and Steph, Mackenzie sank into Steph's low-slung sports car and breathed a gusty sigh of relief. "I hate to admit it, but your invitation was a godsend," she said. "I needed to get away."

"Away from Gage?" Steph asked perceptively as she cruised toward town. "That's the main reason for girls' night out. We've been worried about you. You haven't seemed to be your bubbly, enthusiastic self during our weekly family dinners. Is there trouble in paradise?"

"You could say that," Mackenzie mumbled.

"Well, tonight we're all going to let our hair down, unwind and relax." Steph veered into the parking lot at the local bar and nodded in satisfaction when she spied the familiar cars. "Randi and Laura all already here. Let's treat ourselves to a few glasses of wine and kick back."

Although Mackenzie had never been a partyer she was more than ready to purge her unrequited feelings for Gage with wine, whiskey...whatever. She just needed to let it all hang out, to recapture that part of herself that had gone missing.

The instant Steph and Mackenzie entered the tavern, Laura and Randi motioned them to a corner table. The jukebox was playing one of George Strait's country hits and a string of men had bellied up to the bar. Several chummy couples were cheek to cheek on the dance floor.

Mackenzie smiled in satisfaction when she saw Dex cozied up in a booth with Kristen Barlow, the school librarian. She was pleased to note that her matchmaking had paid off. Mackenzie nodded a greeting as she took her seat.

Laura poured wine into the glasses—except for Randi's. "Designated driver, if it comes to that," Laura announced, smiling at the attractive brunette. "The end of school is always a strain and it has taken me a month to unwind."

Steph lifted her glass in toast. "Here's to your well-earned summer vacation."

Everyone took a drink.

"And here's to overcoming the hurdle of getting my dad and brothers' approval of my hasty wedding," Randi said as she topped off her glass of ginger ale. "Thanks to all of you running interference no fights broke out at the reception. Since our marriage has lasted to the eve of Independence Day, my family has finally decided to accept Vance into the fold."

Everyone took another sip of her drink.

"And here's to surviving the steady stream of wedding rehearsal dinners, family reunions and business dinners I had scheduled from April through June," Steph said. "I never thought I'd complain about business going great guns. But here I am. Whining. Let's drink to whiners."

Everyone tipped her glass then refilled it to the brim.

"And here's to finishing up the final arrangements for tomorrow's Fourth of July celebration at town square," Laura added. "Thanks to all of you, the holiday festivities should be a success."

The women downed their drinks then Steph glanced at Mackenzie. "Your turn. What do you want to drink to?"

Mackenzie raised her glass. "To the effects of wine. I should have grabbed a bite to eat before I came to town." She smiled giddily. "This stuff is going straight to my head."

Chuckling, the Ryder wives knocked back more wine.

"Seriously," Randi said, "What's been bugging you? We really want to know. We want to help."

"We need more wine if I'm going to get into that," Mackenzie insisted. "Long story."

Randi waved her arm in expansive gestures to nab the waitress's attention.

"Man, y'all must be dehydrated," the waitress teased as she set two chilled bottles on the table. "*Bottoms* up, ladies." She leaned in close. "That's the message from the barkeeper. He's a male chauvinist pig.''

"Then let's drink to all the MCP's of the world," Randi suggested, uplifting her glass. "I met my share at the academy and on the Oklahoma highways and byways.''

"I met plenty of 'em while working in Dallas.'' Steph pulled a face. "Can't swing a dead cat without hitting one.''

"The world is lousy with MCP's." Mackenzie took another sip of wine. "There's foreign and domestic MCP's, believe you me. Don't know which ones are the worst.''

"Some of them work in the schools," Laura declared.

"Yeah, well, I married two of 'em," the waitress grumbled as she tossed spare napkins on the table. "You ladies don't know how lucky you are to have lassoed guys who'll show you a little respect.''

"Hey, Wanda, order's up!" the bartender called out. "Quit yammering and get back to work.''

"There, ya see? Wha'd I tell ya? Won't lower himself to bussing drinks," Wanda grumbled. "King of pigs. Enjoy yourselves, ladies, and down a sip for me while you're at.''

When Wanda wandered off Steph nudged Mackenzie's elbow. "So, spill it, Keni. And I'm not referring to your drink.''

Mackenzie had indulged in too much wine too quickly. The stuff was fizzing through her bloodstream like Alka-Seltzer. Her nose tingled and her tongue was entirely too loose. "Well, for starters, my name isn't Kendra. It's Mackenzie Shafer and

I'm not married to Gage. We're just living in the same house."

The women gaped at her in disbelief.

Mackenzie nodded then helped herself to more wine.

"Not married?" Laura parroted.

"Shh!" Mackenzie cautioned. "It's top secret. Gage was assigned as my personal protector."

"What the devil are you talking about?" Randi demanded. "And who, exactly, does Gage work for? I never can get a straight answer from Vance."

"Ditto for Wade," said Laura.

"And Quint," Steph added.

"Can't tell," Mackenzie mumbled. "But I'm swearing all of you to secrecy." She placed her hand over her heart and insisted the other women do the same. "Repeat after me—I promise not to breathe one word of this to anyone else."

The women took their solemn vows then swallowed down another drink of wine. They leaned toward Mackenzie—all ears and wide eyes.

"I'm the potential target of kidnapping or assassination because of my dad," she confided in a slurred voice.

"Are you serious?" Randi grilled her. "Please tell me it's the wine talking and that you have a wild imagination."

Mackenzie shook her head. "Nope, the bad guys want to use me to manipulate my dad into silence. If he blows the whistle on them, they could face twenty years to life."

"Whoa, how bad are these bad guys?" Laura asked warily.

"*Extremely bad,* bad guys," Mackenzie clarified.

"Do our husbands know this already?" Randi asked.

"Yes, they set up the drop zone the night Gage snapped my harness to his and forced me to parachute from the plane."

"What!" Steph hooted. Her silver-blue eyes narrowed in annoyance. "They knew about this and they didn't tell us?"

"I thought there were supposed to be no secrets between us," Laura muttered. "They'll pay for this deception."

The other women nodded in agreement.

"So, your marriage is just a sham?" Steph asked, bewildered. "But I thought you and Gage looked as if you were nuts about each other."

"Well, until a few weeks ago," Randi qualified then frowned suspiciously. "That handsome hunk didn't take advantage of this pseudomarriage, did he?"

Mackenzie sighed unhappily then drowned her misery in more wine. "No, that bozo has enough integrity for both of us. Unfortunately."

"Uh-oh." Steph slouched in her chair. "You're in love with him and he isn't cooperating, right?"

"*Was* in love with him," Mackenzie amended sluggishly. "I decided to stop wasting my emotions on him the night of the wedding reception. He's a hopeless cause."

"Right, and I can tell your strategy is working like a charm," Laura smirked then raised her glass. "That's why you've been moping around for weeks, isn't it? Well, here's to nice try but no cigar."

Everyone drank to that—twice.

"I'm telling you, girlfriend, falling out of love is

like trying to overcome an addiction," Steph insisted. "What you need is professional help."

"Exactly," Randi put in. "And we're all professionals here. We tried—and failed—to get over the Ryder men. There was no solution but to marry them."

Mackenzie's shoulders slumped in defeat. "So you're saying my condition is terminal? No cure whatsoever?"

"'Fraid so." This from Laura. "Can't live with 'em sometimes and can't live without 'em. Doomed."

"Well, Gage can certainly live without me," Mackenzie said deflatedly. "I could throw myself at him—stark-naked—and he'd turn his back and lecture me about how this is his job, that he *is* the job. He wouldn't be interested in making a commitment or putting down roots, even if I planted him in potting soil and watered him weekly." She inhaled more wine to ease the sting of rejection. Since it didn't help she had one more drink.

"I just don't get it. What kind of man turns down a fling with no strings attached? I would've settled for that, pathetic loser that I am," Mackenzie muttered, dispirited.

"You are not a pathetic loser," Randi contradicted.

The Ryder wives agreed wholeheartedly that Mackenzie wasn't a loser. It made her feel better—somewhat, at least. "Thanks, you're the best friends a woman ever had."

"We're on your side," Steph assured her, giving her a lopsided smile. "Maybe if you seduced him—"

Mackenzie waved her off. "Tried that. Didn't work. He went running scared, the big chicken."

"Maybe if you borrow my pistol and shoot him a couple of times he'd be more cooperative," Randi suggested teasingly. "You know, if-you-can't-beat-'em-then-shoot-'em theory. I was saving that as my last-ditch effort with Vance, but he came around before I resorted to violence."

"How about the jealousy factor?" Laura said then shook her head. "Never mind. Obviously the rumors linking you to Dex didn't faze the big lug. Now Dex is with Kristen and she's over the moon for our local war hero." She frowned pensively. "Maybe I could hook you up with a fellow teacher."

"Waste of time," Mackenzie mumbled. "When this threat blows over I'll fly home and resume my life. Maybe when Gage is out of sight he'll be out of mind."

"Right," Steph scoffed. "Did Juliet get past Romeo? Did Mark Anthony get past Cleo?" She shook her red head then held up the half-empty bottle. "The answer is probably in here somewhere. We just haven't drunk deeply enough yet."

"Well, keep looking while I find the rest room." Mackenzie hoisted herself from her chair. The room spun crazily so she braced her hand on the table. "Whoa, head rush. Remind me not to do that again."

"While you're gone we'll put our heads together to find a solution to the problem," Randi insisted. "By the time you return we'll have this all figured out."

Mackenzie was struck by an impulsive thought

when the honky-tonk stopped spinning around her. "Can I borrow a cell phone? I left mine sitting on the charger on the nightstand."

Steph dug into her purse and dropped the phone in Mackenzie's hand. "Don't forget to enunciate clearly when talking," she slurred. "Your words are starting to slur."

"Said the pot to the kettle." Mackenzie smirked as she glanced around to get her bearings. It took a few seconds for her eyes to catch up as she panned the dimly lit tavern. Having spotted the darkened hallway, she zigzagged between the tables and was pleased that she tripped only once on her way to the hall. She halted, propped both hands on the walls and squinted at the identical doors. Through blurred eyes she tried to determine which door led to the ladies' room.

Before she could wobble through the door on the left, an unseen hand clamped over the lower portion of her face and another hand squeezed her throat, cutting off her air supply. Her reaction time was so slow that Mackenzie couldn't defend herself. She was plastered against a solid male chest, dragged backward and stuffed into the supply closet.

"Damn it, sister, look at you," Dex scolded harshly. "Toldja to always remain on alert. You've had so much wine that you couldn't fight your way out of a plastic bag."

She slumped against his muscled torso and grabbed a deep breath when he loosened his grip. "Don't scare me like that."

"You're too soused to be on guard and that's a good lesson for you. Never wander off in dark places alone. Didn't we cover that during our self-defense training? You drop your defenses for one second and your goose is cooked.'' Dex opened the closet door and steered her toward the ladies' room. ''I'll stand lookout until you come back. Next time don't try this solo. Understood?''

She patted his bulky arm clumsily and flashed him a goofy grin. ''Thanks, Dexie. Sure am glad you're dating Kristen.''

''Yeah, she's a sweetheart.'' His arm shot toward the door. ''Now skedaddle. I'll be right here when you come out.''

Mackenzie shouldered into the room then punched in her father's phone number. He answered on the second ring.

''Daddy, I wanna go home,'' she mumbled. ''This is just an empty threat, a scare tactic. I've been here for months.''

'''Kenzie?'' her father chirped. ''What are you doing? You don't sound like yourself.''

She blinked owlishly. ''No? Who do I sound like?''

''Never mind, honey. Are you okay? Is something wrong?''

''Yes, something's wrong. I wanna go home,'' she said sluggishly. ''Can't take much more of this. Driving me crazy.''

''Where's Gage? Put him on the line,'' Daniel insisted.

''Can't do that. Not here,'' she said sluggishly.

''Damn, where are you calling from? Is this line secure?''

Secure line? She stared at the cell phone. ''Gee, I dunno. What does it matter? This is a hoax.''

When Dex rapped on the door she hurriedly ended the call. "Gotta go, Dad. 'Bye."

"Everything okay in there?" Dex called impatiently.

"Gimme another minute," Mackenzie requested.

Blast it, her father was as paranoid as Gage, she mused as she staggered back into the hall. Hide out, lay low, assume an alias, take a cover and watch out for unsecured phone lines. What a bunch of hooey. The Mafia had her dad and Gage running scared and disrupting *her* life. She'd had enough!

"I hope you didn't drive into town," Dex grumbled as he steered her back to the bar.

"Nope, got a designated driver. Not to worry." She smiled up at her concerned friend. At least she thought she smiled at Dex. Her facial muscles felt so slack that she couldn't say for certain. "Go back to your date and enjoy yourself. I'm perfectly fine, Dexie."

His reddish brows bunched over his dark eyes. "You are definitely foxed. Stay with your relatives, okay? Promise?"

"Scout's honor," she promised then patted his cheek. "Now scram. I can take care of myself."

When Dex ambled off Mackenzie inhaled a steadying breath then surged across the room to rejoin the Ryder wives. "So..." she said as she plunked into her chair. "Did you come up with a sure-fire cure-all for falling for the wrong man?"

Laura nodded her blond head. "Yep. We've decided you should tell him how you feel. No more pussyfooting around. Honesty is the best policy."

"Pftt!" Mackenzie propped her elbows on the table to hold herself upright. "I gave you ten minutes

and that's the best plan you could come up with? I am definitely *not* telling him.''

"Yes, you are," Randi insisted. "I marshaled my courage to tell Vance and it turned out that he felt the same way. Hence our hasty flight to Vegas for the wedding.''

"Gage isn't Vance," Mackenzie pointed out.

"Good thing because you and Randi would be crazy over the same man," Steph joked. "Couldn't have that.''

Mackenzie wasn't amused by Steph's attempt to tease her into good humor. "I just want this fiasco to end so I can reclaim my life. My only regret in leaving here is that I'll miss being with all of you. To friendship,'' she said in toast.

Everyone took a drink.

"If I could have sisters then you'd be my pick," Mackenzie added. "To sisterhood.''

Everybody drank to that, too.

BACK AT THE RANCH, Gage was checking his watch and wondering how much longer ladies' night was going to last. He was edgy and restless because he didn't know exactly what Mac was doing, didn't know for sure that she was all right.

"Hey, Cousin G, are you gonna deal or daydream?" Wade asked as he drummed his fingers on the table. "Some fun you've been tonight. You've spent more time looking at your watch than at your cards.''

"Keep it up and you'll have us thinking you'd rather spend time with your supposed wife than your lovable cousins," Vance teased.

"Speaking of your mock bride," Quint said,

"what's up with her lately? Looks like someone implanted a spigot into her and drained out all that spirit and vitality I've come to associate with her."

"No kidding." Wade watched Gage shuffle the cards halfheartedly. "You two have a big blowout or something?"

"Nope," Gage said sullenly then sipped his beer. "She's steering clear of me, as if I've contracted a highly contagious disease. I tried to talk to her about it, but no dice."

"Are you sure you didn't say or do anything to spoil her cheerful disposition?" Quint asked. "Gotta tell ya, I hate to see Gidget moping around. Are you *sure* you aren't the cause of her blue funk?"

"I didn't do anything," Gage defended himself as he dealt the cards.

"Maybe that's the problem," Vance speculated. "She's pining away for you and you aren't giving her what she wants."

Gage stood up, slammed down his cards and glared pitchforks at his ornery cousins. "Don't you imbeciles get it? Gidget is going to return to her dad, just as I got her. No hanky-panky. No reckless fling! I'm a professional, damn it!"

"Jeez, you wanna turn down the volume a few decibels?" Quint tapped the side of his head. "Sexual deprivation is definitely getting to you."

"I wish the hell I'd never dreamed up this cover," Gage muttered, exasperated.

"Why? The M-word scare you?" Wade taunted. "True, the M-word used to make the rest of us twitchy, but not these days. You should—"

"Give it a rest," Gage interrupted. "I don't want to hear testimonials on the benefits of marriage. I just want to keep Mac safe until I send her home. Besides, my job isn't conducive to meaningful relationships and that's fine by me."

Quint shrugged casually as he tossed two chips toward the middle of the table. "You're not as fine as you think you are, cuz. But you better figure out what's making Gidget so unhappy. She's shriveling up before our eyes."

"I'll interrogate her tonight, if she ever comes home," he said, glancing at his watch. "There. Happy now?"

"Deliriously." Vance's dark eyes danced with deviltry.

Gage tossed down his cards and bounded to his feet. He wasn't in the mood for his demon cousins. There were times when their playful camaraderie was like an injection of pleasure, but right now it wasn't enough. Something was missing. Something was unresolved in his life.

Gage wheeled toward the door. "I'm going home."

"Sweet dreams," Vance taunted. "Have fun hugging your pillow."

"Yeah, yeah, yeah," Gage snarled on his way out the door.

He stopped on the porch to grab a deep breath of air. He didn't realize how tense and restless he'd been until he saw Randi's car veering into the driveway. Good, Mac was back so he could rest easier. At least he *hoped* she was back and that Randi hadn't arrived with the grim news that Mac had been abducted during girls' night out.

In swift strides he headed toward the approaching car. He slowed his step when he heard uproarious giggles wafting from the vehicle. It didn't take a genius to deduce that the women had partaken a bit too much of the bubbly. Criminey. The whole lot of them could've been kidnapped! Annoyed, Gage whipped open the door. It only took two seconds to realize Randi was the only sober female in the car. The others were definitely tipsy.

"Hi, Gagie." Steph wobbled from the car and flashed him a silly smile. "How ya doin'?"

Gage smirked. "Hi, yourself, Red. Jeez, who said women were more sensible than men? Just look at you."

"Oh, phooey," Laura snorted. "Everybody knows that when men get together they behave like juveniles. Why should men get to have all the fun?"

When Mac came unsteadily to her feet and then wandered off in the wrong direction, Gage tracked her down then steered her toward his truck. "Good thing Lewis and Clark didn't hire you as a guide. You'd still be lost and the whole expedition would've been a bust."

The women cackled at his dumb joke. Definitely a sign that they were skunked.

Gage turned his disgruntled stare on Randi. "Some cop you are. You should have hauled them in for public intoxication."

"Well, if you weren't such a dunce—" She shut her mouth and glared at him. "Vance is going to hear about this, too."

"Wha'd I do?" Gage asked, flabbergasted.

"Maybe it's what you didn't do," Laura supplied in a slurred voice. "Where's Wade? I have a few things to say to that rascal. None of it's good, believe you me."

"Quint's gonna get an earful, too." Steph meandered unsteadily toward the porch. "Men can be such meatheads."

Gage's brows shot up like exclamation marks. He suspected there'd been a considerable amount of husband-bashing going on over drinks. His cousins thought they resided in matrimonial bliss? Ha! His cousins' wives were gunning for them. Even Randi, who obviously hadn't been drinking, was planning to give Vance what-for—and who knew what for?

Gage decided to let his unsuspecting cousins deal with their own. "C'mon, kid, let's put you in bed."

Mac jerked her arm from his grasp so abruptly that she flung herself off balance. She landed in the grass with a thud and groan. Gage rolled his eyes, hooked his hands under her armpits and hauled her back to her feet.

"I ca' ta' care 'f m'self," she said drunkenly. Despite her declaration she leaned heavily against him as he ushered her to the truck. "'Zit foggy out here or 'zit just me?"

"It's just you," Gage confirmed, lips pursed. "Get in the truck before you fall off your feet, Mac."

She stumbled to a halt and squinted in the darkness. "Which truck?"

Great, she was seeing double. That was bound to make her twice as much trouble for him. "How much did you drink?"

"Not enough, that's for sure," she mumbled as he opened the passenger door and boosted her onto the seat.

Gale piled into the truck, switched on the ignition and headed home. The restlessness that had plagued him finally eased off. Mac was safe in his protective custody—at last.

Mac mumbled unintelligibly during the drive home then konked out before Gage stopped in the driveway. Leaving Mac where she was, he strode off to ensure no one had tried to gain entrance during his absence. Assured that everything was A-okay, he retrieved Mac.

When he scooped her in his arms she cuddled against him and said, "Hi, honey, I'm home. Miss me?"

"Yeah, as a matter of fact, I did." An odd feeling of tenderness washed over him as he carried her to the house. Impulsively, he angled his head to brush a light kiss over her flushed cheek. "What am I going to do with you?" he murmured, both exasperated and amused by the condition she was in.

"You can kiss me like you mean it," she suggested.

Uh-oh. Gage veered down the hall, hoping liquor didn't affect Mac as drastically as that little white pill. His emotions were bubbling too near the surface tonight. He'd fretted and stewed all evening. Having her back in his arms, after weeks of cautious avoidance, felt a little too right, too necessary. His unruly male body was giving him fits.

The solution, he decided, was to stuff her in the shower and sober her up so she wouldn't climb all over him and tempt him until his self-control crumbled. With that plan in mind, Gage toted her to the shower in the master bedroom because it provided more space to maneuver.

Holding Mac in one arm, he leaned sideways to switch on the faucets then untied her shoelaces.

Without the slightest cooperation from her, he removed her shoes then hesitated. Undressing her wasn't a good idea. He didn't need to see too much skin. That would send him right over the edge, for sure.

Although Gage decided to let her shower in her clothes, Mac yanked off her blouse then unbuttoned her jeans.

"No, wait...! Oh, hell..."

His voice evaporated when she stood beside him in her bikini panties and matching bra. Like a sex-deprived pervert *he* looked his fill, while *she* was oblivious to what transpired around her. Damn, she was sexy, he noted as his hungry gaze roamed, unhindered, over her voluptuous figure. His fingers itched to glide over the fullness of her breasts and skim down the flare of her hips. He kept trying to tell himself that seeing Mac in her undies wasn't much different than looking at a woman in a bikini bathing suit and that he could keep his raging hormones under control.

Unfortunately this wasn't just any woman; it was Mac. Mac with those mesmerizing lavender eyes, that all-too-kissable mouth and that glossy raven hair that was a tangle of curls. She looked absolutely breathtaking and he'd be a goner if he didn't cram her in the shower to sober up while he found some place to cool down.

She grabbed the rail and stepped unsteadily beneath the shower. Before he could close the glass door he noticed that her wet undies clung to her body like second skin, revealing way too much for his peace of mind.

"Damnation," Gage muttered as he shut the door.

The glorious sight of that killer body was stamped on his eyeballs. He'd never be able to look at her without seeing her as she was now—very nearly naked. *He was doomed.*

Gage got outta there, PDQ. He needed a drink—or four—to take the edge off his rioting hormones. Barreling down the hall, he grabbed a bottle of whiskey and took it straight—no ice, no glass. But the image of Mac still hit him like a freight train so he took another swig. And another.

There, that should do it. Now all he had to do was pluck Mac from the shower and tuck her in bed. Confidence restored, he headed to his bedroom. In a few minutes he'd have Mac tucked in bed, sleeping off her bout from girls' night out. First and last girls' night out, he decided. The Ryder wives were a corruptive influence on Mac.

In five minutes he'd be home free. He'd have dodged another bullet that went by the name of Mackenzie Shafer. She'd be in her bed and he'd be in his. Problem solved...he hoped.

8

GAGE FOUGHT TO BREATHE when he rounded the corner to see Mac propped against the bathroom door. She'd wrapped a towel around her wet head, but it was her clingy underwear that needed to be covered because it left nothing to his imagination. Those hurried slurps of booze had taken the edge of his willpower, *not* his libido. Desire hit Gage like a heat-seeking missile. He grew hard and needy so fast that blood rushed south of his belt buckle, leaving him light-headed.

To his frustration, Mac pushed away from the doorjamb, cast the towel from her head and weaved toward him. "What is it you don't like about me?" she mumbled in question. She entwined her arms around his neck, pressed herself against him and tilted her head to stare up at him through drowsy eyes. "Am I too short? Not pretty enough? Not smart enough?"

"I like you fine," he wheezed, his body on fire.

"Then prove it."

When she kissed the living daylights out of him Gage knew he was in serious trouble. He'd backed away from this gorgeous bombshell so many times that his common sense finally raised the white flag of surrender. Internal battle over, he realized. There was nothing to do but accept the terms of inevitable defeat. Sighing helplessly, he wrapped Mac in his arms and took what she offered, even though he knew she wasn't functioning at full mental capacity. Which was even worse than all the times she'd purposely tormented him with kisses, just to push him to his limits. Now he was taking advantage of her.

"I want you," she murmured against his lips. "Just once…"

She punctuated the request with another knock-your-legs-out-from-under-you kiss. He lost his slippery grasp on self-control and tumbled into the swirling vortex of desire. He forgot to remember that Mac was his assignment and that he wasn't to take her personally. Forgot that she was Daniel's daughter. Forgot she was the very last woman he needed—and was suddenly the only woman he remembered wanting—to the extreme.

He closed his eyes and kissed her without an ounce of restraint. Devoured her, was more like it. If he was going to commit the unforgivable, irreconcilable sin then so be it. He'd pay the consequences later. No more guilt trips. He put his nagging conscience to rest. There was just the two of them here in the heat of the moment, slaking needs that had broken through the last barriers of his defense.

When he tumbled with her onto his king-size bed her laughter filled the small space between them. She tilted her head back and her glazed gaze focused on his face. He stared at her lush mouth, felt her curvaceous body molded against his and he knew he wouldn't be satisfied until he was inside her, feeling her softness surrounding him. All or nothing. He'd tried nothing and now he'd have all of her.

Like a starving man he claimed her mouth. His seeking hands glided over her breasts, peeling away the wet fabric, kneading the full mounds until she arched against him and moaned. She grabbed impatiently at his shirt and pearl snaps popped. She raked her nails over his back as he bent his head to suckle her nipples. Her muffled groans encouraged him to see what other sounds she'd make when he skimmed his hands down her rib cage to divest her of her bikini panties.

"Gage..." she rasped as his hand slid between her legs.

He felt her shimmering heat burning his fingertips and desire nearly electrocuted him when she all but came apart in his hands. She was so wildly responsive that it blew his mind—what there was left of it. For sure, basic instinct reigned supreme and he was making love to her as if they'd been together forever—or planned to be. As if he had the right and privilege to touch her as intimately and often as he pleased. He wanted to taste her completely, wanted to give her the sun, moon and stars because a woman like Mac deserved nothing less than all the erotic pleasure a man could offer.

Gage refused to be satisfied until he knew her luscious body by touch and taste and heart. He shifted to offer the most intimate of kisses and caresses, because he *needed* to know her in every sense of the word. He *needed* to know how she responded to him because this was the only thing he didn't know about Mac. He'd seen her frightened, angry and belligerent. He'd endured her torment, her defiance and her avoidance. But he'd never seen her go wild—the way she did when he touched his lips and fingertips to her softest flesh and felt the tremors of passion consume her.

She climaxed instantly, clutching at his shoulders as if she were hanging on to him for dear life—sort of like she had the night he'd dragged her from the aircraft and left her free-falling with him through space. But now she was shimmering like liquid fire on his lips and fingertips. And by so doing, she aroused him to the very limit of his sanity—what little he had left of that, too.

Incredible! He'd never focused on satisfying a woman the way he focused on Mac. She was the only woman who'd ever gotten to him on every level. The only woman who'd pierced his protective armor and stripped him down to pure emotion.

Watching Mac tremble and gasp in response to his kisses and caresses, feeling her burn in immense pleasure, left him with the astounding realization that he'd achieved a higher level of awareness. With a sense of wonder, Gage lifted his head and stared straight into those passion-drugged violet eyes that were rimmed with spiky black lashes. Man, she was so breathtakingly beautiful that she bewitched him.

"Love me," she whispered on a hitched breath. "Love all of me with all of you. Just once…"

Mesmerized, he peeled off his jeans and grabbed a foil packet from his wallet. He tore it open and hurriedly covered himself. All the while she watched him with those luminous eyes that held such a fierce gravitational pull that he couldn't look away. He eased his knees between her thighs and braced himself above her. She grabbed a handful of his tousled hair and pulled his head down to deliver a lip-blistering kiss that spoke of her frantic need for him.

Gage drove himself to the hilt—and then froze in stunned shock. "Mac?" he croaked against her parted lips.

"Mmm…" She shifted, adjusting to the unfamiliar pressure of masculine invasion.

"I th-thought," he stammered, battling the natural instinct to move within her. "I d-didn't know… Why didn't you tell me?"

"Top secret, 007." She smiled as she arched sensuously against him. "You're the only one I know with security clearance. But you aren't the only one who operates on a strictly need-to-know basis." When her smile turned impish his heart flip-flopped in his laboring chest. "Now that you know the truth, I'll have to kill you…or love you. You choose."

"Damn, woman, you are full of surprises, aren't you?" he said, smiling despite the inner conflict tormenting him.

"No, I'm full of you." She arched into him, smiling. "But there better be more. I need more," she demanded.

Gage groaned aloud when her seductive movements sent white-hot need blazing through him. "You're a very demanding woman," he wheezed. "Do you always have to have your way?"

"Only with you…ah…"

Her voice evaporated when he drove helplessly into her, yielding to the urgent demands of his body. Desire consumed logic as he moved in the ageless rhythm of passion. Everything inside him responded to the feel of the luscious female body beneath him, responded to the breathless gasp of pleasure and encouragement that tumbled from her lips.

Jaw clenched, he plunged and retreated, knowing

he was probably hurting her, trying to slow the frantic cadence, but unable to stop the roller coaster of desire that gripped him. She felt so unbelievably good in his arms, as if they were one body and soul moving in perfect harmony, reaching for the same shooting star that was just beyond their grasp.

"Gage? Oh, my…"

He knew the exact instant that passion riveted her body because the tremors of ecstasy echoed through him. He shuddered helplessly, clutched her to him and tumbled into a free-fall that was nothing like he'd ever experienced. There were no words to describe the unfamiliar feelings and fierce sensations that converged then exploded inside him. No way did he want to put a name on what he was feeling for Mac because he was definitely feeling too much. And though that scared the hell out of him he couldn't roll away because he simply couldn't find the willpower to let her go. Not yet anyway. Maybe in a few minutes when his fogged brain cleared up and his spent body rejuvenated strength.

She sighed against his shoulder and smiled impishly. "Best bodyguard I ever *had.*"

He chuckled. "*Only* bodyguard you ever *had.* Obviously. Why me, Mac—?"

He swallowed the question when he felt her sag beneath him. He levered up to see her long lashes resting against her flushed cheeks, her lips parted in a half smile. Well, so much for getting answers to his questions. Yet, Gage figured he knew why *him* and why *tonight.* Mac had drowned her inhibitions in a wine bottle and he'd been available and convenient. Plus, she'd teased him about men and their hair-trigger lust.

She'd proved her theory, all right. He hadn't been able to resist her because he'd depleted his supply of resistance—little by little, until there was nothing left but this hidden desire that had finally slipped its leash. It bothered him that, while he might be able to protect her from possible harm, he couldn't protect her from himself. Jeez! His legendary professionalism had taken a direct hit.

Gage could pretty much guarantee that his conscience was going to work him over—but good—come morning. Well, he'd deal with that later. Tonight he'd hold Mackenzie close and savor these totally inappropriate feelings of possessiveness that stole over him. After all, he couldn't undo what he'd done. And some part of him, some ridiculously old fashioned part of him, was humbled and astonished that he'd been Mac's first lover.

He rolled from bed to switch off the volume to the sensor alarm so Mac wouldn't be disturbed during the night. When he settled back beside her he pressed a kiss to her velvety lips. He didn't question why holding Mac while she slept off the groggy effects of wine seemed the natural thing for him to do.

MACKENZIE STRETCHED LEISURELY then felt an unfamiliar twinge. Vaguely she remembered consuming wine like it was going out of style and giggling like an idiot. She opened her eyes then groaned when an invisible sledgehammer thudded inside her skull. Good gad, no wonder she'd never been a party animal. Hangovers were hellish.

Careful, so as not to slosh her wine-logged brain, she levered herself onto her elbows. She raked the curly tangle of hair from her face then opened her eyes, hoping the room wasn't spinning the way it had been last night.

She gasped in bewilderment when her gaze landed on Gage's incredibly sleek and muscular body that was covered—barely—by the sheet. What had she done? The thought no sooner backstroked across the murky waters of her mind when flashes of memory hit her like a strobe light. The details were hazy, but she knew without question what had happened between them.

Before she was prepared to face Gage his silver-gray eyes fluttered open. Her face went up in flames as she self-consciously clutched the sheet to cover herself. She'd waited forever to find herself in his bed, but now she felt awkward and unsure of herself.

"Morning, Mac," Gage murmured.

"Morning, Gage," she wheezed and stared at the ceiling.

She should be exceptionally pleased that she'd finally managed to seduce her dream lover. But, she couldn't remember exactly *how* they'd come to be in bed together.

A hysterical laugh burst from her lips when the irony of it all hit her between the eyes. It was one thing to get what you'd wanted for years and quite another to get it—and not remember it. How unfair was it to make love with the only man she cared about and be unable to remember the juicy details? Good grief, she just couldn't catch a break, could she?

"Hey, sleepyhead, we thought you wanted to get an early—"

Mackenzie shrieked in humiliation when she

glanced sideways to see Gage's cousins logjammed in the doorway.

Gage bolted straight up in bed. "Oh, hell!" His gaze darted to the computer that was flashing sensor notifications of intruders but emitted no sound of alarm.

Mackenzie jerked the sheet over her head and prayed that it was possible to die of mortification. She didn't want to live if she had to endure the Ryder cousins' teasing harassment. Wasn't it enough that the Ryder cousins had seen her climbing all over Gage that first night in the pickup? Did they have to be on hand to witness this milestone, too?

"I'll be outside in a minute." Gage glared mutinously at his cousins. "I have a doorbell. Next time use it!"

Wade chuckled wickedly. "Why? We've been in this house more than you have the past few years. We've always had an open door policy around here."

"Policy rescinded," Gage muttered, giving them the evil eye. "Don't ever walk into my house without announcing yourselves first. Understood?"

"Got it," Wade said obligingly, then snickered.

"Sure, you betcha," Quint said, lips twitching.

"Reading you loud and clear," Vance added. "'Course, before now there was nothing interesting to interrupt."

The three men burst out laughing.

Mackenzie groaned in embarrassment.

"Move it, you yahoos!" Gage belted out impatiently.

Mackenzie waited until the men left then rolled herself in the sheet and sprinted back to her own room. Now what was she supposed to do? Behave as if nothing had happened? Facing Gage was bad enough, but facing his devilish cousins? Oh, God!

Assertive though she usually was, she took the coward's way out and crawled back into bed to sleep off the wine-induced headache. She couldn't face any of the Ryder men until she had time to regroup and recuperate.

GAGE JERKED ON HIS CLOTHES and walked onto the front porch to confront his demon cousins. "Let's get to work," he said as he brushed past them to saddle the horses.

When his wicked cousins began to hum the "Wedding March" Gage lurched around and slashed his index finger across his neck in the universal signal to shut-the-hell-up-or-you're-dead-meat. "Not one teasing word to Gidget. It was her first—" Gage slammed his jaw shut. He couldn't remember the last time he'd blushed, but he was blushing now. For an intel operative he was suddenly suffering from loose lip syndrome.

Three black brows jackknifed and three wry smiles came Gage's way.

"Don't worry, cuz," Wade said. "Turns out that we've been there ourselves. You can't help but admire and respect a woman who knows what she wants and refuses to settle for less than what she knows in her heart is right for her."

"Makes you feel special and protective, doesn't it?" Quint said knowingly.

"Doesn't surprise me one bit about Gidget, either," Vance interjected. "We won't razz her about this because we like her too much. Of course, we have no qualms about tormenting you.''

Gage studied his grinning cousins. Apparently the women they'd married had waited until they fell in love. *Love?* Gage jerked upright. But Mac didn't love him...did she? No, things had simply gotten out of hand after she painted the town red. She liked to tease and torment him, but why would she love him? Gage wheeled toward the house. ''Be right back. Saddle the horses for me, will you?''

Gage strode swiftly to the house. Awkward or not he had to speak to Mac. He barreled down the hall, whizzed into her room and jostled her awake.

''One question,'' he said abruptly. ''Do you love me?''

She thrust out her chin and glared at him. ''Is that the first question you ask the women you sleep with?''

Gage bore down on her, but Mac, being Mac, wasn't easily intimidated. He liked that about her—in a frustrated kind of way. ''Forget other women. I want to know about *you*.''

She propped up on her elbows. ''Why? Am I on trial here?'' she smarted off. ''Is loving you a crime? What's the punishment? Desertion on your part? Do you run and hide if you have an inkling that a woman cares about you?''

He noticed that she was trying to appear sassy and flippant, but she couldn't quite pull it off and he refused to let her use the ploy of answering his question with questions.

''I want the truth and I'm not leaving the room until I have it,'' he said in his best secret agent voice.

Her chest heaved when she drew a deep breath. Gage made a point not to let his gaze drift to her barely concealed breasts. This wasn't the time to get sidetracked. "Answer me."

"If you usually run scared of love, then you better pack a bag and slip on your goodbye boots," she said, not quite meeting his intense stare. "You want the truth? I don't even remember when I didn't love you, not that you ever noticed."

There, she'd taken the Ryder wives' advice and gone for broke. Mackenzie knew it was a gigantic mistake because Gage wasn't your everyday average kind of guy. He was a tumbleweed who needed no roots, aside from an occasional visit to his ranch to see his cousins. He didn't do *love*. She knew that, but it still hurt to realize that loving Gage wasn't enough to hold him. He had no interest in her heart.

He stared at her as if he hadn't heard her correctly. "Is that a yes? I want a straight answer, Mac. Yes or no?"

She shot him a withering glance as she gathered the sheet around her and stood up. "Yes. Just how dense are you, 007? I might've resented you all those years, but that didn't stop me from idolizing you. That was the sublime paradox." She sighed as she raked her hair from her face. "Loving and hating you at the same time. Wishing…" She shrugged. "Well, doesn't matter. You were always oblivious to the way I felt about you."

He lifted his arms helplessly. "Mac, I didn't know—"

"Oh, hush up," she interrupted crossly. "You didn't know because you weren't interested enough in me to even bother looking past the wisecracks.

But don't go getting all apologetic on me at this late date. As far as you're concerned we just had recreational sex last night. End of story.''

"How is it possible that a beautiful, intelligent woman like you never...?" His voice fizzled out as he stared questioningly at her.

"How is it possible? I never stayed in one college for more than a semester. When was I supposed to establish a meaningful relationship? It didn't help that I measured other men up to you. But not to worry, I'm not going to ask you if it was as good for you as it was for me." She burst out in a humorous laugh. "Truth is, I don't remember much about it. You'd be a better judge of whether I enjoyed it.''

Having had her say—which was obviously more than he needed to know—she dashed toward the bathroom to retrieve aspirin. Gage snagged her arm, but she wormed loose. He caught up with her in two long strides and pulled her back against his chest. This time he refused to release her, even when she karate-chopped his wrists.

"You had a great time, Gidget," he whispered against the side of her neck. "Best time ever, in fact.''

Blushing furiously, she squirmed for release. "You know it was the *only* time. Now let me loose. I have a hellish headache. Don't you have some place you need to be right now?''

"Sure do, but I'm not going anywhere until we get things squared away," he insisted.

"Everything's square. You go do your cowboy *thang* and I'll do my holiday-planning *thang*," she drawled sarcastically.

Her protective defenses were finally back up and running, thank goodness. She could deal with Gage without simpering like a heartbroken imbecile. He didn't love her back and she had to accept that. But damn it, how had he figured it out? Had she spilled the truth last night? Or, being the super spy that he was, had he arrived at that brilliant deduction?

"Are you going to town with Dex?" he questioned abruptly.

"Don't I usually?" She congratulated herself on her lawyerspeak. She had implied a *yes*, but she hadn't exactly said *no*, either. "Let me go so I can shower."

He finally released her, but he kept staring at her as if she were a curious specimen under a microscope. "Is that what you meant yesterday when you said you were trying to move on? Is that why you've been avoiding me the last few weeks?"

"Sure, whatever," she sassed as she strode off.

Mackenzie half-collapsed then groaned miserably when she locked the bathroom door behind her. Between the nagging headache and Gage's third-degree she'd about had it. Now that Gage knew the truth—and hadn't returned the heartfelt sentiment, because he didn't love her, because he thought he'd committed the cardinal sin in his professional codebook—she had to skedaddle. She'd put up a bold front for the past few months, but she couldn't live in the same house with him now. It would be too tormenting.

Since she'd told her father that she was ready to quit this place and reclaim her life then that's what she'd do. She wasn't going to be Gage Ryder's assignment or his charity case. She'd adjust her atti-

tude and get on with her life. He'd become the man
she *could have* loved wholeheartedly, forever.

Mackenzie knew what Gage would do with her
heartfelt confession. He'd treat it like intelligence
info. He'd process it through his analytical brain and
study it from every angle. Then he'd dismiss it as
irrelevant—as it pertained to this assignment. He'd
use tact and diplomacy to let her down gently and
try to salvage their friendship—because of his relationship with her father. She wasn't going to hang
around for the *debriefing*. Thanks, but no thanks, she
thought as she grabbed aspirin then stepped into the
shower. She'd pack her meager belongings and
she'd be as gone as she could get—and she wasn't
coming back.

LOST IN BEWILDERED THOUGHT, Gage returned to
the corral to rejoin his cousins. Mac was in love with
him? She'd been infatuated with him for years and
concealed her true feelings with teasing taunts? Yet,
when confronted she had been honest. Now there
was something he wasn't familiar with in his line of
work. Maybe that's why he appreciated her honesty
so much.

*I don't remember when I didn't love you, not that
you ever noticed.* Her words whirled in his mind like
a blender. Now that he had that startling information, what was he going to do with it? What did he
want to do with it?

"So...are you ready to ride or are we going to
stand around here while you get your love life
straightened out?" Wade questioned restlessly.

Vance glanced at his watch. "We're on a short

clock. I told Steph I'd be in town square by five-thirty.''

''And my in-laws will be arriving soon,'' Vance announced. ''We don't have much time to move your herd of heifers to the northwest pasture.''

Gage swung into the saddle then reined south to gather the herd. He kept thinking how his cousins had settled into ranch life, married and become involved in civic and community activities. They'd taken root while he flitted around like a migrating bird. Years ago, he hadn't wanted to come home because he'd been humiliated by a woman whom he'd foolishly trusted to be loyal and true blue to him. Then he'd fallen into the routine of living out of a suitcase and meeting the challenges of international security.

But suddenly, none of that seemed as important as watching Mac stand before him—wearing that defiant expression that was so much a part of who she was—and admitting that she loved him, despite her pride and embarrassment. Honest, trustworthy, loyal. That was Mac, through and through.

Gage had traveled the world and he'd yet to meet anyone other than his own family who matched Mac's character. Plus, she'd thrown herself into the activities of this community, intent on making a difference, giving of her time and herself, because she was civic-minded, energetic, and ambitious.

All these feelings Gage had been battling for months, hoping to maintain an emotional, physical and professional distance from Mac, settled into place as he trotted across the rolling Oklahoma hills. He'd found a woman he could trust, one who wouldn't betray him. And damn if she hadn't been right under his nose for years. She loved him. How about that?

He chuckled, remembering how he'd tried to hold himself in check while she'd played her seductive charade in public. Only it hadn't been a masquerade, he realized. Her hidden feelings had come pouring out and he'd fought like the devil *not* to respond to the loving, playful woman who'd had his hormones exploding like popcorn. That sassy, spirited, provocative woman had gotten so completely under his skin that he'd buckled to impossible attraction. He'd had the best time of his life last night and she didn't remember the incredible details. The irony of that provoked him to laugh out loud.

"You wanna share, Cousin G?" Vance asked. "What's so funny?"

Gage jerked to attention. He'd been so immersed in thought that he'd forgotten he wasn't alone. Even more peculiar was that his demon cousins hadn't been tormenting him while they gathered cattle. What was *that* all about? Gage regarded them suspiciously, waiting for the shoe to drop.

"So, wha'd you do?" Wade questioned. "Stuff Gidget in a closet so she couldn't get away from you, shine a light in her eyes and force her to admit she loves you?"

"How do you know how she feels?" Gage grilled him.

Wade snickered. "Well, duh. We pointed it out to you the first night you parachuted in. We didn't need our secret decoder rings to figure out that she was nuts about you. But apparently *you* did."

"So, what are you gonna do about it?" Wade wanted to know. "Blow off the best thing you've ever had going and fly off into the great unknown when this caper is over?"

"Dunno," Gage mumbled, distracted. "Hadn't thought that far ahead. Damn, this sorta changes things."

"*Sorta* changes things?" Vance cackled. "Nothing like understating life-altering events, cuz."

"They aren't life-altering if Gage doesn't love her back." Wade fixed his intense green eyes on Gage. "*Do* you?"

"I'm not sure what love is," Gage admitted honestly.

Quint shook his head and chuckled. "First off, if you've got the hots for her the way you've never had them for anyone else—except during adolescence when you were a walking hormone by nature—then you're hooked."

Oh damn, thought Gage. The answer to the first question on the In Love Quiz was yes.

"Secondly," Wade piped up, "if being with her makes you happy and content, even while doing nothing more than talking, eating or watching the boob tube then the need to be *with* her, to be there *for* her is intense. You're snared, cuz."

Uh-oh, yes to question number two, thought Gage.

"When the thought of another man knowing her as intimately and completely as you do sends you over the edge then you're sunk," Vance diagnosed.

Well, hell, that described him to a T, thought Gage.

Quint said, "If she's the only one you want in your bed at night—"

"—And if she's the only woman you want to

see," Wade put in, "when you wake up in the morning—"

"—And when you look at her," Vance added, "sometimes it's hard just to breathe because she's so beautiful to you—"

"—Then you're definitely hooked," said Quint.

"Snared," said Wade.

"Sunk," said Vance.

Gage's shoulders slumped. "Well, I'll be damned. Slam-dunked through the hoop of love."

Wade snickered. "That's another way to put it. So, does that clue you in to why you decided to pretend Gidget was your wife, not your housekeeper or long-lost cousin?"

"Did it occur to you that the reason you tagged her with one juvenile nickname and one manly nickname was because you wanted to downplay your attraction to her?" Quint asked.

"Jeez, you armchair psychiatrists are getting to be a bit much," Gage snorted. "If you don't mind, I'd rather not plot out the rest of my life in the short amount of time it takes to drive this cattle herd to greener pastures."

"Hey, when you know, you just know, ya know?" Vance said. "That will teach you never to bring your work home with you. It turned out to be a lot more than a job."

Gage lapsed into silence while he and his cousins fanned out to circle the herd then funnel the livestock through the pasture gate. Well, okay. So he was in love, but how deeply? What about his demanding job and Mac's promising career?

His thoughts trailed off when he glanced westward to see Dex Nolan's rattletrap truck bouncing across the pasture. Suddenly Gage went on high alert. He could see through the cracked windshield to note that Dex was alone. Mac was supposed to be with him. Something was wrong.

"What's Dex doing out here?" Wade asked as he swung from his horse to shut the gate behind the cattle.

The instant Dex piled from the old truck Gage shouted, "Where the hell is she?"

Dex stopped in his tracks. "I thought she was with you."

Gage's mind raced back to the response he'd received from Mac when he'd asked if she was riding into town with Dex. She'd questioned his question with: Don't I usually? And he hadn't called her on it. "Hell's bells," he erupted.

Her evasiveness could only mean one thing, he concluded. Now that he knew she loved him—and hadn't said diddily squat in return—Mac had gotten her feelings hurt. She'd cut and run.

"I saw two nondescript brown sedans barreling down the graveled road from the north," Dex reported. "Oklahoma County license plates. Rentals are my guess. Four men. Gotta bad feeling about this, Gage."

So did Gage. Mac was without a bodyguard and in a state of frustration because he'd mishandled her declaration—badly.

"Meet us at the ranch, Dex," Gage said hurriedly. "Bring all your firepower. I've got tactical communication equipment and the necessary gear for a takedown."

"Oh, great," Vance said as he reined his horse south. "Gunfight at OK Corral on Independence

Day. I thought we had plenty of fireworks scheduled already.''

''Where's Randi?'' Gage yelled as he and his cousins thundered over hill and dale.

''Went to meet Laura and Steph at the restaurant,'' Vance yelled back. ''Gidget is supposed to be there, too.''

''Congregating in the same place?'' Wade howled then took off hell-for-leather. ''Damnation!''

Like the Four Horsemen of the Apocalypse they raced toward the house. This assignment suddenly became as serious and personal as it could get. The thought of Mac coming to harm caused unnerving fear to corkscrew through him. His years of experience and professionalism deserted him when Mac's beguiling face loomed large in his mind. The thought of losing her ripped the breath from his lungs.

Mr. Cool Under Fire hit the panic button in two seconds flat.

9

MACKENZIE SWIPED AT THE FAT tears that dribbled down her cheeks while she drove Gage's pickup toward town. "Stop crying, you big baby," she muttered at herself.

She'd held her emotions in check when Gage demanded to know her true feelings. But once she'd packed and buckled her seat belt she'd realized she'd never see Gage again.

She'd gotten her heart broken for the first—and last—time, thank you so much. Now she'd focus on being the best, most dedicated lawyer in the land. She'd set her sights on the office of attorney general. There would be no distractions because she wouldn't entrust her heart to another man.

Mackenzie blinked back the tears when she noticed two vehicles were blocking the country intersection. Dust billowed around her as she stamped on the brake. To her astonishment, four men burst forth, charging toward her, packing nasty-looking pistols.

"Holy cow!" Mackenzie yelped as she slammed the truck into reverse. Gravel pinged against the undercarriage of the pickup as she zoomed backward.

"Okay, okay, don't panic," she yammered nervously. "You're the one in the off-road truck. Use your resources."

She whipped into the nearest dirt path that led to

the pasture and plowed through the gate. She winced when metal scraped metal. Gage would pitch a fit when he saw the damage to his pickup. Not to mention knocking his gate off its hinges and leaving it in a twisted pile of wreckage.

Mackenzie stamped on the brake, threw the skidding pickup into drive then mashed the accelerator to the floorboard. With both cars giving chase she blazed a trail across Gage's pasture, frantically looking for another gate that led to a graveled road that would take her to Hoot's Roost. She certainly wasn't going to lead these goons—who were taking potshots at her while bouncing over the rough terrain—back to Gage's ranch. No one was home to provide assistance anyway.

According to Dex's instructions the best plan was to lose yourself in a crowd, not hole up in isolation. With the Fourth of July celebration gearing up for tonight there should be plenty of witnesses on hand to discourage the four thugs, sporting Frankenstein monster haircuts, to show their mugs in public.

Pulse pounding ninety miles per hour, Mackenzie set a new land speed record to reach town. She didn't dare take her eyes off the bumpy road to reach into the back seat to fish the cell phone from her purse. Jeez! Did Gage deal with death-defying car chases and bad guys shooting at him on a regular basis? How'd he keep his legendary cool? She, it seemed, was the personification of *panic* under fire.

"Breathe," she lectured herself. This was no time to hyperventilate. "Call attention to yourself." That had been one of Dex's suggestions, too.

Mackenzie switched on the emergency blinkers and honked the horn repeatedly. Unfortunately not a soul was in sight when she veered onto the highway. Hopefully, she'd encounter traffic on the outskirts of Hoot's Roost.

To her relief the two cars—now sporting crunched fenders and bumpers, after the wild chase through the pasture—fell back a half-mile. Mackenzie glanced down at the fuel gauge, wondering how long she could circle town before she ran out of gas. Well, damn. The tank was nearly empty. She'd have to find a place to roost in Hoot's Roost. Someplace where she could find protection and call Gage. Even if he didn't love her he'd race to her rescue. He was *the job,* after all, and he knew what was going down.

She intended to head for the police station adjacent to town square, but the street had been cordoned off as the dance area for the festivities.

"The Palace," she said suddenly. The Ryder wives planned to congregate at the restaurant that Steph had closed down for the day. Mackenzie had intended to lend a hand before saying goodbye to her new friends. Hopefully, Laura and Randi hadn't arrived and Mackenzie could send Steph running for safety before disaster struck.

Casting another frantic glance in the rearview mirror, she noticed the two banged-up sedans were four blocks behind her. Mackenzie whipped into the disabled parking space, lunged over the seat to grab her purse then plunged from the truck. Panting for breath, she charged into the restaurant and locked the door behind her.

When she heard the murmur of voices coming from the kitchen she dashed forward. "You have to get out of here. Now!" she railed urgently. "Steph, go!"

Mackenzie stumbled to a halt when Laura, Steph and Randi wheeled around to gape at her.

"My God, you look like you've seen a ghost," Laura observed as she put away the plastic bags she'd used to haul hot dogs, buns and plastic plates to the picnic area.

"What's wrong?" Randi demanded worriedly.

"Those bad guys I told you about?" Mackenzie said on a seesaw breath. "They followed me to town. You've got to get out the back door!" She waved her arms wildly. "I don't want you to get hurt. Now go!"

The pounding at the back door indicated the bad guys had arrived. Any minute they would pick the lock and be inside.

Mackenzie glanced around frantically then dashed over to grab the two fire extinguishers. "Improvise," she whispered as she handed the units to Laura and Steph. "I'll distract them while you make a run for it." She noticed that Randi had pulled her handgun and refused to budge from the kitchen.

"The first thing we have to do is exit the kitchen. We don't want bullets ricocheting off all these stainless steel appliances," Steph whispered then stared directly at Mackenzie. "Oh, by the way, we aren't leaving you here alone."

"No way," Laura and Randi said in unison.

"You could get hurt," Mackenzie muttered. "I have lots of acquaintances, but you've become my dearest friends and I refuse to let you get involved in this."

"This is the sisterhood," Steph said determinedly. "All for one, et cetera."

Mackenzie dropped onto her hands and knees and

the Ryder wives followed suit when they heard the creak of the back door. "Steph, kill the lights. Everybody grab a cell phone. Once the place is pitch-black, we'll call for help."

"Good plan." Steph crawled toward the back wall of the kitchen to shut off the breakers.

The room plunged into darkness. Mackenzie breathed a sigh of relief.

"Ms. Shafer?" a heavily accented male voice boomed in the darkness. "I believe you know why we're here. We have the front and back exits covered. Let's make this easy on everyone, shall we?"

THE INSTANT GAGE AND HIS COUSINS dismounted to jog toward the house four cell phones erupted. Gage answered hurriedly.

"This is Mac at Steph's Palace. Four goons packing heat."

"Wait!" Gage demanded before she could disconnect. "Don't hang up. We're on our way."

"Keep your wives on the line," Gage told his cousins. "We need to remain in touch without ringing phones tipping off the goons."

On his way to retrieve his rucksack Gage tossed his phone on the sofa. He noticed his cousins did the same. Good, he didn't want the women to hear everything he had to say.

"Damn it to hell!" Wade muttered as he followed in Gage's wake. "Did our wives have to end up in the same place?"

"Probably," Vance grumbled. "Randi mentioned something about the sisterhood when she got home last night. I know she wouldn't leave Gidget to face trouble alone."

"Steph shares the sentiment," Quint muttered. "Now all four of them are stuck in the restaurant. If those thugs decide to put the women on ice in that walk-in freezer, I'm gonna be royally PO'd!"

"Simmer down, Quint," Gage said as calmly as possible. "Nobody is going to turn your wife into a Stephcicle." He grabbed his rucksack and quickly unzipped it. "Vance, call the police chief and fill him in. Tell him we'll insert from above so we don't alert the goons. Have him find volunteers to set up the picnic area for you. Business as usual for the holiday festivities. Don't want the thugs to know they've been made."

Vance grabbed the phone off the nightstand to brief Chief Jackson.

Wade watched Gage fish out headphones, black commando gear and NVGs. "You came prepared for the worst-case scenario, didn't you?"

"Sure did and sure the hell is," Gage grumbled. "I'm sorry your wives got involved."

"You can apologize to them when they've been extracted," Quint insisted.

"Right, I'll—" His voice trailed off when he noticed the sensors flashing coordinates from unidentified sightings on the laptop computer. The instant message signal bleeped at him. Gage hurried over to tap the key that put him in touch with headquarters. When the message that had been relayed through several secured lines flashed on the screen in capital red letters he swore ripely. Daniel was informing him that Mac had called him the previous night from an unsafe phone line. That's how those thugs had found her so quickly, he thought sourly.

"Gage!" Dex called out. "I've got the goods!"

Gage hurried down the hall to see what Dex had in his bag of tricks. There were several lengths of ropes, an assortment of weapons and ammo galore.

"Whoa," Vance hooted. "You definitely have enough stuff to equip a whole squadron of commandos."

"Gotta be prepared for anything," Dex insisted. "Ready to rock and roll, Gage?"

Gage slung his rucksack over his shoulder then scooped up his cell phone that linked him to Mac. Small comfort but better than none at all, he mused on his way out the door.

"Recon time," Gage announced. "Let's go scout our options and find the best place to insert."

MACKENZIE OVERHEARD DEX and Gage's comments then breathed easier. Help was on the way. All she and the Ryder wives had to do was play hide-and-seek in the dark and hope the rescue squad made it here in time.

In the dining area she could hear her would-be captors banging against the chairs and swearing profusely.

"Time to split up," Randi advised quietly. "But don't back yourselves into corners. You need an escape route."

"Steph, you know this place like the back of your hand," Mackenzie murmured. "Where are the best hiding places?"

"The beverage station," Steph whispered. "Laura, take that position. There's a cubbyhole under the cabinet. Randi, the booth in the southeast corner of the private dining area has the largest table and padded seats to sprawl out on."

"Good," Randi murmured. "Maybe I can work my way to the door. I'm sure the tangos put up a blockade to prevent us from making a run for it, but I might be able to clear the way."

"The women's bathroom might be a good hiding place," Steph suggested.

"That'll work," Mackenzie said in hushed tones. With three separate metal stalls to climb over and under it would be the perfect place for what she had in mind.

"I'll be in the storeroom that has two exits," Steph announced. "One to my office and one near the hall leading to the rest rooms."

"Okay then, let's move out. Keep your phones handy so you'll know when to expect the rescue squad. Everything within arm's reach is a possible weapon," Mackenzie insisted. "Use your resources to protect yourselves."

"Ms. Shafer," the spokesman for the goons called out. "We are getting impatient. Surely you're smart enough to realize there is no way out."

Mac stuck out her tongue at the disembodied voice. She wasn't all that smart, obviously. She'd fallen for a man who—upon hearing her heartfelt admission—stared at her as if he'd encountered a creature from a distant galaxy. But Mackenzie was going to do her best to outsmart these thugs.

GAGE STARED THROUGH the binoculars and panned the street where the restaurant was located. The local authorities and Vance's in-laws—who'd volunteered to help—had moved into position outside the building. Although his cousins didn't have Gage's and Dex's spec ops training they were tough, physically fit and held a personal vendetta against these goons. The Ryders were also familiar with firearms. They'd been raised as hunters and knew how to handle a rifle.

"The fireworks in town square are scheduled to begin in fifteen minutes," Wade informed Gage. "The noise will override any racket we make during insertion."

"Vance, where's the staircase that leads down from the second story of the old building to the ground floor of the restaurant?" Gage questioned.

"There isn't one," Vance reported. "Steph's parents removed it a few years ago. They just use a ladder to reach the upper storage area."

"Then where's the former opening?" Dex asked.

"Near the hall leading to the rest rooms," Vance said.

Gage nodded pensively. "Get on the phones and tell your wives we'll be inside in fifteen minutes. Make sure you know exactly where to find them." Gage grabbed his cell phone and whispered, "Mac, fifteen minutes and counting. Where are you?"

"Women's rest room. But don't worry about me. Get the other women out. This isn't their fight."

The grim determination in her hushed voice caused alarm bells to clang in Gage's head. "Damn it, Mac, no daring heroics. Got it?" He cursed when he realized he'd been talking to a dead line. She'd disconnected. Hadn't he told her specifically not to do that? Had she listened? Hell, no!

Swearing colorfully, Gage crammed the useless phone in his pocket and grabbed his Uzi. "Let's move out."

Thanks to the help of the volunteer fire depart-

ment, Gage and his makeshift commando squad
used the hydraulic ladder to reach the top of the
building. Below him he could see the crowd of fes-
tival-goers who had chowed down on hot dogs,
chips and had begun to make use of the dance area.
The crowd was unaware of the rescue operation.
They were as oblivious as the four thugs who were
inside the restaurant.

Good, surprise attacks at night were his specialty.
And if he hadn't had such an intense personal interest in the outcome of this op he might not have
achieved these new levels of cold sweat. He knew
Mac was up to something and that scared the bejeezus out of him. He had to reach her before her daredevil scheme got her in trouble.

The instant Dex secured the rope, Gage rappelled
down the side of the old brick building to reach the
window. He scowled when he realized the sill had
been painted shut and refused to budge. Grabbing a
knife, he sliced the layer of paint from the window.
It took three attempts to raise the pane.

While the other men rappelled to the window
Gage scrambled inside to shine his flashlight over
the area. Apparently this had been living quarters
decades earlier. Now the place was filled with fallen
plaster, cobwebs and several layers of dirt and de-
bris.

"Watch where you step," Gage murmured into
the mike that was attached to his headphone. "We
don't want these creaking floors to give us away."

Hoping to avoid sounds that would alert the thugs
down below, the rescue brigade crept along the
walls to reach the plywood trapdoor where the stair-

case once stood. Gage glanced at his watch. "Three minutes," he said into the mike.

The other men gave him thumbs-up.

It was the longest, most agonizing three minutes of Gage's life. He wanted to defuse this situation and pull Mac into his arms and ensure she was in one piece. Then he was going to strangle her for making that late-night call on a phone that wasn't equipped with a scrambler. He was definitely going to rake her over live coals for that slipup.

THREE MINUTES AND COUNTING, Mackenzie thought as she gathered her makeshift weapons. Although she didn't have much to work with in the rest room she'd gotten inventive and creative. She'd left water trickling into the sinks and plugged them with paper towels so they'd overflow onto the tiled floor. She'd emptied the soap dispenser and left a film of goo to provide unsure footing. She was going for slick and slippery and she hoped that when she alerted the thugs to her hiding place they'd barrel inside and wipe out on their keisters. She also hoped the metal stalls would provide protection in case bullets started flying. But before that could happen she hoped to launch her grenades—the wet rolls of toilet paper that were saturated with soap.

Long story short, Mackenzie had made the most of her limited arsenal of makeshift weapons. Standing on the toilet inside the middle stall, she gathered her soap-soaked grenades then let out a howl that was guaranteed to raise the dead and clue in the goons to her whereabouts. A moment after she yelled her head off she heard bombs bursting in air, signaling the start of the Independence Day fireworks display. She also heard male voices shouting to one another in the near distance.

Clearly the pop, sizzle and explosion of the fireworks in town square startled the goons, made them impatient to beat a hasty retreat with their captive in tow.

"Hey, you big clowns!" Mackenzie hollered. "Yoo-hoo, I'm in the bathroom!"

The clatter and thud in the dark hall indicated the goons were approaching as a single force. They were banging into each other and clanking their weapons against the wall.

Heart racing, Mackenzie grabbed her first soggy missile. The scant light coming through the frosted glass window allowed her to focus on the door. Flashes of colorful fireworks cast eerie images across the walls and sent vibrant reflections shimmering across the wet floor.

Yep, she mused, this resembled a scene from a horror movie. The expansive mirrors were perfectly positioned to startle and alarm the goons when they barged inside to confront their own reflections. Mackenzie could take advantage of their momentary hesitation and launch her attack.

Body tense, arm cocked, Mackenzie watched the door burst open and four gorilla-size goons, packing handguns, plunge headlong into the room. The scene played out just as she'd planned. The goons' forward momentum threw them off balance. Their feet flew up when they skidded on the slippery floor. The men howled in surprise and landed on their backsides, knocking the wind out of themselves and slamming their heads so hard against the floor that it stunned them momentarily. While they were sprawled like targets at a carnival duck shoot, Mackenzie launched one soap-soaked grenade after another.

She knew the soggy rolls of toilet paper found their targets because the men commenced cursing and rubbing their eyes—which worsened their condition. They couldn't see to blast her to kingdom come.

Bounding from the commode, Mackenzie raced toward the closest blinded goon to kick his pistol from his hand. Lo and behold, the sisterhood arrived on the scene to lend assistance. Laura and Steph let loose with the fire extinguishers, covering the thugs with foam while Mackenzie and Randi disarmed the men then held them at gunpoint.

"Nice work, Mackenzie," Randi complimented, then tossed her a disapproving frown. "But you should have told us what you were planning so you didn't have to take all the heat."

Randi had no sooner gotten the words out of her mouth when the commando squad showed up, wearing their black combat suits and shining their flashlights on the foam-covered goons.

"Anticlimactic but impressive." Steph grinned at the Ryder SWAT team.

"You okay, Red?" Quint asked as he carefully made his way over to stand beside his wife.

"Perfect, except that I'm holding Mackenzie responsible for cleaning up this messy trap she set for these clowns," she said with a teasing wink.

Vance stepped up beside his wife. "You okay, Randi?"

"Yes, piece of cake." She pressed a kiss to

Vance's cheek. "You are one handsome hunk of commando, by the way."

"No scrapes, bruises or gashes?" Wade shined his flashlight on his wife. "Damn, Laura, I was sweating bullets."

"I'm fine, honey." Laura set aside the fire extinguisher to give Wade a hug. "Mackenzie stuck her neck out to ensure we didn't draw fire or attention." She stared pointedly at Mackenzie. "You must not have been listening when we made a pact that we were in this together."

Mackenzie shrugged off the condemning stares from the Ryder cousins and their wives. Her main concern was the thunderous expression on Gage's face. Thus far, he hadn't made a peep, just aimed his death-ray glare at her from his position beside the door. Since he looked homicidal she didn't go near him. Instead she kept her gaze trained on the goons she held at gunpoint.

"You all right, sister?" Dex questioned as he circled the group to give her a jostling bear hug. "That's my girl. You made me proud."

"Thanks, Dex, couldn't have done it without your crash course in survival." She turned her attention to the goon who was sprawled in front of her. "How much was I worth?"

The man wiped his eyes, glared at her, then, in Russian, he cursed her soundly and said he didn't understand what she'd asked. Mackenzie posed the question in his native tongue and he swore some more before he claimed he had no idea what she was talking about.

A moment later the local cops arrived, accompanied by Randi's police family. The goons were cuffed, hauled to their feet and marched out the back door.

Mackenzie was grateful the holiday festivities hadn't been interrupted and the threat on her life had been neutralized. There was only one obstacle standing between her and the door when everyone filed out.

Gage planted himself solidly in front of her escape route. Mackenzie braced herself for the inevitable eruption of temper that she could see building on Gage's face. At least he'd waited until they were alone before he bit her head off.

Sure enough, he erupted like Krakatoa. "What in the hell were you thinking, damn it!" he roared. His booming voice ricocheted off the tiled walls and bombarded her from all directions at once.

"What was I thinking *when?*" she smarted off. "You'll have to be more specific."

Gage sucked in a gigantic breath that caused his chest to expand like an accordion. "Damnation, Mac, you never *ever* make a call on a phone without a scrambler unless you want it traced within minutes!"

She winced uncomfortably when he glowered at her. "Uh…sorry about that."

"Sorry? You're *sorry?*" he bellowed. "We had very little warning or preparation time because of *you.* I spent two weeks covering our tracks to prevent this very thing from happening. You wiped out my precautionary defense in five minutes flat!"

Mac had never seen Gage so furious. His face was an amazing shade of red. So were his ears. His lips were curled, revealing his full set of gritted teeth.

His hands were balled in such tight fists that his knuckles had turned white.

She tried to defuse his temper with a smile. "I said I was sorry. I had too much wine last night when I impulsively called Dad."

"You weren't thinking this afternoon when you left the ranch without a chaperone, either," he snapped at her. "You might as well have pinned a target on your chest and waved a banner that said— Here I am. Come and get me."

"Stop yelling at me," Mackenzie muttered. "I've had a bad day and endured a highly stressful situation, you know. What with trying to protect your cousins-in-law who got stuck in this mess."

"The entire incident could've been avoided if you would have stayed put," he shouted.

Mackenzie didn't know why he was so bent out of shape. The situation had turned out fine, hadn't it? No one had been hurt. Although she'd let Gage vent—because she'd botched up his assignment and caused him undo duress by involving his family in danger—she'd been chewed out quite enough. There was a limit to how much she could take from him before she lost *her* temper. It was time to skedaddle, she decided. If she could make it past Gage and venture outside, maybe he wouldn't snarl at her in public.

Unfortunately, when she approached the door he planted his feet, crossed his brawny arms over his inflated chest and glared thunderclouds on her. Fortunately for her, however, a rap resounded on the door and Gage was forced to abandon his position. Growling at her, he whipped open the door.

"Yeah, what is it?" he barked unsociably.

It was Randi, thank goodness. "The chief needs to see you in his office," she reported. "Paperwork and all that. Uncle Tate figured you'd want to clue him in on how to handle the incarceration and extradition."

Gage nodded sharply then flashed Mackenzie a parting glare. "I'm not through with you. This is to-be-continued. I'll see you at home."

When he stalked out, her shoulders slumped in relief. The way she figured it she could enjoy part of the firework display, watch Dex receive his well-deserved recognition and say her final farewells to the Ryder family. She'd drive to Oklahoma City's airport before Gage knew she was gone. There was no reason to stay. The thugs were in custody and she could have her life back.

A pang of regret buzzed through her as she headed out the door. She was sorry that her last memory of Gage was witnessing his firestorm of temper. Oh well, she consoled herself. Maybe if she clung to that vision he'd be easier to forget.

A quiet little voice in her head—that sounded a lot like Gage—said: Yeah, right, fat chance of that, *kid*.

10

GAGE WASN'T SURE HOW LONG it would take for him
to recover from his outrage with Mac and her daredevil confrontation with those thugs. The rescue
squad had been on its way and she'd purposely
jumped the gun with her antics. An eerie chill, the
likes he'd never experienced, had overcome him
when he'd heard Mac taunting those goons to come
and get her. He'd suffered all the torments of the
damned during those agonizing minutes while they
were creeping around the second story to move into
position for the drop through the trapdoor. He'd expected to hear the rapport of handguns filling Mac
full of holes and the thought caused him to come
unglued.

True, he'd been impressed by Mac's ingenious
trap, using whatever makeshift weapons available.
But still!

"Sign these last two forms and you're good to
go," Chief Tate Jackson requested, jostling Gage
from his troubled thoughts. "That was one fine im-
provisation your wife dreamed up to entrap those
creeps. Bet you're mighty proud of her, Gage."

"*Proud* doesn't adequately express my sentiments," Gage muttered as he put his John Hancock
on the dotted line. "The Feds should be here tomorrow to extradite your prisoners." He pushed to

an upright position and nodded gratefully. "Thanks for your assistance, Chief. Sure glad we didn't have to disrupt the holiday festivities."

Tate smiled wryly. "An appropriate day to ensure justice prevailed, don't you agree? Oh, and by the way, congrats on your recent marriage. My niece is really fond of your wife."

"She's—" Gage bit down on the announcement that Mac wasn't actually his wife. He didn't want to be waylaid by a lengthy explanation to the chief. He just wanted to wrap up the red tape and track down Mac because he wasn't finished with her, not by a long shot.

Gage had noticed the dents and paint scrapes on the front and rear end of his pickup when he jogged across town square to reach police headquarters. Realizing Mac had been involved in a high-speed car chase to reach town had fired him up again. None of that would've happened if she'd stayed at the ranch. Gage and his cousins would have arrived before those goons caught up with her. But Ms. I Can Take Care Of Myself had thumbed her nose at his insistence on a chaperone and she'd unnecessarily endangered the Ryder wives.

Although his cousins hadn't lit into him, Gage knew they'd been concerned about their wives' safety. So naturally, Gage had held Mac personally responsible for upsetting his cousins. Hell, he'd held her personally accountable for this jumble of emotions that bubbled inside him like a boiling cauldron. Damn it, that woman was going to pay for scaring ten years off his life.

Gage walked outside to view the last of the spectacular fireworks. During the bursts of colorful lights

that filled the night sky he spotted his family huddled together on a park bench. Gage strode over to
apologize on Mac's behalf for scaring the bejeezus
out of them.

"Hey, Rambo," Randi teased playfully. "Get the
paperwork wrapped up?"

"Yup. And I'm really sorry—" He tried to apologize.

"Sure am sad to see Mackenzie go," Steph interrupted, smiling wryly. "A real shame to break up
the sisterhood."

"Go?" Gage repeated stupidly. "You mean back
to the ranch?" Damn it, that better be what Steph
meant.

Laura shook her blond head. "No, the former,
supposed Ms. Gage Ryder said her farewells before
she headed to the city to catch a flight."

"What!" Gage howled in disbelief.

Wade grinned devilishly. "She took your truck,"
he reported. "Guess the game's over. Gidget's
gone."

"Gone?" Gage echoed.

"Bet you're glad she's out of your hair," Quint
teased. "Now you won't have to bother with life-
altering decisions about your future."

"She asked us to convey her appreciation to
you," Vance imparted, lips twitching. "She said she
tried to extend her gratitude, but you were too busy
yelling at her... So, thank you. From Gidget."

"I need to borrow someone's truck," Gage requested urgently. "She can't leave because I'm not
finished with her."

"Now that's a real shame because I'm pretty sure
she's finished with you." Wade dug into his pocket

then tossed Gage the keys. "Good luck tracking her down."

Driving like a bat out of hell, Gage roared down the highway to reach the interstate. He grabbed the phone to alert the highway patrol to have her detained. He knew that Gidget still faced potential danger until he got the all clear. A short while later he recognized his pickup sitting beside the road.

Muttering, he watched Mac wrestle with the spare tire. Obviously her wild drive across the pasture had punctured a tire and it eventually went flat. Well, at least the inconvenience prevented her from making her getaway.

Gage pulled onto the shoulder and climbed down. He knew the instant she recognized him because he saw her flinch. No doubt, she was expecting him to jump down her throat again. And he intended to. But first things first, he decided as he strode over to grasp her arm.

"Woman," he said, "swear to God, I've never had this much trouble with other assignments. You aren't free to leave until I hear from Daniel. C'mon, we're going home."

Mac set her feet, refusing to budge, but Gage uprooted her and towed her toward the borrowed pickup. "I already proved that I could handle trouble," she reminded him as he shoveled her into the pickup. "I want to go home!"

"That's exactly where I'm taking you."

She eyed him warily as he shoved the truck into gear and made a U-turn. "Are you going to yell at me some more?"

"Absolutely," he assured her as he zoomed off.

"Don't waste your breath because I'm finished listening to you rant and rave."

Now that Gage had Mac enclosed in the pickup he dragged in a deep breath. Finally he could relax and decompress. He plucked up the phone. Since Vance kept a spare key to his pickup his cousins could change the tire and make the delivery at their convenience.

Home at last, Gage thought as he pulled into the driveway. Despite Mac's objections he wasn't letting her out of his sight until he received the call from Daniel and from his bosses. He'd stick to her like adhesive.

"I'm going to take a shower before you fillet me again." Mac hopped from the truck. "I'm covered with soap."

"At least it isn't your own blood," he muttered as he followed her into the house. "You could be dead right now."

"Well, I'm not," she smarted off. "But you'd probably prefer it so you'd be rid of me—for good."

"Don't put any ideas in my head," he scowled as he veered toward his bedroom.

Gage showered in record time to ensure Mac didn't try to cut out on him while he was standing around naked. He dried himself off then glanced at his laptop to notice another message awaited him.

"About damn time," he said when he read the message. The G-men had finally served their warrants to round up the gangsters who'd put the thumbscrews to Daniel. The evidence that he and Daniel had spent two years compiling had finally gotten results. Mac was free to go.

Gage stood there, draped in his towel, letting that

realization soak in. It was over. An odd feeling of emptiness swelled inside him. Jeez, he'd become a sentimental sap all of a sudden. And it was Mac's fault. She'd turned him wrong side out so many times he couldn't function normally.

Wheeling around, Gage strode into the hall. He encountered Mac, wrapped in a towel, heading to her room. She tilted her defiant chin and visually skewered him. He suspected she'd made use of her time in the shower to conjure up some really nasty zingers to hurl at him, if he dared to light into her again.

Unfortunately he couldn't muster much enthusiasm to bite her head off. Furthermore, he'd had an epiphany while he and his cousins had combined forces to save the day. Only Gage hadn't gotten the chance to save the day—and Mac's neck. He'd wanted to be Mac's hero and he'd been deprived of that privilege. Maybe that was silly, but he'd wanted to be there for her. This was the woman who'd alternately idolized and resented him for years, the mouthy minx who got to him more than any woman alive. He'd wanted to be her hero because he'd wanted her to see him as worthy, reliable and capable of taking care of her.

Yet, he supposed that it was right and fitting that she'd stolen his thunder since she'd felt overshadowed by him for years. He'd dropped through the hole in the ceiling, armed with Uzi and flash/bang grenades, ready to take on the tangos to rescue Mac. But she'd felled the goons, armed with soggy toilet paper rolls, soap and water, without firing a single shot.

Gage sucked in a deep breath, let it out slowly and said, "I've been thinking—"

"Now there's cause for concern," she cut in snippily.

When she tried to veer around him, Gage hooked his arm around her waist and steered her into his bedroom. "Sit," he commanded, gesturing toward the bed.

Her chin angled up another notch. "No."

Gage rolled his eyes and sighed. This violet-eyed hellion wasn't going to make this easy on him. Fine, he thought as he unhooked the towel from his waist and let it drop to his feet. He watched in wicked satisfaction as her gaze dipped to note his obvious state of his arousal. Well, what did she expect? That a normal, red-blooded man could stand there, staring at a gorgeous female, dressed only in a damp towel, without reacting? Not *this* man. Not to *her*. One look at her and he went hot all over.

Her mouth dropped open as her shocked gaze leapt back to his smiling face. "Wh—" Her breath came out in a *whoosh*. It was the first time he recalled seeing Mac speechless.

"Drop your towel, Gidget," he requested, smiling rakishly. "You and I have some unfinished business to attend."

"Wh—" She was still dumbstruck.

Gage reached over to remove her towel then roped his arm around her waist. "We need to reenact the best time you ever had," he said before he brushed his lips over her sagging jaw.

"Why's that?" she chirped.

"Because it disturbs me that you don't remember the specifics of the best time *I* ever had."

Her eyes shot open wide as she tilted back her curly raven head to gape at him. "It was?"

Gage grinned. He liked knowing that he'd finally reduced Mac to one and two-word responses. He had her off balance, but he really preferred to have her on her back, on his bed, showering her with so many kisses that she ended up with chapped skin.

"Definitely." His forefinger trailed down her collarbone then skimmed the swells of her breasts. "And seeing as how you love me and I love you, I think—"

"You love me?" she croaked in astonishment. "Since when?"

"Can't say for sure. It just sort of sneaked up on me while I was trying to convince myself that what I've been feeling for you was inappropriate. It's hard to do your job when you're personally involved. Never happened until I was assigned as your bodyguard and you started turning me into a nutcase."

When she flashed him a supernova smile Gage swore his heart melted down his rib cage. God, he was crazy about Mac. His cousins had assured him that he was suffering from all the symptoms and he had finally accepted the fact that he'd contracted a severe case of love—the kind that kept recurring, no matter how he fought against it. So a guy might as well admit it and live with it because he wasn't going to get over her, loving her the way he did.

Still smiling, Mac glided her hands up his bare chest and locked her fingers behind his neck. When she shifted that gorgeous body of hers up close and personal, Gage groaned. His male body nearly went into spontaneous combustion. He was about finished with the chitchat and he hoped she was, too. A guy could only hold a beautiful, naked woman like Mac in his arms for so long before he reduced himself to natural instinct. He was revved up and ready to show her how much she'd come to mean to him.

He slanted his mouth over hers and kissed her with all the love, passion and affection roiling inside him. To his surprise, she reared back and stared at him intently.

"Do you realize this is the first time you've kissed me without my kissing you first? My goodness, I think maybe you actually meant what you said."

"Of course, I meant it," he declared, affronted. "Do you think I go around spouting off I-love-yous to every woman I encounter? Not hardly! Not ever!"

The comment seemed to please her immensely. She smiled radiantly and desire delivered another sucker punch that knocked the breath right out of him.

"So, if I love you and you love me, then—" she began.

"Look, Mac," he interrupted. "You wanna hash this all out now? Okay, fine, but make it snappy because I want to make love with you so bad I'm not sure how much longer I'll be able to think rationally. For my part, I'm thinking we should do it up right. Marriage and family. I also want to make this ranch our home because I don't think I can stand to be away from you during long assignments. That job has got to go."

He took a deep breath. "I want what my cousins have found. If you want to pursue your promising career, then do it. But I really need to be with you because, if being without you all day today is anything to go by, I'll be suffering separation anxiety like you wouldn't believe. Marry me? Please? The whole town already thinks we're husband and wife and I kinda like thinking of us that way, too.''

''Are you sure?'' she asked him very seriously.

He smiled rakishly as he tumbled her with him onto the bed. ''Oh, yeah, absolutely, sweetheart. I've never been so certain of anything in my life. I want to be the first and last man you love. You're mine and I'm definitely all yours. Now hush up and let me show you how much fun it's going to be every time we get naked together.''

When he kissed her again Mackenzie knew her impossible dream had come true. He *loved* her. He really loved her. She'd gone from the depths of dejection to the highs of euphoria when he'd whispered those three little words. But when Gage kissed and caressed her as if she were a precious gift, she knew he meant what he said. This was for real. This was forever.

Her thoughts trailed off when the phone blared, interrupting them in midkiss.

Gage swore ripely. ''If that's my demon cousins calling I'm going to hunt them down and kill them.'' He rolled sideways to grab the phone. *''What?''*

''Gage, it's Daniel. Now that the case has been wrapped up, and the Feds are confident the convictions are going to stick, I wanted to personally thank you for taking care of 'Kenzie. I owe you—big time. How can I ever repay you, my friend?''

Gage stared at Mac. ''You can repay me by giving her to me.''

"What? Give her to you? What are you talking about?" Daniel asked.

"I mean I want to keep her," Gage declared, never taking his eyes off Mac. "As in, do you take this woman? And I do."

After a short pause Daniel said, "Are you serious? How does 'Kenzie feel about this?"

"Why don't you ask her?" Gage handed the phone to Mac. "Tell him you're crazy about me and hurry up about it so we can get back to where we left off."

Mac grabbed the receiver and said, "Daddy, you need to come to Oklahoma for the wedding ceremony and you need to come quickly."

Daniel chuckled. "About time. I picked him out for you soon after I met him. Why do you think I've been singing Gage's praise to you for years? That's also why I insisted on Gage as your personal protector, honey."

"Dad, you're too sneaky," she scolded him playfully.

"It carries over from my line of work," he replied. "I'll be in Oklahoma as soon as I make travel arrangements. After the sting Gage and I set up I'm not very popular in this part of the world. It will be healthier if I take a new position in another country. Definitely time to move on."

When Mackenzie hung up, she turned her full attention to the handsome hunk whose distracting caresses had made it difficult to concentrate on the conversation with her father. Her heart in her eyes, Mackenzie gave herself up to the emotions and sensations that Gage aroused in her.

A long while later, when they were content and

sated, Mackenzie smiled up at Gage and said, "You're right. That was the best time I ever had. But we should do it again to see if it gets even better."

Gage stared into those mesmerizing amethyst eyes that twinkled up at him and knew without a doubt that giving up his current job wasn't going to bother him in the least. He had a new and better job awaiting him—as Mackenzie's devoted husband. And since he *was* the job he intended to eat, sleep, breathe the love of his life from now until forever. Guarding this gorgeous body of hers with his heart, his soul and his life would be his greatest pleasure.

Gage finally discovered what his cousins had found and this time he'd come home to stay. He was exceptionally glad that he'd brought his work home with him—just this once.

* * * * *

She's hip, she's cool...and this heroine's world has turned upside down! Catch a glimpse of Harlequin Flipside, coming to romantic-comedy lovers October 2003.

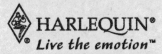

HARLEQUIN Temptation.

AMERICAN HEROES

These men are heroes—strong, fearless... And impossible to resist!

Join bestselling authors Lori Foster, Donna Kauffman and Jill Shalvis as they deliver up

MEN OF COURAGE

Harlequin anthology
May 2003

Followed by *American Heroes* miniseries
in Harlequin Temptation

RILEY by Lori Foster
June 2003

SEAN by Donna Kauffman
July 2003

LUKE by Jill Shalvis
August 2003

Don't miss this sexy new miniseries by some of Temptation's hottest authors!

Available at your favorite retail outlet.

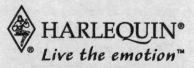

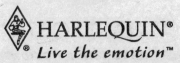

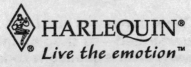